I0668185

STAR ANGEL
DAWN OF WAR

David G McDaniel

TeamStarAngel.com

Star Angel: Dawn of War

Published by
Black Helm Entertainment

Cover design by
Ivan Zanchetta

THE STAR ANGEL PENTALOGY IS:

BOOK ONE: AWAKENING
BOOK TWO: RETURN TO ANITRA
BOOK THREE: DAWN OF WAR
BOOK FOUR: RISING
BOOK FIVE: PROPHECY

TeamStarAngel.com

Anitra is saved but now the Earth may be in jeopardy. Worse, the fate of Zac is completely unknown. The only way to be sure is to go, and the only way to do that is to steal the one thing that can never be stolen.

Once again Jess is faced with the impossible.

And that's not the end.

As a result of her last, desperate act, the very thing that saved a world, a sleeping giant has been awakened, the likes of which has not been seen for a thousand years. Lost for a millennium to space and time, it won't be long before the deadly reality of that threat is felt. An inevitable destiny, and with an unstoppable demon at its helm, it can mean only one thing.

War.

Dedicated to those who do the right thing,
even when it isn't easy.

Thanks to you the world holds promise.

"First comes the Decision. From that all else flows. The Decision is senior to all things."

— from the Codex Amkradus

CHAPTER 1:

THE POWER OF FAITH

JESS SAT UP. Doing so brought on a disorienting moment of transition as her view shifted from the blue sky overhead to the surrounding violence. Willet remained crouched at her side, patient, waiting for her to gather her wits. Behind him, spanning the horizon, loomed fires and burning black columns of smoke, marking the battle that took place just out of sight. Shocking imagery, it was, paired with the sounds that had been there all along, sharply ending the tranquil view Jess had been staring up into; drifting clouds high above, floating in that tiny slice of pale-blue serenity, somehow having managed to put the horrific noises from her mind. Now the thunder of destruction slammed her back to reality. *BOOM!* A blast ripped the air, not far away, closer than the rest. Willet's forced calm, as he tried to be there for her in the wake of her loss, contrasted the intensity of that backdrop.

"We need to get you out of here," he said gently.

A terrible fear began working its way in from the corners of her mind. She fought to impose reason. To accept the consequences of her actions of the last, intense minutes. What she'd done, giving Zac the deep-space Icon and making him use it, making him take Kang to a place where he could do no harm, had been the only option. *It was the only way.* Filled with a hundred reasons why it was a *bad* idea, it was, in the end, the *only* idea, and so she'd compelled herself forward in order to make it happen. Now it was done. Zac used the Icon. He and Kang were gone. Anitra was safe.

And now the real terror began. As she'd known it would. Never, though, did she imagine the fear would be this great. Zac acted on her instructions exactly as she intended, exactly as she demanded, without question, trusting her completely ...

Her stomach knotted. An awful sickness gripped her.

I will *come for you!* her own last words echoed in her mind.

Now, what she had to do in order to make good on that promise ...

Desperately she looked to Willet, who tried to coax her with a mild, yet urgent, encouragement to move. To rise, to follow him so they could get out of there. One danger was past, others were in plentiful supply. Explosions intensified, rocking the air with ever-increasing force. He held out a hand.

But the fear she fought, the terrible intuition, was that Zac had *not* made it. And the panic of not knowing, the sheer emptiness of having no way to know, each moment a critical second in which he could be dying ... now that this bitter moment was upon her, where exactly he was, how she would ever find him again—these things nearly overwhelmed her.

What if he was stuck in deep space?

She took Willet's hand; an effort to distract herself, if only for a moment. To catch her breath and turn her mind from it. To the next thing.

And the next.

She swallowed.

And the next.

Told herself: *Keep moving.* That was all she could do; keep moving. Was what she *had* to do. *I* will *come for you!* For a strange, surreal moment, she tried to beam the thought to Zac. Wherever he was, in whatever condition, firming her own resolve even as she did. Reminding herself of that very vow:

I will *come for you.*

Willet tried to help her the rest of the way but she stood and he released her hand.

He studied her, peering into her eyes, gauging her condition. "We need to get you to Satori."

After a second of that he started them down the small hill, back across the park in the direction of the battle—

which was close, but still far enough away that they could walk in relative confidence. He led her toward the trees. One of Willet's recon team stood in the near distance. The man raised a hand as they passed; Willet spoke to him briefly on the radio, telling him what they were doing as he took Jess onward to safety.

Zac is alive. She had to believe that much. Whether from her own desperate hope or some real, tenuous, ethereal connection, she made herself feel it. Believe it. Hold to it. Deep in her heart … made herself know it. All else was horrible uncertainty, but she clung to the notion of his survival and, reasonable or not, allowed it to buoy her. Made it the foundation for her gathering determination.

She glanced at Willet as they headed for the cover of the trees. From his expression she could see he was still amazed. No doubt he still wondered at the sudden arrival of she and Satori, in the midst of the battle, at her possession of the legendary Icon, her decision to take it directly into the fray, to Zac as he warred with Kang. Willet had done his part, of course, making him as much a player in the heroics, but his understanding of recent events was limited. He'd gone along in order to help Jess pull off what she insisted had to be done, but so far he knew little more than that.

She looked to him as they walked.

They were a team, she and Willet. Satori. Already they'd overcome life-changing obstacles. Jess knew she could count on them. But how far? How would she convince them of what she suddenly had in mind? How would she get them to do what, without question, had to come next?

How would she convince anyone?

* * *

KANG WATCHED THE SPACESHIP hanging in the void before him. A giant, black thing, shaped like some massive, metallic predator. Sleek angles, crisp curves, no windows he could see but he knew there were people inside. There must be. Beings of some kind. Surely they watched him.

The ship had moved in slowly from out of nowhere. Out of the starry black of space, after he popped into existence there in that infernal system of planet and stars.

AAAARGH! He screamed into the void. Silent. No air. No sound. He could feel the tension in his neck, the tear at the corners of his mouth as he raged into the nothingness.

That first instant took him by surprise. One moment he'd been locking in yet another neck-breaking hold on the weakened Horus—*why would he not die?!*—the next ... he was snapping into existence in some other place altogether.

He'd seen the girl give Horus the Icon, knew what it was, knew vaguely what it was capable of, but had no idea what the Kazerai intended. The result had been chaos. A disorienting transformation to this other place, during which he and Horus jerked apart, sending the two of them in opposite directions, the Icon in an entirely different one. In that first instant the shift to the biting cold and the vacuum of space slammed into his senses, gripping him in shock, such that it was several disorienting moments before he gathered his wits enough to determine what went wrong:

Horus had used the Icon to transport them to the void.

Kang could only assume the plan was for Horus to use it a second time and send himself back, to the safety of the girl, leaving Kang there to float harmlessly in deep space. That, of course, had not happened. The limp body of his adversary floated further and further away, not moving. Kang could not tell whether Horus yet lived, but likely as not he did. *I had him!* The Kazerai was nearly broken when the girl showed up. *Bitch!* The same one from before, the one who inspired Horus to such great feats, leading him, ultimately, to the showdown that ended with Kang in this disfigured state. Then, in those final instants, when his greatest nemesis was near gone, she came again, as if from nowhere, inspired Horus once more to action and ...

There he floated.

For several long minutes Kang's seething rage burned with a heat that nearly repelled the intense cold of the void; a roaring desire to finish the fight, to grab Horus and break his neck. Coupled with a hatred of the Kazerai and the girl and what they'd done ... it felt as if he could simply will himself across the gap. *Horus is right there!* Helpless. Ripe for destruction.

But Kang was a slave to physics. Nothing more than a slowly twisting object, moving further and further away from the two things he wanted most: Horus, whom he wanted to finish and, now, even more important than revenge, the Icon itself. The only thing that could get him back.

He watched in impotent fury as both flew slowly from his grasp. Oh so slowly. So close, slipping effortlessly away. Further and further away. Horus one way, the Icon the other. Presumably never to be gained again.

Now this.

A spaceship.

Moments before, as his gaze flicked between the receding Horus and the tumbling, glinting Icon, the bizarre purple planet and this star system's three orange suns—*three suns!*—another object began to move against the curtain of stars.

A speck at first, but soon it began to resolve and, in no time, he could see it was mechanical, moving under its own power, moving slowly and, at length, he'd nearly forgotten Horus and the Icon as the ship came closer and ...

Stopped.

Right there before him, as if on display.

He studied it, wondering what it would do next.

Dying to get his hands on it.

* * *

"YOU HAVE TO COME WITH US." Jess held Willet briefly at the edge of the woods. She needed to freeze this moment; to get his agreement before going further. Get him, in truth, in her corner before facing Satori. The ornithopter could be heard idling just beyond the trees, whine of the steam turbine strong above the sounds of battle. If Jess peered closely she could see it out there in the clearing, Satori's red hair visible through the windows. She wondered if

Satori, in turn, could see them standing in the trees.

Willet was, as expected, confused. His plan had been to get her to the 'thopter and on her way back to the safety of the mountain complex. He himself would return to his recon unit and continue operations behind enemy lines. Now that Kang was gone there was much yet to do to win this battle.

Only, Jess had pulled him up short. And now she was changing the plan.

"I need you," she said.

His confusion only grew. Though she could see it was tinged with the beginnings of concern. He knew what she was capable of. Was well aware of everything she'd already done. Jess was a wild variable, and she saw Willet could tell she was working up the nerve for something even greater. "I'm needed here," he said simply. No doubt hoping that would be enough.

She gathered resolve. It was clear this was going to push him. And for a shuddering instant she had such a crushing feeling, such an absolute fear that there was no time to lose ... she actually staggered. Willet reached a hand to steady her. Every second was killing her. *Killing Zac.* But she could not afford to rush this and risk losing it all.

Did she really need Willet? Could she just do it with Satori? Maybe. But what she now had in mind was so huge, there was so much involved, so many ways for it to fail, she *wanted* Willet. Wanted anyone she could get, and the only two people even remotely familiar with her plight were right there with her.

Willet and Satori.

Her friends.

She glanced furtively across the clearing. If Willet were in agreement it might make it easier convincing Satori.

I need them both.

A series of explosions ripped through a nearby neighborhood and she jumped. Far closer than anything so far. Portions of the battle had drawn uncomfortably near. She looked out toward the conflict. The sun shone brightly on destruction as far as the eye could see; sounds, flashes; crystal clear, hi-def chaos just beyond the buildings. Like a scene on TV from an embedded news broadcast.

Only she wasn't watching TV.

"Zac has no way back," her voice came too urgent, too desperate.

Willet's patience was wearing thin. "You've got to get out of here."

But Jess was emphatic. "When I came here with the Icon I knew this was only the beginning. The first step was getting rid of Kang. We did that.

"Now we have to rescue Zac."

Willet was incredulous. "Rescue Zac?" Then, a genuine question amid rising frustration: "Where did he even go?" Willet had no real understanding of the Icon, but it was clear he'd heard things. "Can't he find his own way back? I thought that thing went to Osaka."

"It doesn't."

He continued to look at her blankly, desperate to just get her out of there and be on his way.

"We *really* got rid of Kang," she said. "That was a different Icon, set to pop out in deep space. I told Zac to use it a second time, which would send him back to Earth."

Willet's head was shaking, trying to understand, too impatient for real effort.

"My world," said Jess.

Willet liked Zac, and he wanted to help, but Jess could tell this chunk of information was more than he could process under the circumstances.

"There's a way to get to Earth," she pressed. "I have to go. I have to find him. I can't just let him die."

For a moment Willet seemed to forget everything else. Focusing, at last, on the absurdity of what she was suggesting. "He's a Kazerai," he said. "I don't think they die that easily."

"He's with Kang and Kang can kill him. Where they went, they went together."

The pause stretched; the sounds of battle weighed heavy on the air and Willet said: "You realize I'm just getting more confused, not less."

"I need your help." She glanced to the ornithopter, wings outspread and waiting, turbine whining and ready. Fixed Willet's gaze.

"I can't do this alone."

"Do what alone?"

"There's a way."

Willet just looked at her.

Then closed his eyes and inhaled, turning his face up to the canopy of trees. As if getting it all at once. Maybe not the details, but he knew he was not done.

Jess still needed him.

Reluctantly she let him have his moment, clenching and unclenching her fists until he opened his eyes, at which point she implored:

"I wouldn't ask if I didn't really need you."

His blank expression became aggravated.

Then annoyed.

"Dammit."

Then, finally, resigned.

"What do we have to do?"

She tried not to let her relief show. "I'll explain on the way."

As if to put emphasis on the moment another explosion, closer even than the last, sent rubble pluming skyward, causing them both to cringe.

Willet placed a hand to his earpiece and, in a terse exchange, informed his team he was leaving and turned over control. Then he and Jess were sprinting from the trees. Satori saw them coming and engaged the wings, obviously impatient herself to get moving. The wide foils began cycling forward and back, gaining momentum as they ran toward the 'thopter—powerful, deliberate strokes— and by the time they reached it their mighty thump was staggering. Crouching low they hurried beneath, straight to the waiting cargo door and jumped in. Satori looked over her shoulder.

"I saw the video from Dox," she said to them both as they entered and closed the door. "You did it. You actually did it."

"Zac did it," Jess corrected, sounding bitter. She felt out of control of her emotions in that moment, stomach knotted with the uncertainty of everything staring her in the face. She made her way forward, Willet in tow.

Satori shrugged. "Hope he was able to dump that son-of-a-bitch." Then to Willet: "I'll get her back safe." She puckered a quick smooch.

Willet kissed her.

Then climbed into the passenger seat.

Satori stared at him as he sat.

"I'm coming with," he said, by way of explanation. Satori's mouth worked for an instant. "You're—" She looked immediately at Jess. The obvious culprit. "Why?"

Jess didn't answer. As she sat in one of the cargo seats and strapped herself in, wings pounding, turbine roaring, Willet finished hooking his harness in the passenger spot and looked to Satori.

"She says she'll explain on the way."

CHAPTER 2:

A SECRET REVEALED

LINDIN NEARLY TRIPPED as he rushed down the stairs to the lab. He had to get his hands on the other Icon.

At the next landing he lunged forward, grabbed a railing in each hand, swung his legs out before him and leapt all the way to the next, hit and did the same for the next, dropped to the hallway below and broke into a run.

Irrational as this mad rush might be, he was not taking anymore chances.

Just minutes ago he watched in shock as the girl, Jessica, handed Zac one of the devices. Before that the entire control room had followed the video feed in rapt fascination as she and Willet made their mysterious approach to the grassy knoll, on foot, everyone wondering what the two of them were up to, exposing themselves so precariously right there in the middle of the park where the battle between the Kazerai and Kang took place. No one at that point had any idea what Jessica planned. The whole spectacle held the entire room transfixed. Somehow, for some reason, Satori had flown out there in a commandeered ornithopter, with Jessica, and that was really all anyone knew. Lindin was aware of what Zac meant to the girl, saw how she fought him so desperately not to leave, and so at first thought maybe she'd gone to inspire him or, maybe, be part of his doom or some other romantic such thing—to die with him, a real-life version of the sad girl in so many tragic fairytales. But as Jessica crouched on the hill, Willet near, their images grainy but clear enough in the feed coming from the recon team, Lindin saw it.

One of the Icons.

Shiny, silver. In her hands. And at that moment the developing scene captured his full, undivided attention. He knew at once what she meant to do. Suddenly it all made sense. She hadn't gone to die with him, she'd gone to give him a way out. And the outrage of the realization of that, that she'd stolen an Icon—yet again—was mitigated only slightly by the small hope that she might, actually, pull it off. As angry as Lindin was some distant, more rational part of him realized the upshot, if successful, was that they would be rid of Kang.

And then it worked.

Jessica slipped Zac the Icon as the whole room watched, breathless. Zac took it, tackled Kang, activated it and ...

The two of them disappeared.

The most dangerous monster ever to threaten the planet, perhaps the most dangerous single thing ...

Gone.

A collective whoop followed. Cheers. Leaping applause. Lindin understood their exhilaration. After what Kang did at the school, after the destruction he'd wrought so far and all the suffering he was no doubt destined to continue, the thought that his threat was removed, all manner of future deaths prevented, the blood of the others avenged, was huge. The whoop moved quickly to a celebration and, for a bit, the battle that yet raged between Dominion and Venatres was forgotten. Lindin shared their zeal, all the while working to figure out exactly what he'd lost.

Then the terrifying thought struck him:

What if the girl had taken *both* Icons?

Followed by:

How did she get them in the first place?

And the rage returned. In force. And he hurried from the room, down halls, to the stairs, to the lab level where he now ran, boots pounding the metal floor in rapid succession as he curved up on the startled guards waiting outside the door.

He waved them aside and ran through. Inside the cavernous space the starship loomed; a massive weight of potential, poised for action.

"Nani!" he yelled for his lead scientist. She had to know how this happened. *She* had to be the one that gave the icon to Jess. He could not, at first, imagine the soft-spoken

Nani being involved, but it had to be her that knuckled under.

"*Nani!*" his voice echoed. The place was nearly empty.

"Here," came a nervous response.

Lindin hurried around the edge and found her on the other side of the craft, near one of her workstations. But it wasn't Nani's voice that answered. It was the girl who came from Earth with Jessica. The other one. *Bianca.* She stood with Nani.

What the hell is she doing here?

Somewhere during the celebrations she must've slipped away.

Lindin slowed to a brisk walk and headed stiffly in their direction. This sort of lax attention to security was no doubt exactly what got them in this situation in the first place. And, as he approached, he could tell by Nani's expression she *was* guilty.

Dammit! He resolved to lock things down.

"What did you do?" he asked, voice harshly accusatory. The Earth girl, Bianca, had a kind of a forced innocence about her, like she was preparing to lie.

Nani, however, was far too pure to hide any such emotion. She was terrified.

"They said they needed it to get rid of Kang," his lead scientist fairly blurted, knowing exactly why Lindin was there, scooting back against the workbench as he stormed up. Unnecessary. He wasn't going to strike her. Though he had to admit he felt a little like doing so.

Bianca interposed herself, trying to defend Nani, seeing lies were never going to work. "She saved us," she insisted. Lindin ignored her, focus entirely on Nani.

"Where's the other one?" The answer to that was more important than anything right then. Punishing Nani could be figured out later. Right then it served no purpose. What was done was done and there would be no undoing it. Lindin needed to assure himself all had not been lost.

Nani didn't hesitate. She went immediately to a strong box at the end of the bench and entered a code. It popped and she reached in and took out the other Icon.

Lindin breathed a sigh of relief.

"We haven't lost anything," Nani tried to explain away her treason, to make okay what she'd done, seeking his understanding. "This one," she handed it to him and he took it quickly—yet carefully, "the one Jessica took ... the coordinates are plugged into the starship and into our computers. We've deciphered it. It's all here. We have it all here. The device is no longer needed."

Of course Lindin knew that.

Nani was shaking her head. "I've got everything we need."

"It's a small price to pay," Bianca added her take on the situation. Repeated: "She saved us." She looked at Lindin, as if to affirm that declaration.

Jessica's actions had, indeed, saved their asses.

But it didn't matter.

"No excuse," Lindin was firm. He glared at Nani. "There was no excuse for letting one of these go."

But the Earth girl wasn't through.

"Go easy on her, boss man." She pushed her hair back over one ear, fidgeting, looking up at him with an uneasy glare. Clearly nervous but standing up for her friend. "You may run the show around here, but Zac just gave his life so we could live. And Jess, who loves him more than anything, gave him the way to do it." She gained resolve. "*They're* the ones that made the sacrifice. Not you. Not me. Not her." She glanced at Nani.

Lindin really didn't have time for this. Bianca's sudden passion, however, did bring his fury down a notch. In light of the fact that they'd lost only the physical device, and in exchange rid themselves of a potentially world-changing threat, he was now mostly just annoyed.

He turned the other Icon over in his hands, cognizant of its incredible power. With a twist it could send a man clear across space, to a point light years away.

"Call security," he instructed. Nani did so at once, without question, and Lindin could see she shook as she worked to press buttons. Probably worried he was about to put her in lock-up. *I should lock both of you up,* he thought, staring hard at Bianca.

He turned and glanced up at the starship.

What technicians were on hand had come closer at the commotion, watching the drama unfold from what they deemed a safe distance. Lindin had no idea if any of them were involved, but his purpose at the moment was not to start passing out sentences. His objective was to get the remaining Icon to safety and ensure no further breaches of security occurred.

"They're on the way," Nani reported.

Lindin suspected no one else at the complex but was nevertheless rattled by the breach. First thing to do was set protocols for the lab. His main objective, now that the deed was done, was to bring Satori and Jessica in for questioning.

Much as he hated to admit it, Bianca made a good point. Jessica was likely already considered a hero following the successful banishment of Kang. As a result he wasn't sure how harsh he could be, but was determined to find out exactly what she was thinking. More than that, what *else* she was thinking. And what Satori was thinking. It was, after all, Satori that gave Jessica the Icon last time, ostensibly so she could go home, thus robbing Lindin and his team of that which they so desperately needed. Leaving the entire project, in effect, dead in the water.

But Satori had not known then what was at stake. Not exactly. Now she did. And if Lindin recognized anything it was that the Earth girl, Jessica, was a wild card. Apt to do anything, no doubt determined once again to get home. To go chasing after her Kazerai boyfriend. And this Icon, this one right here in his hands, was the key to doing just that.

He could only imagine.

Yes. The girl would need to be watched.

* * *

KEL WARLORD ELDRON HALF LISTENED as one of his crew described their slow approach to the monster floating in space. His helmsman methodically aligned their trajectory so the thing would come in range of a bay door on the side of the battle cruiser, open in anticipation of bringing aboard the unusual "discovery". Eldron made a little noise to himself. That thing out there was certainly more unusual than *anything* that had been discovered in their system or any other. He found himself eager to dissect it.

"In synch," came the final report.

Down below a team of Kel warriors, suited up in space armor, were at the open bay, waiting to secure the creature and haul it aboard. That it lived at all was amazing. The best scans they'd been able to direct upon it indicated it had pulse and a heartbeat, lungs, organs and soft tissue, which meant it had internal body pressure, which meant it should've burst in the vacuum. To say nothing of the air it no doubt needed to survive.

Which meant, of course, that what Eldron was staring at was more than just a visual freak of nature. This beast was an anomaly to the greatest degree.

"Grapple deployed."

Eldron watched the video coming from the cargo bay, a line of warriors standing at the edge of space in their dark armor, eyes on the mutated yellow form in the near distance, floating against the backdrop of stars, eyes open and fully alive. Staring back with what appeared to be complete awareness.

Slowly the robotic grappling arm extended in its direction.

For a brief moment Eldron took his eyes from that developing scene and turned to the other body floating in space, drifting further and further away. That one ...

Human.

While they had no record of anything like the creature they now worked to bring aboard, they most definitely had record of humans.

The Fetok, they were called, in the Old Dialect. The "Tolerated". A term introduced long ago when the Kel empire stretched across half-a-dozen worlds. It was a derogatory term, serving well to convey the feelings the Kel held for the inferior race. Much had been lost following the Great War, but prior to that the Kel knew the humans all too well. Ruled them. It was an uprising of the Fetok, in fact, that led to the Wars, which in turn led to the vast and irreversible destruction that, by the end, resulted in the collapse of the entire Kel civilization. The Kel homeworld fell out of contact with its empire, contracting, revolution eventually consuming Kel itself—such that their society fell into a darkness from which they'd only recently begun to recover. In that the Kel thought the Fetok little more than a part of their past, long gone. Now here was one, a human, clearly having arrived somehow with the beast.

The Kel had rebuilt. In the rebuilding Eldron's people pieced together old technologies, old records where they could be found, managing to unite their homeworld once more. A powerful, warrior race, poised for empire.

The old worlds, however, the worlds of the Fetok, knowledge of where they were or how to reach them, no longer existed. Large chunks of the Kel history were lost or buried in legend, and though Kel engineers managed at length to enable ways to power their spaceships to the stars, to rediscover that ancient technology, the cosmos was vast. Only in the last years had they even managed to reach other worlds. None so far had been found with worthwhile life or habitability.

And the Kel were unlikely to look harder. Resources were plentiful in their own system. Due to the brutality of their existence there was no pressing need for population expansion. Simple gaining of new space was not motivation enough. The lessons of the past, perhaps, held them further in check. The Kel desired conquest, not merely new places to call home. War. Empire. Others to rule. The humans, the last known makers of civilization other than themselves, had been perfect subjects for past dynasties. Until the revolt. Now those worlds, long since lost from Kel records, could be anywhere.

Eldron always suspected the humans were still out there. They had to be. Possibly rebuilding, as had the Kel. Surely one of the human worlds had managed to put itself back together. Maybe even advanced. Maybe such a world, should they find it, would give them more challenge than before.

The troubling thing was that this human floating out there in space—Eldron studied the magnified image—like the beast, this human defied description. It was at once proof humans *were* still in existence, and ... a harbinger of frightening possibilities. For, like the beast, the human was also alive. Impossible but true. Unlike the beast the human did not appear conscious, yet its heart beat and it gave off heat.

And this, possibly more than anything, caused Eldron a subtle sense of foreboding. If this was indeed a human he was looking at, and it could survive in the cold vacuum of space, then that meant humans had evolved in entirely unexpected ways. Not just restored lost technology, or lost civilizations, but had, somehow, become more indestructible as a race, perhaps even stronger, and if this were the case then a new war with them might lead once more to the ruin of the Kel.

How could they fight humans strong enough to live unprotected in space?

He would know soon enough. Once the demon was secured they would gather the human next and all questions would be answered.

Eldron's superiors would be quite intrigued with this find.

He turned to the feed from the cargo hold. The robot arm had gripped the yellow, horned form and was curling it in. The sturdy grappling arm was designed for attack, meant to secure other vessels in the act of boarding, to hold them fast as assault parties went across. Now, with nothing else to use in this unique situation, it was being employed to bring in a tiny, living body. Eldron watched the beast grip the thick metal arm as it held him, an appendage that was far too bulky for the task, hoping the arm's operator would be able to apply its hydraulics lightly enough to avoid crushing the small form.

Eldron put his hands behind his back.

They were in the middle of something truly monumental. Two organic creatures, one possibly human one probably not, had just popped into space and were floating out there, helpless but alive.

"Securing the cargo."

Eldron watched the arm reach its retraction point. His team moved in.

CHAPTER 3:

ANATOMY OF A LONGSHOT

"*WHAT?!*" SATORI LOOKED back at Jessica, strands of red hair snapping about her head in the chaotic turbulence of the cockpit. She flew the ornithopter low and straight, headed away from the battle, back to the mountain complex, but as she glared with wide, angry eyes Jess had the sinking feeling she was about to haul them up to a screeching stop, land them right there, march everyone out and start chewing them out. Like Mom stopping the car to scold her unruly children.

"Are you crazy?!" she demanded, gaping at Jess sitting in the rear jumpseat. So far she kept flying. No stopping yet. Willet, in the opposite seat, stared at them both, considerable confusion playing across his expression.

"*Starship?*" he asked for the third time. "What starship?"

"It's the only way," Jess spoke directly to Satori. Satori kept flying, full speed, on target, headed back. Silently Jess crossed her fingers. Hoping the red-headed demon girl would just keep going. *Keep flying,* she willed her. *Keep flying.*

"It's nonsense is what it is!" Satori jerked her gaze back and forth between Jess and the rapidly-scrolling terrain blitzing along scant feet beneath them. Forward, back. Forward, back. It had Jess on edge.

Pay attention to what you're doing! she wanted to scream.

"Starship?" Willet asked yet again. No one was listening.

"I *know* it's insane." Jess wanted Satori to believe she understood. Wanted her to know she, Jessica, realized just how crazy it was, what she was suggesting.

Satori held her eyes forward—thankfully—concentrating as she banked them through a narrow pass.

"I thought he could pop his own way back!" she yelled over the roar of wind and machine, whipping them up a ridge and over it, down the other side, dipping on currents of air that made Jessica's stomach rise.

She swallowed it down. "He can't. It goes to Earth."

Satori executed yet another snap maneuver, sweeping close enough to a stand of trees to count the leaves. "Zac's on Earth?" They were entering the foothills.

"Yes. Maybe."

The circumstances were horrible to be trying to convince anyone of anything. The loud roar of wind, turbine and wings made even yells hard to hear. The erratic flight necessary to clear the outer fringes of battle, the fact that they were even *in* a battle, running for their lives—all these things added up to make it near impossible to make a case.

But there was no time for anything else.

"Why is he on Earth?" Satori was incredulous. "I thought the Icon came back here!"

Willet continued looking back and forth between Satori and Jess. About all it seemed he could do in that moment.

"It goes to Earth," said Jess, wishing this wasn't so complicated. "And I'm not sure he made it. I have a bad feeling." She did. A horrible intuition she couldn't shake.

Satori concentrated on flight. "You mean, maybe he *didn't* make it?" Despite her anger she was working to grasp the situation. "He could be floating in space?" She brought them around a soaring peak and higher, clear now of a direct line of sight with the last of the forces at war behind them. As she did so she glanced over her shoulder once more. Jess knew she had the most horrible look on her face.

"Dammit!" Satori put her attention back on the mountainous pass ahead.

Jess swallowed. "That's why the other Icon isn't enough. It's why we need the starship.

"Only the starship can go both places."

"You just keep pushing!" Satori yelled, exasperated. "Pushing, pushing, pushing! Expecting people to follow! To do what you say! The most absurd things! Now you've sent Zac off and he may be floating in space?! Dammit!" She smacked the console. Then again, harder. So hard it made Willet jump.

"I thought this was over," she kept shaking her head. "Yay! We saved the world from the monster!

"Ha! It's not over. It's never over with you. Is it?" She looked back accusingly. Jess wished she would just keep her eyes ahead. Strands of red hair continued their mad dance about her head, a halo of rage as she flew on, grumbling. She faced forward and said no more.

In that moment Willet fixed Jessica's gaze. Finally, it seemed, he'd found an opening.

He mouthed a single word:

"Starship?"

* * *

KANG WAITED AS THE ROBOTIC ARM brought him in. As yet he had no idea what the mechanics of this ship were capable of, but if they were in any way comparable to those of his own world a hydraulic boom—even one of this size—would be no challenge. Escape, however, was not his purpose. He wanted to get aboard this alien craft and so far the arm was helping him do that. If he broke it, or started fighting before he got inside, he was just as likely to end up spinning off into space as he was to make it aboard, and he was quite certain, if he did that, they would not try again to retrieve him. Looking at the armored soldiers waiting for him in the dimly-lit hold, and having now studied the craft in greater detail, he was confident they would simply try to blow him to bits.

These were warriors.

Seven of the dark-suited men stood in wait. They seemed stuck to the floor of the hold, and as he at last passed within the confines of that room he felt himself pass through an invisible shimmer, the smell of breathable air washing over him, some sort of artificial gravity tugging him to the deck.

Yes! he enthused silently.

He must gain control of this machine.

The arm stopped slowly and released him. He stepped from it; stood naturally, arms at his sides, observing his would-be captors. They were human-like, but definitely not human. Their black armor did not look powered, not like the Skull Boys and Astake of his world; more a suit worn rather than operated. They carried no rifles or sidearms, but each held a club in one hand. The club looked to be made of something similar to the armor and had what he could see were retractable blades. No doubt a brutal, gruesome weapon against a target of flesh and bone.

He grinned.

As he did this they separated a bit, cautious of him now that he was among them. They were slightly taller than he was, making them taller than an average man, uniformly on the slim side, and though he could not see faces through the reflective gold of their stylized visors—a color that stood out brightly against the gloss black of the rest of them—he had a sense they were of some exquisite visage beneath those elegantly shaped helmets. Each sported a long tail of hair that protruded from the rear of the helmet, all but one of them dark. The exception was white. Whether the hair was mere decoration or it was their actual hair pulled through an opening it gave them an air of the living. Otherwise they might as easily have been robots as men.

The white-haired one spoke. Stepped to the side as he did, almost cocky in his movements, and Kang was sure then that they were living. It was the voice of a man, projected from a speaker on the suit, terse and, Kang could swear, condescending.

He couldn't help himself. He grinned wider.

"You might want to show me some respect," he said easily. The man said something else, equally choppy, equally agitated.

It was possible, Kang had to consider, that these aliens were as strong as he. Unlikely, of course, but he'd just appeared in a whole new star system and was aboard an alien ship with beings that were not known to him. Anything was possible. Until someone made a move he had no way of knowing for sure.

He looked to the side, at the bulkhead spanning the

breadth of the cargo hold. It was not a gigantic space, this ship obviously built for war, not cargo, but everything in there was sturdy beyond reckoning. He doubted there was truly anything to fear from these soldiers, however he *did* have doubts as to his ability to enter the ship by force. Maybe he could beat down the outer door. Maybe not. It was a chance he was unwilling to take. For now he would allow himself to be led. Captured, if that was the way they chose to see it.

Unsure how to convey his decision he simply raised his hands. That seemed to work. The group gestured with their clubs, the leader continuing to issue sharp commands, herding Kang to the door and into a smaller room beyond. The door shut on the hold behind them and different air began to flood in, slightly thicker air, richer, giving Kang to assume this must be an airlock. Pressure built, confirming it. The air had a sweet-smelling musk he found at once offensive and ... intriguing.

Once the room was set the far door opened, admitting them into yet another, this one lit just as dimly; an austere, functional aesthetic that spoke of combat and minimalism. The metal was dark green, the lighting green as well, and as Kang swept the room with his gaze he saw three other aliens at the far side, helmetless, waiting. He felt his eyes widen at the sight of their faces.

Curious.

Those three also wore armor, but without helmets he was able to get a far better idea of what he was dealing with. Exquisite, as he'd imagined. Definitely humanoid; two eyes, a nose and a mouth, their features angular, sharper than an average human, more defined. There was a purity to their skin that nearly defied description. Never had he seen such a complexion. They were uniformly pale, each of them male as far as he could tell, each with dark hair pulled tight into a tail that hung from the top and back of their head. The hair was real. Their eyes were bright yellow, and each had some form of unique markings around one or both sockets. Black ink, almost like a tattoo, or perhaps even part of their skin.

No matter, they were not some kind of bug-eyed monster. They were men, of a sort, though definitely not human. The only question remained: Did they bleed?

One of the three helmetless ones took over. Barked a cursory gesture of command and, quick as that, Kang heard a *snikt* to his right and ... decided to hold himself still for the blow that was no doubt coming. One of the soldiers had flung out the blades on his club and, without delay, swung mightily into Kang's back. Had Kang been "normal" it would've felled him. He could sense that. Possibly even killed him. Was that their objective so soon?

The blow was as nothing.

And so the question was answered. These aliens were no more than men in all ways. No superior strength. Nothing to concern him.

He chuckled.

Reached and grabbed the hair at the back of the helmet of the one that struck him; picked him up as the soldier began striking furiously with the bladed club.

Useless.

Kang snatched away the club and threw it at one of the helmetless ones, the one that had barked the command; a casual toss yet it crushed his face and drove him back, nailing him against the wall where he spasmed and fell.

Before he hit the ground, before any of them could process what was happening, Kang ripped the helmeted head from the man he held and struck the head from another, the crack of his fist snapping sharply from the walls.

Pandemonium erupted in the small, green room.

Clubs came out, plus a gun—they did have guns—but the blast, while it definitely hurt and Kang made note of the fact, was not enough to phase him and in a matter of instants, with a flurry of sweeping strikes, he decimated them all, effortlessly. None escaped, though one tried, seeing too late just how futile it was to stand and fight.

In those final instants, however, Kang confirmed, weak as they were, these were warriors. Of course they were weak, and he was glad to have proven that out. All things were weak compared to him. But it was their attitude that intrigued. These were a brutal race. He'd gotten an inkling from the design of the craft, its obvious purpose, but the bladed clubs, with their potential for pain and gruesome injury, the look in these alien's eyes, their mannerisms, unmistakable in any language, the fact that, even when it was clear they would die, all but one remained to fight— these things added up to a race whose philosophy he could appreciate.

He stood tall amid the gore. Breathing in the heady smell of the strange environment.

They bled. Even red, as far as he could tell in the green glow. No more came at first. He was sure others would be on the way. This was a large craft and it no doubt took many to run it. This was a warring race, and they would probably have a small army aboard. Of that he was convinced.

He stepped ahead to the next door, wondering at its function. It slid aside as he reached it. Probably they would begin locking things down. He had no doubt they would. But he would find his way. He would take control of this vessel and make it his own. And, once enough of the crew had died, perhaps they would see reason and follow him.

He started down the buttressed, green metal of the alien hallway.

Thrilled with new possibility.

CHAPTER 4:

RETURN OF THE HEROES

SATORI CONTINUED HER BATTLE WITH JESSICA—battling with herself nearly as much, it seemed—even as she raced on toward their destination. "You know," she grappled hard with the situation, "I thought, We owe you. You wanted to steal that damn Icon and I said, We owe her. For all she's done. And anyway, this is for all of us. Ok. Let's do it. Then it worked. We got rid of Kang.

"But this?"

She kept looking back, as if hoping to see Jess might be joking or something. Trying to make sense of it. Any of it. So amazing, so stupendously absurd was the mere idea ...

"*This?*"

Jess tried to be calm. "It's the only way."

Satori shook her head vehemently. As if doing this crazy thing was actually, somehow, a real possibility and she had to shut it down. Now. "No! We can't steal an *entire starship*." She was adamant. Jess was quiet. Working to keep up the soft sell; to listen, to impose her will, firmly yet gently, hoping Satori would eventually run out of steam.

So far that tactic wasn't working.

"Zac is a warrior," her red-headed adversary went on, talking more to herself, it seemed. "A Kazerai for God's sake. He'll make it on his own."

Jess looked out the window. The sun was at its zenith, high in the sky. Ahead she spotted their destination, recognized it as they rounded the last of the intervening peaks: the mountain housing the chalet, the wooden structure not yet visible, beneath its snowy slopes the top-secret labyrinth. Deep at its core the vast cavern, where sat the ancient Kel starship. Waiting. Ready to go. According to Nani all it needed was a test.

With it they could save Zac.

"How are we even *supposed* to take it?" Satori wanted to know. She gestured with one hand, steering with the other. "I mean, just the fact of—"

"Nani knows how to fly it."

"And what? She's going to tell us how, in the few seconds we have before they charge in and lock us up?" Satori scoffed. Continued to make empty, absent movements with her hand. It was like she didn't know where to begin.

Jess didn't either. All she knew was she couldn't lose them. Couldn't lose Satori. Couldn't lose Willet.

If she even had them.

Willet rubbed his temples. "You know," he said, "I'm getting a headache. Just ... tell me once more: There's a starship, hidden up here?" He pointed: "In that mountain?" No one answered and he went on. "And you want to use it to save Zac."

Jess nodded.

"Who might be floating in space."

"Right."

"Or, maybe, he's on another planet."

"He could be on Earth, yes. That's where he was supposed to go."

"Your planet."

She nodded.

"And you want to use the starship to get him. No time for discussions, no time to ask, no time to talk to Lindin, to get the Venatres involved, no time to do anything other than ... take it."

Again she nodded.

"Steal a starship."

"Yes. If Zac didn't make it ... I don't know how long he can survive." Truth was, she didn't know if he could survive at all.

Willet squinted his eyes, speaking more to himself now, kind of like Satori: "There's a real starship, hidden up here in the mountains."

Jess watched him chew on that bit of info. He rubbed his temples harder.

"We're not taking it," Satori was firm. She shook her

head "no way". Sharp, side-to-side movements, almost childish in their stubbornness. *No way!* "Make your case to Lindin and the lab group. I don't care. Our leaders will authorize it if it's as important as you say. We're not kidnapping our top scientist and making her steal our biggest secret. No way."

Jess was practically in despair. "We're already too late! If we don't do something ..."

Satori kept shaking her head. "We're not," she said, wide-eyed with the impossibility of the scale it even implied, "even if we can. We're not."

"*We have to!*" Jess fairly exploded, withdrawing at once from the force of her own outburst. Satori and Willet jerked around to face her, shocked with the amplification of her will. "I told him I would come for him! He did what he did because he trusted me!"

Consciously Jess reined herself in. But her frustration was not to be denied. She became stern. "We are," she said, more quietly yet every bit as emphatic.

"Look," she made them get it. Willet, who had no obligations in the operation of the ornithopter, kept staring. Satori looked ahead, piloting them on toward the complex. "This is not *just* about Zac. I'm not some stupid girl swooning over a boy." Though probably she was. "We owe it to him to do everything we can, and I'll argue that with you all day. *But.* Outside that, beyond that: the Icon he used connects two points. Deep space *and* Earth. *My* world." She gave that a moment to sink in. "Remember? When Zac and Kang popped out of the park, they went to deep space. If Zac was able, then he used the Icon a second time and ended up back on Earth. If so then all is great. Joy. And maybe we're talking about all this for nothing. Maybe there *is* no dire rush. He'll be fine until we reach him.

"But. You saw how strong Kang is. What if Zac *wasn't* able to use it the second time? There's a chance he wasn't. That means not only is he stuck floating in space," she paused as her voice hitched; imagining Zac floating dead in space was too vivid an image for the emotions of the moment,   "but it also means Kang is on Earth."   She beamed it into them:

"*Kang*, not Zac, could be on Earth."

Satori glanced around.

Jess went on. "If you thought Anitra wasn't equipped to deal with a super monster, Earth definitely isn't. If Kang made it ...

"We have to *do* something. We don't have *time* for discussions. More planning. Agreement. You know that's exactly what will happen, and it could take weeks—if Lindin and those guys even agree at all. We're already too late. We have *no* way to be sure. If Option One happened, and Zac made it to Earth, fine. *But.* If Option Two happened, which is just as possible ... we have to do something. If we take even an extra second to discuss anything with anyone, to arrange a meeting and come up with a plan and ... if we lose a single second, Zac is dead in space and Kang is wreaking havoc on Earth."

Satori made a harsh sound. "So what if we *found* Kang on Earth?! What would we do any different there than here?! This makes no sense!"

"*We shoot him from space!*" Jess fairly screamed. "I don't know! Maybe we should've just done that instead of giving Zac the Icon! I don't know!" She didn't. All she knew—all she knew—was that what was done was done, and if they didn't take the next step, and fast ...

She eased the force of her delivery. "It's quite possible that, in giving Zac the Icon, we only transferred the problem from one world to another. I didn't think this all the way through. We had to get rid of Kang. Maybe Zac *did* get away and make it to Earth. But I'm having serious doubts.

"This is bigger than him. This is bigger than us. We have to follow through and fix the problem. All the way. Giving Zac the Icon was just the first step. We have to finish it. And the *only* way to do that is by using the one thing that can actually end this nightmare. The one thing that may be able to destroy Kang in the first place. If Kang *did* make it to Earth, that ship hidden in the mountain down there," and she pointed out the window, "the *Reaver*, may be able to stop him. And it can get us to him. It can go there. It can go both places. It has the coordinates from *both* Icons."

Willet nodded, almost unconsciously. Jess thought more of how they could probably, eventually, have used the *Reaver* right there on Anitra to peg Kang, possibly, once the bureaucracy of that was overcome, but she did what she did when she did it because they had to get rid of Kang and there was no time for other options. Any other way this might've gone was a waste of time to even think about, because that was the past and this was the present and they had to figure out ...

She took a deep breath.

Satori said nothing. Which, on the face of it, was an improvement. At least she'd stopped arguing.

For the moment.

"When I gave Zac the Icon," Jess added, too worried to let the momentary silence be, "I knew that wasn't the end. I knew I would have to go after him. At first I thought I could do it myself. I knew there would be more to do but I thought I could handle it. Alone. My plan was to take the other Icon. Another suit of armor like last time. Go for him myself and bring him back. No one but me. Icon back, Zac back, Kang gone. Problem solved. I didn't know how I would do that, it seemed impossible, but it was the only idea I had. All I knew was that to save Zac, to save any of us, we had to get rid of Kang. Before anything else, we had to get rid of Kang.

"Now we've done that. And now I realize all the ways it could've failed." She tried to make them understand. "This is why I need you. Both of you. The only way I can do this is with your help.

"Look," she was trying so hard to reason with them, to get through. Any moment Satori was going to tell her to shut up; she could feel it building, but she couldn't stop making her case. "I know the insanity of what I'm suggesting. You think I don't? Look at everything I've done so far. I'm not just, 'Oh, let's go steal an ancient alien starship.' It's crazy. I know. Steal it? But starships, Icons—*none* of that matters when lives are at stake. You, your people—anyone who wants can place all the significance they want on that starship but you know what? It's just sitting there. That's *all* it's doing. If it can be used to save a planet, to save a man, then that's a hundred times more important." Then, with perhaps a bit too much obstinacy but at that point she didn't really care: "It *can* save a man, and maybe even a world, and I'm going to use it. Even if you guys won't help, I'm going to figure out a way."

Satori continued shaking her head, subtly, and Jess wondered if she'd gone too far. Would Satori just turn her in?

But ... Satori's mind was moving in other directions. "We'd need a team to operate it," she said, and Jess felt a surge of hope. Though there was no agreement there, not even in Satori's tone, it was a different sort of resistance. One that had actual consideration behind it. Jess caught her breath as Satori went on: "There's no way. It's never even been taken out of its berth. In a thousand years! How do we even ..." She kept shaking her head, seeing all the impossibilities, all the reasons this would never work. Then: "You can't even be sure Kang made it to Earth."

Levelly Jess said: "*Exactly*," and let the word hang. Then: "That's exactly right. We have to make *sure*. This is far too important to assume anything. We can't sit here wondering if he did. We have to be absolutely certain. If there's *any* chance Kang made it ... we have to go.

"We can't *not* do this just because Kang *might* be floating dead in space. Just because Zac *might've* made it." Still the idea of the alternative, Zac floating dead, even as they argued back and forth, nearly caved her all the way in. The one thing keeping her from those depths of despair was the intensity of the argument and the notion—nothing more than a sixth sense, really, but it was all she had and she clung to it—that Zac yet lived.

The radio blurped and they all jumped. Willet turned to the console.

"Unit Five Seven," he acknowledged after an awkward delay, during which he simply stared at the radio like it was a foreign object.

The operator on the other end didn't seem to notice the pause. "Proceed to Pad Three."

Willet glanced between Jess and Satori. "Sounds like they're expecting us."

Satori looked grim. "Lindin," she surmised. "We're not just going to walk in there," she said. "No matter how many lives we just saved. We took an Icon. They're going to detain us. We're not just going to land, get out, run down to the lab and steal the next item on our list."

The radio blurped again, impatient.

"Acknowledge," the voice demanded, now noticing the hesitation.

Willet spoke to it. "Acknowledged," he said, debated saying something else but didn't. Jess could see this whole situation was going to be far more difficult even than imagined. For all of them. She couldn't get the agreement she wanted. Satori was balking hard. Willet ... Willet just seemed to be wondering what he'd ended up in the middle of.

Lindin was probably standing by to throw them in the brig.

They crested the last ridge between them and the complex, dropping out over the shallow valley as the chalet came fully into view.

And as it did Jess found herself momentarily transfixed by the beautiful structure, an instant of bitter sadness, recalling her last conversation with Zac on the tiny balcony far below, no more than a strip of wood from that altitude, before he leapt away to fight Kang. Leaping without further thought or consideration into the fray, no regard for what doing so meant to his own life, determined to do whatever he could to stop the rampage of a beast that could not, in fact, be stopped.

This was the end of the line. Satori was right. Stealing the starship was fantasy. Now or ever. Even if she and Willet were in full agreement. And even if they did manage to try again "in a few days", after the questions were done and the scrutiny had been removed, even if they did manage to sneak down there, take it and go, it would be too late.

Far too late. Already Jess feared the worst. Those feelings of dread would no longer be balanced by any hope. Even if Zac lived, he would not float in space forever. Days were far too long.

"Here we go," Satori swooped them around the mountain edge, steeply, banking across the far ridge and down toward the giant hangar door that stood open against its side. The g-forces of the heavy, crushing turn, thankfully, swept away Jessica's welling feelings of grief.

How could she give up?

As Satori executed yet another gut-wrenching maneuver and hooked them toward descent Jess took deep, shuddering breaths. Any rescue attempt would now become subject to the formalities of the Venatres establishment. Assuming they weren't sent straight to jail. The idea of convincing Lindin and the rest of those in charge, especially after everything else that had happened, made her ache. The sheer mechanics of doing so were suddenly overwhelming. She felt herself sink into the jumpseat with the weight of it—that oppressive feeling aided none too gently by Satori's continued, aggressive deceleration as she brought them in hot. Satori was the angry type, no doubt, and right then she was angry—at everything, it seemed—but even in light of that Jess wondered why the urgency.

Maybe they could get Lindin and the Venatres to take the starship to Earth. Maybe. To make sure Kang hadn't ended up there, to save it if needed. That was a worthy argument. Maybe she could find some other motivation to inspire them. Maybe. But the crazy adrenaline high of her effort to convince Satori was gone. Crushed beneath the despair of reality: If anything was going to happen it would happen only through proper "channels". And if Jess had learned anything at her young age it was that things—real, game-changing things—only happened when you took matters into your own hands.

Channels rarely got anywhere.

Satori dipped low then up, across the hangar threshold, pulled back on the controls and heaved the 'thopter over the lip to a hover, directly above Pad Three. In one vertigo-inducing moment the machine hung in mid-air then, with a gentle roll forward, dropped to the deck in what felt more like a plunge than a landing. Satori stuck it dead center with a last-second flare of the wings.

As soon as it was down she flipped a series of switches, yanked a lever, killed the turbine, unhooked her flight harness in the same motion and was standing.

"Follow my lead," she said tersely and headed for the rear door. The wings outside were still cycling down. Willet turned to Jess and they shared a questioning look, unbuckled with some hesitation and rose to follow. Quicker, as Satori was already firing open the cargo door and jumping to the ground, fully in action. Out on the pad two waiting guards came toward her, short-barreled machine-pistols in hand. Overhead the large wings were sliding to a stop.

"Lindin wants to see you," the guards placed themselves before her but she kept moving. Jess and Willet jumped out awkwardly behind.

Satori scoffed at the guards. "Where do you think we're going?" She was brusque, impatient—striding at them with no hesitation. None whatsoever and at the last second Jess thought she would walk right into them. Their machine-pistols were leveled and Satori just ignored them, a purposeful look on her face as if they were the least of her concerns. "He just called." She sounded hugely annoyed, not breaking her pace. The guards stepped aside and she was past them, heading toward the far side of the hangar.

The guards weren't sure what to do.

Willet and Jess kicked themselves into action. Jess wiped the look of confusion from her face. Willet wasn't so quick but followed suit, keeping pace as they trailed Satori, past the guards and on across the hanger. The guards remained where they were, the situation clearly not fitting entirely with their orders—probably what Satori gambled on—but if the commander said she was off to see Lindin, and apparently give him a piece of her mind, then, so be it. Maybe their job was done.

When the soldiers were out of earshot Willet looked

across at Jessica. She, too, wondered what Satori was up to. But Satori didn't slow. Marching angrily ahead, leading the way. Jess took a few longer strides to keep up. The hangar was mostly empty but a few 'thopters remained, and it wasn't long until they'd passed far enough away that the guards were safely out of sight.

"What are we doing?" Willet asked when they were clear, voice low.

Satori didn't look back. "Going to find Zac."

And on the confirmation of what Jess had begun to suspect her heart beat faster.

This was happening.

And she felt, suddenly, the rush of camaraderie. Somewhere, though obviously she missed the exact moment, Satori had come over to the dark side. Whether from frustration, a desire to do it so Jess would just shut up—a terrible reason, to be sure—or some real shift of attitude ... somewhere in there Satori changed her mind.

They were doing this.

We're doing this.

Jess steadied her breathing. Set her mind for what was to come.

Willet's participation was implicit. Until that moment he'd been jerked along like a balloon in the wind. Part of that, Jess knew, was due to his shock over the whole starship/Icon/Earth/Zac/Kang thing, of which he'd only just learned the epic details, but the bigger part was that he loved Satori and, in the end, would probably do just about anything she said. In fact, as her junior, it was kind of his job.

They continued on, not slowing, Satori hurrying with feigned, angry purpose—though not breaking into a run that would attract the wrong sort of attention. It was a fine line, rushing toward an objective yet acting indignant, but they pulled it off. Jess followed Satori's lead; even found herself more and more acting the part, stomping along with righteous ire, itching to give someone a piece of her mind. They passed along mostly empty corridors down to the lab levels below, people moving aside for their impatient passage, keeping up the ruse. Willet didn't put on much of a face, and where Satori and Jess hurried without apology he stepped aside here and there, making polite excuses and jogging to keep up.

A few passersby looked as if they wanted to say something more, as if brightening when they realized who the trio was, and from the looks on their faces Jess wondered if they knew what they'd done with the Icon and Kang. It looked like some of the people wanted to thank them, and a few almost got out those words before realizing the three were in too much of a hurry and stopping for nothing.

Soon they were in the wide corridor leading to the lab, heading for the far door. A different pair of guards were there this time, armed with machine pistols like the ones in the hangar. Security had been beefed up.

Guns came up immediately.

"Is Lindin here?" Satori demanded, again not slowing and again not paying the weapons any heed. She marched right up to them. Jess followed, outwardly just as impatient, inwardly going to ice. She did *not* want to get shot. Willet stopped a few steps behind, cautious.

"He's upstairs," one of them said. "In Command. You need to wait here." The guard's tone was firm as he raised the gun higher. His partner lifted a radio and spoke into it.

But Satori was resolute, pressing uncomfortably close. The guards' backs were against the door, Satori nearly in their faces. Jess inched closer too, though she wasn't sure why, eyes flitting between Satori and the guns.

"He told us to meet him here," Satori said, voice filled with agitation.

"We'll see," the one talking insisted, looking to his partner.

And Satori had his gun. Just like that. Snatched away, twisted from his grip and into hers before he could react.

And, much to her own surprise, Jess was lunging at the same time and ... grabbing the other's. *What am I doing?!* As if a signal had been sent, though Satori said nothing— and in fact looked on Jess with equal surprise. In a blur Jess was yanking the gun away, causing the man to drop his radio in the process. Her snatch wasn't near as graceful but the result was the same and, all at once, she and Satori were taking several steps back, holding machine-pistols pointed at the two guards. Both men froze before them.

Stunned.

Jess seemed to start breathing all at once. Reality came flooding back as she worked hard to appear in control. *What did I just do?!* She tried desperately not to let the gun shake.

I'm holding a gun!

And she was pointing it at another person.

Now the whole situation was suddenly very, very real.

Satori glanced at her, Jess still coming to grips with how fast she'd followed her lead. On the floor a voice from the radio called out, asking for a response.

Satori got things moving. She instructed the guards to open the door. They did. She indicated they should go through.

They did.

Jess could not believe how quickly—and effectively—she'd reacted, nor could she believe she was now holding a gun on a soldier who, at the heart of it, was an ally.

Nobody said this would be easy.

She steeled her resolve for everything yet to come.

The group proceeded into the yawning cavern, into the presence, once more, of the giant black starship. Willet followed. Across the threshold Satori stepped wide; Jess kept her gun trained.

"Lock it," Satori ordered. "Seal it up."

Reluctantly one of the guards did so, closing the lab entrance and shutting off the sound of the radio still squawking on the floor outside. Willet stood near, little more than a spectator at that point and, as the guards looked accusingly at him, Jess thought she saw him shrug in response to their hard stares. Almost apologetically.

As if to say: *Hey, this wasn't my idea.*

Or even:

Bitches be crazy, right?

CHAPTER 5:

DOING THE IMPOSSIBLE

"DECK TWELVE," came the measured report from Eldron's chief security officer. This was turning into a nightmare.

"Clear this area," Eldron highlighted a section of the warship's schematic, just beyond the blip marking the progress of the creature. He stood near his command chair on the bridge, watching the security screen intently. The rest of his crew were at their stations, furiously engaging a defensive strategy to combat a threat for which, they were slowly coming to realize, there *was* no defense.

"Can we direct it?"

"Where?"

"Deck Eleven. Here and here." Graphics on the display were highlighted. "Take it to an airlock. Sacrifice a response team and shoot it into space." So many had been lost already, a dozen more Kel soldiers for the cause would be a small price to pay. Otherwise the creature would soon overrun them and the entire cruiser would be lost.

Eldron exhaled. "Try it."

"Executing."

Orders were issued, the drama unfolding from their perspective in a deceptively organized fashion. The command center was a green-lit hive of technology and orchestration, the crew at their consoles looking for ways to resolve the chaos in the bowels of the vessel; a calm mirror of the raging fury below.

It was as if a cancer had taken it.

Eldron paced to the side.

The ship was big, but the beast would eventually find its way here, to the bridge. That seemed to be its objective. It was intelligent, there was no doubt of that now, and after its initial attack and subsequent testing of the strength of their systems its entire focus had been a methodical sweep inward and upward from the point of its entry. Searching, it seemed, for the heart of the ship. Command and control. The bridge, where Eldron and his crew worked furiously to find a solution.

So far nothing had been able to stop it.

"Team moving down. Gathering at intersection."

Eldron watched the schematic overlay.

"Creature is at major bulkhead nine."

Even the most massive internal doors—*bulkhead doors!*— had been unable to hold it. When it reached the first they assumed that was it. There it would stay. Contained. A danger to be sure, but one for which they would find a way to contend.

But no. The door didn't hold. The hard metal slowed the beast, no question, but at length it was able to shatter the lock bars, even the frame around it, sending it crashing through. Worse, once it established that in fact it *could* break the doors, it was as if it became stronger. Confidence powered it, somehow. The next door and the next smashed quicker.

And on it came.

They tried nerve toxin. No effect. Vacuum was useless. Whether the thing needed atmosphere or not, they knew it didn't need it long enough to matter. Wave after wave of response team assaulted it in the narrow passageways, attempting to kill it as it made its way relentlessly upward, weaving through the ship, looking for what it sought. They may as well have been trying to halt a force of nature. It passed through each wave easily; not even their most powerful weapons had an effect. Anything larger—if even those weapons would've worked—was too much to use within the confines of the ship itself.

Now this latest gambit. Perhaps, just maybe, they could lure it to another lock and blow it back into space. Pull about and fire on it with the cruiser's giant plasma cannons. Hit it with atomic warheads. Anything to destroy it. Or, failing that, just let it float like an asteroid, forever if they were lucky. And God help the next world it fell upon.

And so Eldron concentrated silently. Hoping. Wishing

his team success in their sacrifice.

The alternative, if they failed, was grim. He could not unleash this unholy terror on his world. If they could not rid themselves of it, they would set the cruiser adrift. Destroy all controls and send it floating forever into the cold depths of space.

An eternal coffin for the abomination.

* * *

LINDIN LISTENED PATIENTLY as their military liaison briefed him and a small group of officials in the command center. The room buzzed with conversations, isolated pockets of activity as the staff monitored the conflict to the south. There weren't many actual tasks to be carried out—all tactical command was being handled directly from the battlefield, the mountain complex in existence for an entirely different purpose—which brought a certain disconnected sense of intensity as all watched the critical outcomes unfolding.

All Lindin could think about was the Icon.

Before returning to the command center he'd taken the remaining Icon back to his office and secured it. In a lockbox, in his own personal safe, where nothing short of an assault with advanced tools or explosives would break it free.

Of course part of him fretted at the idea of Satori and the girl returning unseen. Taking a crack at it. Somehow, learning where he'd put it and making a bid for it. By now he would not put it past them.

There were far too many things standing in their way but, for some reason, the comfort of that did little to calm him. Though he knew them getting the other Icon was ridiculously improbable, for many reasons, he had a hard time with the impulse to go stand by the lockbox and watch it until he had both of them in sight. But he refused to go that far. The two of them were *not* enemy commandos with an agenda. Just one simple girl who had a habit of ending up in the wrong place at the right time and, of course, a knack for getting people to do the most unexpected things. Case in point: Satori. Jessica had convinced his commander to break more than a few rules. And so, when they *did* turn up, they would be brought directly to him. Those were his orders.

The liaison giving the briefing was indicating the Dominion had managed to hold, deep in Midbay, but that their position was untenable. Venatres forces were being directed from locations to the west and would sweep them from the city, reclaiming it.

There was much anticipation in the air. The Dominion advance was ill-advised, by any standard, and now they would pay. With the loss of their new "Emperor", Kang, and the rest of the losses in their upper ranks as a result of Kang's brief reign (rampage was more like it), the Dominion was about to suffer a collapse. Perhaps fatal. They had never fully recovered from the incidents at the Crucible, and now this.

For an instant Lindin had the unsettling conclusion that, in a strange way, credit for the fall of the Dominion might be given to the girl. *Jessica.* His very nemesis, in a sense, yet her actions had directly driven the destruction of the Dominion stronghold, the Crucible, setting in motion events leading to now. And now, less than an hour ago, she'd provided the means to get rid of Kang.

The truth of it was hard to ignore. The way it might be perceived even harder. She brought down the Crucible. And, with it, the entire upper hierarchy of the Dominion. Then, when Kang showed up, the beast quickly got rid of the rest of the clerics and ...

Jessica got rid of him.

Lindin had, again, the unsettling yet sincere worry the girl from Earth would be seen as a hero.

He had to be careful the way he handled her.

"Sir," the voice of one of his officers got through. Josef. The drone of the liaison was interrupted and now Josef came from the background, inserting himself into the conversation. Lindin looked to him.

"Yes?"

Josef shifted anxiously. "We just got word. The girl and

Commander Satori have returned."

Immediately Lindin was on alert. *Here we go.* Time to get them where he could keep an eye on them.

"Are they arriving at the hangar?"

"They left the hangar."

Left the hangar? Images of the feared commando assault came flooding to mind. Lindin started for the door without thinking, then pulled up short, trying not to give in to that irrational impulse.

"You mean they arrived? They've already arrived? Are they being brought here?" *Those were my orders.* They were to be brought to him.

"They claimed you called them, and that they were on their way to see you, as requested. They got by the guards." Josef was nervous. "We think they may be headed for the lab."

Lindin blinked. Shock then anger passed through him in rapid succession, leaving him stunned. He felt his innards churn.

His mouth worked a moment.

"... The lab?"

Josef nodded. "We've lost contact with units there."

Lindin's mind was racing, alternating between relief and concern. There was nothing in the lab for them to get. He'd already removed and secured the other Icon and it wasn't anywhere near the lab so if they were heading to the lab there was nothing to fear. All was safe. They were on a cold trail. Probably they *were* going for the other Icon, which made him wish he'd been wrong in his suspicions, but they wouldn't find it. Not there. So why was he afraid? What gnawed at him?

Amid the chaos of the battle and all else it wasn't impossible to imagine they slipped back undetected, but he was alarmed they'd gotten past the guards. Did they truly dupe them? Did they overpower them? And if they'd lost contact with the lab ...

It was one thing to steal, quite another to injure. If so, if they *had* assaulted guards, then they'd now crossed a line. Would that make it easier to punish them?

But all those questions fell suddenly away.

And the gnawing fear crystallized.

Now he felt sick.

And with a harried call for *all* guards, voice rising in pitch, calling for every guard in the place, to meet him at the lab, now and without delay, he shoved everyone aside and was off at a full sprint.

The starship was in there.

* * *

"DON'T MAKE US DO ANYTHING," Jess cautioned, working to keep the tremor out of her voice. "We're not criminals. You have to believe that." Now that Warrior Jess had done her part, helping Satori take the guards' guns and hold them hostage, the teenager in her wanted to set things right. It wasn't the best impulse to honor at the moment, she realized, but she couldn't resist the urge to explain. "I don't want anything to happen. To anyone. Don't do anything that would make anyone get hurt.

"Okay?"

The guards didn't respond, but she saw their reluctant expressions at her plea. Perhaps they wouldn't try anything.

And suddenly ... a reality check. *We're holding guns on people,* she couldn't help staring down at the deadly machine-pistol in her hands. *About to steal a starship!* The behemoth loomed in her peripheral vision and, despite her best efforts, she found herself looking slightly in its direction.

How the hell are we supposed to steal that? It had never been flown, it was barely understood—*so massive!*—it was priceless, it was in the middle of a mountain that, until then, she only *assumed* had a way out. That she'd gotten Satori and Willet to come this far, in that instant, terrified her. This was huge. It was sensational.

What have I done?

It could turn out there was *no* way to fly the ship. Maybe it needed weeks of prep. Maybe it needed all kinds of authorization codes. Nani might be unwilling to help.

What if Nani's not even here?! And what about Bianca? Could she leave without her?

Far too much had been assumed.

And it was about to fail miserably.

Jail was now a certainty.

"Let's go," Satori waved her gun, indicating the guards should start walking. She motioned them toward the fore of the craft. That was where the work stations were. Where Nani would be, if she hadn't left. Jess looked up. Way up, and the sheer scale of the setting washed over her. The cavern was so big, the air seemed to have a breeze at all times, temperature differentials at differing heights causing natural circulation. It was a yawning openness, like the inside of a giant football stadium, filled nearly to capacity with the bulk of the giant starship itself.

She had to deliberately make herself not think about it.

There was no going back now.

So far the startling comprehension of the magnitude of what they were about to do was not, seemingly, hitting Satori. At least if it was it didn't show. Maybe all her resistance came earlier. Maybe she'd gotten her arguments out of her system. And as Jess realized this she also realized why. It was because Satori had, by even deciding to do this, invested full confidence in *her*. Whether from her adamant insistence, her own personal, unwavering determination, her past success or something else, Satori, having finally relented, now expected Jess had matters well in hand. Having decided to follow her Satori's own doubts had been put on hold.

Now it was up to her.

No pressure.

"Jessica!" Bianca called from somewhere up ahead. Jess found her and her spirits lifted, briefly. *Bianca! You're here!* Her friend stood in the distance, near Nani—*Nani's here!*—along with a small group of lab technicians. *Yes!*

She wouldn't have to leave her after all.

As soon as Bianca saw the guns, however, her expression went slack. So did most of the others.

Nani put a hand to her mouth.

Bianca's voice dropped in timbre. "Jessica, what's going on?"

Jess hated the extent of the mess she'd dragged her friend into.

And it was about to get worse.

"It's not as bad as it seems," she lied, noting the guards at the end of their guns looked back and forth between her and Satori. She didn't think the two soldiers would try anything, but she caught her attention wavering and made sure not to let it lapse. The next minutes were going to be the most difficult, and she didn't want the tables turned because she was getting emotional with her friend. More than anything she didn't want to pull any triggers.

"Oh no," she heard Nani mutter through her fingers. "No," the blonde scientist looked behind her, as if searching for a place to run. Realizing, of course, there was nowhere to go.

I know that feeling.

Jess and her small group drew up on the work area where a standoff ensued; the handful of lab-coated technicians in various states of fear, Bianca looking to the terrified Nani— even as she fought her own fear; facing across from the two guards tasked with preventing entry, their protectors, now with their hands up at gunpoint. At gunpoint with guns being held by their friends.

It was a terrifying, shocking, confusing moment.

Willet stood off to the side, still looking like he was along for the ride. In fact, to Jess it seemed he was almost curious to see what would happen next.

Satori spoke. "A bunch more guys with guns are probably on their way. We need to keep moving."

Nani actually whimpered. She lowered her hand. "Lindin was just down here," she managed. Now she looked directly at Bianca, and Jess found it interesting—a misplaced regard in that moment—that Bianca seemed to be a point of comfort for Nani. Bianca, who had absolutely fallen apart during the first half of their journey, seemed now to be a source of strength. At least for Nani.

Jess was glad for it. Because for what came next they

would need all the strength they could get.

Satori was all business. Young though she was, here was a seasoned field commander, one who had risen to rank for good reason. "We don't have much time," she informed them. "We need to move." She turned her attention to the starship, eyes roving up and down its great length—even as she kept the guards at a safe distance. Jess shuddered at the presence of the craft. More, at the thought they were about to go aboard.

"Nani," Satori held her gaze, as one might hold the attention of a frightened child, "how do we fly this thing?"

The guards' mouths fell open. So did the mouths of all the technicians within earshot. Nani spluttered, a *what?!* expression crawling across her face. She jerked her head involuntarily, to look at the ship, then back; flipping that wide-eyed, piercing stare between the ship, Satori and Jess.

Absolutely frozen in fear.

Bianca locked eyes with Jessica. Friend to friend. It was as if, for an instant, the rest of the scene, the rest of the players, melted away—for the briefest of moments—and Bianca stood only with her. Just the two of them. Long-time besties. Fellow high-schoolers. Only girls from Boise in the room.

I need you. Jess hoped her friend would stay strong.

"What are we doing?" Bianca's voice quavered.

"We came for the ship," Jess told her. Then, in what felt like an impossible oversimplification but which summarized the moment: "It's the only way."

Nani shook her head. "No, no, no. What are you saying? Take this? Oh, no. If we do that ...

"They'll never let us out."

"You're their best and brightest," Jess thought of ways to reassure her, finding few. "They won't lock you away. Us, maybe. Not you. We're the ones making you do this."

Satori had little time for further discussion. "It won't matter," she said, continuing to eye the ship. "If we don't do something quick this little escapade will be over before it begins."

CHAPTER 6:

A NEW TOY

KANG PULLED WITH BOTH HANDS, hard, exerting a good bit of his full strength to peel back the thick metal of the alien bulkhead. Whatever this machine was made of it was superior to the materials of Anitra. The alien metal was proving difficult to make his way through and, in fact, at first he hadn't been sure he could. After decimating the "greeting" party he'd turned his attention to finding the control center and whomever was in charge, but when they locked the first, massively thick door it nearly thwarted him. Only as he applied more and more force did he finally break through— truly straining; heaving, and as he'd stepped through into the hallway beyond found himself wondering how far he might have to go.

Of course each successive door had been locked. Making his progress slow. But success after several doors built confidence; showed him weak points, taught him where to punch through, where to grip, where to pull. And so yet another door bent toward him and down, enough to allow him to pass. He moved along now with an economy of motion, ever upward, looking for the heart of this vessel so he could command it.

At the last major intersection another assault team had attempted to lure him away. Presumably to blow him into space. He'd killed them like all the rest. Their weapons, their tactics—none of it was proving a match for his strength and his resolve. Already he'd killed dozens of the aliens and would kill as many more as necessary. The reasonable part of him, if such still existed, cautioned against a full massacre, as only the aliens understood how to work this thing, and he knew at some point he must pause to consider that. Enough must be left alive when he was done to follow his lead, to work the mighty vessel at his direction. Looking at the size and complexity of it he was sure he could never run it alone.

At the thought of that a deep, maniacal laugh escaped him, reverberating down the green metal hallway.

It was like a maze. He'd been trying to make sense of any part of it, to find clues that might lead him to what he sought, but so far no luck. Angrily he scratched at his arms, still irritated from whatever toxin they'd released.

Just another effort to stop him that failed.

Next up was another intersection. He strode into it and stopped, checking left and right. There, to the left, toward the interior of the ship, were as many of the alien warriors as could fit in the hall, waiting; manning at least three large cannons mounted on tripods. He took all this in just as the barrage hit him.

CRACK! the electric beams enveloped him. *CRACK! CRACK!* Brilliant blue lightning at the edges of his vision. They hurt, but did not have the push of the plasma used by the Dominion, or even the impact of the projectiles used by the Venatres. Both weapon types failed miserably against the Kazerai, but at least had kinetic energy that tended to drive them back, delaying the attack of the super warriors if nothing else. These alien weapons transferred a far more painful blast—especially the big ones being used on Kang now—but had relatively no inertia.

Making it that much easier to charge.

"AAAARGH!" he bellowed thunderously and leapt against them, hitting the front line in one leap, scattering bodies to both sides. The front cannons went silent as the warriors behind them kept up a furious rate of fire with rifles, stinging him with bright blue beams that flashed the walls like brilliant arc-lights.

In seconds he'd dispatched them all, a maelstrom of solid thunks and flying body parts ...

And the hall was silent once more.

That group had been waiting, he noted, not in ambush but in defense. They were the most heavily armed so far, and their stances had been different; unmoving, looking to protect.

Could he finally have reached the heart? The nerve center of this massive beast? He gazed steadily at the door beyond, reading the meaningless markings on it, feeling the residual sting of the high-power beams radiating from his skin. The markings on this door were larger, more prominent than any yet seen.

He stepped to it and punched through. Just above the lockbars, where he had all the others. Punched in his other hand, took hold and ... pulled. Harder. Pulling it back, feeling the titanic groan of metal as much as hearing it, the strain pounding in his ears as he let loose a groan of his own, followed by a mighty bellow as the door came clear of the hinges.

He flung it thundering into the carnage behind him.

And there, before him ...

Was the bridge.

Yes!

Of the rooms he'd come across so far this was the obvious control center. Long and wide with a low ceiling, lit by the green lights of numerous control stations, manned by more of the aliens. These wore no helmets and looked less like soldiers, more like technicians. At the far end was a screen that covered the entire wall, side to side, floor to ceiling, displaying the stars without. And there, in the middle of the room, the only one standing, was one with a bearing that could only make him their leader. This one's hair was shock white, though the rest of him was as the others; pale, perfect skin, sharp angular features, brilliant yellow eyes and dark, precise markings tracing patterns around one socket.

Kang checked the hall behind, confirming no additional troops approached. No sounds came to him, no sign of movement. Just the bodies piled there, lifeless, pinned beneath the crushing weight of the door he'd just discarded. Ahead was the only threat, and from the look of it the men assembled on the bridge were even less equipped than the others to offer resistance.

Which meant the ship was his.

Their leader began issuing orders, terse, in the sharp

notes of their language, and as others of them hurried to comply Kang began suddenly to fear they might arm some sort of self-destruct. After all, it was clear they'd lost. It was over. He'd won, killing many in the bargain. Surely they must expect him to kill more. To kill them all.

Somehow, after all this, he had to turn things around. He had to make them understand he would stop the killing.

If only they didn't do anything first.

"No!" he said, taking several steps into the large room. They wouldn't understand him, of course, but they were human enough. Perhaps the mannerisms, the intent— these things must surely be clear. "No," he waved his hands side to side; tried to make them understand he meant them to stop whatever it was they were doing. To rethink his presence and see, perhaps, that he was done with the massacre. "No," he kept repeating, walking slowly among them, methodically, waving his hands back and forth in what he hoped would be perceived as a calming gesture. They knew what he'd already done, had just seen him peel through an armored door, behind him the butchery of his arrival. Though he could do so easily, he wasn't killing anyone else. It should be clear he wanted their attention. He was as alien to them as they were to him, and there wasn't much reason for them to hold, he had to admit, but, to his great satisfaction, they did. Curious, it seemed, and the sight of their expressions struck him.

"Wait," he threw in another word, stood straighter and lowered his hands. His voice was deep, grizzled, scarred from his transformation, and until then he'd relished it. Now he wished for something a bit more ... diplomatic. Their voices, at least the ones he'd heard so far, were smooth, and rich.

No matter.

"I wish no more harm," he rasped, deciding that, though the words would not be understood, perhaps some of what he meant might yet be communicated. It was all he had.

"I," and he indicated himself, "want this." He turned in a circle with his arms out, trying to suggest the ship around him. It was hard not to laugh aloud. Should he just kill them and be done with it? Slaughter them all before they could set their plans in action? What then? How long would it take to figure out this technology?

Forever.

He cast his gaze across every surface, bewildered by the myriad of lights and feeds of information. All in an alien language. There was no way he would work it himself. Even *were* it in his language, there was just no way. He'd never been a scientist, an engineer. Hardly. Warrior, leader; these were his strengths.

He needed these remaining aliens.

Like children in command of a world-breaking machine, they were no match for him. Yet he needed them.

The first thing, he decided, was to successfully get them to do something. It didn't matter what. Get them to let him sit in a chair, press a button—whatever. From there he could build his control.

He had an idea.

As non-threateningly as he could he walked across the length of the bridge, away from them, to the giant screen at the front. This was a transmitted view, he gathered, not a window, though it was as clear as one. He'd not seen any windows from the outside. On the screen the edge of the purple planet was just off to one side, the rest of the view filled with stars. He scanned the breadth of it, top to bottom, finding nothing even with his superb vision.

"Where is it?" he turned back to them. The whole of the bridge sat staring at him from their stations, their ribbed black armor, pale complexions, hair pulled tight into queues; pointy ears and faces he could scarcely tell apart. Like they'd all been cast from the same mold. Only the commander stood, mute; wondering, Kang could see, just what the beast was thinking. It almost seemed to him they were shocked he could speak at all.

"Where is it?" he repeated. This was what he would have them do. This would be the first test of his control.

They would recover the Icon.

"The device." He described it with his hands, tracing its outline in the air before him. "The device." After a few attempts it looked as if some might actually get what he was talking about.

The commander did.

"The device," Kang said again, and pointed out into the depths of space. He traced its outline again, then pointed. He did this twice more before the commander issued an order to one of his crew. The man did something at his console and the rest looked up, past Kang; Kang turned back to the screen and ...

There it was. The Icon. Floating against the stars, tumbling slowly, metallic surface glinting with each gentle turn. They must've magnified the screen to bring it into view. Which meant they'd already spotted it, as Kang suspected they would've, along with he and Horus.

Horus.

A dark cloud passed across his expression, he could feel it, but he got control of his anger and pressed on. Horus wasn't going anywhere. There would be time enough for him.

First he would secure the way back.

"Go to it," he gestured. Then refined his gesture, pointing at the floor of the bridge, as if to take hold of the ship, then move it through an arc forward, toward the Icon on the screen. He did this several times, dragging it out toward the Icon.

"Fly the ship," he said. "To it." Pointing. Dragging.

No one budged.

He was sure they must be getting the concept.

"Fly," he said and walked to the nearest console. The man seated there just looked at him and, for a brief instant, Kang admired his courage. Admired all their courage, now that he thought on it. Humans, even the bravest, faced with something as shocking as him, in such close quarters, after all he'd done, would've been cowering in terror against the walls. Screaming, looking for a place to hide. Not these. This was a warrior race. To a man they seemed prepared to die, if necessary. In a way he hoped he might learn more of them, and expected he would, eventually, if he ever got through these initial phases.

For now he wanted them to fly.

"Fly," he touched the console. As he touched it he turned to face the screen, mimicking controlling the ship, steering it this way and that—making it move forward, toward the Icon.

Behind him the commander issued another order. A pair of crewmen seated side by side turned to their consoles and began making adjustments. Imperceptibly Kang felt the craft move. Just barely. The same technology that gave a sense of gravity against the floor must also nullify other changes in direction. However, to his greatly attuned sense of equilibrium, he could tell they had begun moving forward at a brisk clip.

The power of the vessel was remarkable.

On screen the Icon image was adjusted and brought into perspective and Kang could see they were, in fact, moving toward it.

He had successfully issued a set of instructions and the aliens had complied and, now, he was about to achieve his first objective.

Now he did let loose a short laugh. Kept it to a quiet chuckle and reined it in before it rose to the full mania he was feeling. As with other communication basics, he had a suspicion laughter would be readily understood by these aliens, and the cackle of a maniac would be universal.

Best not to let things slide.

He was making too much progress.

* * *

"I think I'm going to faint," Nani actually stumbled and caught her footing as they made their way up the passage. She braced herself with one hand, then continued, leading the small group with faltering but deliberate steps toward a ladder at the far end. Her at the front, Bianca staying close, ready to steady her if needed, followed by Satori, Willet and Jess. That was all that boarded the *Reaver*. Their little band of felons. Halfway up Nani paused to find a control and activate lighting and the alien corridor came alive under mild illumination, tinged with violet, showing details that had, until then, been cast mostly in stark relief from the light of the lab streaming in through the open entry. She set another control and ... the thick outer door closed. A heavy thunk and it notched into its recess, sealing out the lab.

Sealing them inside.

Jess began to panic.

All at once; like a complete inversion of the determination that got her this far. Impossibly everything was falling into place, everything was going as planned and ... suddenly it was too much. Satori had agreed to do this. They got past the guards and the few measures left to stop them. Nani ended up being with the *Reaver*, just like they needed. Bianca, too, was there. Incredible. Then, Jess was able to convince Nani to do what she wanted. Now they were going aboard, so far no one was stopping them and, as it turned out, Nani *could* fly the ship. Alone. She could fly the starship, just Nani and their little group, they could take it out, it could go instantly to where Zac went, even to Earth if needed ... they could go do everything Jess wanted, all of it, everything she'd imagined doing and they could do it now and they were here and they could do it right now— *right now*—they could go rescue Zac, go check the Earth for Kang and ...

All Jess wanted to do was run.

In that very instant the only thing in the world she wanted was to just get the hell out of there.

She reached a steadying hand to the wall. So many things could've—should've—failed. But they didn't. And the impossible was working, this was happening, and it was everything she'd hoped for and the heavy door closed like being locked in a coffin and all she felt in that instant was a scream welling and the overwhelming urge to call it off; to tell Nani to fire the door open so she could flee it all and run away.

Jess found herself holding tighter to the cold, unforgiving metal of the alien bulkhead. Making sure she didn't sag to the floor.

This was all my idea. Nani, Bianca, Willet, Satori ... they all went with her, because of her, ready to embark on a journey the likes of which no human—on Earth or Anitra—had undertaken in, well, in ever, as far as any of them knew. It was epic.

The walls kept crushing in.

Desperately she fought to rise above it, to make herself process the mundane things around her; the basic things; the normal, usual things; how she was standing, where everyone was, what they were doing right at that moment. She noted she and Satori still held the machine pistols. Why, she had no idea. Because there was nowhere to put them. Because they'd forgotten they were even in their hands. They'd kept them trained on the two guards and the gape-mouthed technicians as they walked backwards up the ramp moments ago. No one showed any sign of trying to stop them. Maybe the Venatres still thought her a hero. Maybe they were just too stunned to act. She hadn't thought to ask or demand or bring anyone else, any other technician, unsure of her ability to continue to sway Nani, to influence the others—unwilling to bring more variables into the equation.

Nani, apparently, was all they needed.

Steady breaths.

Slowly she got a grip.

"Here," Nani instructed, voice shaking as she motioned everyone forward to a spot near her. When they'd gathered close she set another control and a second door shut, this one internal, between them and the outer door, creating a sort of airlock against the ship's hull. As that happened, both doors solid and fluid in their actions—remarkably quiet at a thousand years of age—cool air began circulating in the otherwise stale hall. Jess took a deep, shuddering breath.

"They breathed air like ours," Nani informed them. "We didn't have to calibrate anything." Essentially useless information but they were, each of them, thoroughly unnerved in that moment, and talking was better than silence. Jess appreciated it. Only Willet seemed to retain some small semblance of curiosity, looking about at the alien technology with a mixture of admiration and awe. The surfaces were smooth, glossy-black, lit with violet, geometrically interesting trace lights like something out of *Tron.* Part of Jessica admired the craft, but only a small part. Most of her remained panic-stricken.

"This way," Nani went for the ladder.

Then Satori said the words that half broke the spell:

"Are we really doing this?"

Willet shrugged, eyes roving all over. "I'm just following orders."

Nani went up the ladder. Bianca followed as Nani climbed higher, the rest following one after the other. At the top they made their way down another passage.

"The problem," Satori kept talking as they went, "will be if this thing doesn't work. We flip the switch and nothing happens? Not good."

Up ahead Jess thought she heard Nani let go another whimper. Bianca touched her comfortingly on the back.

Nani reached another bulkhead door and it slid open and she was stepping through. Then Bianca. Then Satori. Then Jess, pausing across the threshold, a lump rising in her throat.

"Whoa," Willet said from behind, voice nearly a whisper.

It was the bridge.

Probably about as big as a really big living room, it had a high, domed ceiling, ringed on the floor with half-a-dozen shiny-black workstations, complete with violet-lit controls—hundreds of readings and small screens, on and ready to go. At the center were three more rugged chairs, on pedestals, one higher than the others.

The real gasp-inducer, however, was the external view. The domed ceiling was essentially a video display, starting just above the control consoles at about waist level, all the way around, three-sixty and curving up—wrapping the full upper half of the bridge like some kind of IMAX superdome. It was on and showing the cavern without. Whether Nani turned it on when she entered or it was on all the time, it was an incredible projection of the outside.

There were overlays of information in the alien Kel glyphs, floating here and there ghost-like, other metrics showing steady mechanical heartbeats from whatever things they monitored, but otherwise the effect was like standing on the top of the starship, looking out.

"Can they see us?" Bianca asked, already at one of the edges and looking "down". A few techs were visible on the floor at the front of the ship.

"No," said Nani.

"It looks so real," Bianca said under her breath, touching the crystal clear image.

Nani went to one of the workstations and sat, tapping various controls as if having practiced these actions time and again. But of course she would have. This was her life. Jess could see she was, despite her nerves, completely ready for this moment. Nani's hands were shaking, yes, but they moved with confidence.

Then a troubling thought. There were so many. But this was crucial.

"Wait," she said. Why didn't she think of this? "This will blow the mountain apart when we take off. Won't everyone be killed? It's way too massive." What kind of energy would it take to even lift this thing off the ground? The force alone ...

There was no was she was going to blast out of there in a rain of fire, burning everyone to ash.

But Nani never would've been swayed if that was the case. The answer was as expected. "No," the scientist girl kept bringing up controls. There was no danger of that. *Good.* "Field manipulation," she went on. And, for the briefest of instants, as she successfully brought to life the thing to which she'd devoted so much of her ambition, a flicker of enthusiasm. "If it works properly we should glide out of here like we're floating on air."

Bianca stood at the front, looking out on the cavern and the lab. "How?" she asked. "How do we get out?" There was no visible starship-sized exit.

"There," Nani pointed and, as if extending a magic finger, the entire fore end of the cavern broke along one perfect edge and began sliding to the side. Into a recess, the mechanism so expertly finished that it hadn't even been apparent until activated. The door spanned the height of the cavern and most of its breadth, wide enough (Jess presumed) to allow the Kel warship through.

Nani looked up, done tapping screens for the moment.

"The only risk is that I accelerate too fast," she said. "That could draw a wake behind us and suck people out. I can't hurry until we're clear."

Jess was patient. Made herself be. Her fear was that something would fail; the door would stick, someone would override it; the starship itself would get shut off remotely. So many things could yet prevent them.

Be patient.

They all watched as the giant door continued its to move to the side, exposing more and more of the smoothly bored tunnel through which they would exit. At the far end, beyond the thickness of the mountain, another door could be seen moving aside at the same pace, exposing a clear blue afternoon. Jess still held the gun. So did Satori. Willet stood with them. Bianca at the front, right at the screen looking out; like a kid at a picture window, curious at the kids across the street. Wondering what the day might hold. Nani, their only source of understanding for all this, at her station, preparing. It was kind of a surreal moment. Such a normal, small group of people, standing in the middle of all that technology. All that potential.

And it was working.

"There they are," Nani interrupted their rapture. Everyone followed her gaze to the side and down, at the entry to the lab. Far across the floor a group of armed soldiers had stormed in and were fanning out, Lindin in the lead.

"Damn."

Nani was terrified all over again. She looked to Satori, then Jessica, second-guessing what they were doing. Jess gave her what she hoped was an encouraging look, trying to project the idea of *keep going, this is what we're doing.* Nani turned to the console in earnest, checking and re-checking as she looked anxiously between the lumbering cavern door and the readouts. Jess wondered if the guys on the ground *did* have a way to override it.

"Remember we're holding you hostage," she said, feeling the machine-pistol in her grip. "If anything happens and we don't make it, you're just doing what we forced you to do. You won't get in any trouble." *Keep opening!* she willed the massive doors.

Nani kept checking things. Tapped a few controls.

"There," she said at last. "I think we're clear." And she turned fully to the console and concentrated on what she was about to do. Systematically, one action after the next, keying up controls until ... the ship moved. At first Jess didn't feel it, just saw it. She reached a hand for the closest chair. Then realized she couldn't feel any movement at all. She expected to feel it, but only her eyes told her things were changing position. Like watching a movie on a giant screen. Slowly the ship lifted a dozen feet into the air. Small distance in view of the size of the ship itself, but they rose. There was a thrum of titanic force through the superstructure, echoes of the power involved, but it was of such low frequency it only barely impinged on the edges of perception. It was incredible. The *Reaver* was probably as heavy as a US Navy warship and physics were physics, which meant that however the energy was transferred—with fields or with fire or a sprinkling of magic pixie dust—this was a *huge* amount of mass to move. That it could happen so quietly, with no shock, no evidence of that titanic force ...

But it did. Outside in the lab nothing blew away. People scrambled against the far walls, of course, but not because anything made them. The *Reaver* lifted gently on a distant hum, like a giant magnet, then ... began moving forward. Toward the door and out the cavern.

"You can't even tell we're moving," Bianca marveled.

"Inertial dampers," Nani said, almost proud that all was working as planned. "They're not perfect, but at this acceleration you won't feel a thing."

They passed through the first door, all holding their

breath that it didn't go slamming closed and pin them in. Further they drifted, ever forward, into the tunnel and slowly, slowly toward the other opening at the far end, gradually picking up speed.

Bianca looked back from the front, directly at Jessica.

"We're going home," she said softly.

Jess nodded, knowing that really wasn't the case. Bianca knew it too. They knew their lives on Earth were over. But Jess tried to let the thought of it sustain her. They had hope now. Possibility.

* * *

"*Do something!*" Lindin was practically spitting, stepping first toward the technicians, desperate to get them to do *anything* to stop this impossible thing that was happening, then back toward the starship as it hovered slowly forward, through the massive doors. Hanging over the cavern floor as if suspended from invisible cables. Nice and slow, taunting him. Reflexively he reached out a hand, as if he might take hold and pull it back.

There was nothing to be done.

"What do you mean you can't close the doors?!" He was infuriated. The nearest tech was attempting to explain, something about the way they'd set it up, fail-safes to prevent damage to the starship once it was in the tunnel, how they'd never anticipated a situation like this and blah, blah, blah—even as Lindin wanted to scream at him *of course we never anticipated a situation like this!* but do *something!*

He couldn't bring it down. Not in there. Not that he would. He couldn't close the doors. He couldn't stop it.

The frantic scurrying of bodies eased and now everyone just kind of stood there, stunned. Helplessly watching the inevitable. Unreal. A nightmare come to life. Through the inner door and up the tunnel it went. Huge, black, shining perfection, sweeping out as if in slow attack; shape of it looking as if swooping for the kill, even when barely in motion, moving along an unerring, laser-straight path, up the wide, oval tunnel; too massive to be so smooth, so quiet, "wings" out to the sides like a bird of prey in flight.

Getting away.

CHAPTER 7:

FLIGHT

THE REAVER SLIPPED THROUGH the final, massive door into the sunlight, screen optics doing a perfect job of relaying the view outside. Under the overarching dome it was as if the small group stood atop the ship in the open air, like on the deck of a sailing vessel, some kind of pirate ship of old, or maybe even a Disney ride; something out of *Peter Pan*, gazing down on the splendor of the gray/white mountains as they sailed quietly over the peaks beneath a clear blue sky.

It was breathtaking.

Nani tapped the controls expertly, upped the acceleration and curving them to greater and greater heights. Soon they were high enough to see the ocean to the east, then the curve of the world itself and, soon enough, were fairly racing to orbit. The rate at which they gained velocity became visually alarming. Jess was reminded of UFO "re-enactment" videos, where a giant spacecraft would dart suddenly into the sky at impossible speed. She held tight to one of the chairs, though as yet felt little of the change in direction. It was as if she could easily step away and just stand there, unwavering as they blitzed into space; maybe even sip a cup of coffee, or even balance on one leg. Movement was that imperceptible.

Nani was hugely pleased with the results.

"It's all working," she said as they slipped free of the last shreds of atmosphere. Now that they were clear—*boy are we*, thought Jess, looking out at the rapidly darkening sky—Nani was transforming before her eyes. Lapsing fully into her passion for the machine. Their high treason, for the moment, forgotten. This was, in truth, the thing she'd been working toward for years and, though the circumstances were all wrong, she had at last achieved her ambition.

She was flying the ancient Kel starship.

Outside the black of space soon filled the view, the last wisps of air slipping away. Clouds blanketed the globe below, just like in every orbital video Jess had ever seen.

I'm in space.

She could hardly believe it.

Anitra spread beneath them, further as they rose, defining itself more and more each moment as a giant sphere. Just like Earth. Brown, some green, not quite as much blue, but otherwise a planet. Practically a mirror of her home, filled with life, covered in a nurturing blanket of air. Higher they went, moving further and further away, the globe becoming more and more defined, and she found herself standing at the wraparound screen beside Bianca looking at it receding. She noticed Willet and Satori had joined them.

Transfixed.

After a while Jess glanced to the side. Satori looked more stunned than Jess had ever seen her. In the silence that hung in the air, each of them gazing on that spectacular vista, processing their own thoughts—Nani alone busy, in quiet motion behind them, making it all work—Satori summed up the situation:

"Holy. Shit."

Jess didn't know if that was an Anitran slang too, or if Satori had just heard her or Bianca say it somewhere along the way, but it could not have been more appropriate for the moment.

Holy shit indeed.

At Satori's apt assessment everyone kind of stared at each other, the full import of things seeming to settle over them all at once.

Utterly taken with what they'd done.

Nani had no time for such awe. Her mind was in motion, consumed, continuing her frantic working of the *Reaver's* systems, nearly beside herself. "There's so many things I want to check," she said, filled all at once with a flood of scientific curiosity. Jess looked back at her. Couldn't tell if the flurry of activity was still necessary or if Nani was simply pouring through more information, testing, evaluating. Finally getting the chance she'd been waiting for. Each second her fear of the epically punishable thing they'd just done morphed further into raw excitement.

As if sensing Jessica's gaze her blonde head glanced up from the console and looked across the bridge.

"I'm setting up what we need to go find Zac," she amended her enthusiasm. "I've got to move us further beyond the gravity well." For a brief moment she lingered, admiring the spectacular view herself, having been consumed until then with what she was doing, then put her attention back at the controls.

The *Reaver's* speed only seemed to increase. The entire planet came well into view. Continued moving away. For it to keep changing perspective at that rate Jess knew they had to be accelerating at a tremendous clip. She had no idea how fast, or how fast the ship could go, how hard Nani was pushing it and so on, but they were moving way faster than any rocket of Earth, that much was certain. It would take hours or even days to cover that kind of distance in a regular chemical rocket. Whatever powered the *Reaver* was impressive beyond any Earth reckoning. They were minutes into their flight and already Anitra had diminished to fill only half the screen.

And the *Reaver* could go further. Between the stars, if it worked. That it could be a thousand years old and fully functioning ...

It was miraculous.

Jess looked around the bridge, admiring the power of it, the ease with which this ancient ship promised to bring her objectives to life.

And noticed most of her panic was gone.

After a few more minutes she walked carefully—steadily— back across the bridge, over to Nani, who'd stopped tapping controls and was now scanning screen after screen of information.

"Incredible," she kept shaking her head.

"You think the ..." Jess fished for the right term, "star drive will work?" She felt the urgency of Zac's peril.

Nani looked to the screens. "We'll know in a moment."

Satori joined them. Jess noted both she and Satori still held the machine pistols.

It had been a tense escape.

She found a spot and laid hers down. Satori seemed to notice the gun all at once and put hers down too.

Jess glanced back toward the front, to Willet and Bianca who stood watching Anitra recede. For Willet his home, for Bianca an alien world, the mark of her first step through the looking glass.

"We need to go to the last point," Jess tried to think of the best way to describe where they had to go. Where Zac would've gone, and where he might still be. "The one the second Icon was set to. You can reference that, right?"

Nani nodded that she could. Checked some more readings. Jess turned to look back across the bridge, at the colorful world that kept getting smaller and smaller. Anitra's moon had come into view, looking like another world in itself, floating in the black of space in the distance, off to the port side. Polarizing filters kept the glare of the orange-tinged sun to a dull fire, giving everything a crisp visual edge.

They were covering distance at a truly amazing rate. Jess was having a hard time getting over it. If this were Earth they could've been halfway to the moon by now. It was absolutely stunning.

"Ok," said Nani. "We're ready." She continued checking things, tapping now and again, setting whatever was involved in making the jump.

"We should probably sit," she advised. "I don't know what effect the state-shift will have on our physiology. We may lose our equilibrium." Willet and Bianca turned from the fore screen as Nani continued: "We don't actually travel *through* space, in the sense that we understand it. Just shift from one location to the next. The effect should be near instantaneous, from our perspective. I just don't know what it will feel like."

Jess figured it was probably like an Icon transfer, of which she and Bianca were the only ones there that had any experience. It was disorienting, yes, but the feeling passed quickly.

She and Satori looked at the available seats. The three at the center had to be command chairs; five more around the edges were control stations like Nani's.

Willet came closer, looked at Jess and extended a hand to the central, highest chair. The one clearly reserved for the captain.

"It would only be fitting," he said. Jess looked at it. Was about to defer then realized it was a stupid point to argue and, in the end, it really didn't matter. Without comment she stepped over, stepped up and sat in the large, comfortable seat. It was big but not overly so. The Kel were clearly more or less human in size and so it fit. Settling in she looked around the bridge, feeling very much like Captain Kirk or something, ready to take command. Not only that—and though this was never intended—everyone's plain, black Anitran clothes, what they all just happened to be wearing, almost made it look like they wore uniforms.

Like they were a real crew.

Willet took a seat in the chair to her right. Satori sat in the other, to her left. Bianca went and sat at the station near Nani.

When everyone was in place Jess gripped the arms of the chair and looked ahead.

"All right," she said, thought for a surreal second to add something like, *engage*, maybe even point a finger toward the forward screen, but said instead: "Let's go get Zac."

* * *

HE'D DONE IT. Kang had the Icon. With less difficulty than he imagined he'd directed these aliens across the void to retrieve the shiny device, and now held it in his hands. As he walked the corridors back to the bridge he looked down on it, catching his stretched and deformed reflection in its curved metallic surface.

The aliens had pulled alongside it with the same bay they'd used to retrieve him, making use of the same grappling arm—made all the more unwieldy by the size of the Icon itself. But he refused to go to the edge or in any other way risk the chance they might contrive a way to be rid of him, making them get it instead. And so now he had it. Raising the next most obvious question:

What to do with it?

All he knew of the Icon was as a holy relic. He'd never thought of it in terms of a portal device, but clearly that's what it was. It had transferred him and Horus. Would it send him back? Surely it must. Using it again—however one used it—must return him to Anitra. But how much would be transported? Would it take only him? Would it take the whole ship? Whatever he touched? When Horus activated it they brought grass and bits of the park with them. Was that just a localized effect?

One thing was for sure, if he used the Icon and it returned only him, and not the entire ship, this opportunity would be lost. Even if he then tried to pop back here it would only put him right back in the void, and there was no way he would get back aboard. And as he thought of that he realized the first thing he had to admit was that taking guesses at the Icon was foolhardy. He had no idea what exactly it did or how it worked.

But there was someone who did.

Horus.

He and his small group of escorts passed through the destroyed bulkhead door, last before the bridge, and stepped through, back into the busy command center of the mighty alien craft. The commander was there, impassive, staring at him with his unreadable yet brutal gaze.

Kang came to a stop and stood among them. Interrogating Horus had to be next. His nemesis knew the Icon, at least enough to use it. Perhaps the girl told him other things in that final moment, before he lunged at Kang and sent them both hurtling here, to this completely different star system. Ordering the aliens to blast Horus, floating helpless out there in space, had been forefront in his mind, his next action as their leader—to watch his enemy vaporized by the mighty warship's guns—only now …

Now he realized he needed him.

If Horus knew something, as Kang was forced to admit might be the case, he must come to yet another change of heart. He must be smart about this. He must extract information about the Icon from Horus. The thought of doing so, the difficulty it would no doubt present, troubled him. But it was the only way. Whatever Kang had stumbled into, knowing the secrets of the Icon were, at the moment, paramount.

He must yield to reason.

Staring at the commander he grinned, though he was certain the alien leader had no idea why. Just another maniacal gesture from the crazy monster. For Kang the moment was a revelation. It seemed not long ago he'd been contemplating the end of all challenge, the conquering of Anitra imminent. Now this. It was as if some divine entity had opened up a brand new opportunity. His grin widened; turned to a low cackle.

All on the bridge stared at him.

Holding the Icon carefully, uncertain as to what might trigger it, he went to the forward screen and began looking for Horus among the vast backdrop of stars. So that he might set his puppets off on their next objective.

And as he searched the starry depths alarms began to sound.

* * *

BIANCA RETCHED. It was a dry sound, punctuated by groans from Willet and Nani. Through squinted eyes Jess saw Satori heaving forward in her chair.

The leap through quantum space was disorienting, to say the least, more even than it had been using the Icon, but it was over in an instant.

Nani was checking controls. A massive purple planet had appeared directly ahead, quite suddenly. One second they were clenching in nervous anticipation, looking out at Anitra and its moon in the distance as Nani told them to hold on and ... those worlds shimmered and shifted, replaced abruptly with a vastly different star field and the purple gas giant. Now everything held steady. A new view, a new location.

One very, very far from where they'd just been.

Jess struggled to orient. An influx of information was already grabbing Nani's attention. Alarms. At first Jess thought the warnings meant something went wrong, but the ship was whole and—though the sudden appearance of the giant purple world was shocking—nothing seemed broken. And though expecting it, for her it was a double shock to recognize the scene from pictures on the laptop. Photos taken by travelers from Earth who made the same transition to that very spot, confirming with icy reality that the contents of the laptop were no myth. Not that she'd doubted it, but here it was, live and in person, and it was very real. What she saw before her was just like in those images. They'd gone to the right place. This would've been Zac's first stop.

But something *was* wrong.

"There's another ship," Nani practically gasped, not believing what she was seeing.

"What?" Jess and Satori spoke as one, looking to the blonde scientist as she herself looked in disbelief at the information pouring in. The alarms weren't shutting off. The *Reaver* was telling them things were not right.

They were not alone.

Jess staggered from the captain's chair and went to Nani's station, looking back and forth, at the vastness of space outside the dome, left to right, top to bottom, trying to see anything against the brilliant backdrop of stars. Trying to find the ship Nani was talking about.

Trying to find Zac.

Did he make it?

"Another ship?" She scanned the myriad displays, digital readouts, signals, images moving and rotating on screens at Nani's station. The Kel information was hieroglyphics as far as she was concerned but Nani knew it cold. "Like, another starship? Like this one?"

Now Satori was standing beside them. Each trying to

understand what they were looking at, glancing at the starry expanse outside to see if any visual confirmation would appear. Though the Kel text was meaningless, there were now graphical elements on the displays that were unmistakable. The computerized outline of another starship, different in aspect from their own but just as lethal in profile.

Nani poured over the flood of data. Responding to inputs, tapping out instructions, fingers grazing the touch displays with fluid comprehension, having practiced with the *Reaver's* systems to the point of perfection. If she understood the controls, however, she was utterly confused by what they were telling her.

"It's another starship," she confirmed. "There's another ship out there."

* * *

"WHAT IS IT?" Kang whirled from the commander to the vast viewscreen at the front of the bridge, trying to grasp what was suddenly transpiring. At the first sound of alarms he'd assumed it was some new effort to be rid of him. As if they were alerting all hands the monster was in position and execute Plan B now, or some such nonsense. It didn't concern him overly—he knew there was no way they could stop him—but it gave him pause and he wondered once more if they might be working up some way to self-destruct or otherwise eliminate themselves and, hopefully, he with them. Blow up the ship, blow up the monster. They seemed to possess the sort of warrior mentality that would do such a thing.

But those thoughts were supplanted rapidly by the realization that, to his surprise, their abrupt leap into action did not concern him at all. It was an outside threat, and for an odd moment it was as if he was forgotten. He stood there among them, holding the Icon, a spectator as they hurried to respond to the blaring alarms, warnings, changes in lighting and all else that indicated danger. Was there a problem with the ship? Was there about to be a catastrophe?

He found himself actually stepping to the side, making room so they could do their job without the impediment of his presence. He assessed what he could, listening to them bark orders in their curt dialect, peering at information scrolling across screens and trying to learn what drove them. At length he was able to determine the cause for alarm was external. Some sort of intruder had arrived. Someone else from Anitra? Another Icon?

But it wasn't another individual, or even a group. It wasn't another Icon being used to bring more people.

It was another spaceship.

Like this one.

He saw it now as they called out directions, the commander hurrying to stand beside him—out of necessity, not out of any desire to come near—pointing to the large forward viewscreen, issuing orders as a section of space was magnified and there, sitting motionless against the starry backdrop, was another craft. Shiny black, outswept formations at the rear like wings that gave it a deadly profile. In many ways it looked more menacing than the one Kang was aboard. He wondered how big it was, and whether it was the enemy of the alien warriors.

Was there about to be a battle?

Would he die in a fight between starships?

From the responses of the crew on the bridge, however, the arrival of the ship was more a surprise than anything. He observed them. These were not the reactions of warriors coming face to face suddenly with a known threat.

These were the reactions of people who had no idea what was happening.

CHAPTER 8:

RESCUE

"They're moving on us!" All at once Nani was frantic. "What do I do?!" Her rising reaction only made the knot in the pit of Jessica's stomach clench tighter. For the first time Nani was at a loss as to what button to push or what control to activate. Jess scanned the lighted Kel panels, their incomprehensible glyphs scrolling madly, wishing there was some way she could help. Satori, too, looked pained at the feeling of uselessness. Jess could almost see Satori's fingers twitch, as if wishing for a trigger, a joystick—something, anything with which to take action.

But were they sure they were in danger?

"Can you tell if they're hostile?" Jess asked. That seemed more the source of Nani's panic. She had no idea *what* to do. It wasn't a lack of knowing *how* to do it, once a decision was made. She just needed a nudge in the right direction.

"Are they moving fast?" Jess looked back and forth between the readouts and the view of space outside. Still no visual of the other craft. "Like, getting ready to attack?"

Nani managed to work through a few controls. "Here," she tapped an input and turned to the domed screen. Everyone looked with her, watching as she brought a section into magnification and there it was. The other ship came into sharp relief, dark against the colorful curtain of stars.

It certainly *looked* hostile.

But then so did theirs.

From that perspective the purple gas giant nearly filled the image, and soon the alien craft was moving in front of it, heading across its colorful bands at a slow clip. A sleek, dark blot against a canvas of violet hues.

"Wait." A new alarm caught Nani's attention. "They're

sending signals," she worked to process everything at once. She was running the whole ship, Jess realized, and if they ended up in an actual firefight Nani was it. She wondered if Nani would snap. A leisurely passage through space was one thing; the intensity of battle would be something else altogether. Nani was on her own.

And for a moment Jess reeled; caught herself with a hand on the console. They were aboard a starship, in deep space, in another star system, around another planet, in a standoff with *another* starship.

This was no movie.

She gripped the console harder and made herself stand straight.

This is real.

Nani cursed, something Jess had, so far, never heard her do. She fumbled with the controls then got the results she was after. "It's a little larger than us and more massive. From what I can tell it's less advanced. Definitely weaponized. Lots of weapons, energy signatures. It's a warship." Then: "... wait a minute." Now her expression changed, briefly, to one of curiosity—a scientific reaction, it seemed—then quickly back to alarm. Jess watched her intently, as did the others; hanging on her every word, her every change in expression, her every movement as the brilliant scientist, their only hope of salvation, poured through what was becoming a cascading overload of information.

"Hold on," she continued to tap inputs, check results and pull up queries. Everyone gathered closer, one nervous eye on Nani, the other trained on the deliberate passage of the alien warship, its dark outline cutting an ominous path across the cloud-striped surface of the giant planet.

Nani sat back all at once. "Impossible."

"What?"

"What is it?"

"The signals," she turned her full attention to the closing ship, away from the blinking controls, "the language they're using."

Everyone looked at her, a silent *Yes?* hanging in the air.

Slowly Nani shook her head.

"It's Kel."

Jess felt her mouth drop.

"Kel?"

The others were also stunned. "Same as the language of the people who built *this* ship?"

Nani nodded, not believing it either. "Different," she said, glancing once at the screen before her to confirm. "A little different, but definitely Kel. They're broadcasting in Kel. I've sent no signals. There's no way they could've extracted our language base." Her disbelief was clear. Jess felt it too. How was any of this possible? Even within the context of the utterly fantastic, which was no doubt the nature of the adventure they were on, how could any of this make sense?

Jess heard herself ask a logical question:

"What are they saying?"

Nani turned back to the controls. So stunned was she by this discovery that the scientist in her—which was to say the real Nani—had returned and was in danger of becoming consumed with this new mystery. Forgetting they had a bigger issue to be solved.

"Um," she bit her lip as she tapped and dragged, piecing together the information she had so far. "Hold on. It seems their general intent is ... It's an order," she looked up, growing concerned again. Frightened Nani was back.

With a vengeance.

"They're ordering us to surrender and prepare to be boarded."

* * *

KEL WARLORD ELDRON took a deep breath and held it, watching the activity on the bridge around him. This duty rotation had gone from boring routine to history-making—and not in a good way—and it just kept getting worse. As if the rampage of the beast had not shaped things in ways that would have repercussions for all time, now an alien spacecraft was sitting out there, having popped into existence at the same spot where the beast materialized. All Eldron could think was that it was a ship full of them, and the idea of that sent chills up his spine. So far the alien ship was just sitting there, not responding, but Eldron's burning impulse was to blow it out of space without further consideration and worry over the consequences later. The question was, could they? Scans indicated it was made of materials more advanced than their own. The data they had suggested it would likely break under a sustained onslaught, but retaliation would surely come before that end was met.

Furtively he glanced at the beast, standing there holding its shiny prize. No doubt the thing that brought it. If that ship had more of these monsters aboard then engaging with the intent to destroy was the smartest thing he could do. What other advanced devices did they possess? And would shooting the ship out there send the beast into a rage? Probably. But that didn't matter. As long as they had time to finish the job. Already Eldron had been debating setting a course for the gas giant and flying straight into its core, ending their lives and the life of the creature in one fell swoop. The best thing he could do would be to finish it right here, right now.

"Charge weapons," he ordered, keeping a nervous eye on the horned monster. So far it just stood there, watching.

"Weapons online," came the reply. His crew were running through all information they could gather, sending signals to the intruder to stand down and prepare to be boarded. The alien ship remained unmoving. Completely unresponsive, just hanging there where it arrived; brazenly ignoring them, as if they were beneath its notice. Eldron had no intention of risking a boarding. Nor did he expect the intruders even understood what was being ordered. There was no protocol for such an event, but he was determined to stay the aggressor until he figured it out.

Then he would destroy it.

"Sir," one of the crew got his attention. The bridge was a flurry of commands and relayed information, the beast so far watching from the wings.

Eldron looked to his crewman.

"They've begun a signal array of their own," the man

checked what appeared to be an influx of new data. "Hitting us with what looks to be a communication dump. Almost like a translator routine." He paused as he confirmed more readings. "It's a blast. A massive flow of data. Alien language paired with ... hold on." Others near the station looked at what was streaming in, this development slowly becoming the new center of attention.

Then: "It's Kel, sir. It's a translator dump of Kel and another language."

Eldron hesitated, but only briefly. "Put it through."

And a garbled voice came from the speaker. Quiet fell over the bridge as what sounded like a female repeated a few key words in a strange tongue.

"A translation to Kel is part of the stream," the operator informed his commander. "They're saying they mean no harm."

Eldron noticed the monster had, at hearing the female voice, straightened. Quite dramatically. The yellowed beast stepped forward, now fully involved in what was going on, horned head cocked toward the source of the sound—as if the words spoken by the voice coming over the speaker had meaning.

As if it were a revelation.

* * *

"No change," said Nani. "Weapons are powered up. Closing." She checked the feed. "I'm broadcasting on the same channel they used. They have to be receiving it. I've sent them an entire cross reference between our language and theirs. Nothing. So far no response."

"We have to find Zac," Jess insisted. Already the problem of the alien craft had distracted them from the real objective. Aliens could wait. Zac, however, would not last in the cold depths of space.

If he was even here.

Did he make it through to Earth?

Did they both?

At once she began dreaming up other possibilities. What

if the alien craft captured him?

What if they killed him?

Then, the terrible, impossible misfortune of it:

How is there a frickin alien ship—a Kel ship—right here?!

"Can you see him?" She tried not to voice the mashup of anger and terror she was feeling but failed. "Is he out there?" How did she allow herself to become so sidetracked, even for a second? Even by something as significant as this.

Nani spared a moment to shift efforts, dialing in other adjustments, directing her focus away from the other spacecraft—of which they knew about as much as they could—to search for a human form.

"Got him," she said almost immediately. Jessica's heart leaped into her throat. *He's here!*

But that meant ...

"Reading at these coordinates," Nani zeroed in on the scrolling figures. The tension among the small group was palpable. The approach of the warship, whose intentions grew more ominous with each passing second, the unfamiliarity of everything, now coupled with the discovery of Zac ...

Jess blurted: "Is he alive?" The intervening pause as Nani checked for that answer was unbearable. She found her hands actually shaking.

"I think so," came the answer and Jess shuddered all over, the tension of that fear falling away.

Even as new fears continued to take hold.

"Only him," Nani reported. "I have life signals. No sign of Kang. And ... no sign of the Icon." She turned from the console. "It would appear Zac got left behind. Kang and the Icon are gone." Then: "Kang could've made it to Earth."

"Get Zac," It sounded like an order but Jess didn't care. It *was* an order. "Go. Hurry."

And Nani set them in motion. The screen-in-screen image of the approaching warship remained framed at one edge but the view on the rest of the dome shifted as they swung abruptly away and accelerated toward Zac.

"Could that other ship have captured Kang?" Bianca

wondered aloud.

Satori was incredulous. "Captured him? I don't think anyone is going to 'capture' Kang. Besides, why him and not Zac?"

"It doesn't matter," said Jess. "We have to rescue Zac and get out of here. Kang is long gone." Then, with the same volume of fear in her voice but speaking more to herself: "It's exactly what I was afraid of. Kang got away. Kang is on Earth."

Nervously she looked at the dark vessel on approach, becoming increasingly well-defined against the purple backdrop of the gas giant. How fast could it move? If attack was its objective why didn't it just leap at them and pounce? Or open fire? According to Nani it was filled with weapons which were active, in a ready state, continuing its methodical march toward engagement, even though they'd sent a return signal saying, basically, they meant no harm. A friendly signal, in a language the aliens should understand. Now the *Reaver* was suddenly on its way to get Zac. Would the other craft speed up? Pursue?

Nani's voice snapped her from her dread. "We're pulling alongside," she said. "Zac will be out the airlock. Go get him aboard." She pointed toward the door. "I lit the halls to the bay."

Bianca turned to Nani. "I'll stay and help."

"Come on," Jess motioned for Willet and Satori. They rushed with her to the door and went below, following the trace-lit halls to their destination. Jessica's mind raced. Their own ship, the *Reaver*, was a thousand years old. That one out there looked increasingly of similar design. And it was broadcasting in the Kel language.

Was it fallout from the Great Wars? From a thousand years ago? Was it as old as the *Reaver?* Or was it newer? Had the Kel rebuilt their Empire? If so how much? Could that ship travel between the stars?

Would it follow them?

That was a terrifying thought.

She ran for the hold below, Satori and Willet in tow. No time for any of that now.

Zac was out there.

CHAPTER 9:

ESCAPE

KANG STRODE SIDE TO SIDE, baffled by what he was hearing. The audio message—he assumed it to be coming from the ship out there—was in the Emperor's language. Anitran, English; the voice of a female, saying over and over: "Attention. We mean no harm. Please respond. Identify." Repeat.

Who's on that ship?

So far the whole situation had spiraled beyond his comprehension. He couldn't decide whether to keep watching the alien crew react or inject his own demands into the mix. How was there a spaceship out there broadcasting in English? His first thought was that it followed him and Horus, but that was absurd. Could there have been an alien race monitoring Anitra? Keeping tabs on things until the Icon was used then following to see what happened? Immediately he thought of a dozen more ideas, most of them equally improbable. For some reason, however, the most ridiculous was the one that stuck. That the Venatres had, somehow, developed space travel. In secret, using the info from the stolen Icon, perhaps, and with that technology had come racing after Horus.

As the idea of that took hold the ship out there began to move.

Immediately the chatter on the bridge intensified, the alien crew hurrying to action. On screen Kang watched the ship gain speed, accelerate forward, turn and bank sharply—the whole sequence of actions so abrupt as to be alarming. One second it was just sitting there, as it had been from the moment it arrived, the next it was curving away, darting off screen.

The commander ran to his chair and sat, barking orders. Kang bristled. Unsure what was happening, unsure of the intruder's objective, unsure of everything in that moment but not liking this new development. He noticed it wasn't coming at them. Rather, it was headed in another direction altogether. Maybe it decided to run away.

Then he saw it.

"*NO!*" he bellowed. Reflexively, loudly—far too loud for the confined space—causing everyone on the bridge to throw hands to their ears and cringe. The commander stood and yelled back at him, furious, forgetting for an instant he was reacting to the very creature that had killed dozens of their number and, for all intents and purposes, taken control of their ship. Kang let his insolence go. He needed to be rational if he was going to get their compliance in such short order.

Something must be done.

The intruder was heading straight for Horus.

"No!" he said firmly, at a lower volume this time, striding over to the giant forward screen and pointing. He pointed to the ship, making sharp gestures, slicing motions, both hands, one—trying to make them understand. They needed to stop what was happening. It looked as if the ship was heading to recover Horus and that could *not* be allowed to happen.

"No!" he repeated, frustrated by their distraction. Now, rather than the ship, their attention was on him, on what he was doing, what he might be saying, trying to figure it out—all the while Horus was about to get away.

Kang pointed frantically, watching as the other ship closed on the tiny, distant, floating form of his arch nemesis. Convinced now the ship *was* Venatres, and that they had come to retrieve the traitor.

Surely the aliens could use their guns.

"Shoot it!" he commanded, gesturing with great urgency to the other ship, knowing they couldn't understand him but figuring they must understand the basic concept he was trying to convey. He made trigger motions—he knew they had triggers on their rifles—directed at the target— even made rasping *pew! pew!* noises and an exploding pantomime to simulate firing at the other ship and its destruction.

Nothing.   They continued staring at his ridiculous display.

Furious, unable to maintain the forced calm, he lunged toward one of the consoles and took it as the man there moved aside. He began hitting controls, searching for any kind of weapons or way to move or attack or otherwise prevent the horror happening before his very eyes.

But it was fruitless. Something on the console blinked; he activated something, but nothing with any control or usefulness. The man at the console kind of got the idea, though, came closer, made a call to another station across the way, reached and ... fired a shot, random, a bright bolt of energy that lanced into space and was gone. *Yes! Now you've got it!* Desperate to turn that action into a result Kang tried to motivate him to action, to an understanding that he must do it again—with aim this time ...

Too late.

There on screen, as he watched in impotent rage, able to do absolutely nothing to prevent it, the intruding ship closed the final gap on Horus and pulled alongside. Horuses' tiny form was on the opposite side as it curved to him so nothing could be seen. Tense moments passed, the crew frozen by Kang's actions, then ...

The intruder leapt away. Gone, into the void.

Leaving nothing behind.

Horus had been taken.

* * *

JESS SAT ON THE FLOOR of the airlock, cross-legged, holding Zac's head in her lap. The effects of the quantum field washed over her in a buzz of infinity and the accompanying, sickening sensation flowed and went, leaving behind the same yawning emptiness with which she'd become so familiar. The dramatic sensation of fantastic displacement. She shuddered, felt another shudder building and held herself still before she started to shake.

Satori sat on the deck beside her. Willet too. Before her

lay Zac—*Zac!*—on his back, head in her lap, eyes closed as if he were merely sleeping. Breathing now, unlike when they found him—much to her growing relief. As they worked desperately moments ago to drag his heavy body aboard, lifeless and cold, through the shimmering containment field that shielded the *Reaver's* hold from the vacuum of space, feeling the ice on his skin, Satori assured her the Kazerai didn't really need air and that Zac had probably just shut down. Like in a coma or something.

So far she was right. Once aboard he started breathing again, came immediately to life and flushed with warmth. Though he remained unconscious.

"Oh, Zac," she exhaled, near breathless herself, running her hands through his hair, not caring what Willet or Satori thought. They knew how she felt. She bent forward as far as she could, over him, bringing her face close to his, hair falling all around him, on his chin, his cheeks, draping onto his neck.

He was whole, if a little bruised, and looked as healthy and as perfect as ever. His skin, icy to the touch just seconds ago, had returned to its natural glow, any remnant of his ordeal in the cold of space already gone. He was warm. He was alive.

I came for you!

She felt a thrill wash over her.

I did it.

Just like she said she would.

Zac!

He was safe. She raised her head a little and stroked his cheek. *I love you!* She had to catch herself as she nearly cried with the strength of it. It was unreal, just being there with him, now, after everything.

Nani's voice over a speaker interrupted the tranquility.

"We're here," she said, the omni-directional intercom in the small room coming from all sides.

Jess sat straighter and looked around the confines of the airlock. Voiced the first concern on her mind: "Were we followed?" And at the same time realized: *We're back.* She'd known the transfer to Earth would be as instantaneous as the other. Still, it gave her a sudden tingle to think they were actually home.

"Not so far." Then: "They shot as we were leaving. We probably got away just in time."

Then Bianca's voice: "It's Earth, Jess." Her tone was hushed: "You've got to see this. It's beautiful."

Satori stood. Willet with her. Reluctantly, after another long moment savoring Zac's incredible presence, knowing they needed to keep moving, Jess slid his head to the side, being very gentle as she did so—and had the odd, momentary epiphany that it didn't matter how gentle she was. Zac, so real, so human, she cared for him so much ... her impulse was to handle him with such absolute tenderness, especially as he was injured and unconscious, but the fact was she could probably throw his head to the floor, leap up and down on it, bang his skull into the deck, kick it, shoot guns at it—they all could—and it wouldn't make a bit of difference.

The Man of Steel.

Carefully she set him down and got to her feet.

For a long moment the three of them stood in a small circle, looking at each other, at Zac on the floor; violet tracer lights and the clean, shiny black surfaces of the Kel airlock a technological mockery of their human imperfections.

Willet glanced down.

"Well," he looked Zac over, "at least now there's another guy."

Satori cocked an eyebrow.

He held out his hands and Jess could see this was about to be a typical Willet remark. "I'm just saying," he shrugged. "This ship is full of women. At least now there's another swinging—"

Satori smacked him.

"Watch it," she warned. "The girls are still in charge."

Willet pretended to be hurt. Nani's voice came over the intercom. "I'll meet you guys outside the airlock."

"Ok," Jess agreed, speaking to the walls. "We'll wait for you here."

Willet bent to grab Zac's shoulder.

"You *are* going to give me a hand though, right?" He got under one arm. "It's like he's made of lead."

Satori bent under Zac's other arm and together she and Willet lifted him. Satori was nearly a foot shorter than Willet, who himself was shorter than Zac, so the arrangement made for an awkward, lopsided drag of Zac's limp body. Jess was about the same height as Satori, more or less, so there wasn't much else she could do. For now she put a hand on Zac, steadying his body between them as best she could.

And with that she fired open the inner door and the motley group stepped into the clean, alien hallway beyond.

* * *

LINDIN COULDN'T STOP PACING. Striding, back and forth, a fury in his steps that wasn't diminishing. The rage, the sick feeling in his gut, the numbness in his skull; these things drove him, no direction, no center for their release. His mind raced, his heart raced.

All was lost.

Now the girl had taken the starship.

Jessica.

Took.

The starship.

The emptiness in the cavern, the great, yawning, emptiness; the sheer weight of the void in its absence bore down on him. As if it would crush the breath from him.

Nani! She was the one with all the control, and she was the one that flew it. Why had he blanked that entire possibility? Why had he never considered it? *Never* given it an ounce of thought.

Because of everyone who might, she was the only one who wouldn't. Timid, hyper-intelligent Nani, and there she went. Whether at gunpoint or not, the fact remained she had the ability to do it because Lindin had never prevented it.

Consequently the impossible had happened.

"Close the doors," he ordered, eyeing the gaping tunnel

leading through the mountain to the blue sky beyond. Around him the others in the now-empty space were in a state of confused motion. Bodies ran this way and that, no real purpose to their action. He and his pacing were hardly noticed amid the confusion. Technicians scrambled to find a way to follow his earlier command, to use their equipment and send signals to the fleeing craft, to take control and direct it back. None of that mattered now. The *Reaver* was gone. *Long gone*. Tracked to a distant orbit, it then disappeared from scans altogether. No doubt having activated the quantum drive and gone off to whatever destination the girl had in mind.

Earth. Had to be.

Jessica.

As before Lindin found himself furious, apoplectic, seeing red quite literally with his lack of foresight where she was concerned. She was an alien, she was a radical, and once again he'd let her be with little more than a cursory thought as to her observation. Free to roam, free to engage others.

Free to steal the starship. *The whole goddamn starship!* Heart of the Venatres' future.

Gone.

No one in the cavern had any idea what to do next, least of all him. Still they ran, checking things, considering other options. The giant doors at last began to close. Moving back toward their notched recesses, smooth in their ancient grooves, slicing off more and more of the sky until, as they sealed tight with a mighty boom, everyone had finally gone still.

And, for an ironic moment, Lindin realized he'd accomplished exactly what he originally set out to do—and lost everything in the bargain. In his quarters, in a locked safe, he had the Icon. The Holy Relic, so closely guarded by the Dominion for so long. Now he had it. It was all his.

It's all mine!

And he'd lost the whole reason for having it.

A manic laugh escaped him. He shut his mouth at once, eyeing the fearful faces staring back.

Such a tangled web. The Icon, taken by Zac under the

direction of Venatres double-agents, then used unexpectedly by Zac to go to Earth and return, bringing Jessica with him.   Jessica, wild variable who'd managed to direct the actions of others—to the point the entire Crucible was destroyed and much of the Dominion leadership killed. A significant blow. Only, in the aftermath she'd managed to leave, taking that very Icon with her.

When that happened they were worse off than they'd ever been. At least when the Icon was in Dominion hands they could go after it. With it gone, back to Earth, there was no way they could ever hope to retrieve it. Leaving the *Reaver* project, for all intents and purposes, completely dead. Nothing more could be done.

It had taken some time for Lindin to get over the effects of that.

Then the girl returned. *She came back! Yay!* As if on a whim. *And*—and this was the most amazing part—she brought a *second* Icon. More pieces of the puzzle. Greater understanding of the Kel and their ancient technology, the effects of their past and so forth. It was all starting to come together.

Hah. As far as Lindin was concerned Jessica was public enemy number one. At first he'd thought Satori might be the one causing all the trouble. After all, she'd let Jessica go the first time. And she'd just now helped Jessica take the other Icon out to Zac, so he could use it to get rid of Kang. Now she'd aided Jessica with the theft of the starship.

But it wasn't Satori.

Jessica was the common motivator in each of those capers. It was Jessica, not Satori, driving each. Satori was, at worst, an accomplice. More likely than not she was just a pawn.

Yes. Jessica was the one he should've been watching. How he, with years of experience in the command of men, then years more as the head of the intelligence branch— tasked specifically with figuring out the human mind and what it might do next, the actions of entire governments— how *he* could've let this happen escaped him. Maybe the girl *was* some form of angel, as their misguided allies, the Conclave, believed. Maybe she *did* have some sort of divine hand at her back. As ridiculous as that sounded, it wasn't much more ridiculous than smart men and an entire government being duped by a teenage girl.

He certainly had to give it some thought.

The bigger problem, of course, was that nearly everyone considered her a hero. Perhaps that gnawed at him more than anything. Only a handful of Venatres knew the absolute critical significance of these Icons. Fewer still knew about the starship. The other 99% of the world knew only that Jessica used the Dominion's own Holy Relic to bring about the collapse of the Crucible and weaken the Dominion itself. Then, as if for an encore, she saved them; saved the entire world from the brutal reign of an unstoppable beast. Kang. Using the Relic once again to do so. From their point of view she *was* an angel. One who kept popping in and saving them.

Lindin realized he'd been grinding his teeth. He made himself stop and look around; take in his surroundings. Most of the technicians and even a few of the guards had fallen into loose groups, talking about what just happened, wondering what came next and otherwise expressing their disbelief. The doors were closed, the cavern empty—so empty—now that the starship was gone.

"Agnet," he called the senior scientist. The older man stood with a small group of others in lab coats, debating the impossibility of it all. Agnet worked directly for Nani. Lindin was confident the man knew everything she did.

He turned. "Yes?"

Lindin waved him over. Conversations quieted as the others turned an ear toward whatever Lindin might say. He was, after all, their leader, and now that the chaos had passed it seemed as if he were ready to make some decisions.

He was.

"The Icons," he said as Agnet stopped and stood before him. "How much can they transfer? How much mass?"

It took Agnet a moment to understand the question. Then:

"I'm not sure, exactly. We know the girl went with a suit of Skull Boy armor and returned with that plus the other girl. However, we also know from reading the information on the computer device that the agency on Earth tried to use one to move larger masses and was unsuccessful."

Lindin was reminded of the "laptop" brought by Jessica. It contained a wealth of information on the Earth agency and the data *they* gathered on the Icon.

"I would say not much larger than the mass of a Skull Boy to be safe," Agnet surmised.

Lindin began to formulate an idea.

"Get me all the information from the computer device," he ordered. "And the interviews with both girls."

Agnet nodded. Lindin turned and started off toward the exit, heading back to his quarters.

Once word of this got to *his* superiors there was no telling what hell he would have to pay.

But ... he *did* have one Icon. And that one went where Jessica was almost certainly headed.

Earth.

There had to be a way.

This was not over yet.

CHAPTER 10:

HOME

KANG STOOD AT the wide viewscreen boring holes into space, catching himself each time his fists clinched in anger—withholding the force that might so easily crush the Icon. He looked down at it, held tightly in his hands. The aliens had been useless in those final moments, more concerned with him and what he was doing than with stopping the escape of Horus. Now they sat frozen, staring at him with their blank expressions, though he noted a few continued to analyze information in earnest at a console.

He had the vague feeling they were analyzing *him.*

He could activate the Icon. He turned it over in his grip, wondering how exactly that was done. If he could figure that out he could use it; go back to Anitra and find Horus. He had no doubt that was where the other ship took him. Back on Anitra he, the mighty Kang, could continue his rise to destiny, assuming his place as Emperor of the entire world. Horus might be safe in that other starship, for a spell, but he would have to come out at some point, would have to face Kang, and when he did ... this time Kang would forgo the sport of it. He would go right for his neck.

But using the Icon in that way, impulsively, would be foolish. A limited view. There was monumental opportunity right here, aboard this alien craft, in this other star system. If he could but figure out a way to capitalize on it. This ship, and the others no doubt commanded by these aliens—for there had to be others ... *that* was the future. Not a return to Anitra and the path he'd been on. Here was the path to true power, to command of an army that could conquer the stars. Not just one world.

Many worlds.

He exhaled. The starship that came for Horus, whatever and however it was, could not represent a larger force.

There was just no way. The Venatres had clearly been hiding it. And it *had* to be the Venatres. They knew to come for Horus; he was the object of their effort, the purpose for their being there. If they had more than one of those ships then, surely, they would already have unleashed conquest of their own, subjugating the Dominion and bringing the entirety of Anitra to heel.

No, that ship had to be some sort of experiment. A proof of concept that actually worked. Something so advanced would've been known of otherwise. Would've been impossible to hide. The fact that the Venatres had only used it just now, to rescue Horus, was evidence enough. Before that they must've been working on it, waiting for the right moment to test.

There were other, possible explanations. A million possible explanations. It mattered little. Whether the ship was indeed Venatres or something else, the fact was if he went back to Anitra now he would be right back where he started.

But these aliens—and Kang looked around the bridge now, at their curious, expectant faces; elvish warriors each of them, fearsome to behold, nothing more than ants to him—these aliens held real power. As yet he had no confirmation of it, but he had no doubt this ship was not alone. It *must* be a component of a much greater armada. If he could tap that, control it, unleash it …

He could begin a reign so great, so vast … the Empire of Anitra would pale in comparison.

It was folly not to figure a way to make that happen.

And so using the Icon now, in his rage, was not an option. Could not be. Doing so would end that dream. He rolled it around in his grip. As long as he held it, as long as he remained aboard this alien warcraft, the larger plan held hope.

Perhaps the aliens would be smart enough to understand it. The Icon. Perhaps, if so, they might even be able to divine from it the location of Anitra. Could these ships travel the way the other one just did? Could they pop between locations? If so perhaps he might follow. Aboard a starship of his own. At the head of an entire fleet. Go after Horus and Anitra and go after all worlds.

Yes.

These thoughts began to take shape; to mold the core of new ambition. Such ability to travel, at the helm of such power, to pop in and out of existence, must open up all manner of possibilities.

He must find a way to command.

"This," he held up the Icon for all to see, drawing their attention, "can do that." He pointed with his other hand at the screen, to the point in space where the other craft just disappeared. He mimicked using the Icon, then made a sort of "poof" motion, as if to simulate the fact that the device would make the user disappear, just as the other ship had. He made the motions a few more times. When it seemed they had the concept, vaguely, at least, he added: "This," and he pointed again to the device, then to the floor, the walls—indicating, he hoped, their own ship, "can make your ship disappear. Go where that one went." And now he undertook an elaborate series of gestures, speaking slowly: "This makes the ship disappear, follows the other ship, reappears where it went." Most simply stared at him and he began to feel stupid—the concept he tried to communicate was too much, and he wasn't even sure it was correct—but those same few continued working in earnest at the console, only seeming to grow more interested as he spoke, not less. He wondered what they were so desperately trying to figure out.

And as he made a few more gestures he again had the thought: How much could the Icon transfer? It transferred he and Horus. Would it move the whole ship? Would it take whatever he was in contact with? He was fairly confident it would take only him if he twisted it now. However, what if it were strapped to the bridge? Would it only take the parts it was in contact with? Would it take the whole ship?

"How?" came a question from one of the consoles, where the aliens worked, heads down and concentrating.

"I don't know," Kang shook his horned head. "That's the point." Then: "How what?" and it hit him, in one mind-expanding flash. The voice was artificial. It had come not from the alien crewmen but, rather, from the console itself, and, more than that—so, so much more …

It was in English.

The computer voice expounded. "How can it be as you say?"

Kang's eyes were wide. Astonished. Suddenly so astonished he couldn't speak. His own words of a second ago echoed in his head. His answer to their question, spoken on impulse, in that instant between instants before his mind processed the fact that:

They're speaking my language!

He stood mute. All the elfin warriors had stopped what they were doing and were looking to him. Waiting. Keen, it seemed, to hear what he might say in response. Confident they'd managed to communicate something he understood.

He chuckled. Could not control it. The cackle came and it was some time before he was able to stuff it back down and form a simple sentence:

"With your knowledge," he said carefully to his waiting audience, absolutely filling with glee, "with your technology we will discover how."

Blank faces as they listened to what must be a translation of his words, then a response:

"Our technology can make it so?"

Again Kang held back a joyous laugh.

"Yes," he said. "Your technology can make it so."

The last barrier was gone.

Already he had the physical strength to subjugate them. Now, with language, he could tell them exactly what would be done. He could relate plans, vision. Learn their secrets.

He could lead an army.

The likes of which Anitra had never seen.

He threw back his head and let the laugh consume him.

* * *

"LAY HIM THERE," Nani entered the Kel infirmary, pointing to one of the three beds in the small room. The door hissed aside briskly as they entered—just like the doors in any good sci-fi movie—the room that same glossy black as the rest of the *Reaver,* slick panels on every surface, purple neon tracing patterns around the edges. Too perfect, too clean. Jess helped Satori and Willet carry Zac to one of the beds. "Beds" that were really just molded ledges protruding from the walls, about the length of normal beds with a perfectly shaped pillow and what appeared to be soft mattresses with no sheets. Stark like the rest of the ship, projecting that same no-frills sterility. At the center of the room was a curved desk with more controls, lit with Kel glyphs and glowing graphics.

Nani helped and together they lifted and positioned the heavy Zac. Jess adjusted his head on the pillow and the others stepped back as Nani went to the central console and began tapping controls. Bianca had remained on the bridge, so it was just the four of them, plus Zac. With a quiet hum another ledge extended overhead, above him, with what appeared to be sensors or other objects that activated and bathed him in colored light. Jess moved away.

"We were never able to learn much about the Kazerai," Nani said as she worked, reading the information that began flowing in. "But if they're under enough trauma they can shut down. That seems to be what happened."

Jess glanced across to Nani.

"The good news is he's alive," she studied readings. "Very much so, it appears. Most of these metrics are off the charts." Then: "This is fascinating. Our medical experts studied Zac when he joined our side. I read some of the reports. Obviously we tried to learn everything we could, since he was the only Kazerai we ever had access to."

Jess swallowed her emotion. Her feelings were crazy all over the place. Joy that Zac was here—*we found you!*—to fear he was in a coma from which he might never awake, or that he might never be the same if he did and every other possibility between. What if he had amnesia again? What if he didn't know who she was? So handsome lying there under the lights, so strong, so perfect and so hers, so safe and out of harm's way, with a future that could not have been more uncertain. Hers, his ... nothing to cling to. Like a terrible freefall, hand-in-hand, she and her true love, together yet ...

Totally, utterly apart.

The sudden threat of a meltdown gripped her.

"What did they learn?" she managed. "When they studied him?"

Nani shrugged. "Basically what we already knew. That the Kazerai are impossibly strong. Probably indestructible."

Only, thought Jess, *Kang killed three.* She couldn't believe Kang didn't kill him too. Was Zac stronger than the others? Had his will just been greater? When she found him in the park it looked like he was done. Like Kang had already killed him. Maybe she'd come right before the killing blow. Prevented it somehow. All she knew was that Zac broke free and came to her, found within him the strength—from whatever source—to rise, to cast off his would-be killer, take the Icon and heave both him and Kang into deep space.

Behind her Nani shut off the scanning device. The overhead ledge slid back into its recess.

Jess turned. "Will he be okay?"

"Everything is what I expect to see. Of course, with this equipment and my limited knowledge of his specific physiology it's hard to say. Still, it seems he's just in some sort of coma, like we suspected."

"When will he wake up?" Though she knew there would be no way to know.

There wasn't.

"Not sure," Nani looked to the others, worried, it seemed, she wasn't giving the right answers. Clearly she didn't want to upset Jess.

Jess turned her attention to Zac.

"Can I have a moment?"

The small group hesitated only briefly. Out of the corner of her eye she saw Willet and Satori turn, heard them go with Nani, heard the door hiss open, hiss closed as they left and they were gone. Leaving the room in silence.

There were no beeping monitors. No clicks or steady sounds of respirators or other devices. None of the expected hospital-type noises. In fact the small infirmary was deathly quiet, like a tomb, and as her ears adjusted all she could hear was Zac's steady breathing. That and the beating of her own heart.

Wake up. She willed him. It seemed more like he was in a trance, not a coma. He looked totally fine. Even the small cuts and bruises were starting to heal, looking like they were already days old. His skin was flush, breathing steady. Everything about him was just like it had been, as perfect as in his most perfect moment.

She began arranging his arms, wanting to do something, anything, then his legs, so they were as straight as possible. Sturdy, heavy limbs. First a little this way, then that way, feeling silly after a while and stopping. She pulled off his boots. Comfort hardly seemed to matter. None of that mattered. For a long moment she looked up and down the length of him. Tentatively she reached a hand and laid it on his bare chest. *So warm.* The beat of his heart was strong. Everything about him seemed entirely human. *He* is *human,* she told herself. Despite any super-human abilities he was, at the core of it, human. He was a man. Had been fully human once, before the transformation to Kazerai.

She shuddered but kept her hand pressed against him. His eyelids seemed barely closed. As if they might flutter open at any instant.

I love you. She thought the words that were, at times, so hard to say. *I love you!* she imagined more forcefully, letting herself go; feeling that emotion so powerfully it made her buzz. It was complete, and as the power of the moment washed over her she felt the heat of little tears stinging her eyes.

She leaned over his face. At first with the idea to kiss him, maybe on the forehead, like a mother kissing a child, then, as she bent closer ... with the fleeting image of a fairytale. Maybe her kiss would break the spell. And with that ridiculous notion floating through her mind, along with a certain giddiness to be kissing him in such a state, she touched her lips to his. Gently, and the sensation was magical. She pressed harder, tasting the salt of a few of her tears as they fell, a sense of despair washing over her as she lingered, imagining she might actually do it, might actually wake him with nothing more than the magic of her love ... but as she pulled away, slowly, staying close to his soft lips, expectant ...

Nothing.

He remained as he was.

Of course he did. This was no fairytale. It was a fantastic, incredible tale—utterly fantastic—but it was no fairytale.

She watched him. How long she didn't know, but at length she ran a hand through his hair, gave him one last kiss and left the room.

Back out in the halls she found her way to the bridge. Again she felt that panicked, closed-in sensation; less from the terror of being in a confined space in the middle of the void, or even from being alone in the alien passageway, more from the impossible *alienness* of the Kel technology itself.

Soon she was entering the bridge and found Satori with Nani looking over screens of information. Bianca and Willet stood at the viewscreen, gazing out. Bianca turned to her, filled with wonder.

"Look," she enthused.

Unnecessary, as Jessica's full attention was already locked to the dominant image on the video dome.

Earth.

Curving across the breadth of the screen, bottom edge to bottom edge, blue/white crescent—lots of blue—peppered with brown and green and layered in clouds.

Slowly she moved toward it, drawn to it, the rest of her surroundings fading. Emotions of just moments ago fluttered away, forgotten for the moment in the face of this, her home, spread before her in all its majesty. Only as she felt Bianca squeeze her arm did she realize she'd come closer at all, and that she now stood beside her friend directly up against the screen.

"Beautiful, isn't it?" Bianca breathed more than spoke. The hemisphere they looked at was clouded over and not much could be seen, most of it in daylight, the line of night approaching at the far edge. Was the sun going the right way? For a disorienting moment Jess struggled to gain her bearings.

"Which side are we on?" she asked.

"That's Madagascar," Bianca touched the image. The clarity of the screen was such that it appeared to have actual depth, as if they peered out a real window, and only as Bianca touched it did the illusion collapse. "We're flipped over," she said. "There's the south pole." Jess followed her outstretched finger, to the top of the image, recognizing Antarctica. They were in an inverted orbit.

"We didn't come out over the house?" she stood transfixed, seeing now the eastern edge of Africa and feeling, so used to looking at the globe with the north side "up", the strange sensation of hanging upside down. Vertigo tingled.

"I used the location pair for the second Icon," said Nani, voice at first distant across the small room. "Figuring that's where Kang would go. It appears over the mountains you call the Rockies, so the QE drive bounced us. It has a non-interference filter that restricts movement near massive objects. It brought us out at a safe distance. I've just moved us up to this location. Right now I'm trying to build a passive model of your world." Jess pulled her eyes from the screen, glancing back at Nani who worked intently as she spoke: "You have a *very* complex communications backbone. More so than Anitra. Way more." Nani shook her blonde head. "Lots of active systems looking, listening. It's like we flew into a web of sensors, some coordinated, most not. Our countermeasures are contending, I think, but so far I'm trying to lay low. At least until I have a better gauge of what we're up against."

"You think anyone sees us?"

Nani shrugged, eyes glued to her console. "Maybe."

"But no sign?"

"Not yet."

Jess looked back at the Earth.

"The good news is," said Nani, "with everything running through one, giant network like it is, everything is, eventually, connected. Makes it way too easy. With one solid hook we can plug into your entire world. It's just a matter of breaking down the right doors. It actually makes it *easier* than if the tech was lower. Isolated, disconnected info is much harder if not impossible." Nani was suddenly a kid in a candy store. "But you guys have *everything* plugged in. Once I get in ..."

Then: "I really can't believe how advanced your world is on this front. You guys don't have space travel?"

"Not really. Kind of. We've been to the moon."

"Amazing," Nani continued the disbelieving shake of her head. "With this much technology you should have bases on the moon. Amazing," she repeated, more to herself— becoming consumed with each new discovery. For her it was like a cascading revelation.

Jess focused on the staggering view.

Earth, her home, spread out before her; it was such an unreal sensation to be standing there, looking down on it from the bridge of an alien spaceship. Like the whole thing, everything that had happened so far, would turn out to be a dream after all. Like she might actually wake with a start in a warm bed in her room back in Boise. Reality just seemed so ... impossible. For a moment she lost herself in the memories of that former life. Posters on the wall. Childhood trophies. Smell of fresh baking drifting upstairs. The sound of Mom working in the kitchen. Amy in her room, talking on the phone.

All of it, right down there.

Behind her she heard Satori speaking with Nani. Nani was explaining this or that function as Satori made an effort to understand.

Jess inhaled. Heard Satori asking: "So no sign?"

Nani clicked her tongue as if concentrating. "The Icon would've dropped him over Point Two. I'm moving us back around to an orbit above that area. We'll take a closer look from there. So far no evidence of anything that would indicate his presence. Nothing coming over communication channels about a monster or an attack or any sort of activity like that. Of course, there's so much to sift through there's no way yet to be sure."

Kang was who they had to worry about now.

"It hasn't been that long." Jess wondered if Kang *did* suffer an accident in transit. Or maybe the Icon failed. Or, and this was possible, maybe that other ship back there blew him up. Maybe they were about to fire on Zac when the *Reaver* showed up.

"From what I saw on the laptop the place in the Rockies where the Icon connects is pretty remote. Maybe he popped through and is laying low."

Satori snorted. "Kang?"

Jess had to admit that wasn't likely.

"Or, maybe he just hasn't made it anywhere yet."

"Didn't your government build a base there?" Nani asked.

Jess nodded.

Bianca piped up. "Maybe he went into a coma like Zac."

That gave them pause. Was it possible the mighty Kang, killer of Kazerai, could be lying in the mountains out cold?

It was an interesting thought.

"We'll know soon enough," Nani worked away at the screens. "I'm tapping the global network. Putting it all together, decoding what I can. I've got a few of the major encryptions cracked and have already gained access to your key networks. Believe it or not, the hardest part so far is identifying what data is important and what's not. The sheer volume is overwhelming."

Again Nani marveled at the advancement of Earth: "I just can't believe how much information you're throwing around! Only a fraction of it seems to have any relevance to anything significant. The rest is pure garbage. Music, movies, pictures ... All personal stuff. Nonsense."

"That's Earth," said Jess.

Starting to wonder how exactly they would stop Kang once they found him.

And once they stopped him, what then?

CHAPTER 11:

A TERMINAL SITUATION

KEL WARLORD ELDRON stood face to face with the monster, barely two paces away. In its hand it held the silvery device it had been so keen to retrieve which, according to it—and in line with what Eldron had suspected—was what brought it and the other creature, the human, to that deep space point in the Kel star system. "It" called itself Kang, and Eldron had been speaking with it back and forth in the somewhat stilted dialog that began once they realized the newly acquired language base could be used to talk to it. Whatever data feed had been broadcast by the intruding vessel was a near-perfect correlation of Kel and the language spoken by the beast. Once confirmed it spoke eagerly, rasping as their computers ground out translations and, in turn, spoke Eldron's responses back in the alien tongue. So far the creature was proving as maniacal as it looked.

"Does that make sense?" the thing asked. "I know you understand quite clearly." The delay through the computer was slight, overlaying his rough, grotesque voice with the smooth Kel translation. Eldron found the whole process grating.

"We understand you."

His bigger concern, however, had become the alien craft. He regretted he'd not followed through on his instinct and destroyed it, or at least attempted to, when he had the chance. Kang was a threat to ship and crew, yes, but Eldron had already made the decision to sacrifice both. They were isolated with the beast. It could cause no harm elsewhere. That alien ship, however ... *that* was indicative of a much larger problem. What if it carried more like Kang?

Why did I not engage it!?

Immediately upon its escape, as the current standoff with Kang developed, he'd instructed his operators to relay everything from the encounter back to Kel. This was now being processed. Information regarding the earlier rampage of the monster aboard their ship had already been sent and, as yet, no response forthcoming—though news of the intruding starship yielded additional traffic. An armada was assembling and would arrive shortly at their location. Eldron debated requesting the ceremonial destruction of his own ship, by the same armada, accomplishing a purge of the beast and seeing that as a far more honorable way out than plunging into the gas giant, or simply destroying all controls and drifting off into space. However, when the beast began communicating he rethought that idea. Opting instead to share the ongoing transmission. Therefore his debate with Kang was now being listened to by his commanders back on Kel. Perhaps they would have a different take on the situation. An idea as to how to preserve honor and, perhaps, even save his crew.

His men were good warriors. They did not deserve to die over some freak such as this.

"Why do you hesitate?" Kang asked through the translator. Eldron could see the beast was irked. His elation at discovering he could talk to them had been quickly replaced by agitation at their failure to jump to his suggestions. Eldron could see Kang was a highly emotional creature; was probably unstable in all ways.

"Answer me," Kang repeated, false calm in his voice.

Eldron remained impassive.

"You do not enjoy the position of strength you think you do," he spoke clearly, eyes locked to the monster's red/yellow orbs. As the computer finished its translation into Kang's crude tongue the beast frowned.

"What do you mean? I can destroy all of you. This whole ship if I choose."

It was not a threat. More of a confusion, and Eldron sighed at the level of creature he was being forced to deal with.

"If I am to understand your ambition," he spoke slowly

for it, "killing us and destroying this ship are not your plan. That is the *last* thing you want to do. Would you not agree?"

"I will," it said. "If I have to."

"Nothing, surely, is stopping you."

And it stood there. Seething.

Eldron stood taller. "I suggest you use your precious device and go back. There is nothing for you here."

"No," came a voice at Eldron's console. A different voice, from his commander back on Kel. He and Kang both looked at the console with equal levels of concern.

"No?" Eldron queried. Kang watched him, suspicious.

"Don't antagonize it."

The computer had been instructed to skip this translation. To relay only Eldron's direct words to Kang, nothing else. Eldron spoke to his commander directly, in Kel, in open privacy.

"You see value in it?"

Hesitation on the other end. Then: "No decision has been made. However, based on everything so far we feel it would be foolish to let it escape."

"Let it escape? It holds us captive, not the other way around."

"There may be a connection between the device it holds and the vessel that breached our system."

Kang interrupted the dialog he could not understand: "If you won't accept my demands I'll kill you all. If it takes time to learn the operation of this ship then so be it. I will learn it. I *will* have this."

"The controls will be destroyed," Eldron said matter-of-factly and the computer translated it, Eldron barely turning his attention from the voice of his commander. "The ship will be useless to you. A coffin."

"Wait," the commander back on Kel instructed. A moment later he continued. "The fleet will take up position at your location. We've confirmed the other vessel arrived using a similar method of travel as the one used by the creature and its device. Both seem to employ the same quantum-flux systems. The connecting points could be anywhere but, based on the arrival signature, wherever that is we do believe both the beast and the craft probably came from the same location."

It was as Eldron feared. There could be a whole world of these things out there. And now they knew how to get to Kel.

"The size of the device is remarkable," his commander went on, and Eldron couldn't tell if it was his own marvel or if he was relaying that of the council from where he spoke. "We must have it. Much has happened in a short time, but we must use forethought. The ship has escaped. The creature and the device are still ours. How can we retain them?"

Eldron stared at Kang. The expression on the thing was near unreadable. Eldron knew it was angry, but even in the few moments of revelation, such as when it realized it could talk to them, the heavy brow and blood-red eyes conveyed static rage. It seemed it was in a perpetual state of displeasure.

He wondered just what they were getting themselves into.

"It wants this ship," Eldron said, watching Kang warily as he spoke to his console. "And our subjugation, from the sound of it. You've heard the dialog so far. If we make gestures toward this end, at least in promise, it might be led. If it looks like we're going to give it what it wants.

"But I cannot stress enough the extent of its strength. This is like nothing we have ever seen. I don't believe we could ever contain it. Destroy it, perhaps, but not without massive collateral damage. Right here, right now, we have it aboard one ship. If we relinquish this opportunity to destroy it there's no telling how difficult that might become later." It felt odd to be talking so openly about killing Kang right there in front of him. Already the creature grew increasingly annoyed, listening to the back and forth that was clearly a conversation about him. Surely it must assume they were discussing how to be rid of it. How much longer would it stand there quietly?

The pause on the other end stretched.

"What are you talking about?" Kang asked in his gruff voice, filling the silence.

"Whether or not to destroy you," Eldron said honestly, satisfied to make the thing worry—if only a little. Many Kel lives had been sacrificed; Kang would realize they were a race of warriors, unafraid to die. Maybe they *would* leave him floating there in a metal coffin, the beast seemed to be thinking. Eldron could see the gears turning in its head.

Then, when it seemed as if Kang would leap over the edge, restore himself to a full rampage and kill them all, Eldron's commander came back on the line.

"The Praetor will meet with him."

The Praetor?! Unprecedented. Consul to the Tremarch herself? What need did they have of such elevated rank?

And ... *meet?*

"The Praetor intends to come here?" Eldron could not disguise the disbelief in his voice.

"He will come aboard, yes. He will meet the creature face to face and negotiate for the device."

Eldron was stunned.

Kang stared hard at him, the beast chewing on its own doubts. As if wondering whether to act, or to continue letting them debate among themselves. Eldron wondered how they might possibly negotiate with it. Yet, considering the scale of their entire civilization, pitted against a single monster it was possible that, with the right degree of reason, they *could* get through. Come to a compromise. Get their hands on the device. If nothing else Kang had so far demonstrated raw intelligence. And enough reason to at least stop himself short of a full massacre.

Eldron looked at the device, closely for the first time. Such a simple looking contrivance. Smooth. Mirror-like reflectiveness. No moving parts to be seen.

Somehow it could transport individuals across vast distances, just like a full-scale starship drive. A personalized way to travel between worlds.

Incredible.

"Very well," he said to his console. "How should we proceed?"

"Inform it. Remain on station until the fleet arrives. Once command has been transferred, return to Kel at once.

"The Praetor will meet you in orbit."

CHAPTER 12:

INDECISION

"STILL NO INDICATION ANYONE'S SPOTTED US." Nani's evaluation of the Earth and its infrastructure had hardly slowed as they moved cautiously around the planet in high orbit, positioning themselves discreetly over North America. As more of the flood of information was catalogued and cross-referenced, connections made and the database built, their scientist guide seemed to be settling into the discovery of a new world. "I would've expected to pick up some reference to us by now. It looks like we haven't been seen."

Jess was amazed. Weren't people and machines always searching the sky?

"We've been mostly over the daylight side," Bianca noted, idly; eyes glued to the screen at the console at which she sat. "Maybe no one's looking up?"

Jess looked across at her friend.

"Our countermeasures exceed your detection ability," said Nani. "But we're still visible. I haven't tapped all your secure networks yet. It's possible *someone's* seen us, but so far we haven't made the news. We haven't been mentioned."

Since they arrived they'd been listening to Nani's ongoing wonder, backed by occasional comments from Satori, and as the two Anitran women talked Jess found herself curious as to how Anitra worked. Her time on their planet had consisted primarily of fleeing this or that danger, charging *into* danger or otherwise finding herself in a series of challenges and violent ends. She hadn't had the chance to really observe, to see how they reported news, how they stayed in communication with each other and so on. To hear Nani, and even Satori, describe it, the sheer glut of information being transmitted on Earth was staggering in comparison. Part of her wanted to ask questions, to learn the differences. But now was not the time.

"We can't ignore the Kel threat," Nani was multi-tasking. Jess saw she'd shifted attention from whatever process she was running on various bits of Earth information, turning to the screens she had up on the Kel. "I haven't found anything to change my assessment." She'd been studying the Kel in parallel, pouring over and analyzing the snapshot of data she got on the Kel warship and the other star system.

Jess, for her part, kept trying to shove the stark images of the alien Kel from her mind. Earlier, when Nani showed them the graphic pictures of the aliens, from archives aboard the *Reaver*, Jess found herself utterly shocked. Everyone was shocked, of course. None of them—Willet, Satori, Bianca—had ever been faced with images of a real alien. After the encounter with the Kel ship, after the stunning discovery that the Kel were still very much alive and well … to then pair that wake-up-call with example pictures of the aliens themselves, visages of beauty overlaying deadly purpose …

Yes, the others were shocked. None, though, as much as Jess. For the others the images were merely faces to go with the rest of the facts. For her the Kel were far too …

Familiar.

Pale, perfect complexions; youthful yet ageless elfin features; shock-white hair and yellow eyes.

It was a difficult feeling to shake.

"That was definitely a Kel warship," Nani was saying. "Like this one, but an entirely different generation. Modern but less advanced. A whole different configuration. They've lost ground in the last thousand years. If I had to guess I'd say they had a dark period of some sort, loss of technology, and then rebuilt. I can tell you, though, they haven't changed in terms of their purpose. At present, as in the past, their entire culture is geared for war. Now that they've seen us … now they know we're out here, we're going to become their objective. I can guarantee it. Nothing I see in the data I captured indicates they know where we are, and I'm pretty sure they can't follow us—I can't even do that with the *Reaver*—but their entire purpose will become Find The Humans. We—Earth, Anitra—need to prepare for that. It will take time to bring ourselves up to a level to even fight them, and there's no telling how fast they'll be able to find us. With the *Reaver* technology we can—"

"I think we're getting a little ahead of ourselves," Satori interjected. "Obviously there's a whole crap-load of things staring us in the face that weren't there before. Things we had no knowledge of. Ignorance is bliss, and right now we know too much. In the short term we've got to finish what we came for and get this back. Let the smart people figure the rest out." She looked to Nani. "No offense. In all honesty you're probably smarter than anyone. But you know what I mean."

Nani did. "It needs a high-level discussion, I agree."

Doesn't seem to me like we've had a lot of success with big-wigs making decisions, Jess wanted to say.

"There's no sign of Kang," Satori went on. "Maybe the Kel blew him up before we got there. Or maybe he used the Icon and it malfunctioned and he's gone. Either way, it looks like he never made it here."

Nani was back at her screens. "I've gone over everything on the laptop," she left Satori's statement as a general comment, choosing not to take it up further. "I've reviewed all the info on the Bok and what the Project knows of them," Nani brought their attention to the ancient secret society on Earth, and Jess knew she was talking now mostly for her. "The Bok, as we know, are directly linked to the ancient Kel. If I can find anything on them it might give us some clues. I've got feelers running, for anything else I can dig up. Executing routines against Earth databases and so forth. So far the Bok are turning up as un-crackable to me as they have been for the Project."

Satori looked like she was going to say something, but held her tongue. The undercurrent of tension in the room was growing.

Earlier they'd discussed the Bok briefly. Nani was curious to learn what they knew of the Kel. She believed that, if there was a past connection between the Bok and the aliens, any information the modern Bok on Earth might hold could be exploited. Furthering the understanding of the Kel was, as far as Nani was concerned, vital. Mapping the overall approach to their future threat, a critical next step.

Consideration of those things, however, only seemed to drive Satori's impatience. As Kang failed to turn up in scan after scan Satori had begun losing faith, convinced the monster didn't make it and ready to move on. To say she was antsy would've been putting it mildly. Jess found it hard to disagree. Kang was likely gone. She'd fully expected to see a swath of destruction, to find news channel after news channel with reporters standing before screaming people and raging fires, talking of the horror that had been wrought.

So far nothing.

Hopefully Zac could shed some light. Jess wished he would just wake up. What happened after he used the Icon? Did he know why he was floating alone? Did he know what happened to Kang? *Did* Kang use the Icon a second time? Did that other ship shoot him? She shuddered. Whatever happened, wherever Kang was, at least it didn't happen to Zac. Zac wasn't shot out of space by an alien spaceship. Zac hadn't used the Icon and disappeared forever into the void. Zac was right here, with her, safe. After everything she found her knees weak with that reality. They were both alive.

And we're together.

She looked around the bridge. Nani hard at work, piecing together the bigger picture. Satori growing more doubtful each minute. Skeptical of why they were still there. What they were doing. Willet, sitting in one of the command chairs, leaning comfortably to the side, gazing at Earth on the forward screen—lost in what thoughts Jess could only imagine. And she herself, alternating between walking around the room and stopping to stare.

Bianca brought the only human counterpoint to the scene. An Earth-ish reality missing from the rest. Sitting at the next console over, avidly looking things up on the internet as the rest of them talked or pondered. Earlier Nani figured out how to access Earth's information superhighway in a way that was familiar enough for Bianca to use; a sort of Kel browser she could operate and, of course, she dove right in. Since then she'd been giving the human-interest angle to the story. Though Bianca's "research" was restricted to the public web, no different than if she were sitting at a computer back home, the internet was nevertheless a wealth of information, and so she'd been contributing to the overall in her own way, adding to the more meaningful information Nani worked to dredge from tighter channels.

As Jess watched her hunched over her console, Bianca shook her head, scrolling through various pages, checking what she could on their disappearance and, as far as Jess could tell, had at the moment shifted to items of personal interest. Hollywood sites, the latest gossip, etcetera.

"They really miss us, Jess."

At first, when Nani got them connected, Jess and Bianca both rushed to the controls, Bianca ending up in the driver's seat and Jess leaning impatiently over her friend's shoulder, all the suppressed fears and concerns for family and friends rushing to the fore. As Nani secured the more important information—tactical threats, information on the Earth and the Kel—the two Earth girls occupied themselves catching up. The chaos in which she and Bianca departed left disaster in their wake, that much was quickly confirmed, but what had been said? During their time on Anitra, unable to do anything, not even able to *know* what was happening, Jess had managed to shut off the spinning wheels in her head, the worry and morbid speculation concerning Mom, Dad and Amy. But what happened after she left in a blaze of glory?

Slowly, looking at every bit of information they could think of, she and Bianca managed to verify all members of their families were safe and at home. Nani had even been able to look at their houses from afar. They saw Amy arrive home at one point, distant images, but it was her. They saw Bianca's mom go into the back yard. Both were poignant moments, but no tears were shed.

Jess could only imagine the grief their families were feeling.

Frankly she was blown away by the extent of the cover-up. It seemed near impossible that so much could remain unchanged. Yet it had. The significance of what happened the day of their violent departure was so far beyond anything that had ever happened on Earth, she was convinced she would return to find her family gone, locked up, taken away, her house cordoned off and all else. News stories, the Earth in a state of shock ...

In fact the opposite was true. Somehow, some impossible way, the Project had covered it up. Mostly. It could never be swept totally under the rug, of course. Too many people saw. However, after reading all they could find on the matter Jess found herself stunned with the degree to which the Project *had* made those events disappear. There were comments, posts, but none of it had become a global sensation. Military-grade helicopters unleashed missiles in the city. *Missiles!* In downtown Boise. A building had been brought down. Both helicopters were shot out of the sky—by a suit of alien powered armor wielding a plasma cannon. *Alien powered armor!* With a plasma cannon. A neighborhood was lit on fire. That same suit of armor ran through town, leaping pedestrians and crashing through buildings. A hundred smart phones must've witnessed these things. All followed by a blowout gunfight in the warehouse district. Two girls went missing in the wake of all that. Other people were no doubt dead.

Most of it squashed.

Impossible.

But true. The events were, expectedly, blamed on something difficult to disprove: a top-secret military experiment, a rogue operator that was taken in and being held or something like that. Not terribly original but what else was there? As far as Jess could tell in her searches answers were still being demanded, but not nearly as loudly or as widely as should've been the case. Had people really become that dulled? Had the attention spans of the world truly become that short? It was probably a combination of all those things; short attention spans, the conditioning to move quickly to the next sensational headline, along with clever, plausible explanations and an amazing spin that had been put on the whole thing.

She wondered what the Project told their families. If they told them anything. Part of her *wanted* to go back. Home was right there. *Right there!* She could swoop in, get out and go inside. But of course that could never be. Not yet. Maybe not ever. She'd thought of at least making a call, but even that would be too weird. Too painful. There was no guarantee she was coming home. For now she comforted herself in the fact that her family was safe. She had no doubt they were being watched but, for the moment at least, they were being left alone.

Then there was the secret society. She couldn't stop thinking of *that* as she scanned the planet below. Nani was looking for them even now. The Bok—the Esehta Bok—described on the government laptop, arch-nemesis of the Project, and now they had Nani's scrutinizing eye. So far nothing. A secret society with an agenda to rule the world. *Esehta Bok.* She rolled the name in her mind. And the very real probability they were hiding yet *another* Icon. Perhaps more than one. Other things. Knowledge of the Kel.

She wondered if Nani could crack them.

That the Project was a US government agency only partially made her want to see their side of things. What they'd done, the way they'd come after her ... Truthfully she wasn't sure how to feel about them. Both the Project and the Bok were secretive organizations, out to control exclusively something that was potentially world-changing.

She stood straighter and sighed.

The Kel. The Bok. The Project. And before her the breadth of the globe, spanning the viewscreen, side to side and huge; blue oceans, brown and green lands, white clouds swirling and streaking and clumping from daylight to night. A freeze-frame of motion. Massive. Host to seven billion people. Peaceful from this vantage. Calm.

So much more going on down there than most of those

seven billion had a clue.

And so the burning question became:

What now?

Satori was chewing hard on that very thing. No doubt brewing answers of her own. Jess hazarded a glance across the bridge at the red-headed commander. Satori wasn't looking in her direction but her arms were crossed tightly in unspoken disagreement; glaring as she watched over Nani's shoulder, reviewing the same screens of information, posture speaking volumes of how she felt. As if saying, *We rescued Zac. There's no sign of Kang.*

Time to go.

Jess looked away.

She didn't want to go.

Suddenly Bianca giggled. Out of place with the current mood on the bridge. Jess could see she was caught up in some image or comment on the screen in front of her, tittering under her breath. The soft glow of the screen accented the curves of her cheekbones, flickering on her exotic complexion, highlighting her dark, raven hair, making it shine blue-black. *She really is beautiful.*

"What's so funny?"

"Nothing. Toby. He put up a rant on cosplay."

Jess felt her skin prickle. "Where'd you see that?"

"On his page."

Her worry spiked. She should've known to set some guidelines for this ...

"On his page?" Then, spine tingling: "Did you log in? Tell me you didn't log in."

Bianca turned from the screen, a look of concern crawling across her face. "Was that not a good idea?"

Jess took a step toward her. Abruptly, in frustration, before she knew what she was doing.

Bianca began to look mortified. Jess didn't believe for an instant there was anything about them that wasn't being watched, including their personal accounts.

This could be bad.

Then Bianca admitted, having a hard time even saying the words: "I also clicked Like."

"*You what?!*" The others stared between the two girls, not understanding the specifics of what was going on but getting the magnitude of the breach.

"Bianca we're gone! Remember?!"

"I'm sorry!"

"That's even worse! Now everyone will see that!"

"I'm sorry!" her friend tried weakly to defend herself. "I got caught up. I spaced. I forgot we're fugitives, okay?"

"Forgot we're fugitives?!" Jess was incredulous. She pointed emphatically to the front of the bridge, where the Earth covered half the video dome. "We're in frickin orbit!"

"I said I'm sorry!" Bianca turned and tapped the screen on the console. "There. I signed out."

Jess didn't want to be mad at her friend. Not after everything. Especially not now, when they needed unity more than ever. But how could she lapse? *Everyone* Bianca was friends with—which was many—would see she was online and had posted. Even the simple click of a Like button. Bianca was popular. It would probably come up on hundreds of people's pages.

It would probably even make the news.

Jess exhaled and turned.

"I'm going to check on Zac."

CHAPTER 13:

MOTIVATION

ZAC LAY ABSOLUTELY STILL. His chest rose steadily. Up, down, barely perceptible, but otherwise he did not move. No shifting, no twitching of limbs. Not even a finger. No flutter of eyelashes. Jess watched those most, studying his eyes, hoping for any movement—maybe even a quick dart beneath his lids, any sign of life—willing him to stir awake. So far he was as motionless as if he were a mannequin. A warm, soft, oh-so-life-like mannequin, breathing just enough so you could tell he wasn't dead.

She'd been watching him for what felt like hours. No one else joined her. Maybe they wanted to leave her alone. Maybe they'd found something interesting. Whatever the cause she was glad for the solitude. She had no way to tell the time, or even whether it was night or day on Earth below. There were no viewscreens in here. When she left the bridge the sun was setting across the mid-west. Was it dark in Boise yet?

It was disorienting there in the small, alien room.

Up on the bridge Nani was no doubt continuing the search for signs of Kang, the Bok, mapping the infrastructure of Earth, fulfilling her scientific curiosity and otherwise learning things. Jess was becoming more and more convinced something went wrong with the Icon, some sort of failure and Kang was gone. Like Satori wanted to believe. Despite that, Jess nevertheless had the terrible sense Kang could pop out at any moment.

She reached and stroked Zac's cheek. There was a slight, darker shade along his jaw, hints of a beard growing. It gave his smooth skin just a touch of roughness.

She sat back.

Since leaving Earth the first time, back when she and Zac popped out of the playhouse and appeared over Osaka, a city at war, she'd been fairly clear each step of the way what needed to come next. Everything had been driven by obvious necessity. The need to handle threats. There was a bit of a lull after she returned home, where she mistakenly thought she could slide back into a normal life—only to discover just how wrong she was. More threats, more calls to action, and she'd been forced to continue her painful journey.

Now ...

She'd always yearned for something more. Greater purpose. Until that first trip to Anitra she hadn't even really known why. The shock of that transfer triggered many fears. Then, once on Anitra, her burning drive was to get back home. "Normal" never looked so good. And though most of her life had been dedicated to getting away from the usual, once on Anitra that first time the quest to get back to "normal" drove her to amazing feats. Impossible, improbable feats—for an individual of any caliber, let alone a high-school girl. Yet, even as she accomplished those goals and made it home ... doubts remained. In a weird way, once home she felt less alive; certainly less than she had during her time in mortal danger. Some deep-seated part of her had been awakened, spurred by the life-in-the-balance terror, as if brought into being, and she began to think Earth might not be where she belonged. Weird, very weird, no doubt, but it nagged. A feeling that at length began to burn intensely within her. And so it festered. And though she took no action toward it, when the crux of the moment came, where she was forced to make the decision to run, to *return* to Anitra, to once more leave home ... that same part of her felt relief.

Perhaps even a thrill.

And on Anitra the chase began again. Immediately, with baggage this time in the form of Bianca, and she had, once again, felt the impulse to go home. It was frustrating to be torn between those two desires. Yet, this last time the feeling to run home brought with it more clarity. And she recognized the urge, not primarily as the wish to return to something normal but, rather, the desire to run from the challenges before her. She saw it for what it was. A weakness; a wish, to escape what, quite oddly, she felt she was supposed to be doing. To flee her destiny, and that impulse came from fear, not longing. A subtle but significant difference.

Now she was home. Again. Made it. Rescued Zac.

And here she was again, torn.

The door to the room slid open. Satori stepped in and it slid closed behind her. There she paused. Jess just wanted to be left alone—*I wish everyone would leave me alone*—but they *had* been leaving her alone. A long time had already passed and no one bothered her. Satori looked her usual, mildly annoyed self, which meant things on the bridge were probably pretty much the way Jess left them. Impulsively she sat straighter. Waited.

At length Satori broke the standoff.

"He looks healthier," she commented, then came over and stood near. Satori's bright red hair and black military uniform made her look like she'd just stepped out of some sort of future-perfect anime. Or was about to step into one. Gorgeous, a real-life fusion of the Asian/Anglo features, so popular in a million mangas. Against the setting of the stark alien room, with its gloss black walls and precise lighting, she was a veritable snapshot of that style. Of all of them she fit within the Kel surroundings the most.

Jess pulled her gaze from her and looked back to Zac. Most of his cuts were indeed healed or fading, bruising all but gone. It truly looked like he could rise from the bed that instant, say Hello and get right to it.

"Can't say I've ever seen one hurt like this." Satori was standing right beside him, right by Jessica. "Kang was some kind of monster."

Impulsively Jess reached a hand to Zac's shoulder. Thinking of all the coma stories she'd heard, of people being asleep for years, wishing she could just shake him awake. Part of her wanted to try.

For a long moment both of them stared at his motionless form.

Then Satori said: "I got Nani to risk some directional

scans. Active scans. Right at the area where Kang would've fallen." She paused. "Nothing. There's nothing there matching any of his signatures. No sign that any object fell.

"I think we can be pretty sure he did *not* make it through." At that she turned to face Jessica, unspoken questions in her eyes.

Jess had no answers.

After what became an uncomfortable silence Jess drifted back to Zac, where her attention had been for so long. It was easy to fall into him, to lose herself in his presence. Handsome, perfect Zac. Healing before her eyes. The stubble on his chin was darker at that angle, and if she looked just so she could imagine him with a full beard. Against the youthfulness of the rest of his face it ended up looking, rather than tough, or even manly, kind of cute.

But Satori hadn't turned away.

"We have to go back," she said, and a little shot of ice ran through her. Though Jess knew it was coming. "We can't keep this here. We did what we came to do. Zac is safe. Kang is gone.

"It's time to take it back."

She meant, of course, the *Reaver.*

When Jess failed to meet her gaze, unable to confront what must be faced, Satori went on. "You've got some decisions to make. We all do, but especially you."

Jessica's mind buzzed. She could feel her head thrumming. The sheer uncertainty of the moment had her receding.

"I can't go home," she said, voice distant in her own ears; not sure whether she told Satori in the hope she might have an answer, a way out, or if she even told Satori at all. Maybe she told no one, simply stating aloud that which she could not yet believe.

Satori studied her, then glanced again at Zac. Made the kind of observation only she could.

"You're afraid to leave him."

Jess tried to speak but couldn't, able only to shake her head. The emotions of the moment were piling on. Her lip trembled.

"He loves you," Satori drove the sadness deeper—though Jess knew it wasn't on purpose. "If you stay he'll try to stay with you. If he's not awake we can leave him with you, but I don't know how that will work on your world. He'll be quite an oddity."

"I can't stay," Jessica's voice dropped. She looked up at Satori. "Don't you see? I have nowhere to go."

"You have choices."

"I can't go anywhere." And she wondered, had the forced ambivalence of her life been merely a shield? A way to protect herself from the very pain she was feeling now? After all, if you didn't really care about something how could losing it hurt you? Had she never allowed herself to fully embrace the joy of friends and family—all so she never had to experience the agony she now felt? Because right then, the stark realization that those relationships were all but gone, in such a permanent way ...

She ached. No way to comfort it away. There was nothing to be done, no hope to put in its place. No substitute for the pain. Now that the moment was finally upon her, no longer just a future speculation, no longer merely a bridge she would cross eventually ...

The bridge was here. She was standing at the edge, now, and she must, without question, cross it and leave behind her old life; and, though made true from the moment she ran for the Skull Boy in the barn, gun in hand, bound for Anitra one last time, the moment of permanence had finally arrived.

She drew a shuddering breath.

"I have no idea what to do."

"Well you need to decide."

Satori's lack of sympathy twisted the ache harder.

"Kang could still—"

"Kang's not here and he's not coming."

Jess swallowed. Hating her right then.

"We don't know that for sure."

"We know it well enough."

"We don't!" Jess recoiled at her own outburst.

She needed time.

"We don't know what happened to the Icon *or* him," she calmed her voice. "He could still come through."

I just need time! If they left now ... it was forever. Once they took the *Reaver* back to the Venatres ... It was over. And though she had nothing to go back to on Earth, no feasible way to return, the thought of actively deciding to accelerate that moment, to leave it behind for good, once and for all—now that they were *here*, now that she was *back*—had her nearly panicked.

She couldn't leave.

She couldn't stay.

Satori glared at her.

"We're taking this back," she said with finality. "You need to decide whether you're going with us or staying."

And with that she turned and walked from the room.

The door hissed shut, marking the end of that passage of time.

Jess watched after her bitterly, staring at the closed door long after she was gone. Crushed that Satori, the one person who should understand her plight, who should at least have something kind to say—no matter how hardened she was—showed no compassion whatsoever.

She put her face in her hands.

CHAPTER 14:

AN AUDIENCE IS GRANTED

DRAKE HAUER TOOK A SIP OF COFFEE. He held the cup halfway to the desk as he was setting it down, a new bit of information on the computer screen catching his eye. At some point he realized his hand was hovering and finished the action, placing the cup in its spot amid the clutter.

"Did you see this?" he called out. A moment later Bobby came from the bustle taking place in the other room. His junior agent grabbed the door frame and leaned around, sticking his head and most of his shoulders into the relative quiet of Drake's office.

"What's up?"

"This info on the access point." Drake pointed to his screen. "It came from an ISP in New Zealand."

"From the girl?"

Drake nodded. "That's where the signal jumped on."

Bobby stepped more fully into the room.

Drake looked up. "Does that make any sense?"

"I guess. I mean, there's been nothing else."

Drake turned his eyes back to the screen. This odd, random "Like", from the girl's friend, Bianca Devnani—or at least from someone using her account—was bugging him. Now they'd determined whoever it was accessed the internet in New Zealand.

Strange.

What were they doing there? They already knew the two girls blinked out of existence back in Boise, using the other device—the one Jessica Paquin somehow ended up with—along with a very alien piece of military hardware. A suit of powered armor that laid waste to a dozen city blocks. Could the Jessica device go to ... New Zealand? That was ridiculous. Based on what little the Project knew about the teleport devices they were crafted by an ancient alien race and used to travel between worlds. Not between landmasses around the same globe.

Drake cleared his mind. He had to stop obsessing over this random occurrence. It was a fluke. A spoof. Something. Someone found a way to get logged on as her friend, Bianca, and click a button. Drake's group captured the login and the click, but would never be able to confirm who actually did it. If it *was* the girl, and she was dumb enough to do it once, why hadn't she done it again?

And how the hell was she back on Earth?

He'd already spent too much time chasing this small lead.

He noticed Bobby staring.

"I've got to let this go," he echoed his own conclusion.

"We're all a little stressed." Bobby paused, then left to get back to what he was doing.

The shock of what the two girls had pulled off still seethed within the whole agency. It had taken way too long to identify Jessica from the chatter—months—and when they finally *did* ID her the execution of her capture was beyond sloppy. The result was a fiasco, ending in the loss of not only the device she held but the one the Project had as well. They'd gone to get hers, and she got away with theirs. She got them both. Admittedly they'd exhausted every form of study they could on their own, but the loss was huge. And not just a little embarrassing. The wake of destruction had been massive, all driven by their botched attempt to nab a teenage girl, and every aspect of that incident tested every last bit of the Project's ability as a bottomless budget, limitless access operation.

Now they had no alien technology.

None.

Drake leaned back. The chair creaked as he turned from the screen, running his palms over his dark, close-cropped hair. He stared at himself in a mirror on the wall. Though his eyes were bloodshot he still managed to look fresh, blessed as he was with good genes. A handsome Hispanic with a medium-light complexion, he had an athletic build and a razor-sharp intellect. The good looks and an innate sense of style gave him an extra edge of professionalism, no doubt, but it was his mind that had propelled him to the rank he held within the Project: Running the operation to capture the girl (which had so far failed; he had no illusion of finding her after she transited to God-knew-where using the other device), simultaneous with being in charge of the efforts to gain insight into, if not the outright capture of, the Esehta Bok.

He glanced at the activity in the other room. Bodies moving back and forth, calling out information—preparing for a mission that would achieve that vision in a big way.

Since the Esehta Bok first came on the scene the Project had been in a losing battle to learn what they were hiding. It was possible that, at the end of all this, the Project would learn the Bok had nothing. No other devices. Nothing else. So far, however, based on what *was* known, that was not likely. Nor did Drake actually believe it would prove true. The Bok were hiding something. They displayed too much knowledge, projected too much power (helicopter gunships right in the American heartland, for crying out loud!), their tendrils ran too deep, their understanding and speed of reaction was far too great ...

The Bok knew their game. They were for real and, the more the Project managed to uncover, bit by agonizing bit, the more those discoveries painted an increasingly disturbing picture. These guys had been around at least a thousand years. The Bok knew of the device held by the Project, most likely had one of their own, if not more, and their (claimed) ties to an ancient Space Opera society had, so far, borne out enough to give the Project every reason to believe the Bok story was legit. And now a breakthrough. Thanks to the ego of their newest leader, Lorenzo, the Project was about to get a whole lot closer to the truth.

Lorenzo Fertiti. Current head of the Esehta Bok. A self-described vampire type who was having delusions of world domination. The Bok modus operandi until then, all through the centuries, had been to remain securely in the shadows. Lorenzo was bringing them into the light. He was tired of hiding and saw the Bok as superior to "normal" humans, imagining the Bok and their pedigree as somehow "superhuman", intending to corral the cattle of the world beneath Bok rule. According to what little the Project knew the Bok background included religious doctrines that taught ways to tap universal sources of power and bring psionic abilities to life. That was all a bunch of hooey as far as Drake was concerned, but in the face of everything else he had a hard time simply dismissing it out of hand. So far no credible evidence of such things had been found but, from Lorenzo's increasingly easily intercepted manifestos, the Bok believed that sort of power was real, believed they possessed it and intended, with it, to gain dominance and rule the world.

Now, remarkably, due to that cavalier bravado, Lorenzo's overconfidence—call it what you like, the Project knew where he and some of his cronies were going to be. Drake and his team had specifics, and, thanks to Lorenzo's careless lapses, a trap was being set. Most of the team working in the other room would be transferred shortly to a safehouse in the target country, to continue preps and stage that operation. An operation that, if successful, would expose the Bok secrets once and for all.

* * *

KANG WATCHED with growing fascination as the world before him resolved, moving closer, growing larger on the wide forward screen until it swept in a massive arc from side to side, filling the lower half of the view. There the Kel warship came to a stop, imperceptibly; held above it, the movement more like watching a film than actually changing position in space. There was no sense of real motion he could discern. It could all have been a dream.

As it came to a halt he gazed down, feeling as if a god looking upon a new kingdom.

The commander—Eldron—had informed him of his audience with the Praetor of their world. Kang calmly accepted that—thrilled he was getting his way, in fact, but trying not to show it—and the intervening wait had become interminable. Soon enough, back out near the purple gas giant, dozens of other ships arrived, several of them looking more daunting even than the one on which he stood, each bristling with weaponry—confirming his suspicion that these aliens indeed commanded a mighty army. By then he realized the Kel must want the Icon he held and, perhaps to a lesser degree, him. At least inasmuch as they feared him and wanted to understand this new threat. The purpose of the arriving fleet, from what he could glean, was to take up guard in the event the intruding spaceship returned.

Eldron's ship then departed for their homeworld, a trip that was near instantaneous. The crew went through a multitude of actions, lights dimming and warnings sounding as they prepared for the transit. Each took their seat, even Eldron who had so far only stood. No one suggested to Kang that he do the same. Of course they knew he was indestructible. Maybe they hoped the leap would somehow injure, or maybe even embarrass him.

It did neither. Activated, whatever propelled the ship moved it, feeling not unlike the action of the Icon itself, now that he recalled it, delivering them to an orbit above their homeworld, the planet he gazed on now. The sensation of that transfer was strange, perhaps even amplified by his greatly attuned senses, but it did not wobble or fell him. He stood firm, easy; impressed with the power of the ship more than anything.

Eager to learn everything these Kel could do.

From there the ship began moving forward in a more usual way, if impossibly smooth, impossibly quick. The warship changed position with hardly a lurch or sense of acceleration. Whatever means they used to hold everything in that artificial gravity also seemed to nullify the action of movement. At least to a great degree. Such that they slid forward rapidly, reaching proximity to the world in no time and coming to an equally fluid stop in close orbit.

Kel.

A dark world, Kang mused, even there on the daylight side; covered in vast swaths of what appeared to be black, volcanic rock, near-black inland seas, all of it split by one massive ocean of a color that was not much lighter. White covered the poles and the many peaks—Kel was a rugged, mountainous world—snow blanketing the persistent black. So black and white was it, in fact, he wondered how it supported life at all. There was no green to be found.

But this world clearly had air. The haze of atmosphere wrapped it, clouds here and there, some formed into the swirls of storms; seas and oceans, snow on every surface, as far as the eye could see. It had water, it had air. He looked back across the bridge at the crew.

It had life.

He found himself quickly unconcerned with particulars. Only that he was here and that these Kel were powerful beyond any reckoning. He looked down at the Icon in his hands. With the Kel—*with this,* he thought, gazing at the Icon—he could rule many worlds.

Eldron spoke and the computer echoed his words with a translation. Kang had learned that when they spoke directly to him the machine ran its routine. The rest of the time it remained silent, allowing them to scheme their plots right in front of him.

The situation was far from ideal, but already he'd made progress. They would try and subvert him. Of that he was sure. Probably even try to kill him. But he would have his way. Their intentions would fail.

He would rise superior in the end.

"Praetor Voltan is on approach," the computer told him. This Praetor was going to come in person—a gesture that continued to garner his respect. So far he liked the warrior mentality of the Kel. He also realized this was his first real test. Threats, sheer physical force would get him no further. Now came the moment of reckoning. He'd never been a politician, never a negotiator; never in his life. Even as a Kazerai results were gained through domination, not talk. Now … after all he'd done, he had to bring this Praetor around through communication alone. After his opening salvo of violence he must talk. Convince. The fact that their leader was willing to meet in person was a start. Kang's goal was to earn their trust. To do so he must become something he was not. In some ways, he thought, he must become an actual emperor. That thing he'd always dreamed of, that mantle he snatched for himself back on Anitra with simple brute force, no one able to stop him. Now he must become it for real.

But the *promise* of force ...

That would certainly help.

A wicked grin found its way across his face and he turned from the others to hide it. Not that they probably noticed. Or would even read into it. His random facial expressions likely meant nothing to them at that point. Still, he wanted to prepare for what was to come. He stood a little taller; adopted the bearing of a leader.

Again he smirked. Felt like a child that couldn't stop giggling. Determined, he gathered his composure and looked out the view screen at the vast openness.

Other vessels moved in orbit above the world, in irregular patterns, other objects floating in space that appeared to be base stations or satellites. The Kel moved through the void much like the Dominion moved on the ground, vehicles in motion here and there, destinations to receive them. The concept of harnessing what he witnessed was thrilling.

Among the bustle he caught glimpse of a smaller craft, probably some sort of shuttle, heading their way, moving from the clutter. It had an escort of sleek craft that looked to be fighters. It was the Praetor, he decided. Soon it reached them and the crew announced its arrival.

Eldron rose.

"Come," he instructed. Kang followed, allowing himself to be led off the bridge, down a corridor to a large stateroom. The room was modestly furnished, though by the minimalist standards he'd seen elsewhere on the ship it was lavish. It had a small screen to one side which gave the appearance of a window, looking out into space. On it two of the three orange suns hung visible in tight opposition; titanic dance partners, gripped in thrall.

"The Praetor will meet you here."

Eldron locked eyes with him, held his gaze an instant ... then turned and left. The door shut behind.

Doors, rooms—none of these things mattered. They could never seal him away. All these Kel might hope to do would be to kill him. Perhaps they could devise the technology to do so. Kang certainly wouldn't put it past them, based on everything he'd seen so far. For now, though, he was an impossible problem, something they had no way to contend with and, in order to maintain the advantage, he needed to keep it that way. Keep them on their heels; off balance in such a way that they never quite got control. At each step of the process he must determine where to give ground, where not. Enough so that they, in turn, eased their desire to be rid of him. It would be difficult, he could see. But perhaps, and this was his true desire, in doing so he might work out a co-existence. Such that they *wanted* to follow him.

He turned the Icon in his hands, cognizant of its hidden power. This was the first key, the first thing they would want. And he would give it to them—as he, too, wanted what it promised—but only on certain conditions. In a sense it was his first bargaining chip.

Unexpectedly soon the door opened and a tall Kel warrior stood without. Taller, more broad, more fearsome than any Kang had yet seen. Unconsciously he pulled himself a little straighter, making sure to rise to his full height. This was the Praetor, Voltan, he knew, and he was surprised at first, having expected a withered, politician of a man. He could see at once how Voltan rose to his place as leader: through physical prowess as much as cunning. That was no doubt how things worked in this culture. The weak were left behind; the strong rose to rule.

His estimation of the Kel grew still more.

"I am Praetor Voltan," the tall Kel confirmed, voice rich, overlaid by the tin of the computer as it echoed the English version. Voltan's hair was shock white, pulled high into the same queue as the rest, skin the same perfect alabaster with inked tracers on his cheek and around one brilliant, yellow eye. Over the other eye he wore a patch; the pelt of some white-furred creature draped his shoulders. The pelt was an unusual contrast to the hard black armor, and had the effect of making Voltan's already wide shoulders look even wider.

"I am Kang." His response was, in turn, through the computer, spoken back in the language of the Kel.

Voltan entered the room alone, just as he had arrived, and the door hissed smoothly closed behind him.

He faces me alone, Kang thought. Of course, a hundred escorts could've done little to protect him. Probably Voltan realized that. After all, he'd chosen to come in person for a reason. Personal safety was not it.

More likely it was to make a statement. Kang could see that now. To show courage, flex the might of his presence. As if to say, *I do not fear you.* Kang sneered, not caring how the expression would be interpreted. He could see that, behind the bravado, lurked the very fear Voltan tried to conceal. Now that the Praetor was there, standing before him, the Kel warlord realized Kang's power. Kang was everything his men said he was. And more.

But, in keeping with his prior determination, Kang deferred. Relaxed a bit of his posture and, not knowing how it might be taken, apologized.

"I am sorry for the deaths of your people," he said. As the computer translated he could see at once this was not the opening the Praetor expected. No doubt he'd come there with several possibilities in mind, any good negotiator would, but an apology was not one of them.

He stood for a long time, looking hard on Kang, scrutinizing his every aspect. Kang thought to say more but the Praetor spoke.

"They claim you have immeasurable strength," he said. "I've seen evidence of your work. How is this possible?"

Kang listened to the intonations in Voltan's voice, trying to see how they matched the words put forth by the computer. Did the translator get them right? The computer had a tone of curious awe about it, though Voltan's own voice sounded simply annoyed.

Kang thought of an answer; wondered if it might go too far but, at the same time, determined to keep them guessing.

"Perhaps I am a god," he said.

Voltan considered that. Made no remark against it.

"Are you, then, unique?"

"There are none like me."

"So there are no more on your world?"

What was he driving at? Already Kang had said so; there was no way to amend that, though he saw no immediate reason to do so. Whatever Voltan was attempting to divine mattered little.

"On my world I am legend."

That seemed sufficient.

"Where is your world?"

"I don't know 'where'. However," and Kang held up the Icon. "This can take me there."

Voltan's one good eye locked to it—unable to hide his fascination. He clasped his hands behind his back but the action did little to conceal his greed.

After a long moment he looked up and held Kang's gaze. Though the other eye was covered by the patch, it was as if he bored into him with both.

"It returns to your world?"

Kang wasn't entirely certain of that, but determined it was best, in that moment, to display utter confidence.

"Yes." He had confidence enough.

The Praetor seemed to mull things over. At length he inhaled.

"We must decide what comes next," he said. "I will contact the Tremarch."

"Wait here." And he turned. Kang watched him as the door opened and he left, fur of the decorative white animal pelt dancing lightly in the air where it lay wide across his shoulders. The door shut behind him.

Kang could sense a bit of acceptance in his inquisitor. The Praetor knew what he was capable of, yet left him in the room as if expecting Kang would simply wait there with civility, as would anyone in the midst of serious negotiations.

Kang grinned.

Determined that things would continue to go his way.

CHAPTER 15:

THE TREMARCH

JESS LOOKED AT HERSELF in the reflective surface of a control panel outside the bridge. Her eyes were red-rimmed, expression drawn. She ran her hands over her face and pushed back her hair, stretching the skin around her mouth, over her cheekbones, trying to freshen her look.

It didn't help.

She'd been standing in the corridor, just around the corner from the entrance to the command bridge, working up the nerve to face the others. After a long session of sad, then angry, then sad again introspection, alone in the infirmary agonizing over her indecision, she'd come to no conclusion. More than ever she felt the desire to just put all this behind; mark it as a possibility that was forever lost; a feeling that went smack up against the undeniable yet inexplicable impulse, an almost deep-seated conviction, that now was the time to seize this opportunity and do something.

It was a terrible contrast of emotions.

She took a deep breath.

Sadly that inexplicable conviction brought with it no clarity. There were too many things she needed to process and the confusion was obviously getting worse, not better, and so, finally, she decided to simply rise and come here. She knew only that she needed more time. Satori was in a mood to go, and if Jess didn't stop her—if she didn't come up with a viable alternative—Satori would make them leave and all would be lost. Only, they *couldn't* leave. Not until she knew what to do. Until then she couldn't allow anyone to move. Until the rest of her life had been figured out and she knew exactly what she wanted and exactly what she was going to do no one was going anywhere, and as the sheer hopelessness of that hit her she nearly collapsed.

She watched the pained expression pass across her face in the reflection of the control panel and made herself stand straighter. Tall and firm. Blew a strand of hair from her eyes. And for an instant, beneath the odd glare of the alien lighting, her eyes flickered gold.

The color was gone as quick as it came.

She tried to recreate it. Turned her head just so until ...

There. Her pupils came alive in shining yellow.

Whoa. She scrutinized them.

Wild.

Like cat's eyes. It was an optical illusion, of course, but the sight of herself in the shiny surface, face set with entirely alien eyes, sent a chill down her spine.

What's happening to me?

Of a sudden it made her feel powerful, not freaked like she would've expected, and as she stood holding the reflection so the color remained she rode that strange sensation, letting it grow, visualizing herself as some sort of ...

Warrior.

Am I? The thought struck her. After everything, after everything she'd done, after everything she'd been through, would it be wrong to think of herself that way? Had she not been a warrior all along?

She slumped to her usual posture and the reflection of her eyes snapped to their normal color.

Brown.

Just a girl.

With a deep, deliberate breath she mustered a fresh surge of determination, turned from the panel and strode the final steps to the bridge. At the door she paused.

Opened it and walked in.

Willet and Bianca were the first to turn. Satori and Nani were side-by-side at one of the consoles—engrossed with the study of All Things Earth. Satori turned to see her standing in the doorway. Everyone just kind of stared, any discussions they'd been having falling silent. The bridge became uncomfortably quiet, in fact. Jess could feel the tension in the air; could almost hear the echoes of their conversations of seconds before. About her. About the situation.

It wasn't like she hadn't expected it.

She fixed Satori's gaze. Slowly Satori stood, getting the unspoken signal. With a glance to the others she went and, when she got close, Jess stepped from the bridge, Satori followed her out and the door shut behind, leaving them alone in the hall.

Jess took a few steps back and stopped. Satori stopped and stood close—a little too close, and for an instant Jess felt intimidated. Satori knew why she was there. Knew she was there to convince her. It was almost as if Satori were already setting her will against her. Already had.

Of course she has.

"I'm sorry I've been a pain," Jess tried to mend fences. Satori was silent. They were almost eye to eye, Satori only a bit taller. In fact the two of them were nearly the same size physically, but in that moment Satori seemed bigger. The battle-hardened commander, firm gaze merciless in a stare-down. A contest of wills Jess felt suddenly ill-equipped to win.

She tried to conjure the brief sensation from the reflection, that feeling of power as she looked into her golden eyes. Reminded herself of all the things she'd already done.

"I'm just worried," she said.

"I know what you're worried about," Satori cut her short. "But it doesn't change anything."

"You said I had to make a decision."

"For yourself. Not for the rest of us. You've presumed too much already, done too much already. Dragged too many along in your wake. Now it's time to make up your mind. You and Bianca need to decide what to do. I already know what *we* have to do." Then: "Your friend wants to go home, by the way."

For a painful moment Jess imagined all the things they *had* been talking about. All the decisions they'd probably already made without her. Making plans as she sat in the infirmary alone, pouting over her troubles.

"She can't go home anymore than I can."

"That's up to her. I don't care what you guys decide to

do. There's a real war going on back on Anitra, with real consequences for a whole lot of people." Satori put her hands on her hips. "This can't be about you."

Jess snapped.

"*It's not about me!*" Then: "*You think I want this?!*"

Satori pulled back, but not much.

Jess felt her eyes go wide and couldn't stop it. "You think I asked for this?" She held out her arms, indicating the starship and everything around them. "I didn't ask for this responsibility!"

Where was this coming from?!

Satori's jaw hung open. "Responsibility?" she gaped. "What the hell are you talking about? This is *my* responsibility. *I'm* the one that let this happen. And *I'm* going to fix it."

Jess inhaled. Shocked but suddenly seething.

"I've changed one world without even meaning to!" Frustration gained steam. "How was that my destiny?!"

"Destiny? What—"

"Yes!" Jess plowed on. "Now here I am, back on Earth, where, oh, by the way, I've managed to make myself a fugitive here too! I've screwed myself, Satori! I'm so screwed!" Anger was pouring off her without warning in hot waves. The words almost didn't matter. She could've been shouting *Blah! Blah! Blah!* It was raw emotion, erupting like a volcano from some source she hadn't seen coming, and out of nowhere she was blasting Satori with it full force; every anguished regret, every pent-up remorse. "Now I can never go back! Earth, Anitra! I can't go anywhere! All I've done is make a mess of my life! Everywhere I've been! I'm only sixteen and I can't go anywhere! Decide?! Ha!"

Satori's mouth worked, temporarily mute, but it didn't take long to regain her composure and blast back: "So figure it out! All I know is this is bigger than you!"

Jess felt completely out of control. "*Exactly!*" The rollercoaster of emotions running through her was unbearable. Something ugly had been dragged to the surface and she wanted to cry, she wanted to scream; she wanted to run off the ship and leap into space. "Don't you get it?! This *is* bigger than me! It's bigger than all of us!" She wondered if the others could hear through the heavy bridge door. "Bigger than you, bigger than me. More complicated. More problems. I *can't* just decide for myself! *Don't you get it?!* Not like you want. Not like you mean and not anymore. And that sucks! I *want* to decide what's best for me! For Jessica!" She smacked her chest. "But I can't!" Her eyes darted back and forth, drilling into Satori. "So what now? Kang is gone! Maybe you're right and hooray if he is! But it isn't over! You think that's the end?! Ha! It isn't! It's like it never ends!" Satori's mouth was still working as Jess plowed on: "I just want out! But I can't get out! I want to walk away but I can't! I'm in so deep! There's nowhere to go. Nowhere to run. I *do* have to decide. But I have to decide for an entire world, Satori. *We* have to decide. Get it? *Two* worlds. It *isn't* just about me. You're missing, somehow completely missing what that *really* means. This is *huge*. We're nothing. This is nothing. Too much is at stake right now and I'm not just deciding for me. *You're* not deciding. I can't just pick up and go home and neither can you.

"I have *no* idea what to do."

Satori was amazed. "You've lost it."

Jess glared at her, Satori's red hair bright in the lights of the alien hall, framing her piercing blue eyes.

"Even if I wanted to go home," Jess tried to be calm, "I can't. You think that doesn't kill me? I'm right here, looking at my house. It's right there!" she pointed through the floor. "Do you know what that feels like?"

"So go back to Anitra. Like I said I don't—"

"You don't get it! Whether I go back to Anitra or not it's over!"

"What is your problem?! What do you mean over?!" Satori's hands, her face—her whole body was animated. "You need to get a grip!"

Jess was done with this conversation. "I do," she said. "I just ... I do. That's exactly what I need to do. Get a grip. Right now we're not hurting anything. Right now we're not in any danger. As soon as we leave ... anything is possible.

Right now we're safe. Right now nothing is changing." She took a deep breath. "I need to think. I need time to think. That's all I'm trying to tell you."

It was all too much. Most people got second chances in life, even third and fourth chances. Her life was officially over. There was no way she could ever have a second chance. Not now. The defenses she'd managed to erect against that horrible feeling, telling herself this or that thing to chase away the sinking fears—the lies she'd managed to make herself believe—crumbled. There was no way back. No clear path forward. Grief gripped her.

But Satori had no soothing words.

"You're better than this," she said, almost with disdain. "At least I thought you were."

Jess stared at her through blearing eyes. Hating her refusal to understand.

But against that continuing, utter lack of sympathy ... found a rock. In freefall, abrupt and unexpected; an unyielding place, at the bottom of the well, that solid foundation that had redirected imminent collapse before. Inner calm; a fortress from which Jess the warrior gathered her charge.

Her core.

"We need to stay," she said, simply, her ordinarily soft voice coming out clear and strong in the confines of the alien hall. Eyes clearing. This was not yelling. This was confidence. "That's all I know right now. We need to stay and we're not leaving. Not yet." Her face was probably flushed, eyes holding the remnants of tears that had just been forming, but she was strong. All at once, and she felt that calm certainty rising. It was a simple statement, *we're not leaving*, but it held force. She was done arguing. She may have had no idea what exactly to do but she knew she needed time. Leaving was not happening.

Not yet.

Indecision fell away.

Satori looked at her matter-of-factly. Crossed her arms.

"You figure out how you want to be involved," she said, "but we *are* leaving. We're taking this back."

"We're not."

Satori waited for her to say more, but she was done. And in that hollow moment, as if stumbling upon a gaping pit of power, such simple, attackable words hanging empty in the air, assailable, "we're not", how weak, how lacking in force, so easy to brush away, to knock aside and replace with a much firmer decision—which Satori thought she already had—in that sickening instant where Satori *knew* Jess was through and that, in fact, much to her shocked realization, Jessica's will *had* been imposed, Satori took a small step back. Blinked. Confused that, somehow, some way, the discussion was over.

Undeniably so.

As before the words meant little—meant nothing. It was the intention. Jess pierced Satori's gaze with it, vision beyond seeing, feeling the sheer power of her own decision flow from her as if a tangible force, radiating from within, wondering if her eyes were glowing in that moment, recalling the sight of their golden authority; almost felt a perverse sense of satisfaction at buckling Satori's will so handily, her own resolve dominant beyond reckoning. But she pushed those feelings aside. Left things unemotional. A mere decision that was and would be.

They would stay.

Yes.

And Satori knew it.

We're not leaving.

The discussion was over.

* * *

KEL TREMARCH CEE RANOK sat languidly in her throne, legs to the side. The throne was a massive, obsidian construct, a piece of art, wide, with swooping arms and a back that shot high above her head, fanning out to either side like dragon wings. It sat at the center of a fittingly vast room, dark beams arching overhead to form a towering dome; austere, empty, the great room holding nothing within it save the enormous throne and a giant screen that spanned one wall.

"I can bring him before you, my queen," her Praetor, Voltan, spoke from the screen, image of his fur-wrapped shoulders and handsome head towering before her. The eye patch only made him more fearsome, not less. "I can get him now if you wish." The screen rose half the height of the cavernous room, dwarfing the throne and Cee sitting before it. Voltan addressed her from orbit, aboard the compromised warship. The "him" he referred to was, of course, the beast.

Kang.

Cee regarded Voltan's giant image. "Our scientists say this Icon, as he calls it, may indeed be a relic from the Fifth Dynasty." She sat a little straighter. "What is your take on it?" Already their brightest minds had studied every picture of the device, poured over every scan they'd been able to engage, data from its identification in space, other readings from its time aboard, securely in the grip of the beast at all times.

"I believe he will part with it," said Voltan. "Under the right circumstances. He sees it as an item of trade. A lever. He has only that with which to bargain and knows it. His obvious ability to resist us is key, but in the end that alone will not get him what he wants. He recognizes the weakness of his position."

Cee let a little smile escape her lips. "I think perhaps your view is too narrow."

Voltan betrayed no reaction but she knew her Praetor. He did not like being made to feel ignorant. No one did, but Voltan had a particular dislike of being uninformed. He had designs on her throne; felt he, not her, should have ascended to that position. That he, Voltan, should sit at the head of the Forever Dynasty.

Not her.

"The thing he holds is not the only prize," Cee said simply.

"You consider," Voltan worked to piece together what she might mean, "he himself might somehow be useful?"

"Do you not consider it?"

Again the absence of reaction, behind his eyes flickers of anger.

But perhaps it was best not to goad him.

"Imagine if we can control him," she said. "Perhaps even replicate his power. His abilities. With this Icon, if we can unlock the stars, and with this creature unlock such raw potential ...

"Wresting this device from him, or making some exchange, is only part of the picture."

"You see value in the beast?" Voltan remained incredulous.

"I see opportunity."

"What, then, do you command?"

"I would speak with him. Bring him."

Voltan bowed his head curtly. "At once."

And he was gone from the screen. Off to fetch the thing called Kang. While Cee waited her highest ranking bishop entered the room. She listened as his booted footsteps clacked across the cavernous floor, drawing closer though she did not turn. Soon he came into view and stopped. With a cursory glance she directed his attention to the giant screen; nothing was now on it but the background of the shipboard room in which Voltan had been standing. Together she and her high bishop waited in silence.

Then the Praetor returned to the image, with him the horned, yellow-skinned monster. Though they knew what to expect Cee noticed the bishop take a step back—noticing she herself reacted, sliding involuntarily in the seat in that first instant.

Consciously she held herself straight; kept her image firm.

The beast, Kang, stood before her. Colossal on the giant display. Voltan moved several steps behind, just at the edge of the image.

"I am ruler of the Kel," Cee announced to the yellow monster, "as you would understand it. All obey my command." The beast's language had been captured during their encounter with the intruder vessel, which remarkably possessed a full translation between ancient Kel and the language spoken by Kang. The dialog was crude but was so far working. Refinements had already been made to their analysis but Cee guarded against subtleties that might be misinterpreted—in both directions. It was important to listen to what the beast said, carefully. Which made the politics of the discussion that much more uncertain.

"I am Kang." Its voice was scratched, harsh, no more beauty in it than was in the beast itself. Kang, in all, was an abomination.

But where was the individual? Surely there must be something in there that could be reasoned with.

"Why are you here, Kang? Why have you come?"

"I am here by accident. I was fighting the other. The human that appeared with me."

The Fetok. "Was the human as powerful as you? How could you be challenged by a mere human, when you killed so many of our soldiers so easily?"

This seemed to rile the beast.

"I was not challenged. Horus is not as powerful as me." Then: "But you should know he *was* stronger than an average human. Strong enough to resist me. Long enough, at least, to use this and bring us here." He held up the shiny device.

The Icon.

"We fought on my world," he growled. "His goal was to bring me here and leave me to die in the cold of space." He lowered the Icon from view. "It didn't work."

"Did Horus know of us?"

Kang laughed. Powerful; a sudden outburst that spiked the audio feed for an instant as the electronics compensated. In the background Cee saw Voltan cringe.

Even the beast's laugh was a force to be reckoned with.

But Kang realized the power of his presence. He bit back the laugh, though a crooked, fanged smile remained.

"He did not know of you. None of us knew of you."

Cee wondered how much Kang actually understood. Was he just a monster from his world? Or did he truly move in their circles of power? There had been other bursts of energy in the past, like the one that deposited Kang and the Fetok, Horus. Those bursts had drawn the Kel's attention and they set up the very outpost that captured Kang. Surely those bursts of energy were others from his world using the Icon, in which case they would at least, by then, know of the presence of the Kel. That was only logical. Kang acted as if this were the first time the Icon had been used.

"What of the other craft?" Cee asked. "Did that not come from your world?"

"I don't know," he admitted. "That ship is unknown to me. My world has no such technology. What I suspect is that it was found by others. I thought they probably came to rescue Horus."

"Did you know it was one of ours?"

This confused him momentarily.

"One of yours?" He didn't understand.

"Indeed." Cee nodded. "It was a Kel warship." She gave that a moment to sink in. "Ancient, no doubt, but one of ours. From the last great period of our rule, near as we can tell. And that, perhaps as much as anything, is a terrible mystery. That ship should not exist. There was a time, long ago, when we reigned over many worlds, some of them human. That ship is from that period. All was lost in a series of great wars. It should not have survived."

Now there was a glimmer of understanding in Kang's eyes.

"Our history speaks of a Great War," he rasped, the computer overlaying his voice with a smooth translation, "when worlds fought."

Cee tilted her head slightly. "That must surely be the same."

"But ... that was long ago." The beast's expression had softened in contemplation of this possibility and, for an instant, as it did, Cee saw a face within that horrible mask of destruction. A face that looked almost ...

Normal.

Suddenly she was curious.

"Have you always been like this?" It struck her that he may not have been.

"A monster?"

She appreciated the frankness of his response. Kang knew what he was. She nodded.

"I was human once."

"What happened?"

Clouds of anger returned. "I was caught in an explosion. It transformed me."

"Before that you were human?"

"I was like Horus."

"A powerful human?"

"More powerful. After the explosion I've become indestructible."

Cee decided to leave it at that. If she had her way they would soon know all they needed to of how Kang came to be, how he got his power and how they, too, might attain it.

And, if needed, how they might destroy him.

"So there are other powerful humans on your world?"

"There were five. I was one. Horus was one. After the transformation I killed the others. Horus was rescued and must've been taken back. That would leave him alone, but Horus was near dead when we came here. Horus I will finish myself. All I need is to get my hands on him."

So many questions fell into that void. How did Kang expect to get to him? If he intended to use the Icon to do it, why hadn't he done so already? But she knew the answer. Kang meant to rule the Kel, to lead an army against his own world and have the Kel as his puppets. And so he entered into these negotiations. Cee could see the process irked him.

However there was something about Kang that intrigued. Now that she had him before her she began to realize her original imaginings were correct. He *could* be used, just as the Icon could be used. Perhaps in ways she herself did not yet see.

She leaned forward in her throne. "You may leave us."

Kang wanted to say more, but acquiesced and left the screen. Voltan stepped back to stand before her as Kang walked out the door of the stateroom. The Praetor looked to his right to confirm the door had closed and the beast was gone.

"We are alone?" Cee asked. Voltan looked down at something before him, checking information.

"He has returned to his room. We are alone."

Cee turned to the side; placed a leg back over the arm of the throne and let the other dangle.

"If this device can truly open our ancient space lanes," she said, "and with it a world ripe for conquest ... perhaps this may be exactly what we need."

"We know the Old Worlds are out there," Voltan agreed. "They must be. As to whether this is one of them ..."

"There would be no other explanation."

"The Progenitor were prolific, my queen. Records tell us their influence was vast. It is not unreasonable to think there might have been—"

"Kang is from the old Combine. He and that other, the human, are descendents of our ancient subjects. I have no doubt of it."

"As you wish."

Cee stared into him, piercing the giant screen; image of his head larger than she and her throne combined. Standing in front of her the bishop was dwarfed before it.

Her voice had an icy edge to it. "Our Dynasty stagnates," she informed him—needlessly, of course. "We bloat under the weight of our limited horizon. If the Kel do not find challenge—external challenge, not some silly war games— we will again fall into revolution. You know this. Like before, we will be ruined.

"The One God has delivered us something, Voltan. This is a boon. And a puzzle. We must execute wisely."

"It is a hazard." His barely concealed antagonism remained. "I caution you. Nothing more."

Cee let him stand there, waiting. At last she spoke; adopting a tone that indicated she'd moved on.

"What do you feel we must offer in order to get the device?"

"He seems bent on the subjugation of his own world. Were we to offer him that, he would comply. I am certain of it.

"However, I do not doubt for a moment he also sees us as his eventual pawns. He would rule us."

"He will not rule us."

"This is no wild beast we can simply corral. Were he to be unleashed on our world there would be no containing him. I've seen what he can do, seen how our technology has failed to stop him. All he would need do would be run amok. We would lose much before he could be destroyed. If he could be destroyed at all. He may yet prove indestructible, as he claims."

"Bring him here," she said. "To me."

Voltan faltered visibly, a little tremor in his stance—though Cee knew he'd seen her demand coming. Knew he realized what her decision would be. That she would order the presence of the beast.

But he played his part. "My queen," he said. "That is far too dangerous. As I say. Here he is contained. Once off this ship he will be a plague. One we will never get back in its bottle."

"I will handle Kang."

Voltan was unmoved.

"Bring him to me." Cee repeated. "We will give him a reception due any dignitary." She could see Voltan waver badly. He said nothing. "In the meantime ensure our scientists redouble their efforts. Study every bit of information we have on him, every scan—all we currently possess and any new data you can gather. I want to know how to destroy him."

Voltan nodded. "Yes, my queen."

And he signed off. The giant screen went dark.

Cee turned to her bishop.

"This may be the beginning of the end," she said to him. Then imagined the possibilities. "Or it may be the start of the most glorious chapter in our history.

"Either way, the time for change has come."

CHAPTER 16:

A NEW WORLD

"THE DOMINION IS IN CHAOS." Everyone in the room looked to Chom as he spoke. He sat at the edge of one of the living room couches, making his point. "The Emperor is gone, his body violated and thrown to the wind. Now Kang is gone— after turning the entire place upside down. Before all that the Icon was stolen, the Crucible destroyed, the Shogun and the entire religious Council killed. Most of our military is across the ocean, fighting on against the Venatres in a war that will leave the Dominion forces broken.

"Our government is a shell. Osaka is a tomb. In shock, waiting for the next blow. If ever there was a time it is now."

The small group of Conclave leaders sat crowded into Darvon's living room. As always, it seemed, trying to make sense of recent events. Working up the courage to act. Darvon's daughter, Egg, watched from the wings, as she had on so many occasions.

"Kazukhan," Chom spoke directly to the Daimyo, their most distinguished member, reclining in the largest chair in the room, Darvon's own recliner, relinquished for the Conclave boss, listening to the debate of the others. "The Dominion leadership is crushed," Chom seemed to plead. "First the Shogun, the entire upper echelon, then their replacement by Kang and, just as the people were grasping the shock of Kang himself and, perhaps, even coming to grips with the idea that he, in his rage, might at least deliver us the world ... now Kang is gone. Utterly. Dispatched with the very Holy Relic once so safeguarded, so untouchable for so many years. What more do we need? The way is open." He looked to the others. "What more impetus is required to finally act boldly? To become that which we have dreamed of for so long?

"True revolutionaries."

Egg watched her father rock ever so slightly, back and forth at the edge of his seat. Events of the past days had driven his enthusiasm for the Prophecy and, specifically, the role of Jessica to new heights. When word reached them that the angel was the one that banished the murderous demon Kang—and that she did so using the Holy Relic— he'd nearly thrown a party right then.

Egg looked across to the Daimyo. He maintained his pensive repose, as he had since arriving and sinking into her father's cushy chair with a glass of wine. Whether he was truly pensive or just tired was hard to tell.

Chom went on. "In my mind," he said, "Yamoto is the key. Yamoto is a general at heart. A military man. Not a Shogun. Yamoto has never been a proper Shogun. He was lost before, now doubly so. And he holds the Dominion's top position."

"Yamoto *is* shaken," one of them agreed. "But what can we do?"

"What of the giant spaceship?" Grisha's question was off the current line of discussion but he was confounded that they were talking about anything else. So were some of the others. "Why don't we speak of that? That surely is the most shocking bit of news. Right? I mean, what have the Venatres been hiding from us? They were supposed to be our allies."

"They *are* our allies," Chom sought to dismiss those events, as he had already several times that evening. The others weren't so sure. Egg herself was intensely curious as to just what the mysterious spaceship was. Reports were spotty, but apparently the craft emerged into airspace over the battle at Midbay and took to orbit, only to fly off into space and disappear. Like some great, shared hallucination. The entire capital was buzzing.

Chom stayed on point.

"We've known they were working on a secret project," he said. "So many things have happened, so many unexpected things ... we can't waste time speculating over something that has no consequence for what we're doing right now.

In fact, that bit of news only adds to the chaos I describe. On top of everything else, the news that the Venatres might possess a super weapon has driven our people further into confusion Not toward cohesion.

"As I say. The time to act is now."

The Daimyo spoke, finally, and a certain quiet descended on the rest as they listened intently to what he might say. Egg, too, paid close attention.

"It's true, Yamoto was only ever a military strategist," he said and paused. Everyone waited. Just as it appeared he would say no more, or had gone back to his quiet introspection, the front door burst open and in rushed Egg's younger sister. Seeing the grave expressions of the people gathered in their living room gave her sudden pause, but only for a moment.

"Sorry," she said. Then: "Hi, Dad." She waved across the room. Darvon smiled and waved back.

"Hi, sweetie. Did you have fun?"

"Yep." And she was off to her room in a rush.

She, like Egg, was used to these meetings.

When she was gone the Daimyo picked up his train of thought.

"I think," he said, giving his next words consideration, "we might arrange a meeting." He looked around the room at each person there—even pausing briefly on Egg. A sense of the momentous ran through her; like she was being included. It was the first time she'd felt that way, though she'd been attending these gatherings as a bystander for years. The invisible girl who brought them wine and the occasional snack.

It was an unexpected thrill.

"Now may be our chance to bring together both sides."

He turned specifically to Chom and issued instructions:

"Make contact with your highest level liaison among the Venatres," he told him. "Make it known we want to broker a meeting. Between Yamoto, our Council, and their leaders. Venatres and Dominion, here in Osaka. Gauge their response."

Egg wondered if she gasped audibly, though there

seemed to be a collective intake of breath in the room. What the Daimyo proposed was probably more than Chom was suggesting yet ... made perfect sense. Why not go all the way? Bring both halves of the world together in one place.

Little bumps tingled on her skin. There she was, one person in a room of few—in her own living room, for crying out loud, crappy furniture and all—not some great political hall or even a public venue—preparing to arrange a meeting of Anitra's greatest leaders. An act, an effort at peace that could forever change the course of their entire world.

The fate of Anitra was being planned right before her eyes.

"While you do that I will meet with Yamoto," the Daimyo finished. "This will inevitably show our hand. Let us hope that it works.

"If it does not ..." he paused. A long pause, during which he took a sip of wine. After he swallowed he finished with: "One way or the other this will be the end of the Conclave."

* * *

IN SUCH PROXIMITY the Kel warship hung in the air like a mountain set free from its base; impossibly huge, filling Cee's vision. Black, sleek, colorless against the white sky. Slowly it came, having appeared first at a fast clip, dropping from orbital heights above and materializing through the clouds as a ghost; fog wisping away around its sharp edges as it came lower, gaining substance until it was at last on final approach, descending to the sprawling port, headed for the giant berth cleared and awaiting its arrival. Cee, her delegates and closest aides stood atop a high platform, in the open air, watching. Other warships crouched in berths scattered across the facility, dark hulls of varying size stretching into the distance. Only one of the other craft outclassed the arriving cruiser, a dreadnought which sat close enough to gauge its massive size in relation. The Kel fleet boasted hundreds of such ships of the line, thousands of smaller vessels.

Far too much arsenal for a race with no enemies.

Soon that will change, Cee thought, watching in breathless anticipation as the cruiser's shadow loomed, seeming to come in right on top of them—an illusion that was real enough to instill a thrill of fear, as if they were about to be crushed. And as it settled the final distance to ground she realized that fear came not only from the proximity of the great warship, but from the consideration of its deadly cargo. Aboard was the beast.

This will be the hallmark of my rule.

With the beast came yet more to drive that thrill. A relic from their past. A device that could, quite possibly, open ancient space lanes, a way to move their vast fleet beyond the borders of their own star system. An opening for conquest, if so; a way to redirect their might. A new direction for their warlike impulse.

If true it could not have come at a better time.

"Is the beast as hideous as they say?" asked one of her delegates. As the cruiser landed it gave off little noise, inertial drives all but silent. Only the inevitable sounds of moving such a titanic shape through the atmosphere— even slowly as it now traveled—preceded it. The push and pull of great volumes of air, displaced ahead of and around its gargantuan form. Once it settled fully into the walls of its berth the spaceport fell heavy with quiet.

Even the frigid air was still that day.

"It is," Cee's high bishop answered. "Truly an abomination."

Cee ignored their exchange, eyes glued to the gleaming black flanks of the warship and the small door through which the arrivals would emerge. A gantry moved into place against its side, squaring up with the portal, all aspects of this arrival pre-arranged. Cee's delegation consisted of a dozen officials and, stationed all around the berth, a legion of Kel soldiers, heavily armed and assembled specifically for this occasion. This was not a civil event. There were no citizens present for the spectacle.

Flurries had begun to fall, gently, fluttering nearly straight to the ground in the absence of a breeze. All around them was like a giant, open-air tomb, deathly quiet beneath the vault of a cloud-laden sky.

The gantry notched solidly into position and the heavy clunk echoed across the snowy landscape. Senior commander of the legion present ascended, trailed by three of his officers, their figures pitifully small against the smooth flanks of the cruiser. Bugs, walking toward a huge black wall. Their white faces and hair were like stark little dots, dark armored bodies blending with the black of the ship itself.

Cee felt herself move closer to the edge of the reception platform as the four officers reached the top of the gantry, assembling outside the troop door. She put her bare hands on the icy railing. For a long moment she stood like that, then reached and pulled her fur wrap tighter about her shoulders. The luxurious white animal hair was long, warm against her cheeks.

Snow fell; the legion of troops below motionless, as were the officers waiting on the gantry; one of her delegates coughed, a dull sound in the cold air.

And the door opened.

As Kang stepped through into the light all but Cee and her bishop reacted, Kang's yellowed, disfigured form stark against the rest, but something in the reaction of one of them took Cee off guard. She turned to him.

"What is it?"

The man stammered. "It's ... The Prophecy."

Cee froze. Fury rose hot in her throat, though she nearly saw the man's words in his eyes before he spoke them. Nearly knew they were coming.

"You dare!" She stepped to him and he recoiled. "You are among the elite!" She herself had made the connection upon first seeing Kang; upon hearing the description of him, in fact, as the drama of his arrival aboard the warship unfolded via their comm channels. But she buried it deep, secretly hoping no others might draw the same conclusion.

A foolish hope. Surely all would who bore witness.

The legends of the Prophecy could never be fully crushed.

"Shall I have you killed?!" she closed the gap, pushing

the man against another such that he could retreat no further. Time to make a statement; a pre-emptive strike here, before her highest leaders. "Now?!" She leaned in, face directly in his. The others would know exactly of what he spoke, were no doubt thinking the same—if they hadn't been already. But none dared utter those thoughts aloud.

How dare he!

Perhaps she *should* kill him. Make a bloody example, such that no other present so much as *thought* to speak such blasphemy.

The delegate was horrified, saw the murder in her eyes, but all he could do was point a trembling finger at the monster.

Cee did not want to release him from her rage, but her own curiosity compelled her to follow his outstretched arm, to turn her attention back to the beast as it departed the ship. Kang stood on the gantry among the Kel officials, gripping the shiny device in one hand. Her Praetor, Voltan, stood near to him, others positioning themselves accordingly, in preparation to escort the monster. Kang's crooked horns, his yellowed hide, bloodshot eyes; sharp, uneven teeth even from that distance, fangs that could not be fully concealed even when his mouth was fully closed ... It *was* the Prophecy. And no matter how she might turn her mind from it, the thought could not be denied.

Damnation!

The delegate's voice snapped her from her thrall.

"My queen—"

She whirled on him, spit flying with lost composure. "The Witch is dead! I will not have her words uttered! *Nothing* of her words will be repeated! *Nothing!* Do you understand?" The delegate trembled. Cee looked to the others. "Would that I could burn those memories utterly from our past! This is a new age!" She got back in the delegate's face. "Who have you spoken to of this?"

"No one my queen!"

She glared at him, piercing his eyes, boring deep into him—in the hope he would be so cowed as to never think on this again.

Still she thought of killing him.

But the deep draw of a bone horn brought her back to the moment. It's rumbling, discordant sound echoed across the expanse of the port, directing everyone's attention to the passage of their guest.

Cee turned. The hornsman stood alone atop a tall, narrow platform, put there for that purpose alone, looking out over the berth and the assembled legion. A proper herald for the arrival of a dignitary. Kang, Voltan and the others passed along the wide walkway, drawing up on the larger platform on which Cee stood with her delegates. The thin, white fur of the pelt draped across Voltan's wide shoulders moved gently in the still air as he walked. With one last, deadly glare at the blasphemous delegate, she stepped further apart from the others and drew herself straight, regally, preparing for the encounter.

Kang and the group ascended the final bit of stairs and stepped onto the platform, Voltan in the lead. Her Praetor came to her. Behind him Kang snorted, like a true beast, frozen air shooting from his nose in a jet and Cee held herself from a start. The impulse to jump passed through her and she looked hard at Kang. It was some sort of natural action, like a sneeze; not an effort to create an effect or make his presence known. She steadied herself before him. In such proximity he was truly fierce to behold.

Voltan, for his part, seemed used to Kang's peculiarities. He spoke as if no sudden outburst had occurred.

"My queen, I give you Kang." He stepped aside and looked between them. One of the officials in their group held a translator and positioned himself accordingly, as Voltan continued the introduction: "Kang, the lady Cee-Ranok, Tremarch of the Kel, queen and ruler of the Forever Dynasty."

Kang bowed his head, then looked to her.

"How shall I address you?" he asked in his deep, scarred voice, the translator doing its work. "I have only one name: Kang. You are Tremarch, queen, Cee-Ranok. How should I call you?"

"For now Lady Cee will do," she decided, the uniqueness

of the situation dawning on her as if a revelation. This was her first encounter with anyone outside the Kel universe. Until that time there had been no call for special means of address.

Lady Cee. Impulsive, but she liked the sound of it.

"Then I am honored to meet you, Lady Cee."

"Welcome, Kang," she warmed to him. Live and in person she saw more of the face that underlay his disfigurement, judging that at one time, by the standards of humanity, he might have been striking, in a rugged way. The beast's manners were certainly coming through, especially in the wake of his violent arrival—though she suspected much of this newfound pleasantness came directly from the desire to get what he wanted.

He took a sweeping look of the entire facility, horns exaggerating the movement, looking out over the legions of troops assembled in waiting, out across the facility at the mighty ships on display. He looked all the way, turning fully in place, taking in the mountains and the land as well, then back to her. "Impressive," he said. "Again I apologize for the destruction I've so far caused."

"I consider that two powers of war have come in contact," said Cee. "Such contact is inevitably brutal. Today we come together to discuss an arrangement." The sense of danger in the beast's presence was intense, but she thrilled with it. And as she stared into his bloody eyes found herself not afraid but, rather, encouraged.

"I'm not much for pageantry," he said.

The edges of his discourse were quite rough, and his impatience was tangible, but standing there in witness of him she was ever more strongly of the belief she could harness him. Properly directed, she imagined, he might move the War Council in ways she herself might not.

It was gripping.

"For one of such power," she said, "who has survived in the depths of space, you may not appreciate discomfort, and thereby comfort, but my citadel awaits our discussion. Let us make our way there."

"As you wish."

She turned to depart the platform, watching him over her shoulder as she did, the fine fur of her wrap tickling her face. A breeze was picking up, swirling the light flurries into a whiter current. Soon it would snow harder.

Kang followed and she looked ahead, speaking to him as she walked. She listened to the footsteps of the group as they followed in order, down the stairs of the royal platform to the beautifully lamp-lined walkway that led directly to the royal transport monorail in the near distance.

"I would give the Icon, as you call it, to our scientists, that they might study it." She held her eyes ahead, on the sleek black train waiting at the end of the walk; her private coach that would take them from the port to her citadel.

"The Icon is all I have to bargain with." Kang's voice was gruff. "Without it I have nothing."

"Absurd," said Cee, hoping the translator managed the subtleties of her inflection. Already she was getting used to the intermediary device, its neutral voice overlaying the sing-song of her own and the bestial utterances of Kang. "You can lay waste to us if you choose. Regain it should we attempt to steal it. The worst we could do would be to destroy it." She determined to project absolute frankness with him, such that he felt she was being thoroughly honest. An apparency of truth was the best way to ensnare him. "But what purpose would that serve?" she wondered, for his benefit. "We would lose the thing we also want, and locking you here … our civilization would be ruined before the wrath of your rage. I doubt we could stop you." Kang's footsteps clomped the snow-dusted walkway beside her, distinct from the others.

"You could use it without telling me," the beast grumbled. "Make me believe it's indecipherable while you secretly use it."

"Unlikely," she said and, again, hoped for the veracity of the translation device. "But no matter. There are a hundred possible outcomes. If any of this is to work we must first lay a foundation of some degree of trust. We have trusted you in bringing you here. Aboard the warship you were at least contained. Here our entire world is at risk. But we have trusted you. I invite you to trust us in return. If only a little."

They reached the shiny black monorail and its wide entry door. Warm air drifted out, mixing with the bite of the increasingly cold outside. A storm was picking up. Cee looked at their reflections in the glossy black surface, distorted by the curve of the train's body. Kang behind her to the left, visage fierce, Voltan at her right, the others grouped nearby. Delegates, the other military officers. She made eye contact with Kang in the reflection then stepped aboard.

"This can get you to my world," he said and followed, the rest of the group boarding. Cee stood near the front of the starkly furnished yet opulent coach. Kang stood across from her, Voltan to her side. The delegates and officers gathered within, the door closed and the train pulled away, inertial dampeners holding them perfectly steady, as on a starship, as it accelerated to speed. Outside the large windows the port fell quickly away and soon the soaring trees of a great, dark forest were blurring past as they gained velocity and raced through it.

"If you were to understand it it might, in turn, show you the way," said Kang. "Like a key."

One of Cee's delegates, a scientist, spoke: "It is arcane technology," he confirmed, looking as well as he could at the device in Kang's grip. The translator picked up the translation as all the rest. Cee frowned a little. Not only that he spoke out of turn, but that the translator used the same neutral voice for him as it did for her. Her translated voice was not unique.

Kang studied the device in his own hand. Everyone else had been staring at it, fascinated by the power contained in such a simple thing.

"If we are not mistaken it should contain a quantum entangled location pair," the scientist went on. Cee watched him, deciding to let him continue. "Which should shift between locations."

"My world is at the other end," said Kang. "Ripe for the taking." A bit of the rage simmering within him passed across his face, ever boiling beneath the surface. "My armies were engaged with the enemy. I would soon have ruled them, then this." He held up the Icon. "I was about to use it to return, after we retrieved it, but by then I'd had a chance to witness your people and what they were capable of. It led my thinking in a new direction."

"You see us as yours to use," said Cee.

"Not entirely," he said, and she found it telling how little he rejected the idea. Almost as if he considered it a valid prospect, but agreed they would likely not become his absolutely. As if they might, in the end, retain some autonomy. Such arrogance! He was rife with it, barely able to hold the façade of diplomatic discourse he knew he must in order to succeed. The banter of politics, the give and take of such a conversation nearly eluded him.

Kang would, truly, be a challenge.

He phrased his words carefully. "The Kel would also stand to gain from the conquest of a new world. Knowing nothing more of your people than I do I know this: Everyone needs territory. You commit to me the resources of your world, in return I give you the resources of mine.

"My belief is that an arrangement can be made."

Cee looked ahead, out the window of the speeding train as it curved from the deep-green forest, flecked with snow, rushing onto a vast plain that led to a deep valley. Immediately her citadel sprang to view, massive obsidian walls climbing the side of a mountain as if the whole structure clung to it, crawling ever higher until its uppermost turrets jutted like dark fingers into the sky. The host mountain sat at the foot of the range, at its base a wide, snowy expanse that stretched to the forest, black rocks of the mountain blending with the black stonework of the citadel itself. The clean fusion of mountain and structure made it look as if the fortress had been formed from the same natural forces that birthed the mountains, rather than crafted by hand. As if the citadel were, indeed, itself a mountain.

Cee watched from the cabin as the train tracked rapidly along the raised monorail, lead cars heading like a shot into a dark opening in the base of the cliff ahead. Within moments theirs zipped in behind and the blackness consumed them.

CHAPTER 17:

A DISCUSSION OF POSSIBILITIES

JESS WALKED THE *REAVER'S* CORRIDORS, feeling trapped within the stark black surfaces, wishing the halls were longer. Wishing for any distraction to save her. She needed room to wander. To get her head straight. The confines of the starship grew tighter each day, leaving her desperate to get off. An unceasing, low-level panic that, by now, she fought constantly.

Dinner minutes ago had been a strained affair. As had been the case with every gathering since her confrontation with Satori. Even Bianca gave her wide berth. The standoff with the others had become excruciating, and as she ate just now she tried to focus on the bland food prepared from the ship's stores, the surroundings, the cool water they drank, anything. None of it diversion enough. Nothing worked to ease the restlessness—or solve her dilemma.

Satori had it all figured out. Whatever force Jess exerted in that difficult yet decisive encounter in the hall was fading. The anxiety of indecision was settling and Jess knew if she didn't come up with something, and soon, Satori would snap out of it and Anitra would become their permanent future. Jess couldn't let that happen. Because once they went ...

She had no confidence in anything beyond that.

If only they could expose themselves to the world. Stop hiding, light up and wave flags "Hey! We're here!" It seemed such an easy—and obvious—answer. Bring the Kel technology directly to Earth and usher in a New Age. Simple. Unlike the rampage of a single Skull Boy there was no way any Earth agency, no matter how powerful, no matter how clever, could cover the presence of an untouchable starship, broadcasting everywhere from on high.

Of course Satori would never go for that. After all, why give this to Earth before Anitra?

Jess sighed as she walked, breath echoing in the narrow space.

Somehow, some way—so far—Satori was adhering to her unspoken command. So far they hadn't left. But she and Jess were on edge, a rift Jess could hear cracking, ready to break, and her hold was slipping. Something would soon give.

Nani had reached a sort of "neutral buoyancy", collecting data and mapping the capabilities of Earth, managing to hold the *Reaver* beyond detection even as she continued to mine the world's information. She, of all of them, was fine either way. Content to be building her store of knowledge, piecing together the data she'd gathered on the Kel and, Jess suspected, in no hurry to rush back to whatever fate waited them on Anitra. Bianca held her tongue, but Jess knew her friend longed to go home and take her chances. Maybe she should let her.

Much to Jessica's curiosity Nani had begun infiltrating the Project in real-time. It was an amazing feat and one which Jess found hugely interesting, but she dared say little about it. Not in the current environment. For Nani—and Jess, privately—learning what the Project and, especially, the Bok knew was key. The Project knew about the Bok, and the Bok could reveal big chunks of the overall puzzle. The Kel were paramount, in her mind, and the Bok were once part of the Kel. And so as the other pressures built so did that one, for Jess, and her urge to expose the Bok had become unexpectedly strong. She wanted them. A compulsion for which she had no reasonable explanation, yet there was no denying the deep-seated desire to rip that ancient society from the shadows. The Bok had secrets. Deep secrets. Nani had confirmed that conclusively. Ties all the way back to the last time human and Kel were in contact, and the Project, top secret agency belonging to the most powerful country on Earth, had made the Bok their top priority. No effort spared.

Could she, Jessica Paquin, with the help of Nani and the

technology at *their* disposal, do any better?

As interesting as the prospect was, she had no dream of convincing Satori of doing anything about *that*. There was no way Satori was going to agree to a treasure hunt—no matter how fascinating might be the promise of the results.

And so life on the *Reaver* had become a slow agony that made Jess want to scream. The greater part of her was slowly coming to grips with the idea she might—in fact, likely would—end up having to live the rest of her life on Anitra. And probably a good chunk of that as a prisoner. A sad prospect to be sure, yet one which she might be forced to accept. It was also possible she could parlay the *good* things she'd done to regain position and at least stay out of jail. Remain a player, of sorts. The idea of coming back to Earth with the Venatres as a liaison was probably shot. That might've helped her avoid a prison sentence on Earth. Maybe. Right then, though, no solution was shining through.

Hoping to avoid jail on two worlds did not exactly inspire one to action.

She reached the infirmary and entered. The door hissed closed behind her and she went and sat in her usual spot, next to Zac.

"Hi," he said.

She screamed and jumped up.

"*Zac!*" She stared down on him, eyes wide.

And for a moment couldn't move.

"You're awake!" she managed.

He grinned. She practically fell on him, gripping her arms across his wide shoulders and hugging him in absolute joy.

"*You're awake!*" She was smiling so wide it hurt, cheek pressed against his, the stubble of his newly growing beard tickling and she pushed tighter, squishing against him. Warm tears fell from her eyes.

"I'm awake," he confirmed, a little hint of amusement in his tender voice.

She hugged him tighter, if that was possible, and felt his arms come up to encircle her. She squeezed him. Then pulled back to look into his eyes, noses brushing, debated kissing him and did. As their lips touched, hesitant at first, he pushed up with unexpected passion and she gasped and kissed him harder. In an instant they were locked in a deep, shuddering embrace. It rocked her, and all at once she was shaking so badly she had to pull away. Only slightly, but far enough to put some space between them. She hovered directly over him, face inches from his as he looked up into her eyes. Searching; looking into her; so deeply, so completely, she shuddered again.

Slowly she climbed onto the narrow bed and scooched in to lay beside him. He slid to give her room and she straightened and propped herself on an elbow. He slid further, turned himself to the side and did the same. Together they lay there, on their elbows, staring into each others' eyes, inches apart. For an instant she thought it would look bad if anyone walked in, but almost laughed with how much she didn't care.

Another shudder ran through her. *You're awake!* She smiled with the joy of it, intensely amused with herself, teetering on the brink; feeling she was about to absolutely lose it and loving that it would've been the most incredible thing if she did.

Zac!

He reached his free hand and touched the corners of her mouth.

"I knew I'd see that smile again."

And she smiled wider; too wide, she worried, and for a weird instant inverted from the joy and hoped her after-dinner breath didn't stink.

"How do you feel?" she asked.

"Fine." He withdrew his hand and flexed his free arm, back and forth, watching the perfect muscles in his forearm and bicep contract. There he lay, right there, bare chested and wonderful, flexing his studly arm and Jess found herself getting lightheaded again. Desperately she put her mind to other things.

It was almost as if he didn't know just how amazing he was.

"How long have I been out?" he asked.

"Not long," her voice caught and she cleared it. "A couple days, I think. Maybe more." She tried to sound composed. "We've been in space since we rescued you. I'm kind of losing track of time."

He looked around suddenly. "We're in space?"

Oops. Totally forgot he needed to be caught up.

A lot had happened since the fight with Kang.

"This is the Kel starship," she said, hoping that wouldn't freak him out. "We used it to rescue you."

He kept looking around the alien room, trying to understand exactly where he was. So caught up had he been in her, it was almost as if he'd entirely missed everything else and now, as he looked around ...

"This is ... We're on the Kel starship?" He remembered the ship's name. "The *Reaver?*"

She nodded. The reality of what that implied dawned on him like a ton of bricks.

"You used the ... How did you ... ?"

"We used it to rescue you." It really was quite incredible, she had to admit, and it was hitting him all at once. There was no denying the conclusions detonating in his mind.

"Then we came to Earth," she added.

Now he pushed up. "Earth?" Then: "You ...

"This is the Kel ship?"

She nearly laughed, his reactions were so sweet, but it wasn't the time for laughing. "It's a long story," she said instead.

For a moment he couldn't speak.

His clear blue eyes were so wide.

"And now we're on Earth?"

"In orbit but, yeah."

And more details came flooding back; like he was just now remembering the particulars of how he'd ended up there, of what was going on.

"How ... ?" He tried to collect his thoughts, tried to come up with an intelligent question, but at last was only able to repeat:

"How?"

In response she shrugged.

He regarded her in hushed awe. "You came for me," his voice was filled with it. "Again you came for me. You came and you saved me."

Quietly, almost shyly, she answered.

"I said I would."

He stared at her. Admiring her; taken with her; utterly, completely, enthralled by her. With no words, without a sound, with no more than an expression and the emotion in his eyes he was so taken with her she could feel it.

It made her belly tingle.

At length the attention became too much, his inability to put into words what he was thinking and the silence that entailed unbearable, and she had to redirect.

"You've got a beard coming in," she said. She reached and stroked it.

It was enough. He'd apparently been as stuck as he looked. He put a hand to his own face and stroked it too—slightly perplexed by the stubble.

She took away her hand. Asked: "What happened out there? With you and Kang?"

Zac shifted. Put the buttload of impossibilities to the side for the moment and simply decided to move on.

"Kang is strong," he settled slowly back to his elbow. "It was a shock. I recall an instant in the vacuum, the cold of space and ... I blacked out ..." He fell into the memory of that event and gathered his thoughts. "That's all." He looked around. "Did he make it?"

She was hoping he would have answers. "We don't know. The Icon was supposed to come here. We came looking for him."

"So he may be on Earth?" Zac looked around the infirmary. Suddenly ready to move.

She put a hand on his shoulder. "So far there's no sign."

He considered this; seemed to introvert.

"I failed," he said.

"Failed?"

"I was supposed to leave him. In space. You were supposed to come here to rescue me. Not come here looking for Kang."

"Zac. You saved Anitra. You did more than anyone ever should have. You put your life on the line and took Kang to deep space. You saved us all.

"You're a hero."

"But now he may be a threat to your world."

"He isn't," she said. "He isn't here." And at last she really believed it.

Kang was gone.

Zac just kept looking at her, piecing together the significance of all she'd done. When she handed him the Icon back in the park it was in a deadly rush, no time to explain. He'd trusted her and simply did as she said, taking Kang and using the Icon and disappearing into the void. Now it was as if he was understanding the full measure of her plan, how she must've managed to get him the Icon in the first place—then got an entire starship in order to come after him ...

"I really can't believe you. You took this?" Again he looked around the alien room. "It's like when you came for me at the Crucible. Crazy. Just ... crazy."

She looked away.

"What about the Icon?" he wanted to know. "If Kang isn't here what happened to it?"

There'd been no sign of it. And with the other starship waiting for them back in the Kel system there hadn't been much time to look.

"I was hoping you might know something," she said. "We didn't see it where we found you. There was another starship waiting so we didn't have much time to look. We had to run."

"*Another* starship?" At this Zac leaned straight up, nearly sitting.

It really *was* a long story.

"Where did I go? Where did the Icon send us?"

Jess shook her head. "All I knew when I gave it to you was it went to somewhere in space. After that it was supposed to go to Earth." Again she was so weak with relief that things had turned out the way they had. Zac was safe, he was alive, he was well, he was awake and he was with her.

"When we came to get you Kang and the Icon were gone and there was another starship waiting.

"Kind of like this one," she said, overwhelmed all at once. Where to begin? "I actually thought you might know something about that, too." Clearly he didn't. "Nani thinks it was a less advanced version of this one, which seems impossible, but we now know the point where the Icon dumped you guys was actually the Kel star system, and what we saw was one of their current warships. Like what might have evolved after the fallout of the Great War. This ship we're on, the *Reaver*, was one of their ships from right before that time.

"At any rate it seemed hostile so we got you and got the hell out of there. It shot at us but it didn't follow. We figure it can't travel like this one. There was no sign of Kang, or the Icon, so we assumed he used the Icon and came here to Earth.

"Now it looks like he didn't."

Zac was shaking his head.

Jess gave him her assessment. "You were floating in space, untouched. What I'm beginning to think is that Kang used the Icon and somehow it malfunctioned. Maybe it got damaged in the fight. There's no sign of him here on Earth. Nothing. No news, no path of destruction. It's been days. There's no way he's just down there laying low."

Zac considered this.

"So maybe ... he's gone? Totally?"

Jess shrugged her one shoulder as she continued to lean on her elbow. "That's starting to seem the most likely explanation. I've been fighting to keep everyone here, to make sure, but Satori is antsy to get back." At this she looked down, toward their feet, lost again in her own head.

There was just no easy way out.

Zac seemed to become further aware. Of course Jess wouldn't have come alone. "Who else is with you?"

And she realized yet more of the picture was missing. "Nani, Satori, Willet, Bianca." She shifted a little. "Satori and I have been arguing. Now that we rescued you, and especially now that Kang is nowhere to be found, she wants

to return the ship. Use it to help win the war on Anitra.
Nani, on the other hand, thinks we need to address the Kel
threat. They're probably both right."

Zac studied her face. As if paging through her thoughts,
looking for what troubled her.

Reading her like a book.

"So what do you want to do?" he asked quietly. Intimately.
This was the source of her personal dilemma and Zac saw
it clearly. He understood her indecision, recognized the
difficulty she faced, and while he couldn't solve it for her,
especially not without knowing what she wanted—she
didn't even know herself—he looked deeply into her eyes,
ready to help. And this unspoken understanding, the
deeper meaning behind that simple pause—that he knew
her, that he loved her, that he wanted to be there for her,
whatever her decision—touched her.

It gave her strength.

"I don't know," she admitted, and it didn't hurt now as
much to say it.

He sat all the way up; a slow, easy action, but it
nonetheless took her off guard. She watched as he slid off
the end of the infirmary slab and stood.

"Come," he held out a hand. "Let's go say Hi."

* * *

CEE KEPT A CERTAIN DISTANCE from the throne, choosing to
stand and discourse with Kang as equals, the scale of her
citadel sufficient to act as reminder of who held the power.
Her delegates were still with them, senior representatives
from each major area of the Kel dynasty, standing in a
loose group around them as if mingling at a party. Voltan
stood outside the group, though near. A cordon of warriors
and military officers had also accompanied the entourage
to her throne room and now ringed the walls at the ready,
weapons across their chests. Cee had no doubt there was
absolutely nothing they could do if Kang snapped. He
would kill her instantly, then the rest. The delegates. All
of them. It was a unique rush of emotions to be standing

there that vulnerable, keeping death at bay with nothing more than the power of her own words. Her will against the sheer might of the beast. Her leverage: his desire to have the allegiance of so powerful a race as the Kel.

"If we go there with an armada," he was saying, "even a small armada, a handful of your best ships, Anitra would be ours in a day." Already he was on to particulars, barely having begun the conversation and already making great assumptions. Cee continued to be impressed with the degree of his desire. His complete disregard for the finer points of negotiation, to presume such vastness of action—and that it would be undertaken so quickly—at his mere wish—was fascinating to behold.

Following a great deal of convincing on her part, asking that bordered on pleading—an impression she sought desperately to avoid, both before her delegates and for her own sense of pride—Kang finally relented to hand over the Icon, so they could begin studying it. If they were to do anything they must start with that. Surely he saw the logic. No armada would be sent anywhere if they had no destination. Once he relented, once he realized that in order for his own vision to go forward he must, in fact, give up his only perceived bargaining chip, Cee's lead scientist summoned his peers and together they took the device off under guard.

Once done, however, Kang's insistence only rose.

"Why are you so eager to see your world subjugated beneath the Kel?" she queried.

"Not just my world," he said. "Even when I was snatched away by the Icon, I was near ruling it on my own. The people of my world had no way to stop me. I had half a planet worth of army at my command. The rest would've fallen soon and I would've ruled it all.

"But what then? Already I'd begun to feel the fear of that. What was I going to do? I look around here and see much the same thing. You've got order, full control, full power. No challenge. Aren't you empty?"

Cee was shocked that such a seemingly dull beast had just driven right to the very heart of the Kel dilemma. She worried her expression betrayed her, or that one of her delegates, who knew full well the plight of the Kel, might speak out of turn.

But Kang pressed on, making his point, not noticing the subtle changes in the room.

"If the Icon unlocks the stars," he said, "or at least tells you how to travel between worlds, how much more is out there?" He looked around, up and out, as if he could see the universe without—the turn of his head, as always, exaggerated by the sweep of his crooked horns. There was poetic intent to that longing gaze, but his twisted form projected little more than the ignorance of a sad monster. *So many things in one being*, thought Cee. Kang was a brute, he had no grace, yet was driven by the same impulses that moved the Kel. He was ignorant, somewhat in intelligence but mostly in his knowledge of things, yet possessed insight far beyond the crudeness he embodied. She tried to see beyond these lesser traits. Decided to find and work only with the useful things. More and more she was convinced it was possible he could be controlled as she imagined. Kept to heel even as he was given rein, perhaps at the head of vast fleets sent for conquest, unleashed on world after world. Yielding, in the bargain, freedom, power, and untold new territory for the Kel.

She began to hope fervently that her scientists could unlock the device.

CHAPTER 18:

DECISIONS

JESS WALKED ONTO the bridge behind Zac, holding a little back. She wasn't surc she was ready to face everyone just yet but Zac was determined. The rift between she and Satori was so strong that, despite Zac's miraculous appearance, Satori's first reaction to her arrival was the same stony expression that had been passing between them since their falling out. That faded quickly, however, as Satori processed the fact that Zac was actually standing in the doorway, live and in the flesh. She straightened, trying to conceal her surprise.

"Look who woke up."

"Welcome to the party," Willet chimed in at the same time, immediately enthusiastic. "Have a nice nap?"

Satori came closer, still snubbing Jess but clearly interested in the Kazerai. "How do you feel?"

Jess took a steadying breath. With Zac awake possibilities shifted. New decisions might be made.

He pretended to check himself over. "Fine, actually." Jess noticed Bianca staring not so discreetly at the bare-chested Zac. Even Satori, gruff mood or not, stole a furtive glance as Zac looked down at himself. Only Nani among the girls seemed immune. Her interest was, as always, scientific.

"I examined you thoroughly," she said. "Everything seems in order. You just shut down somehow. Now that you're awake, physically I think you are, in fact, fine."

"Fine indeed," Bianca snarked, an impulsive little comment meant to be funny. It fell flat. Jess could see her friend flush in embarrassment.

Zac didn't notice.

"So what's next?" he asked. Satori shifted and Jess recognized all too well the bristling defensiveness in her stance.

The commander's response came at once: "What's next is we're going home. Now that you're awake it's high time." It was as if she finally snapped from the tenuous trance that had been holding her.

Zac looked between she and Jess.

Then said to Satori: "We should stay." It was a simple statement, and it jumped right to the crux of the matter. No sense wasting time, thought Jess, and prepared herself for the fight ahead.

Satori crossed her arms and looked angrily at her. Jess wanted to assure her this was all Zac, did not want to keep making an enemy out of her, but at the same time wanted to see how far Zac would get. For the moment she remained quiet.

"We're going home," Satori informed him. "We're not hanging around just because. And I don't care if you can break us in half or beat us into paste or whatever. This isn't about you and your muscles. I know you're hooked on Jess and before you say anything else I can already see you're under her spell—" Jess almost blurted he wasn't but held her tongue "—and I know you'll do anything she says, but this isn't happening. We've sat here long enough. I don't know why I haven't put a stop to it sooner. Maybe *I've* been under a spell. We all know what she's capable of." And she shot another pointed stare. "Nani has all the data we could ever want on this lovely little world. It's time to take this ship back and put it to good use."

Of any of them, if anyone was going to rise in her defense Jess expected it to be Zac but, to her surprise, it was Bianca.

"Why are you being so bossy?" she asked. Satori snapped her attention to her. Just as surprised to hear from the other Earth girl; shooting her a look filled with anger. "I mean," Bianca held her ground, "I like you, we've been through a lot, but you're acting like you're in charge or something."

"I *am* in charge!" Suddenly Satori was beside herself. "I'm the senior officer at this little party! Has everyone forgotten?"

Jess could tell she shouted out of frustration, not for

effect. Satori was starting to lose it.

They probably all were, to some degree.

"This is Venatres property and I've already gone too far! *Way* too far. I don't know how I let myself get talked into this but I'm turning it around. Now." She began to move, as if preparing to take control of the ship right then.

"I should tell you," Nani interrupted, another unexpected voice and everyone held, waiting for her to continue as she glanced between consoles. "I found something." They all listened. Whether because she was the smart one or because she was the least likely to jump into the fray, she had their full attention. The pause stretched, and Jess couldn't tell if Nani was working up the right words to say, oblivious to the tense impatience of her audience, or if she paused for dramatic effect. Probably the former. Nani wasn't much for drama.

"Something else," she said, just before Satori continued into action. "I mentioned a few things earlier about my investigation of the Project. Well, just a while ago I discovered more. A little more from the laptop and I've checked it against live feeds." She looked directly at Jessica. "Confirmed. Turns out the Project *is* planning an operation to capture the head of the Bok." Now she glanced at the group. "I've correlated what I found to their active transmissions, things they're talking about right now. With a little more time I can find out how and when they plan to move." She looked at the people on the bridge as if they totally got how huge that was. Jess looked around the room. No one got it. *She* did, but no one else knew what this was all about.

Almost she said something but again held her tongue. Choosing to let this play out a bit further.

"I've been piecing it together," Nani went on, "and according to what the Project is saying they have a window and it's soon. A chance to capture the head of the Esehta Bok. The Bok, the one group with direct ties to all this." She gestured around the bridge. "The Kel and their entire history. I say this only because it occurs to me we may have an opportunity." Jess held her breath as Nani continued.

"I haven't been able to find anything on the Bok, and believe me I've been digging. Now this. And the Bok ... the Bok, as I keep saying, are connected to the last Kel, from a thousand years ago. They are a direct, living link between humans and Kel. If we can get inside their organization, peel back the covers ... they *will* know things."

Jess couldn't believe it.

It was like Nani was reading her mind.

Satori was already reacting but Nani cut her off with a raised hand. "Listen," a little out of character for the shy scientist, and as she went on Jess found herself staring anxiously at Satori's angry red head. "I know there's some argument about what to do." Satori kept her mouth buttoned as Nani continued. "Well, here it is. We could undercut what the Project is planning. Get to the Bok before them. The society who, in their past, were allies with the ancient Kel that built this ship. The society with a direct connection to the Kel we found in that other system. Separated for a thousand years. Who knows what records they hold? They must have incredible archives, even legends. We can put that with what I have right here, from the *Reaver*, and with it piece together the final bits of history following their demise. That information could prove critical. I can't stress enough how important it is that we know everything we can about the Kel." Nani truly believed in the alien threat. She shifted in her seat. "Also, the Bok may have one or more Icons. I think they will. The Project believes they do. Those could be cracked to unlock other locations, probably other worlds.

"We can't let this opportunity slip."

Satori was speechless.

Jess wanted to scream *Yes!*

This was exactly what they should do.

"We're already here," Nani went on, bordering on a sense of passion, which Jess found intensely perfect in that moment from their scientist savior, "and with this new information we have a chance. Once the Project acts we lose the opportunity and the Bok might never surface again. At least not where we could find them." She looked around at everyone, not just Satori. "We're here, and this operation by the Project is coming soon." She inhaled, revealing her idea for the way: "Zac could easily crash it. Bypass the Project and get what they're after." She let that sit for a perfectly timed second. "We crack the Bok and then go home. With every single bit of information we can."

Zac, Jess noticed, had warmed to the idea. He looked to her, seeing the excitement in her own eyes, then turned to the others. "Crack the Bok," he agreed, going right along with Nani's developing plan. It was insane, it was cool, and Jess knew the mere idea of it was flying right in the teeth of every bit of Satori's reason.

The commander found her voice. *"Crack the Bok?"* she spluttered. "This is not some personal warship!" She looked around the bridge, seeing nothing but crazy people. To Jessica's mild surprise Satori seemed to be getting no immediate support. Even Willet appeared willing to listen. And now Nani, of all people, was suggesting—just suggesting, mind you, but it was out there—something more extreme than anything Jess herself could've dreamed up:

Run a counter sting to capture the head of the Bok.

For the moment Jess decided to continue staying out of it.

"You're all mad." Satori looked like she'd just had an epiphany. The sudden realization that she truly was smack in the middle of the nut farm at recreation time. Jess imagined how she saw them right then; white robes, shuffling around, holding little cups filled with meds. Nani their silent ringleader.

About to take control of the asylum.

Satori leveled her intense focus directly at Zac. "We came to rescue you," she said. "That's how I got talked into this little escapade. I fell for it, we did it, then we had to come make sure Kang wasn't here." She turned on Jessica. "Though I still have no idea what we were supposed to do if we found him." She looked back around, at all of them. "Now you want to go off chasing some secret society? Just because we're here?" She was shaking her head stiffly. "We're done. Done with all of this. This has gone way too far."

Jess worked hard to digest everything, the surge of possibilities at what Nani suggested ... She had to push in the direction toward it. This was the right way to go, even if it was so far little more than an idea. Things were clarifying. Like a film of dirt or a fog being wiped away. Not totally clear yet, but getting there.

She made her mind as calm as she could, as certain. All she knew was that this was a crux, right here, right now—this moment, right there on that bridge, in that very second—and she had to speak before everything degenerated back to a full-blown argument.

Rationality was a hair-trigger from being shot to hell.

"I agree with you," she spoke directly to Satori, trying to think fast. "Believe it or not I do." She gave that a moment. She'd never been a group leader, now here she was, all eyes fixed firmly to her. Expectant. Demanding.

But though she'd never led a group she'd caused outcomes no mere group leader ever had. She'd done things that affected millions. She reminded herself of this and pressed on.

"The problem," she said, "is that we can't make decisions based on the things we've always known. You want to. *I* want to. But we can't. We can no longer decide what to do based on what you—or any of us—simply assume is right. We can't go by Venatres law, or military regs, or Earth protocols or rules or anything we've always gone by. We're outside that. Beyond it." She gave everyone a breath to think, though not long enough to raise objections. "We make our own rules now. See? Whatever we decide has to be based on a new set of codes. Our codes. Our decisions. Our rules. And those have to be—*have* to be—based on the present. Based on what we know *now*. Everything we used to know has been swept away." She brushed an arm as if sweeping aside the Old, ushering in the New. "It's up to us," she told them. "We have to be incredibly bright, smarter than we've ever been, before we make *any* decision. Before we take *any* action."

She wasn't sure where this new logic was coming from, but as it gathered form it brought with it additional clarity.

"Do you see how we've risen above that?" She directed the question to all. "We have to look to the greatest good. We have a responsibility now. And while, on the surface, going back may *seem* like the right thing to do, is it? Is it really? That's where we have to be smart. Take this ship back and maybe, just maybe, do something to turn the tide of a war? From where we sit, from this new level of responsibility, is that the right thing to do?" She didn't want to insult Satori but she had to make her see. "In this moment, in this place—we're beyond all that.

"And I don't want to keep arguing, but there *are* six of us. We've stepped far outside the bounds of convention. We should vote on any decisions. Including who should be leader. If we even need a leader."

It was a perfect time to stop talking and she did. Her words hung in the air, soaking into everyone's skulls; thoughts stirred to fresh considerations, begging for just a little more that wasn't forthcoming. Silence, and for a moment no one moved to fill it.

"Maybe we *should* start voting," said Willet, right as it seemed Satori would resume her tirade. As soon as he spoke Satori glared at him, causing him to withdraw quickly from the tentative proposal. Yet a small wave of agreement had already begun.

"We should," Bianca agreed. The first person she looked to was Nani, and Jess watched the unspoken exchange between them.

Nani, in turn, looked to Satori. "You guys dragged me here against my will," she said. "This was all Jessica's idea. She's been the one behind it." Not exactly a vote of confidence, and for an instant Jess worried she would lose the popular support. Until Nani continued: "But," she said, "however we got here we are, in fact, here. Jess is right. We're *here*." She looked around the bridge, circling her arms as if to say: *Stop and look. Really look at where we are. At what we're sitting in the middle of.*

She lowered her arms and continued. "We have some

big decisions to make. No matter how we did it, no matter how we got here, we're *here*. And starting now it would be best if we decided on things as a group."

Satori bristled. "We're not—"

"Listen to what she's saying." Zac implored. "Things are different now. This isn't the same situation we were in just a few days ago. We've done what we've done and now ... The past is behind us. That may sound dumb but it's true. This is the present. The now. A clean slate, and we have to be careful how we make the future. I know I just woke up, I know I missed a lot, but we *do* have a responsibility, a new responsibility, to more than just our people back home. Our responsibility is to mankind. Right here is a whole other planet, full of people just like on Anitra." He pointed until everyone, even Satori, turned to the front of the bridge and the spectacular view of Earth. "If we have a chance to do something greater," he said, "we have to do it. We have to base our decisions on that. Not past ideas.

"Look," he said, and Jess absolutely loved the way he was charging to her support. "We're halfway into this already. Let's not turn around. We're here, now, and according to Nani we can do something.

"And no, I'm not going to impose my will. I'm not going to pinch your heads and make you do what I say. You're my friends! My best friends, each of you. I love each of you and would *never* hurt you. In fact I'd die to keep you from harm.

"I very nearly did."

Satori was unmoved. "Mankind?" She kept her arms tightly crossed. "We're talking about trying to kidnap the head of a secret society. You guys are all over the board."

Jess looked at her. "The Bok know things. Probably lots of things. Things that will get us closer to understanding the Kel. No matter how removed they seem right now, the Kel are the next threat."

"Ridiculous."

Jess caught the outburst that almost came, not wanting to derail this developing moment. "You're smart," she calmed her voice, "Satori, and you've got to start looking at what we know. I'm going to keep saying it. This is now. This isn't just about Anitra." As she spoke she found herself steadily gaining conviction that this *was* the right thing to do. This was something that actually *needed* to be done.

She wanted the Bok.

Nani stepped in. "This may be our only chance to uncover what they know. And that could become critical very soon."

Satori remained adamant. So solid Jess felt she could probably shoot her and the bullet would bounce off. It was becoming a game, fighting her every step of the way. But Jess was leading the charge—she realized that would probably always be true—and in the interest of politics knew she had to give a little ground and come back to the vote. They had to decide as a group, to be fair.

"So we need a vote," she said. "Do we do this?"

Bianca raised a hand, just a little, out to the side, but it was indication enough. "I vote we do it."

"Of course you do," Satori flashed her a look of disdain.

"Remember I'm giving up a bunch too," Bianca said meekly, defensively, and Jess looked at her with a deep appreciation.

Her friend *was* giving up a lot.

I love you. It was in Jessica's eyes, and Bianca saw it.

Willet looked at Satori. "Going undercover on another world? A human world? I mean, this is what I do." He wilted under her angry stare. "But I ... I'll go with the group."

"You know my feelings," said Zac.

"I'm in," said Nani.

And with Jessica's vote it was decided.

* * *

THERE WAS JUST NO WAY. Lindin had been over and over the info from the Earth "laptop", and there was no way one man, or even a few—all the Icon could reasonably transport—could go to that exit point and make any headway against an entire world. They spoke English on Earth, which meant he could engage them in dialog, but from everything he could tell there was no way he, an ambassador from Anitra, could hope for anything short of an insane asylum if he showed up and tried to enter into a discussion. Even with bits of unique technology to corroborate his story. Anything he offered would likely be taken away for secret study, he locked away in the process, meaning it just wasn't a good plan. And if Jessica took the starship there, as he expected she had, there would no doubt already be chaos.

He looked at the shiny chrome device on his desk. The original Icon. The one that could take him to Earth, if he dared. Beside it the laptop, computer from Earth. On its screen the last page he'd been looking at, a discussion by the Earth agency, the Project they called themselves, owners of the computer, detailing some aspect of a secret society on Earth known as the Esehta Bok. He'd read it all. Everything, again and again, absorbing it. The last few days he'd insisted on being undisturbed, ignoring progress reports on the war to the south—unsure even if the Dominion still attacked. After initial, heated inquiries from his superiors as to the loss of the starship, cut short by the pressing demands of the war—though he knew there would be more inquiries coming, a reckoning he would have to face—as soon as he could after that he'd begun looking over all stored files, anything and everything the laptop held, anything to divine the reality of Earth and what he might expect to find there. By now he almost felt like an Earth man. Like he could walk into one of their department stores and make a purchase and eat at the food court and not be suspected of being from another world. He was as human as any of them.

Which of course kept reminding him, how was that even possible? Lindin had never wondered so greatly at that curiosity as now. Jessica was obviously human but until then it hadn't really diverted his attention. Now it was. How could he be sitting here on Anitra and there be another world, Earth, that was nearly identical? Legends told of a far distant race, a precursor to them all, that came long before the Great Wars, before Kel and human alike.   The Kel were a sort of ruling race at the time of the Wars, over Anitra and, presumably, other worlds.   Had Earth been one of them?   From records on the laptop it didn't seem so.   The Bok went to Earth to get away from the Wars, to escape the rule of the Kel, which meant the conflict never made it to those shores.

Which meant the Earth and Anitra had a much more distant connection.   They had to, if identical humans were to be explained.

He turned from the Earth laptop to his own computer screen.   His desk was a mess, covered in scribbled notes, diagrams, the laptop from Earth, the Icon, his own computer and a dozen other objects related to his search.   Including, at the moment, a fresh cup of tea.   He reached for that and took a sip as he brought up a video.

Jessica's face came on, as recorded when he interviewed her and her friend, Bianca, directly after bringing them to the chalet.   The frame was paused, her expression in the middle of speaking.   She had a certain innocence about her that was disarming.   With her messy hair and the frumpy Dominion clothes she'd been wearing at the time she managed to look helpless.   Younger, even than he knew her to be.   Like you *wanted* to help her.   Take care of her. Do what you needed to get her home safely.   Just like last time.

Damn!

How had he failed—twice—to contain her?   He'd been lulled by her, even though each time he saw it coming.

He clicked Play.

"... mind, rationally, I expected something like that. I wasn't sure how I could keep hiding the Skull Boy armor, and I figured sooner or later someone would find it.   Somehow I managed to put it in the back of my mind. Almost like I was able to make myself forget about it, day after day.   But it was there, and I knew it would have to be dealt with eventually.   I just figured it would be on my terms.   Only, if there's one thing I've learned it's that the perfect moment never happens.   You end up forced to act, and you either do or you don't. Once they came knocking, I chose to act."

In the video background Lindin's own voice questioned her: "When these agents came, did they tell you at first that's what they were there for? The armor, or the Icon?"

"No. I just assumed. Then, when I got in the Skull Boy armor they kidnapped Bianca and demanded "the device" in exchange. It was then I knew they were definitely on to me."

Lindin stopped the video. The Earth-based Project had made their own dossier on Jessica, quite extensive, leading to their attempt to bring her in. The details of that planned operation were here for his reading pleasure, right up to the execution of their attempt to nab her. Of course none of that operation had been recorded as, during the attempt, the Project apparently failed miserably and Jessica stole their laptop. And their Icon. Lindin knew all too well the outcome of those events. Their Valuable Target got away and made it back to Anitra.

Where she promptly stole his starship.

Single-handedly one girl had thwarted two massive government agencies. On two different planets.

In a way he felt sympathetic to the Project agents on Earth. Like maybe if they got together they could all sit around over a drink. Maybe form a club. The "Jessica Totally Screwed Us" club. Oh, she did that to you too? Yep. Ouch. I feel your pain. Raise a glass. Here's to bringing her to justice.

But ... how could Jessica be the crafty power she appeared? By all indications—having met and talked with her himself, adding to that all the info the agents gathered on her on Earth—there was no way she could be anything other than the average teenage girl she most certainly was. The Project certainly had no higher estimation of her than that. And yet, witness all she'd done. The impossible she'd managed to pull off. Everything, right up to this latest caper, stealing an entire starship.

An entire starship! He slammed a hand on his desk and nearly spilled his tea. How the hell did she even *do* that?!

He couldn't believe it. No matter how many times he said it, no matter how many times he looked at the videos of the event, watching it transpire. No matter how many times he walked into the giant, yawning emptiness of the cavern where the starship once sat.

He just couldn't believe it was real.

What was her motivation?

He knew she wanted to get home, at least she did the last time she was there, though he wasn't so sure what drove her now.

He took another sip of tea and forwarded to the part of the video he'd watched the most.

"So you don't see any hope for your family?" his voice asked from off-camera.

"That's not what I mean. I love my family. But I don't know how I can ever reconnect. Not now. I can never go back to my old life, and I don't want them involved in this one." She sniffed, becoming sad as she pretended to try not to think about it. *What an actor.* "I ... have to focus on my life now. I'm too young to have to be this grown up, but I can't change that. I hope to see them again, but for now I can't think about them."

He paused the video and leaned back, Jessica frozen in still-frame. Innocent, angelic face. Sitting there tearing up, looking oh-so-helpless.

You're good.

If she were Anitran he'd put her to work right away. She'd make an excellent addition to his group.

Though, he had to admit, she *did* try to save them from Kang. But that, too, could've been driven by selfish desires. Send Kang and Zac to that other point, then hope Zac could make it to Earth then go save him with the starship. That was indeed the sort of self-centered motivation he could see driving the actions of an average teenage girl. But how did she then manage to pull them off with such god-like effect? No single person, even a trained specialist, should've been able to do anything she had.

So what was it? An average girl with uncanny ability? Could anyone have that much luck? Or was it something else? The Conclave, that small group of revolutionaries within the Dominion, believed her to be a prophet or a herald or something. Maybe there was some truth to that. Could she be a super being? An angel, as they said?

Unlikely.

Instance after instance of impossible good fortune. Did she merely *seem* to be an average girl? One with a great cover, backed by an agenda he could only guess at? Could she somehow be part of the Bok on Earth? That super-secret organization Earth's greatest minds seemed to know nothing about?

She could be either. A lucky girl or a trained specialist with carefully laid plans. If she was the former then she just needed to be stopped. If she was the latter ... if she was the latter then he wanted to know just who the hell she was and what, ultimately, she was after. Even the Project, her own government, had no more speculation on her other than that she was just an ordinary girl who got caught up in something fantastic. Only after they'd made that careful assessment did they get a chance to experience how wrong they were. One way or the other, Jessica was no ordinary girl.

But if he was to go after her ...

The Earth was divided even more than Anitra. Far more complex. Jessica lived within the territory of the most powerful government, but judging by the info on the laptop that government was fraught with more subterfuge than he would've thought possible. It made his head spin. If he did go there, where would he go first? He was a commando once, in shape, but no longer in shape enough to run a Skull Boy from that drop point all the way to the Project's headquarters. At least not according to the maps he had.

The Icon he held dropped over her house. And that, Jessica's house, was the first place he could think to look. Maybe she had a secret lair. In the laptop's documents the house was where the Project tracked her and where she spent her time. Whatever else she'd hidden, whatever else she knew, it must be there. He doubted he would find *her* there, she was probably with the starship, square at the center of any chaos she'd caused, but anything else she held would be there. And, perhaps, by going there, he could exploit family or some other connection to bring her to heel and get back his goddamn starship.

This is such a longshot. He ran his hands through his short, graying hair and slumped. Exhausted. Most of his determination had faded, at least for the moment. He inhaled and pulled himself straight.

Plus her house would probably be swarming with Project agents.

What bit hardest, oddly enough, was much more selfish in nature. Childish. The fact that he himself had never used an Icon. Jessica used one three times. *And* gave one away, for Zac to use on Kang. Lindin had never flown in his own starship. Now Jessica had. He'd never gone anywhere, and she'd been using these things like they were bus passes.

Part of him wanted to use the Icon simply because he could. Simply because he *hadn't.* He looked at it on the table. Saw his reflection in it. Right there. And he realized, as he sat trying to rationalize why he should go chasing after a stolen starship with an Icon that only went one place … he realized there was no rational reason to do so. In summary, looking back over the last days of agonizing analysis and evaluation, each of his conclusions led him to the same decision:

There was nothing to be gained by going.

But he *wanted* to go.

And so after everything, after everything he'd done to get where he was, to rise to the rank and the privilege he had, that small part of him that did not want to finish his life having missed an opportunity—no matter how ill-advised— rose to the fore and decided.

He would make contact with another world. Their first contact, as ambassador from Anitra. He would take his chances.

He would go to Earth.

Then, with any luck—after all, why should Jessica be the only one to have that much luck?—with any luck he would find her and get his ship back.

CHAPTER 19:

BALLER

"This isn't going to be easy," Nani said under her breath, face bent over the console in a pose she'd barely altered for what seemed like hours. Bianca and Jess were with her, alone on the bridge.

"The only easy day was yesterday," Bianca commented, adopting a kind of a good-ol-boy twang as she spoke. She was drilled into the screen in front of her, in some ways a mirror of Nani, pouring over information just as eagerly— though Bianca's searches were much less relevant to the task at hand. After her little "mistake" of a few days ago, her Internet boo-boo that risked flagging their presence, Bianca had gone back slowly to browsing—with permission of course—double-checking everything she intended to do, tentatively at first but growing more confident until, by now, she'd returned to full immersion. Though all it took was a glance from Jess to make her nervous all over again.

Jess could see, though, she was being careful.

She clarified her comment. "Heard that once on some special on the SEALs." Her eyes remained glued to whatever she was scrolling through. Then, as if to be clear she would *not* have been watching a show on Navy special forces on purpose: "My brother was watching it, not me." And at that she looked up. Realizing, as if having forgotten, her brother was a thing of the past. Home was a thing of the past. Rather than grow sad, however, as Jess suddenly expected her to, Bianca let it go. Now that her head was up she glanced for a bit at the Earth, not too longingly, then turned back to the screen and sank back into its depths.

Remarkably Bianca seemed committed to helping. Jess kept expecting her to change her mind and ask to be taken back but so far she showed no sign. As if, for now, she'd shifted to this new thing, happy, even a little excited, to be a part.

Jess leaned back. For the moment she sat at one of the consoles near the edge of the domed viewscreen, gazing over the spectacular view of their homeworld. The Earth spanned the entire width of the dome, so far away yet so close, wispy white bands covering the surface in random splotches. There on the daylight side the sunlight was sharp, the shadows of clouds starkly outlined on the ground directly beneath their puffy white shapes. The proximity to those outlines was an indication just how far up the Kel starship was parked. In most cases the clouds would've been ten, twenty, thirty-thousand feet or higher, yet from that distance looked almost as if they and their shadows touched; white blankets laid just above the surface. Wave caps spread across the oceans here and there, making for a calm day the world over, wrapped at the edges by a thin haze of atmosphere that hugged everything close. And there, flickering at points in space; the satellites of Earth, glinting as they caught the sun, little twinkles of technology in orbit. Jess had been staring at the breathtaking scope of the stunning image for some time, peering at this or that familiar feature, wondering at the sheer volume of activity going on down there, unseen. Bianca, on the other hand, no longer paid it much of any attention. Mostly she continued surfing the information channels of Earth, even as Nani searched deeper into their objective.

Jess found herself relaxing in the relative quiet, absorbing Nani's soft, intent tapping on the screens, balanced by Bianca's equal focus on the latest social trends. The concentration in the room was tangible; a subtle, busy sort of quiet, leaving her long moments in which to reflect.

Rest aboard the *Reaver* was fitful, but after days of little to do she wasn't tired. She was clean and fed. The ship had some sort of ionizer which made their clothes fresh and kept them fresh as well. Already she'd taken several "showers". There were food synthesizers. She wasn't hungry. It was all very austere, of course, showering in faint particle beams, eating what seemed like paste and wearing the same clothes day after day, but it was not uncomfortable. Just boring. What she wouldn't give for a cheeseburger. And there were millions of them just a few hundred miles below.

Billions and billions served.

And as she sat there on the bridge, looking for the tiniest things she could find on the surface of the Earth below, imagining where all the burger joints might be, she made herself, for the moment, stop thinking. Things had lined up, more or less. The only real difficulties lay ahead. As Bianca said, the only easy day was yesterday. Right then things were serene.

The calm before the storm.

"I still can't believe how advanced your electronics are," Nani commented in the long silence. "With this much technology, how are your machines behind ours? It's like your machinery is one generation behind, yet your networks are a generation ahead." She shook her head, then more to herself: "It's quite curious."

Jess nodded absently. "Fifty years ago we put men on the moon," she said. "Now the average person carries around more computing power in their pocket than it took to do that. Yet still no moon bases." She shifted in her chair. "It's like we've gotten worse. In all that time, if it didn't have a transistor it didn't advance. We're still flying the same planes we were decades ago, they still work the same way. Cars still work the same way, ships still work the same way, rockets still work the same way, powerplants still work the same way—everything works the same way. Except computers. We've got screens, communication and computing power the likes of which we never imagined back then. And all the things we *did* imagine—flying cars, bases on Mars—none of that happened." She shook her head, not sure whether Nani fully listened or not. "We can sit and watch a digital creation of what it would be like on Mars, we can even have a war on Mars that looks totally real, in three-d, eight-k resolution on an eighty-inch screen in the comfort of our own home and it would blow the minds of people from the sixties. But go to Mars? Boy would they be disappointed. Something happened and we failed. Completely. No progress. In all that time we've just sat around and dreamed up more and more ways to entertain ourselves." She sighed, not wanting to rant. "With enough distraction, I guess, you start to forget you're actually stuck."

Suddenly Bianca gasped. "Oh my god, Jess. Look." She motioned for her, staring intently at something on the screen. The first thing Jess noticed, however, was not what was on the screen, but that Bianca was picking her nose. Like, really picking. In earnest.

Jess tried to ignore it. "What is it?" She rose and came over.

Her friend scanned the screen, picking harder. Really digging, and Jess kind of twinged. She'd never known Bianca to be that unconcerned with image.

"They're holding a vigil," and as Bianca said this she struck gold, pulled out a nice little nugget, examined it absently and ... wiped it under the seat.

Jess was shocked. *"Bianca!"*

Her friend snapped her attention to her, startled.

"What?" Did she make another mistake? she seemed to be thinking. Should she not be on this web site? *What did I do now?!*

But that wasn't it. Jess hissed: "You're wiping boogers under the seat!" She glanced across at Nani, who of course didn't react to the outburst. Engrossed in her screens, ignoring the two girls.

Bianca seemed relieved she wasn't in real trouble. "So?"

"*So?!*" Jess was nearly speechless.

Her friend shrugged. "The air on this thing is dry."

"Yeah but come on! This is a frickin starship! A thousand years old! It's worth more than the entire Earth! Are you kidding me? You're wiping boogers on it?"

Again Bianca shrugged. As if to say, *No biggy.* "Gives it a human touch," she reasoned. "Like wiping boogies under the car seat. You know. Makes it feel like home."

Jess could not believe her.

Bianca moved on. "So what do you think?"

"About what? The vigil or your boogers?" It seemed as

bad as tucking a quick one behind the Mona Lisa.

"The vigil. Crazy, huh?"

Jess sighed. "Why? What's it for?"

"Us."

At that she studied the screen more closely, the page Bianca had pulled up. It still felt strange to be looking at a normal human web site with normal pictures and writing, framed in a makeshift Kel browser on the Kel screens, aboard the Kel starship, with the Earth looming out the window.

So weird.

"They're holding it at prom," Bianca tapped a few links. "We're going to miss it you know." Her disappointment was clear. "This would've been our first high school prom. I think Toby was going to ask me."

The thought of Bianca and Toby going together brought the image of Jessica's own once-boyfriend, Mike, to mind. That relationship seemed lifetimes old, though in truth Mike was probably still in shock, just like everyone else must be at their sudden disappearance. Absently she wondered what he was doing. Would he ask someone else? Would he even go?

"They're actually holding a vigil?"

"Yeah." Bianca started picking her nose again.

Patiently Jess reached and pulled her hand away. "Stop," she admonished and went back to the screen. There on the prom page, along with other pictures and the theme and all the other nonsense that went along with High School Prom, were their pictures. Jessica Paquin and Bianca Devnani.

The missing girls.

Eyes fixed to the screen Jess scooched into Bianca's seat beside her. Bianca slid over to make room as Jess began to read, taken with the fact that the whole school seemed poised to make such a grand effort in their honor. Some of the wording was quite touching, actually, and she found herself, to her mild frustration, moved by it.

As she was contending with that emotion she saw Bianca's hand sneaking toward her face again. And, as she was about to reach and yank it away, the door to the bridge hissed open and Zac walked in. Bianca jerked her own hand away, pretending to be doing something else.

Apparently Zac was worth hiding it from.

"How's it going?" he asked as the door closed behind. Jess felt herself smiling. The wording from the vigil was still on her mind but a fresh wave of contentment washed over her at his arrival. She put an arm over the back of the chair and turned to look at him in welcome.

"Good."

He stood there, all shirtless and handsome. There were no other clothes aboard the *Reaver* and so everyone was pretty much come-as-you-are. Which meant no shirt for Zac. Which of course Jess didn't mind one bit. Neither did the other girls, she was pretty sure.

He came closer. "I can't get over this thing," he said. "It's incredible." He spared a glance and a nod for Nani. She acknowledged his arrival but was right back to what she was doing. Bianca gave a little wave.

"Small inside for such a big ship," he came all the way over and stopped to stand beside Jess and Bianca. The two of them fit together in the Kel chair but it was snug. Suddenly Jess felt like a child sitting with her friend in one seat. Slowly she got up, trying to make it look natural.

"Power generation," Nani commented without taking her eyes from the screen. "Weapons and armor. Half the interior volume is dedicated to systems."

Zac nodded. "It's got other ships, too. Two smaller ones."

"Fighter escorts," Nani confirmed, and Jess found herself curious at what the other ships were like. The fact that this larger one carried its own escorts was cool. She needed to do her own, more thorough investigation.

"Back at the lab we almost took one of them out and tested it," added Nani, "while we were working on this one. The fighters don't have quantum drives, just wave-field powerplants to move at sub-light speeds. By all indications they should be fast."

As Zac stood there Jess realized she was staring. Captivated by him; his cowlick, worse than ever, sticking up on one side at the back of his head, a smaller one at the front; stubbly shadow of a beard; bare chested and perfect, alive and whole and he made it and she rescued him and they were together ... Fortunately she caught herself before he did. Casually she leaned against the console and turned to something else, just as he looked in her direction.

"I still can't believe you guys took this thing," he said.

Nani made a little snorting noise but kept her attention on the console. "I'm afraid to go back," she said, then broke her trance and looked up at all of them. "Now that we're here, now that we've done what we've done, I'm in no hurry. Maybe we'll find something. Maybe we'll make a big discovery. If we do it would be a whole lot better than showing up with nothing." A moment after she said this her expression changed and she looked at Zac. "Sorry. I didn't mean to make it sound like rescuing you wasn't—"

"I know what you mean," he raised a hand, completely unoffended. "Lindin must be steamed right now. We come back after what amounts to taking this thing out for a joy ride and we're all getting locked up."

"Yeah."

Then Bianca asked: "How would they lock you up?" That wasn't the point, thought Jess, but she understood the question. How *would* they punish Zac?

"I'm not sure," he shrugged. "But I think we'd want to be accepted back into Venatres society, not end up as outlaws."

A moment of silence passed. Then Jess asked Nani: "What have you found? Anything else?" Though they'd been sitting together for hours it had been a long time since she gave an update.

"So far we know a few more things. I've managed to flesh it out." Nani tapped her console and looked up, over their heads to the front of the bridge. Jess turned to the front and there, overlaying the Earth, was a display of information. A screen-in-screen, text and a few images, most prominent of which was a snapshot of a man's head and shoulders. An official-looking man, young, early thirties, in a suit and tie, looking like an agent of some kind.

"That's Drake Hauer," said Nani. "He works for the

Project. He's heading up the sting."

For an instant Jess felt a sharp, unexpected flash of anger, mixed with sadness. Seeing the leader of the group that had brought her so much pain, now knowing more of what they'd been up to; the guys that chased her from her home, sent her running back to Anitra and triggered the series of events leading her here brought a harsh moment of reality. Here was a face to go with her mental image of the Project. Nani continued:

"In addition to the sting operation they've been watching your house," she said, and Jess was instantly on alert. Why hadn't Nani told her that before? "They think the Bok may also be watching for your return. From what I can tell the Project seems to be making sure your parents and sister are not nabbed."

Really?

"They're protecting them?"

Nani shrugged. "I guess. I don't think it was ever their intention to hurt you."

Bianca twigged on this. "See?" she said, "I told you," reminding Jess that was exactly what she'd said before; that the agents wouldn't hurt her if Jess took her home, after they first escaped to Anitra. Neither Zac nor Nani knew anything about the particulars of those events, but didn't ask. Bianca's tone was mild. Just stating a fact. Those events were far behind them now.

"Anyway," Nani went on, "I'm just putting some of this together. As we know the purpose of the sting is to nab the head of the Bok, Lorenzo Fertiti. I've got more info on him." The image changed to show another handsome young face, this one Lorenzo; angular features, dark hair slicked back, very much Mediterranean. He had a cold look in his eyes, even at the distance from which the photo was taken. At the time of the pic Lorenzo had been on a large yacht of some sort, out to sea. "Lorenzo is the new leader of the Bok," said Nani. "The Project has been building a dossier. I've matched everything in real time with the records from the laptop."

Jess recalled the info on Lorenzo. Twenty-eight, painted

as a power-hungry playboy in the Project's records. He certainly looked the part.

Nani kept narrating. "He's been hard to track, if not impossible, but unlike his predecessors Lorenzo has been flamboyant, almost disdainful, like he's tired of hiding, which of course has worked to the Project's advantage. His ego has exposed him enough that they now believe they've intercepted the info they need to narrow down a window, a time and a place where he'll be."

"So it's confirmed?"

Nani nodded. "From what I can tell, their confidence is high. They are in motion and moving toward it. Their intention currently is to strike."

This was getting closer to reality. Discussion aboard the *Reaver* had gone from a bright idea to a slowly forming plan to mirror that of the Project and beat them to the punch— though as yet Nani had not enough details to make final decisions. She would soon, though, at which point they would need to figure it out. And—if they were really going to do this—commit to the steps required to pull it off.

Jess looked up at Zac. Thrilled despite her rising anxiety. Happy that he was ready, eager even, to back her up, to go with her on yet another adventure.

"Where's the place?" she asked.

"Somewhere in Spain. Still trying to get details."

"And they don't know we're spying on them?"

"Not as far as I can tell."

Jess looked back up at the screen and the images of the key players in this little subterfuge.

Drake Hauer, leader of the Project.

Lorenzo Fertiti, leader of the Bok.

She noticed Bianca grin.

"This is such a baller move," her friend observed.

Zac, who'd been pretty good so far at keeping up with the girls' slang, had a look on his face. Like he kind of got it but didn't want to ask. Nani was so used to their little comments being part of the background she didn't even notice. She just kept doing her thing.

Jess explained for Zac. "It's like, I don't know, like

something the average person would never try, but only a total badass could pull off. Something amazing."

Zac nodded.

To which Bianca grinned wider, as if to confirm it:

"Baller."

CHAPTER 20:

A LAST-SECOND BID

YAMOTO STOOD ALONE IN THE Shogunnate chamber, high above the city, pondering events. After all this time there was no more sign of the murderous Kang, and Yamoto was certain the beast was not lost or sitting quietly somewhere on Anitra, waiting to be found. All evidence suggested Kang was gone, Horus with him, the Icon as well, and that chapter of their history was, finally, put to rest.

In many ways this was good news.

The bad news was the aftermath. In the wake of those events there was division within the Dominion ranks, specifically the forces engaged across the ocean at Midbay. Things had been falling apart since the order to attack was given, since just before Kang swept in and was subsequently swept away, and even now Yamoto's generals at Midbay battled on, though he'd given clear orders to withdraw and regroup. The attack had been Kang's orders, not Yamoto's. Retreat was the only way to salvage their position. They must give back Midbay, at least for now. However ... Yamoto's generals had all but formed a coup in their refusal to comply, putting the cohesion of the entire Dominion at risk.

Yamoto himself had been a general not long ago. Top general, made Shogun against his wishes; for the good of the Dominion, it was claimed, and he regretted ever allowing that to happen. After the radical shifts of the last weeks and months, the very men he once worked with—many directly—now rebuked or outright ignored his command. Pushing forward on their own agenda. They would fail. But he had to consider the possibility: what if they didn't? What if they claimed that land? In whose name would they claim it?

The *real* news, even beyond all that, was, of course, the

spaceship. There was no other way to describe it, really; a craft that emerged from a hidden mountain base, flew into the sky over the battle and ascended rapidly out of sight. Ground stations tracked it to orbit, then beyond, where it continued moving away at an alarming rate, like nothing they possessed until it simply ... disappeared. Many resources had been called into play to evaluate that event, to analyze every bit of info to which they had access. Yet another shock in a string of shocks that, soon, Yamoto feared, would be the ruin of them all. Along with the chaotic results of Kang's brief rule, the loss of the Crucible and the Council before that, the current dismantling of Dominion unity by rogue generals across the sea, growing unrest at home, the discovery of what the Venatres might've been hiding—a working starship ...

Yamoto anticipated revolution.

"Sir," one of his aides entered the chamber.

He turned from the panoramic windows overlooking noon-day Osaka.

Maybe revolution was exactly what they needed.

Everything had already been turned on its ear; their dogma, their beliefs, their most sacred religious artifacts; after everything, maybe it was time to put an end to the Emperor's legacy once and for all. With each new blow the Dominion kept trying to hold itself together, to maintain the way things were, but the position of "Shogun" was tired. As were many of their institutions. It was time. Time to get rid of all of it, to bring his wayward generals into line. Give the people of the Dominion something real to believe in.

Yamoto nodded to his aide, who waited patiently at the door.

"Daimyo Kazukhan is here," the aide announced.

"Send him in."

And the aide withdrew.

Kazukhan. Yamoto rolled the name in his mind. Too militaristic a name for a noble. One of the Emperor's gifts, as was Yamoto's own name, from a time when nobles were warriors. Or so it was claimed.

All of that gone, revealed as farce. The Emperor, his holy

form untouchable, locked in the hallowed Vivitak, violated before Yamoto's eyes, torn from its sarcophagus like so much rotting dust, Holy robes ripped away by the abomination Kang yet ... nothing changed.   No Holy Retribution fell upon them, no wrath.   No blazing return of Kagami on a golden chariot.   The Emperor's legacy was at an end, just like that.   It only now seemed to be sinking in.   Everything they'd built, all their rules and beliefs, everything they'd lived by for generations, waiting, the foundation on which their entire society had been laid, was a joke.

Yamoto made a little sound beneath his breath.   A scoff.

The door opened and the aide entered with Kazukhan, showed him in a few steps and withdrew.   The Daimyo came closer to Yamoto and stopped.

"My Shogun." He bowed.

"Daimyo." Yamoto let the title pass.   *Shogun.* He didn't know what he was anymore.

"Thank you for granting me audience."

Yamoto tired of these exact sorts of pleasantries.   His military was disobedient, his nobles were fawning—there was no satisfaction to be had, no worthy people with which to deal.

But he played along.

"I've not heard from you in a while, Kazukhan.   When I received your request I was curious.   What news have you?"

"Not news, lord.   At least, not anything that should not be obvious."

Yamoto waited.   Held his pose, arms behind his back; forced a benign smile.

Then his Daimyo shocked him.

"The Dominion is in a state of collapse," he said.   "This is not news."

Yamoto felt his smile drop, but only after it had.   Too late to pretend he hadn't reacted.   He looked on Kazukhan, his first impulse to be offended, as protocol would dictate.   A lesser noble, accusing him of failure?   So bluntly?   It was dishonorable.   It was punishable.

But it was true.

Could he berate him for speaking the truth? Should he? And wasn't he just thinking how they needed change? How difficult it was to find strong-willed, like-minded people within the upper ranks?

He spoke carefully. "What, then, is the purpose of this audience?"

Kazukhan bowed again, a short bow, as if to let his Shogun know he meant no disrespect, with what he said or with what he was about to.

"I propose a solution."

Despite the basic courtesies Yamoto felt as if Kazukhan addressed him as equal. The initial pretense of his Daimyo's greeting had fallen away and before him stood a man of obvious conviction. Yamoto was not yet sure what that conviction was, or even if he would like it, but for the moment felt a bit of his inner conflict fall away.

Here might be someone with whom he could speak.

"A solution to which ill?" He decided in that moment to be frank. To not dance around, to not make the Daimyo explain himself. They both knew things were not well. "A solution to the fact that our Imperial prophecies have been cast aside? A solution to the chaos left behind by the beast? A solution to the war across the ocean? Or perhaps a solution to the decay within our citizenry? To what do you propose a solution?" It felt liberating to speak so candidly.

Kazukhan's gaze was steady. "To all."

Yamoto studied him.

"I hope you've not come here to waste my time."

"My proposal may fail, in which case I suppose I have. But we won't know until that time. Here and now I come with an idea. One that, I believe, wastes neither your time nor mine."

"Go on."

"A summit."

Yamoto cocked an eyebrow.

"With the Venatres."

At that he blinked and knew he looked surprised. For once he didn't care.

"With their highest leaders," said Kazukhan, continuing with his idea. "You, our ruler, our Shogun, and the leaders of our enemies. Here in Osaka."

Yamoto tried not to stutter. "To what end?"

"An accord."

"An accord?" And he slipped: "Are you mad? Our agenda is the destruction of the Venatres, control of the world. An accord is—"

"Our agenda is old." It was true. Yamoto listened as his Daimyo went on: "Tired. That is the Emperor's outdated agenda. He's dead, his body cast away. That was the agenda of the High Council and the witch. They too are dead. That was the agenda of Ashikagi, Shogun before you. Dead. That was the agenda of Kang. Kang is gone, no more. That remains the agenda of your rogue generals, who defy you, but it is not *your* agenda. It cannot be. It is *not* the agenda of the people. This I know. Soon the Venatres will rally back. We are too far gone. With our disunity, with the state of our affairs, with all we've lost in recent months the Venatres—not us—will rule this world when the fighting is done. You know it. I know it. If we continue this conflict we will lose. The end of the Dominion could not be more at hand.

"However we yet hold power. If we talk, discuss conditions, we yet have the strength to dictate goals. We can set a course into the future on our terms. Anitra can come together, at last, and work toward the next objective.

"If we continue on our current path our final collapse is assured. And at the end of it we will have nothing."

Yamoto knew Kazukhan was right.

But an accord!

The gall.

He found himself warming to his Daimyo.

"How would such a meeting even be arranged?"

"If it please my lord, I will act as liaison." The Daimyo lapsed to a more respectful protocol. "With your agreement, I am determined to make this happen. I will arrange it. Somehow. Some way. I will exploit whatever resources are needed in order to do so.

"I will bring the leaders of the Venatres to us. I feel strongly that this is the way."

Yamoto wanted to resist, but recognized those impulses as yet more old ideas struggling to hold on. Just as Kazukhan said. He was right in that regard. And in that Yamoto suddenly saw a glimmer of hope. This was the clean sweep he'd been imagining. Why *couldn't* they do it?

He had no idea what the outcome of such a meeting would bring, but in that moment was supremely intrigued by the thought of it. Parley with their enemies, perhaps even to make allies.

He turned from his Daimyo, back to the panoramic windows.

"Let me consider it," he said, wanting at least to give the impression of resistance.

Though in truth his decision was made.

* * *

MUSIC POURED from the walls of the bridge, the quality of the sound amazing. The *Reaver's* audio system created a depth, a richness that would've been an audiophile's dream. Jess had no idea if the Kel designed the system with music in mind—maybe they had Kel rock bands a thousand years ago—but the fidelity was perfect. At the moment they listened to a track from an artist named DJ Fujito, a trance/step piece with throbbing bass, and it was like standing inside a pair of high-end headphones.

Nani killed the track.

"That's some of his music," she said. "He'll be at a club in Segovia for a one-night show. Just outside Madrid. Lorenzo will be there." She'd called everyone together to report on the latest. The last bits of the puzzle had been pieced together and she now knew where Lorenzo, the Bok leader, would be, when, and how the Project was preparing to execute their plan to kidnap him.

"So how are we going to do it?" asked Bianca.

Nani swiveled in her chair to face them. It was clear she'd already been thinking of ideas.

STAR ANGEL: DAWN OF WAR

"We beat the Project at their game. They're planning a covert grab after the show. We grab him first."

DJ Fujito was apparently Lorenzo's favorite DJ and the Project expected Lorenzo to make an appearance. They had no idea how or in what fashion, but they expected him to be there.

"We grab him first? How?"

"I've ruled out a few things," said Nani. "I think the best way is low-key." She looked at Zac. "Zac and either Jessica or Bianca could go to the club as a couple. That would be the least conspicuous, based on everything I understand about the situation." She looked directly at Jess and Bianca. "You both know Earth culture, better than anyone here. One of you needs to go with him. We need someone who can blend. Zac is perfect for an operation like this because, well, he's the man for the job. With no additional weapons or equipment he can beat out the Project, nab Lorenzo and make a getaway. But he'll be out of place in his mannerisms. He has to be with someone. Also, from what I've read, these sorts of clubs aren't likely to let in a single guy." Jess was impressed with Nani's understanding of the dynamics of such an Earth social event.

Satori, of course, was skeptical. "Go *into* the club?"

"That's where Lorenzo will be. Until he arrives we won't have a lock on him."

"It should be me," Jess interjected, wanting to make sure that was settled before anything else. If anyone went to the club with Zac it would be her.

"Why not just wait outside?" Satori kept up her line of questioning. "Or swoop in?"

"We could," said Nani, "but we don't know when Lorenzo will arrive or even how. The Project isn't sure if he might come in via some secret entrance, or how he will arrive or exactly when. They only expect him to be inside the club for the show at some point. They're planning to have someone inside waiting for him. I think it's best to mirror their actions, then move before they do. We shadow them, then, when the time is right, we strike first. Beat them to the punch.

"The Project has the proper lead-up. This is not a brute-force action. Once in the club Lorenzo can be identified, then they plan to execute a grab. With Zac we can beat them to it. It should be easy enough."

Jess stood a little closer to Zac and held his arm, imagining doing this mission with him. In truth she could hardly believe it had come to this. Not only were they planning how to actually make it happen, Satori was, so far, not protesting.

"So how do we get in and not be seen?"

Nani turned back to her screens and tapped a few things. "The club is very exclusive," she said. "We can't just barge in. We have to gain entrance as legitimate fans of the DJ. This is really the only tricky part. I've looked over the layout of the venue, done some research on clubbing," the matter-of-fact way she said this fascinated Jess, "and I think any more than two of us is going to stand out. The best way is not to go as an individual, not as an odd-looking group, but as a couple. Zac and one of you—Jess," she amended. "Based on what I've seen about the atmosphere of the club, that will have the best chance of success. We have to pose as legitimate club-goers and be admitted inside."

Jess imagined posing as a couple and making their way in, like some kind of secret spy James Bond move, and while part of that intrigued her—and some of it, she had to admit, made her giddy—most of it just made her nervous.

They were going down to Earth. Where she was a wanted criminal.

Satori asked: "So we get in, fine. But how do we get *to* the club? Won't this attract a little attention?" She looked pointedly at the bridge around them and, by extension, the *Reaver* itself.

Nani answered simply: "We'll use one of the fighters."

"Still a little obvious, isn't it?"

"I've figured out a way we can land without being seen. Probably."

"Doesn't this thing have a transporter?" Bianca quipped. "Like *Star Trek* or something?" No one laughed. "You know." She made a *boo-eee-ooo* sound, complete with a timid little wave of her fingers to simulate someone beaming in.

"A what?"

"Never mind."

Jess gave her a "really?" look.

Nani continued. "I believe I have a way to get a fighter down undetected." Then: "I'll stay aboard the *Reaver* and run things here. Since Jess will go down with Zac, Bianca can stay and help."

Nani turned to Satori and Willet. "Which means, I thought I would show you two how to fly the fighter. Seems the most obvious choice. With the right descent path at the right time you can drop through the airspace over the area and get to ground. The fighter uses the same wave-function propulsion as the *Reaver*, so if you go slow it should be silent and, potentially, near invisible at night. Active countermeasures should keep you off their electronics. I've sighted a few possible landing sites."

Jess continued to be impressed. Nani was taking charge. So far everything made sense, though, like Satori, Jess wasn't entirely convinced an ambush outside the club wasn't a better idea. Mentally she reserved the right to make changes, but for now it sounded workable. As Nani said, with Zac it would be easy. Zac made all of it, in fact, easy. Presumably Jessica's only role would be to provide legitimate cover—a date—for him to enter the club.

She stole a quick glance at him.

"And so how does this play out?" Satori asked. "We go to this club and ... what?"

"Overall it's simple," said Nani. "The Project expects Lorenzo, and probably a few of the other, younger Bok, to be at the club to see DJ Fujito. They know Lorenzo is a fan, it's one of the few things they do know about him, and that he's shown up all over the world at Fujito's shows. They've connected the dots and believe he'll be at this next show, at a club on the outskirts of Madrid."

"They believe?" All of a sudden Jess could feel Satori putting on the brakes. "I thought you said—"

"The Project is committing resources. Their confidence is high. Remember, until Lorenzo came along they were never able to pin the Bok anywhere. The Bok have been living in the shadows of the rest of humanity. Until the Bok attacked the Project back in Earth's twentieth century no one even knew they existed. No one knew anything.

"With his overconfident attitude Lorenzo has finally, unwittingly, opened things up. So, no, they can't be a hundred percent sure he'll be there and neither can we. There's just no way. But the Project has every reason to believe he will. Based on what I've seen I do too.

"This is our chance."

Jess wondered if Nani now knew more about the Earth than she herself did. After days of near-sleepless, non-stop analysis of Jessica's world, was the brilliant scientist girl suddenly more of an expert on her own home?

"So Zac and I pose as a couple out for a night at the club," she said, "go in and pretend to be there for the show and wait for Lorenzo. Then nab him."

Nani nodded. "The Project will have the place covertly surrounded. They'll also have agents in the club. They don't know how Lorenzo will arrive, but they plan to wait till after the show and get him as he leaves. At first they were going to tail him but decided that was too risky. Capture and interrogation seem the best solution. I think that's what we have to do as well. They're not coordinating with the host country so this is covert for them too."

"So Zac grabs Lorenzo before they can."

"Essentially, yes."

"What then?"

"Well," Nani had clearly thought through every aspect. "At that point we'll use the fighter. You capture Lorenzo," she looked to Zac and Jess, "Willet and Satori fly in, pick you guys up and return here. That will expose us, yes, but once we have Lorenzo it may not matter. Stealth will no longer be an issue."

"See?" Bianca was determined to make her joke. "That's why we need a transporter. Then we don't need Zac, the fighter—none of it. *Boo-eee-ooo.*" Everyone looked at her and she added sheepishly: "I'm just saying."

Nani continued. "From there we figure out the rest. All

Zac has to do is get him away from the club, far enough and fast enough so that we can pick them up. People may see the Kel fighter, yes, but we'll have the head of the Bok and, after that, things change drastically anyway.

"Obviously we still have some particulars to work out," Nani admitted, "but that's the general idea."

Satori shook her head. "I still don't get why we're doing this."

"Because they hold the key to tying everything together," said Jess.

"I don't see how that's as significant as you keep insisting. It seems to me this starship is way more relevant than any ancient secrets, probably skewed or lost by these guys. We don't even know. We have no idea what we're getting into."

"They could be holding another Icon," said Jess.

"Could be."

"Maybe more. Icons with coordinates for other worlds. If they still have anything from that ancient period it's more valuable than gold or starships. There were other worlds back then, other things known by the Kel and humans of that time. We've got a chance to pry it out into the open."

"Even if that's true, how? So we capture their leader. What good does that do us? Don't the rest then scurry deeper underground? We'll never find them. Not only that, as soon as we tip our hand we can no longer move in stealth. Once we're exposed ... how do we even go after anything else?"

"Lorenzo will tell us what he knows," Jess looked to Zac. "And we've got the means to get at it. Nothing down there can stop us. *We* put together the pieces of the puzzle, *we* control the dissemination of facts, and we work out a way to introduce Earth to Anitra and to figure out a solution to the Kel and everything else." Putting it like that made it seem a far bigger task than it was already.

Jess forged on. "Like we agreed, we have to look at things from a completely different perspective."

"I never agreed to that."

"The entire existence of two worlds is about to change," said Jess. "Drastically, and we're at the center. With everything that's been exposed, if we just walk away ...

"We, the people right here on this ship, this small group, have a chance to make a change." It was everything she'd ever fretted over, after her return home from Anitra, trying to decide what to do with the Skull Boy in the barn, the Icon, how or if she should use them to make a difference. To wake the world from its sleeping delusions, to bring it to the next level. Now she had an even bigger Skull Boy, the starship, and she still hadn't figured out the solution. "We have to take this chance."

Back then she'd never done more than dream about it. Thinking of ways it might work, realizing, sadly, how it never could. Forced to admit all the ways it could fail and lead nowhere, or even make things worse.

Now was hardly different. There were a hundred ways this could also fail, could also make things worse, not better. Only now the cat was out of the bag. And whether they did anything or not, things were going to happen. If they didn't find the Bok the Project would. Those secrets, whatever they were, would be exposed. The Project knew nothing of this starship or Anitra or, really, for that matter, the Kel. Now the Kel were aware of the humans. Whether they could ever find them or not remained to be seen, but humanity could not wait for that encounter. Humanity had to be as prepared as they possibly could. That meant someone needed to hold all the cards. Not one group with this bit of info, one group with that bit of info, none talking. And so this group right here, on the bridge of the *Reaver*, holding the biggest card of all, would be that someone. Jess, Nani, Zac—all of them. They would strip the Bok of what they knew and decide how to bring it all—all information, all knowledge, two human worlds and all else—together.

She felt her head spin. Dramatic, world-shattering things were in play. Not much had changed in that regard; she was still at the crux of monumental events, same as she had been from the moment Zac arrived in the woods behind her house, but as everything continued to escalate she wondered when her life would ever be any less epic. If it ever would. Would calm ever again prevail?

Satori let the discussion go. Resigned herself to what would be, at least for now. Jess squeezed Zac's arm. She could tell he wasn't worried. And why should he be? At least in the short term, for this mission, there was nothing to fear. He was a Kazerai, indestructible under these circumstances. Nothing on Earth could stop him. He was stronger than a hundred men, battle hardened from the wars on Anitra. In fact he almost looked eager.

But she was looking ahead. Wondering just how difficult Lorenzo would be under interrogation. Would they truly be able to make him lead them to the rest of the Bok? If not, what then?

And as she thought of this she realized her mistrust of the Bok had only been growing. As they talked about it, making preps for the kidnapping, she'd come to want Lorenzo far more badly than seemed natural.

She found she wanted the Bok very badly indeed. And everything they were hiding.

* * *

"You fell there." Jess highlighted an area of the display, zooming in. "That's where you popped out over the woods."

Zac pointed. "And that's your house?" He sat with her alone in the *Reaver's* small observation room, chatting and looking over the Earth below. One wall was filled with a wide viewscreen that appeared, for all its display technology, exactly like a clear window, looking out from orbit, and they sat together up against it, leaning toward it the same as if peering through real glass. They'd ended up in the small room, chatting like a couple of teenagers and she had to keep reminding herself, as it was easy to forget, caught up as they were in such fantastic events, that she and Zac *were* teenagers. Just two crazy teens, way out of their element with a mind to change the world.

"Yeah." She gazed at the highlighted area around her home, no real details visible at that magnification. Little brown and green roofs dotted the carefully manicured landscape of the affluent neighborhood, curving tastefully along friendly lanes and cul-de-sacs. "I've been afraid to look any closer." The ship's optics could drill down tighter, but it was easier to hold at this range. Nani had been scanning close-ups since they got there, but Jess didn't want to see any closer. It was already hard enough.

After a moment of silence she realized Zac was staring at her. She turned to him.

"What?" she laughed nervously.

"Why are you doing this?" he asked.

"Doing what?"

"Getting everyone to go along with this plan. To kidnap the leader of the Bok."

"Me? It was Nani's idea."

"Yeah, so."

She turned it back on him. "You were the one that jumped on it."

"It's what I thought you wanted."

"Liar." He was so handsome, sitting there in the soft glow of the Earth. He was always handsome, no matter what he was doing. There was one scar left from his fight with Kang, one visible at the moment, anyway, nearly healed, on his cheek just above the stubble of a beard. Somehow it made him look even sexier.

"So why?" he persisted.

"I don't know," she couldn't hold his gaze. "I don't actually know. All I know is we're doing the right thing. It's like I told Satori. I mean, we need to keep finding out. The way I see it we've only raised more questions with all this, not solved anything." She turned her gaze back to his. "Why not keep going? If we stop here, go back, things are still going to happen, only without us involved. We might as well stay out front. We need to. Besides, if we don't do this now we lose what might be our only opportunity."

He accepted that. Then sat there looking at her until it became nearly unbearable. She looked away again and he asked: "Where will 'back' be?"

She had no answer.

"After it's all done," he said. "After this is all sorted out, what then? Where will you go? Where will you make a life?"

She searched his face.

And it was his turn to look away.

Make a life? She looked at his eyes as he, in turn, stared out at the Earth. Ice blue eyes, so sharp, so reflective at that angle they were hard to read. But she saw a certain longing in them.

"I don't know." She swallowed. "What about you?"

Though they'd both made declarations of their love, being with him still felt like a first date. Like so much had yet to be determined. Like the awkward phase was a long way from over. Of course it did, and of course it was. Though they'd been through Hell together, there was a lot of getting to know each other left to do.

"I'll go wherever you go," he said quietly, then fixed her gaze. "If that's what you want."

She took his hands, feeling the warmth of his strong palms. Tried to clear her head. For a moment she had a hard time rectifying this current, shy Jessica with the one that stood and fought. Why was talking to Zac so hard sometimes?

"It is," she said. "A life with you is my dream." She made herself be stronger. "One day we'll have that."

Zac smiled. "I can't wait."

Her heart fluttered. She loved him so much. Very nearly said it right there; really, nearly, very nearly almost poured her heart out, gushing like a big romantic, saying things that would be too much for the moment, but held short. Right then it would've come out way too emotional. It wasn't the time for that sort of passionate pronouncement. Zac knew how she felt. Instead she decided to lean forward and give him a kiss. A quick peck, right on the lips, and as she pulled back she smiled.

Zac laughed. "Can you imagine? You doing the dishes and me mowing the yard?"

To that she gave a sly grin. "Who says I'd do the dishes?"

He laughed again. "Ok," he conceded. "Can you imagine *me* doing the dishes?"

At that her grin expanded. "Would you wear an apron,

rubber gloves—the whole bit?"

Zac smiled and agreed wholeheartedly. "Absolutely."

And she laughed and kissed him again.

CHAPTER 21:

CHANGE OF HEART

"WE NOW KNOW how powerful the other ship was," Voltan stood before his queen. Ccc watched him calmly, even as he began to annoy her with his rising insistence. "We've had time to analyze information from the encounter, and what we're now certain of is that what we faced out there was one of our own. A starship from the last Dynasty." He gave particular emphasis to this. "That makes it near a thousand years old. And, from what we can tell, more powerful than our own. It would take five of ours to match it. Five!

"We don't yet know enough of this to make such a rash decision. Please, heed my warning."

"The vessel was handled clumsily," Cee told him. She sat in her throne, trying to remain unconcerned, trying not to be baited by his council. "From everything we know it was manned, not by warriors or ancient Kel, but by someone who knew little of its operation. Their use of the odd, Fetok-style language is proof enough. Whoever flew that ancient ship found it, probably. That they only bothered to gather the other human then flee is further reason to believe this is no more than an anomaly."

"An anomaly?" Voltan acted stunned. "We encounter one of our own ships, a starship from our distant past—*from the last Dynasty before our ruin*—and you would count it as no more than an anomaly?"

Cee thought to put him in his place, to send him away. But it was only the two of them in her cavernous, domed throne room, and at times the rantings of her Praetor brought insight.

"That is exactly what it is. Forgotten, lost somehow through the ages, discovered on the world which Kang calls home, by his people, restored by them, brought into operation. They then followed him here. Nothing more."

"Speculation. That explanation is no more than Kang's own guess as to how it came to be. The beast knows for sure no more than we. Why stake so much on his claim? It could be a trap. He could be leading us to ambush."

Cee allowed herself a chuckle, finding the notion silly.

"Why? To what end? And further, How?" Then: "Kang is not making this up, my Praetor. He genuinely has no idea, and the mere fact of *that* should assure us of its truth. How could he exist on a world where those ships were common and not know of it? That it was a hidden, forgotten derelict is the *only* explanation for its existence. Were it otherwise the armies of his world would surely now be landing on ours."

"Perhaps they prepare for that even now."

"Your arguments go nowhere. Where is the brilliant mind of my Praetor?"

"Too many fantastic improbabilities have occurred in too short a time. We have not spent near enough effort on the evaluation of this action. To have our scientists work feverishly to dissect this device, to learn its use and apply it to our own craft, so that we might then fly off at once to this monster's world and throw ourselves upon it ...

"Madness."

Cee had been before the War Council. The backing of their greatest commanders was hers. She was sure there was dissention, there must be quiet discussions at some level, talk of the risk of undertaking such a blind attack, but in all the reception of her plan and the device was overwhelming. So many saw opportunity, furthered by the secret desires they no-doubt harbored to appease her, to gain favor. Voltan was in the minority, yet he had been valuable in too many things not to hear his advice.

"There is little doubt of what Kang claims," she said. "We will not find a world of advanced warcraft ready to destroy us."

"It could be a world filled with others like him."

She paused. "I will grant you that. It *is* possible he lies to us in that regard. He could hope to lure us to a world filled with super beasts, which he could lead to overthrow us.

"However I do not intend to engage whatever awaits us on the ground. We will conquer his world from above, and in that action discover exactly what we face. If it is more like him, we destroy the world utterly and him with it. If it comes to that, that is what we do.

"Whether that bears out or not, if we unlock the secret of this Icon—as he calls it—then the stars are ours. Either way, the Kel win. My dear Voltan, this marks the beginning of Empire."

She knew, could tell, her Praetor saw full well the possibilities locked in that one device. The "Icon" that flung Kang and his foe across unknown light years of void, the technology of which no doubt also powered the ancient Kel intruder; these devices, these Icons, had been crafted toward the end of the Great Wars. The Kel knew vaguely of them. Used by the rebels of that time to move individuals or small groups from place to place. All were lost following the Wars, when worlds fell into darkness—including, and perhaps most especially, Kel—but with the discovery of this one it appeared all had not been lost. Some must remain, somewhere out there, and here was one that connected right there in the Kel star system, on one end, at the other to an ancient human world ripe for conquest.

And Cee would have it.

* * *

THIS ICON CONNECTS *over Jessica's home on Earth,* Lindin reviewed the details of his upcoming attempt, knowing that once he went there was no coming back. Not to safety, at least. *It returns over Osaka.* Airborne exit points at both ends, too high for a man to survive the fall. Thus, even if, upon arrival at Earth, he decided against this crazy idea, when he returned it would be right over the heart of the enemy. At the moment he was safely in a mountain hideaway, in his own land, far enough from any real threat. *Twist this,* he held the Icon gingerly in his grasp, *and I leave it all behind. I transfer in a flash.* Across enormous distance, to another world altogether. *And a return that puts me directly in danger.* As yet he had no idea how he would escape Dominion lands when he *did* return. One man, high-ranking leader of the Venatres, avowed enemy of the Dominion. Square in the middle of their capital. Whatever waited on the other end was mystery enough, though he had less fear of that.

I can't do this.

No matter the strength of the impulse driving him, there just wasn't enough sound planning behind it. The pendulum had swung and he was back to doubt. No matter how he tried to make the idea work, it was too much whim and not enough real possibility. Don a suit of Skull Boy armor and leap off to an alien culture? Rummage around for clues belonging to a girl who stole a starship? Come back to the land of the enemy, clear across an ocean? Somehow find refuge and make it all the way back here?

He looked around the prep room he'd assembled, not having clued anyone to his intentions. A suit of Skull Boy armor stood to the side, waiting, mighty rail gun strapped to its back. The Icon was there, in his hands, a little slippery now that he'd begun a cold sweat. Other provisions he expected he'd need, ready to be fixed to the powered armor. He looked at his strained expression in the chrome surface of the Icon.

Wondering how he'd let such a childish notion take him this far.

"Sir?" a voice on the room's intercom startled him.

"Yes?" Carefully he set it down.

"The president is on."

For an instant he thought his boss had somehow learned what he was up to. In a way Lindin was on house arrest, waiting for tensions with the war to ease enough to facilitate a thorough investigation into what happened with the starship, along with his role in that fiasco. If the president knew what he was about to do …

But he wouldn't, of course, and the worried thought passed—replaced by other speculations. Why *would* the president be calling? Why now?

"I'll take it in my office," he said and left the room.

On his way up he sorted through a myriad of possibilities, none gaining much traction. The president may have taken it upon himself to contact him directly to discuss the incident with the starship, man to man, friend to friend. They knew each other from decades of public service in different quarters. Private conversations with the president weren't unusual, though they had become increasingly infrequent over the years.

Lindin passed through alternating busy and near empty halls, arriving shortly at his office. The door closed behind him as he entered and went to his console.

"Yes, sir?" he said as he flicked it on. The president turned to the screen from talking with someone else. President Felana was a thin man with gray hair, a long neck and severe features, though at sixty-something he was quite robust. At the moment he looked concerned and, Lindin thought as he began speaking, a bit ...

Intrigued.

"We have an interesting development," he informed him. "The Dominion has requested a summit."

The way he said it, with little preamble and no buildup, didn't register at first. Then the full import of what that meant hit Lindin and he sat slowly.

"A summit?"

"Yes," the president alternated between having his attention on him and other things developing off-screen. In fact, now that Lindin noticed ... there was a high degree of activity taking place at the presidential office.

"This came to us yesterday," he said. "We've been evaluating sources and confirming. A time and place has been arranged. I would like you to attend."

Lindin steadied himself. Moments before he'd been in the midst of trying to follow through on a hair-brained idea to go to Earth. Now it seemed a decision had been made for him.

"Of course," he said. "This is good news?" He nearly shook, the combination of what he'd been about to do and the promise of this new twist hitting him all at once. *What was I thinking? What if I'd gone?*

"Yes," said the president. "We believe so. The stated purpose of the summit is to negotiate an accord."

Lindin flexed his hands, mind turning to this prospect.

If true, this was historic.

Monumentally so.

He maintained his poise. "Departing from your location?"

"Yes."

Lindin nodded. "I'll be on my way."

The president's attention was being drawn evermore to the activity taking place on the other end.

"Very well," and he signed off.

Lindin leaned back.

This would take priority now.

* * *

KANG GAZED OUT over the Kel capital from high above, standing at the windows of a soaring tower. He'd been given these chambers as his quarters, shown a high degree of respect over the last days and even what might be considered hospitality for the war-like Kel. In turn he'd been doing his best to reciprocate with his own civility and decorum. Playing along. Controlling his urges. Finding it not as difficult as he expected, in that the Kel so closely mirrored his own way of thinking. They valued power, brutality; awarded it with rank and privilege. Upon his insistence, appearing before their War Council with the Lady Cee, he'd been able to persuade them. They saw in him the epitome of their culture, and though the Kel projected a veneer of beauty—aesthetics he most assuredly did not—he was nevertheless, despite the horror of his outer shell, a shining example of the power and brutality they so idolized. With this newfound civility he had quickly become a symbol of hope. Their existence was stagnant. He promised new birth.

Cee-Ranok assured him of these things. Spent time with him following their series of meetings, going on about what an impact his presence made, how it swayed the minds of those who might otherwise have resisted such an engagement of their resources. Such quick and dramatic change. For so long had they moved at an unchanging pace, to now have such opportunity—and she insisted it *was* opportunity—they were just as likely to do nothing as to act. Kang understood. On his world, Anitra, even as Emperor it took great force to cut through the bureaucratic machine, to generate fast action. Here, with the help of Cee, they managed to impel the Council to gear for war on short notice. An attack fleet was being armed even then, prepared to employ the technology of the Icon—when and if its secrets were cracked.

No time would be wasted.

Kang hoped the Kel scientists would not come up empty. Prayed against it, to whatever god would listen. If they found the Icon useless for their needs ... he did not yet have a plan for that eventuality. Likely as not he would simply take it back; wrest it from them if he must; use it to return to Anitra and do what he could to rule that world completely.

But how could he leave this fantastic opportunity behind? He couldn't, in truth, and so the idea of failure to understand the Icon was impossible to dwell on.

Around and beneath him the dark metropolis spread far and wide, other towers, other buildings as high as the one in which he stood, black and slate, foreboding structures every one, blanketed in white, bordered in the distance by black-rock mountains and more snow, more ice. The sky itself was leaden with clouds that would bring a fresh round by nightfall ...

This system's impossible three suns, tiny and bright orange, hung in the sky, hazy through the upper, thin bands of atmosphere, setting in such a way that this world had both day and night, not unlike what he was used to. The Kel were not so inhuman, their world not so alien as to be difficult to bear. He quite enjoyed the gloom of the icy, perpetual winter. As part of his welcome Cee had given him his own fur wrap, the pelt of some local animal reserved for warlords and their highest commanders. He wore it now, wrapped needlessly about his shoulders. A point of pride, more than anything. Mere decoration.

He had no need of warmth.

He opened the door to the balcony and stepped outside, into the biting air. To the railing he went and stood, looking down at the city far below. Kel traffic crisscrossed at different levels in orderly rows. With his keen eyesight he saw far and wide, could make out whatever he put his gaze to. The city was alive with purpose. A perfect compliment to his own desire. News of his arrival was everywhere. News of the promise he brought ...

The Kel were nearly in celebration.

He breathed in the sounds, the energy of the vast city. As he let out his breath he turned the steady exhale to a snort and a long plume of frosted air shot from his nostrils. It dissipated far out before him in a billowing cloud in the cold air.

Cee had been sure to show him everything. To make him aware of all things. In some ways he'd grown to admire the powerful queen. She held the reins of this world. She was confident, did not seem to fear him—or at least held her fear in check when in his presence—and professed great interest in what he proposed.

In addition she was beautiful.

The Kel were, in a way, a refinement of the human form. Kang was certain that, even as a human, he would've found Cee attractive. With her exquisitely smooth skin, sharp, angular features, captivating yellow eyes. Even her pointed ears added to her appearance rather than detracting.

As the beast he'd become, however, with the changes he'd undergone, he found himself of even stronger views. Though he could imagine his reaction to Cee as a human, in his current state he found her ...

Compelling.

But this was not part of his agenda. Not yet. For now seeing to the understanding of the Icon's secrets, followed by their application to the fleet and a summary conquest of Anitra ... these were his objectives. There would be a long road beyond that. One filled with victories and, perhaps, even queens.

CHAPTER 22:

NO ESCAPING THE PAST

CEE-RANOK STOOD a little behind and to the side, watching as the beast, in turn, looked out over the activity in the street. Kang seemed fascinated by the daily business of the Kel, the orderly procession of vehicles and bodies, the routine of their lives. Cee and a small delegation had brought him out into the public domain, giving her an opportunity to observe, to understand him better, that she might continue to sow plans for this powerful creature.

"How many are you?" he asked, holding the stylized translator wand to the side as he spoke, eyes on the traffic. Elegant, custom versions of the wands had been crafted to fit the demands of Cee's aesthetic.

"Six-hundred million," she said into hers. "On this world. There are other outposts in the system, but our greatest numbers are here." Kang had become quite curious, though she found it only natural he would be building his own store of knowledge on *them*, even as they sought to learn how better to control him.

She feared and was yet drawn to him. Kang stimulated a certain thrill in her, one she realized had been missing. He was dangerous. Overly so, and the terror of instant death as she manipulated him to her ends was equal parts exhilarating.

She glanced around at the delegates, the cordon of guards present on any such outing of dignitaries. Armed warriors, more than usual; formidable under ordinary circumstances.

Nothing before Kang.

As he stared in the other direction she found herself studying the curve of his hideous form, such that the angry shouts and yelling in the street had reached a frenzy before she noticed. Her military escort had already reacted and was bringing order to the developing scene, positioning themselves against a small crowd that was gathering. Kang, too, seemed not to have noticed, and he and Cee turned to the chaos as one.

"The demon!" a voice among them yelled, and the call was taken up by the rest. "The demon!" Twenty or thirty more clamored against the barrier of bodies now being created by the soldiers.

"The Prophecy!" came another cry. Louder than the others and Cee sought the face of the offender.

The Prophecy?! Her blood went to ice, then boiled. They dared utter such blasphemy?!

"The demon has come! It is the Prophecy!"

And they began a chant that nearly sent her into a fit of rage.

"Allow the Codes!" And: "Allow the Old Codes!"

How dare they?!

She found her voice. *"Apostates!"* she screamed. Pointed: *"They have forsaken the One God!"* Yelling almost on automatic, the words coming as a recital of the law, the mantra, so suddenly enraged was she. "Kill them!" she yelled to her soldiers, all she could think to do in the face of such outrage. In that instant she was blinded to all reason. "You know the penalty! *Kill them!*

"Kill them all!"

The guards hesitated, frozen with the unexpectedness of this turn of events, but driven by her wrath rose quickly to their duty and brought forth guns. To Cee's horror the small crowd held firm before their fate, martyrs, and she should've seen that they would be, none flinching as the Kel rifles hummed and cracked, delivering electric death— convincing her this was no spontaneous gathering. Of a sudden, too late, perhaps, she realized these were zealots, bent on drawing attention with their sacrifice, and she feared the public display they'd already made, terrified at the potential fallout it would generate. She felt herself start to shake, a delayed reaction, and held her hands still. All eyes were on the carnage in the street. The developing scene was rapidly spreading.

But the zealots were dying. Background noises returned as the last crack of rifle fire echoed into the distance and the last body fell. The delegates with her stood hushed by the massacre. Spectators, too, standing silent at the outer edges of the carnage, only the more distant noises of the city impinging. Cee noticed Kang had a malign grin on his face, almost of satisfaction—approval?—but could not divine his emotion.

"Have my Praetor waiting," she snapped. Then to Kang, too curtly but the words came before she could adjust: "Return to your tower. Wait there until called."

And she whirled and swept away, waving an arm in the direction of her driver and getting at once into her personal car. Still furious but fearful of the unrestrained, impulsive order to Kang, she thought to go back. She could not risk sounding too imperious, must phrase such things as a request—he knew nothing of this aspect of Kel history, after all—but it was too late and she decided not to try to amend it now. Only as the driver raced them away did she feel herself again start to shake.

She glanced out the rear window at the yellow-skinned monster, watching him fade with the crowd into the distance. Her senior officer on the scene was conferring with the delegates, no doubt debating how to triage the situation. Kang, in turn, stood watching her personal hover car as it sped away.

If she could not correct her error then she must own it.

She faced forward.

* * *

CEE SWEPT INTO her citadel, making straight for her throne. The head and shoulders of Praetor Voltan loomed on the giant screen before it, waiting. He spoke as she stormed across the empty expanse of marble floor.

"I was on my way to brief you," he said, "when I received your summons."

"They've blasphemed the One God!" Cee yelled as she stomped to her throne but did not sit. "They call for the

Prophecy!"

"My queen?"

She looked up at his towering image, calm, collected, even as she herself strained with fury.

"The Prophecy!" she fairly screamed. "On the street! A group, organized against us! They knew where we would be, they were gathered there for that purpose—"

"We know of no such groups—"

"Of course we know of no such groups! They would be rooted out and destroyed! I had them killed on the spot." She fumed. "They *knew!* They claimed Kang to be the demon! The very thing the Witch foretold! They knew this!"

Voltan was unsure what to say. "Information is a difficult thing to suppress. We know these legends are still whispered."

Cee whirled in place. "We should've expected some fanatic would turn this into a cry for the Prophecy."

Voltan shrugged. "History cannot be fully erased," he said, and Cee hated that he remained so calm when it came to these matters. "*We* know of these things," he said. "We must, that we might be watchful for them. But in the knowing, as carefully controlled as that knowledge is, by the mere fact of preserving it we leave it open for continuance.

"It is inevitable these legends persist."

She bore into him. "Why did you not predict this?"

"What could I have done? What could any of us?"

Cee turned to her throne in frustration. Stared at it but did not go to it. "Now this thing will be twisted. Kang will become the beast from the Prophecy. He will become the demon."

"That is to be expected. It *is* what was predicted."

Cee cast her gaze over her shoulder, back at the screen, glaring at him. Voltan said: "Surely you had the same thought when first you saw him. We know others of our station did. Kang is the very epitome of that which the Witch described."

"None should mention these things!" Cee turned on him; rushed the screen and stopped. "None!"

Voltan held his expression blank.

"Her infernal Codes were our downfall!" Cee fumed. "The Great Wars, all of it. Rebellion *over those Codes!* Have you forgotten? The Witch and her deceits. We fought to abolish the scourge of the Amkradus! Our civilization was near lost! We vowed *never* to allow that insurrection to rise again.

"Never!"

"My queen, It is not in danger of rising—"

"I will not have my people fall prey to the fantasies of self-proclaimed gods!" Cee stared at him. This was the Prophecy come to life, and it was scaring her. That a simple priestess, from so long ago, could so clearly describe a future that so closely mirrored the present was ... frightening.

And that the tendrils of that same Witch's fear-mongering could reach so far across time infuriated Cee even more. Here was Kang, here was ... the demon, and Cee had chosen—*I chose!*—to bring him among them, to make him part of their future. To ignore the rest and focus on what they might become.

What else could I have done?!

Was she herself merely a tool in that ancient foretelling?

"This is our strongest Dynasty," she seethed, holding to her anger that it might supplant the terror. "The Forever Dynasty. For ten generations we have rebuilt from the ashes of the Wars. The arrival of Kang could not have come at a more perfect time. With the device he brings, if it unlocks our drives ... we are now poised to reclaim our dominance. Over not just a handful of worlds but dozens. Hundreds. Empire. We will find them, all of them that were lost, and we will start with his. From Kang's world we spread to the stars. We will find the Old Worlds and reclaim them. The Kel will be great again! Under my rule, Voltan. I swear it!" She rambled, she knew, but in that moment it was all she had.

Voltan bowed his head, something he didn't often do, and Cee got the sense he was ready to end this line of discussion. Her fury, however, had not run its course, and as she was building the elements of her next tirade, secretly fearing the Amkradus and the hypnotic control that small group of rebels had cast over Kel dominion a thousand years ago; the Amkradus Codes, themselves built upon an even more ancient discovery, pieced together by the witch Aesha and brought to the worlds of the Fetok when her people, the Kel, shunned them; a way to attain individual power, of a sort and a nature that would've made civilized worlds, a controlled and organized populace all but impossible ...

Before she could begin Voltan, head still bowed, spoke.

"My queen," he said firmly, "as I mentioned, I was on my way to brief you."

This held her tongue, for an instant, and she redirected her next words. "On what?"

"The device."

Now she nearly forgot what she was about to say. Her tirade shattered and fell away. The device? What news? Had progress been made?

With her Praetor it was impossible to tell.

"Speak, Voltan. What of the device?"

"Our scientific team has unlocked it."

Cee blinked. This she did not expect.

Not so soon.

Voltan went on. "Graetan, our lead on the project, has come with me. Shall I bring him?"

"At once."

She watched her Praetor walk away on the giant screen, then went to the throne and sat. First at the edge, then forced her usual, regal pose into her limbs and reclined to the side. Waiting.

Voltan stepped back before the screen a moment later and extended a hand, summoning Graetan. The scientist stepped into view and bowed.

"My queen."

"Tell me of the device," she pushed past his protocol. "You have unlocked its purpose?"

He straightened. "Yes. It was far less complicated than we expected. We've confirmed it to be technology from our own past. We were able to extract the coordinates and can match its function to our own drives. It seems our rebuilding efforts over the last generations have stemmed from a very similar base—"

"How quickly can our ships be prepared to use it?"

Graetan paused. "Our ships? It should not take long, my queen, now that we see—"

"Do it at once." Her statement was firm, and it took a moment for the scientist to process the demand. He'd been prepared for a much longer discussion, perhaps with more scientific explanations or questions. Cee had no need of that.

Graetan bowed. "Yes, my queen." And, with a glance to Voltan—who nodded that he should proceed—turned and left.

When he was gone Cee spoke.

"If this leads to Kang's world, as he claims, we will go there as soon as the fleet is readied.

"See that there are no delays."

Voltan paused. Then, looking as if he wanted to argue but seeing she would not be persuaded otherwise, said: "I recommend a smaller fleet be dispatched on the first wave. In the event we are met with more resistance than Kang claims. We should approach this in the form of an expeditionary operation. One which we can turn quickly to conquest if we find his reports to be true."

"See to it. You will go with Kang at their head."

Voltan was clearly not expecting *that* twist.

Cee confirmed: "You are the best suited to manage him, next to myself."

Hesitation, then: "Of course, my queen."

Cee could see this did not sit well with him. She didn't care.

"This could not be more perfect," she worked to steady her anger, so recently boiling over, now replaced with fresh possibility. "Our people demand action," she told him. "Now more than ever. These zealot freaks in the street, what they've done will no doubt inflame old desires, which in our stagnant state would do naught but fester. The attention of the people must be redirected. At such scale, with such glory as to eclipse all other distractions. With this news we will give them exactly that. Something so incredible, so monumental as to draw their minds from any such idle thoughts."

To that Voltan did agree. "This will indeed be met with enthusiasm."

Cee sat straighter. "We will wipe away any lingering memories of the past once and for all. I will draw any and all outcry from this event and put their minds back where they belong. On conquest and empire."

"Yes, my queen."

"Send Kang to conquer his world," she said. "Without delay. That it may not only give us new purpose, but break the thrall of this subversive prophecy."

CHAPTER 23:

EARTH

"MIS PANTALONES huelen a queso," Bianca over-enunciated the Spanish pronunciation, stretching her mouth wide with each syllable. Jess laughed.

"What the hell?" she shook her head. "My pants *what* like cheese?" She and Bianca were slouched in comfy chairs in one of the *Reaver's* staterooms, shoes off and lounging tiredly. They weren't really tired, in fact Jess was quite awake, even a little keyed up, as they were finally expecting to get things rolling, but it felt good to totally flop the way they were.

"Smell," B explained. "My pants smell like cheese."

She finished saying this just as Zac walked in. He raised an eyebrow. "Your pants smell like cheese?"

Bianca giggled and Jess straightened, pushing a few strands of hair out of her face. They'd all been going a little stir crazy aboard the *Reaver*, she and Bianca smack in the middle of what had degenerated into a goofy session of Spanish practice. By now it was mostly just Bianca cracking wise.

Jess had to admit it was some much needed hilarity.

"We were practicing Spanish," she explained. "Bianca knows more than me. She's in Spanish Four."

"Mis pantalones huelen a queso!" Bianca announced with a flourish and Jess laughed, a little too loudly. They were both pretty far gone.

Zac's next question, however, was along a different line. "Spanish?"

And she was reminded, again, he was not of their world.

"We're going to Spain," she explained, realizing they hadn't really talked much about that aspect of the mission. "They speak Spanish. Bianca thought it might be a good idea to bone up."

"They speak a different language in Spain? Why?"

Bianca scoffed. "There's like, a hundred languages on Earth."

"A hundred!" Zac was incredulous. "Why so many? You guys communicate instantly according to Nani. Holy ... You must spend all your time translating. Why?" He still couldn't believe it. "A hundred? Really?"

Bianca shrugged. Jess didn't have a better answer.

Zac tried to imagine it.

"That's why we're practicing." Bianca remained slouching in her seat, feet way up the wall, hair partly covering her face. Every now and then she would blow a few strands up, ineffectively, not really intending to make any change. The hair would fall stubbornly back across one eye.

Zac looked at them both. "And so knowing how to announce that your pants smell like cheese is something I should know? Do I need to know this? Or should I just make sure to keep my pants smelling fresh?"

Jess smiled and saw he was into it.

Bianca ripped off another one: "Y su cabeza es una aceituna!" She waved her arms.

"My head is an olive?" Jess was able to figure that one out.

"Nice," said Zac. "I can see you guys are really prepping." There was no doubt they were both a little punchy. Bianca especially.

"We should be able to get by with English," Jess admitted. "We'll be American tourists. But knowing a little Spanish won't hurt."

Zac nodded. "Well, it's time to put your Spanish to work. Nani sent me to get you guys. She's got everything loaded and we're ready. Next stop, Spain."

The target weekend was upon them and, after much planning and preparation—including Bianca's impromptu Spanish lessons in these final hours—they were about to do this.

"I'll meet you at the bays," said Zac, with a wry turn of his lips. "It looks like you need a few more minutes." And with a wink he was gone and the door shut behind him.

Jess felt her heart skip, getting nervous all over again, but she was ready and, truthfully, this last little bit with Bianca had helped bring a ton of perspective to what they were doing. This was going to be easy.

"You know I'm kind of glad we're doing this," Jess said as she stood and stretched.

"Why?" Bianca wanted to know. She stayed where she was.

Jess shrugged. "It's like this is what I'm supposed to be doing. I feel like I'm supposed to be here."

"What does that mean?"

"I don't know. Don't you feel kind of like this was meant to be?"

"No."

"Just get up. Come on. They're waiting on us."

Bianca rose, reluctantly and with much theater, moaning in an effort to get her body up and in motion. They both put on their shoes and headed out of the room, back through the gloss-black, tracer-lit halls of the starship to the fighter bays. It was a short walk from the observation room.

Zac, Nani, Satori and Willet were waiting.

"Here it is," Nani held out a small device as the girls walked up. She stood with Zac and the others, eager. "Should be ready to go. Everything is set in English, the interface is like I showed you. It's a computer and a communicator."

Jess took it. In size and shape it was like a tablet from Earth, scarily so; a small one, or even an overlarge smart phone. Its function was the same, though she imagined the Kel technology was far beyond any Earth device. *Apple would probably love to get their hands on this.* She turned it over in her hands. Matte black and smooth, dark screen, no visible lines or buttons. Bianca leaned in for a look.

"I've put all the relevant info on it," Nani informed them. "It can tap most Earth networks and has direct frequency communication with us and with the fighter."

Jess nodded. The device felt rugged. She wondered if it was made of the same composites as the armor of the Kel ship. It kind of felt like it. Like it would take a lot to break it.

"It's very durable," Nani confirmed. Then: "I've considered other precautions we might take, but any more than this will just be too hard to conceal. Honestly, with Zac, you don't need anything more."

Biance nodded her head knowingly. "Damn straight," she said, an "ah yeah" tone in her voice. "Jess and her OP boyfriend."

Nani pointed to the tablet—even as Jess tried not to react to her friend's comment. "If anything else is needed we can link and load it directly. This will be your intelligence on the ground. I've tested it. From what I know about your culture it should conceal easily as one of your own personal devices. At least at first glance. It works the same, keyed to your biometrics and Zac's. It should fit easily in a purse."

Jess nodded.

And that was their first stop after landing; picking up— stealing was the right word—a bag and some local clothes. They were dropping over the target in the middle of the morning, and with Bianca's help Nani had identified a boutique where Zac would break them in and they would get a purse and the clothes they'd need to fit in at the club—critical to the success of the mission—along with clothes for the day in the city. Zac still had no shirt. Jess had on the basic Anitran garb she'd worn out to the field of battle. At the boutique they'd clothe themselves as inconspicuously as possible, get the things they needed for the club, spend the day in town then don the club garb and execute their mission.

Jess remained nervous about much of it, but she had to admit she was a little excited about spending a day in Spain with Zac. Though she'd been to another world, flown on a starship and otherwise traveled beyond the experience of any other person on Earth, there was yet something romantic and quite appealing about hanging out in Europe with the boy she loved.

The small group stood looking at each other.

This is it.

Satori and Willet had gone through a battery of drills with Nani leading up to now, and even when Nani thought they were done Satori demanded more, practicing simulated flights of the fighter until Jess wondered if she was just doing it to keep her mind off the impending thing they were about to do. The upshot, however, was that she now knew the Kel fighter inside and out.

"All right," she said, and for an odd moment, as Jess looked at her and her bright red hair, she found herself wondering what kinds of hair dye they had on Anitra. *Better than any on Earth, that's for sure.* Even Satori's roots were still the same flaming copper-red they were way back when they went to deliver the Icon to Zac in the field fighting Kang. "Everyone double-check. Make sure we're ready to drop."

Jess was actually glad for her thorough preparations. Satori's experience as a military commander—and Willet's— would be huge on this mission. The two of them would get the fighter safely to the ground, then back to orbit once Jess and Zac accomplished their objective. They would also be on hand if anything went wrong.

Jess made a show of checking over the few items she would bring. Zac carried nothing extra. Satori and Nani had stowed what they thought would be needed aboard the fighter.

Only part of the craft was visible in the hold. Like boarding an airplane, you could see the skin of its hull around the door and a little bit of the nose; more shiny, gloss-black metal with a few of the violet Kel markings, but otherwise the rest was hidden, nestled into its recessed hold aboard the *Reaver*. Around a corner on the other side, out of sight, was the second craft. The *Reaver* had two, for escort or to deploy for special operations, extra defense or attack, etc. The fighters were about the size of a bus, sleek, and sported large powerplants, proportionately overpowered guns and an array of fighting electronics. The small craft were designed primarily with that purpose in mind—fighting—but there was room aboard for a small contingent of warriors.

"Well then," Satori deemed them ready. "Let's get going."

And, to Jessica's surprise, Bianca teared up. They weren't leaving for long, but the circumstances of the moment were, suddenly, overwhelming. Jess couldn't blame her. As hard as they'd worked each second to hold it together in the face of all that had happened, not to mention the hopelessness of their future as a continuation of the lives they once knew ... it was a wonder they weren't both permanently curled up in a ball on the floor weeping. And so, after just having engaged in such a ridiculous session of goofiness, "learning" Spanish, Bianca was suddenly serious and looking sad.

"I'll be fine," Jess assured her. "Zac will take care of me."

"I know." Bianca sniffed. Then she turned to Zac: "You better."

"I will."

Bianca smiled through the welling tears. She looked to Jess. "Guess you'll kind of get to go to prom after all. The club is like a dance. You can pretend it's prom."

Jess gave her a long hug.

She loved her friend.

Without further ado Satori stepped through the hatch, followed by Willet, Zac and, slowly, Jessica. They each filed in and Satori went to the controls, arming systems and wasting no time as the heavy door began notching closed. From inside the fighter Jess waved to Bianca and, just as her friend started crying openly—*Whunk*, the door locked into place.

They were now solidly aboard.

"Will we heat up on entry?" Jess asked. Not that she cared, or that Nani wouldn't already have it figured it out, but all at once she needed to speak, to turn her mind from the panic suddenly closing in. It was the same as when the door first closed on the *Reaver*, all that time ago. By now she was used to being aboard the *Reaver*, but here she was being locked inside an even smaller tin can and it was freaking her out. Just a little.

"Heat up?" Satori was bringing up more systems,

prepping for flight. Zac took a seat and motioned Jess over beside him. Jess looked around nervously. The interior of the fighter was more of the Kel design, a smaller version of the black surfaces and purple neon trace lighting of the mother craft.

Forcing herself to move she went over and sat by him. "When we go through re-entry," she explained for Satori. "If we heat up and make flames it will make us visible."

Satori continued the launch process. "We're not doing a ballistic entry," she said. "This will be a controlled descent with maximum countermeasures. There won't be any heating." She pointed out a few things to Willet at the co-pilot position beside her, then, before Jess could ask any more said:

"Here we go."

Jess braced herself; took hold of Zac's hand and ... the fighter slid from its notched recess and away from the *Reaver*. No jarring, nothing abrupt. Totally smooth. As they separated the view screens popped and came alive, long screens on each side, just like windows, at the front and overhead. For a moment, in the face of the staggering view, all her fear melted away. Overhead the belly of the massive *Reaver* flew gently away, seeming to rise even as they fell. To the sides and below the horizon-spanning, hazy blue-white curve of Earth came into view. Their trajectory was so mild she was again impressed with the advancement of the Kel. Like the *Reaver* itself, the screens on the fighter were not actual windows but created the visual perception of clear glass. Almost as if the big, rectangular screens were actual holes in the hull.

Slowly they began to turn, continuing their drop. Jess watched Satori as she tapped controls and checked readings. Willet followed along, watching, ready to assist but clearly not needed. They maneuvered what seemed to be slowly but was likely quite fast, heading from the daylight side into the band of night. Jess looked back up and the *Reaver* was gone. They were angling down now, bit by bit, the continent of Europe coming into view. Soon she could make out the dark mass of the Iberian peninsula—

Spain—dotted with scattered concentrations of lights in the night. It was about 3 a.m. local, the best time for their approach, it had been decided, and as they drew ever closer she found and focused on the blob of city lights that was Madrid. Segovia was just to the northwest of that brilliant cluster.

After a few minutes of trying and failing to pick out details she had a thought and took out the small Kel tablet.

"I'm going to test the comm," she announced.

"Go right ahead." Satori was concentrating. This was her first real flight, unsimulated, and while Nani had assured her the simulations were exactly like the real thing it must no doubt feel very different to be at the helm of a few hundred tons of metal on a controlled fall miles above the ground. Everything right then was up to Satori. Their lives depended on her.

Of course, Jess imagined, the Kel technology was so advanced she couldn't believe the fighter would simply fall out of the sky. It wasn't like flying an old bi-plane. Satori would likely have to fly it into the ground on purpose. In fact if she got up and walked away from the controls Jess doubted it would crash. It would probably just hover or something.

She activated the tablet. It was, indeed, similar to the tablets and touch interactions she was used to on Earth. Eerily so. The interface came up. She tapped the 'call' button and a second later Bianca answered, face searching her out on the screen.

"Jessica?"

At first Jess thought to make a joke. To say something like, "No, it's your mom," or something of the sort—*Duh! Who else would it be?* —but stopped herself short.

It just wouldn't be funny.

"Thought I'd check this out," she said. "Can you see me? I see you perfect."

"Yeah, I see you."

"How's everything?"

"We're watching you. It's like watching a UFO from above or something. Creepy. Only this UFO is you. You're inside."

She almost teared up again but firmed her expression. The tracks of her tearfall from moments ago were still evident.

She sniffed. "Be careful down there, ok?"

"I will."

For a long moment they stared awkwardly at each other on the small screen.

Then Zac, sitting to Jessica's left, leaned over.

"Mis," he felt his way through the pronunciation, "pantalones?"

Bianca's expression broke. She giggled and Zac grinned. "Good, eh?"

"Perfect," she agreed.

Jess looked admiringly at him. Taken with his effort to lift their spirits.

"How does the rest go?" he asked. "Mis pantalones smell like cheese?"

"Mis pantalones huelen a queso."

"Got it," Zac nodded and repeated: "Mis pantalones huelen a queso."

"Good!"

He turned to Jess. "Do they?"

She shoved him. "Get out of here."

He allowed himself to be pushed, announcing as he leaned: "Mis cabeza huelen a queso!"

Evidently he'd been paying closer attention than she thought.

"Yes!" Bianca enthused from the small screen.

"See?" said Zac. "Mix and match. You see the way I did that?"

Jess shook her head.

"Queso pantalones!" he said. "Cheese pants!"

"That's not exactly the way—"

"Mis queso pantalones huelen a mis cabeza! My cheese pants smell like my head!" He looked at Jess directly, eyes wide and feigning great amazement with this new language skill.

Declared: "I am so ready for this."

She laughed and shoved him again. "Shut up."

"You two having fun?" Satori asked from the pilot's seat.

She sounded annoyed.

Jess looked down to Bianca on the tablet screen. "Call you later."

"Okay. Bye."

And they hung up.

She giggled a little more with Zac, under her breath, thoroughly enjoying the back and forth, then the terrain below had moved close enough to command their full attention. Dark, empty patches were visible, areas with no signs of habitation, some quite large, there in the foothills of the mountains. Satori brought up scanning and telemetry info which played across the screen, set to display in English. It was a recent feature Nani figured out in order to make the Kel technology easier to use: having the alien glyphs display in English letters with full translations. That action alone seemed to have turned the *Reaver* all at once into an advanced American starship, rather then a purely alien craft.

They headed lower, toward the area Nani picked, so far no need to make any changes, no need for correction. By the time they were directly overhead the lights of the closest civilization were far enough away that, in the final stages of their descent, Jess could only vaguely discern details that told her this or that light in the distance was a car, or a house, or a green or red traffic light and so on. Unless someone was on the ground camping near the vertical column down which they approached it was likely they went entirely unseen. Nani assured them the craft itself would not be picked up by any electronic means such as radar. There were no outside lights. And the only sound the fighter gave off was, apparently, little more than a low-frequency hum.

All that should add up to make them very difficult to spot. A true UFO, coming in invisibly.

In short order they'd landed in a remote clearing. A shudder gripped Jess as their descent stopped, Satori shut them down and the entire craft was silent.

She was back on Earth.

CHAPTER 24:

GEARING UP

IT WAS ANOTHER LATE NIGHT. No one had gotten much sleep since the Project team arrived in-country and set up. Drake looked around the room. A dozen agents at work, sleeves rolled up, screens flickering on tables and walls, remains of earlier tapas and empty espresso cups here and there. He held a fresh one firmly in both hands, savoring the warmth. Gently he blew across the porcelain rim, watching the steam waft off. He stood near the back of the small planning room, which was in fact the living room of a non-descript white-washed house at the edge of town, far out in the gypsy quarter, and even as he scanned the room his focus was far beyond it.

For what was, in essence, such a simple operation, the planning and intelligence being brought to bear in that small house was incredible. They were there, in Spain, completely under the radar, no local awareness whatsoever. This could not, would not become an international incident. No foreign power, Spanish or otherwise, was involved in any way. What they were about to do was completely clandestine. Only their best and brightest were involved; there would be no other intervention if things fell apart. This was about to be a big, potentially noisy incident right there on Spanish soil.

And they were on their own.

His right-hand man, Bobby, sat nearby, clicking through images on a laptop. Looked up. "I think that one will work," he said, confirming a decision they'd been trying to make.

"Good," Drake took a sip of the strong Spanish coffee. *Good stuff.*

He projected his voice to the room: "All right," he said. "This is it. Tomorrow we catch our rabbit."

* * *

JESS LOOKED AHEAD through the trees, to the lights of Segovia just beyond the concealing darkness. It was going on four in the morning and they'd arrived near their first objective. Earlier Zac ran them in from the landed fighter, getting them from that remote location to here, close to the edge of town. During that brief sprint she once again thrilled to be in his arms, pressed against his bare chest, wind howling across her ears as he carried her over hilly terrain, up and down gullies, through the woods and across fields beneath the moonlight, the whole experience an absolute rush.

She tingled in fresh memory of it.

He stood beside her now as they held short, still within the depths of the woods, allowing him time to see what he could, or hear any dangers that might be waiting, or otherwise perceive the status of the area where they were headed.

To her the town looked totally asleep.

Around her the night air was crisp, spring chilly there in the Spanish foothills. Adrenaline at the thought of what they were about to do was making her heart race, her skin flush with heat; such that when the memory of being carried by Zac passed through her it was amplified to a shiver. Her life, it seemed, had become one big rollercoaster of emotion. Maybe that's what being on the run was all about. Others had called her a hero. She could only think of herself as desperate. And desperation, she'd discovered, brought with it the most extreme emotions. Happiness. Fear. As she stood there, worrying of what was to come, processing the fact that she was back on Earth, standing on it—*I'm standing on Earth*—the steady, low-level nerves had her guts in knots. She was certain she must be growing an ulcer.

She took out the Kel tablet. So far Zac had spotted no danger. Unlikely, of course, hours before sunrise in a friendly Spanish town, but they were preparing for everything. Not even police had been seen. Jess checked aerial views on the tablet thru the *Reaver's* optics; tapped other information, marking their destination on the screen, determining distance and best approach. Between that and Zac's own super-senses they shouldn't be surprised by anything.

"Looks good here," she said. "Look good to you?"

He sniffed the air. Concerned.

"What is it?"

"I smell something."

She tried to imagine what he could possibly smell, anything that could be identified as dangerous merely from its scent. That was, however, the advantage of Zac. He could sense things.

"Cheese pants," he said, very seriously. "I smell cheese pants."

It took her a second, but only a second, to smack him. He wasn't giving that a rest.

"Would you stop already?"

He grinned and she couldn't help smiling—despite a supreme effort not to. And the thought sprang to mind that Zac could indeed smell stinky pants, stinky anything with his greatly attuned senses, and she had to shove aside the embarrassing idea that she herself might stink, in some way; the same desperate worry she got every time she thought of his extreme abilities.

What if her pants *did* smell like cheese?

God!

It was tough having a super boyfriend.

She accelerated the moment. "Ready?"

"Ready," he took her hand and gave it a squeeze. Gentle, infinite power behind it. A large, warm, strong hand, attached to a strong arm, a strong shoulder, a wonderful, handsome boy who would—and could—protect her to the ends of the Earth.

She smiled up at him in the moonlight.

It was also *awesome* having a super boyfriend.

Together they picked their way to the edge of the woods, hand in hand, pausing just inside the enveloping shadows to gaze out into the lighted areas beyond. The buildings on this side of town were built one against the next, small one- and two-floor shops and houses, rambling along narrow sidewalks and cobblestone streets, none of which seemed to go in an exact straight line. Meandering, everything, street signs stuck to the walls.

As they paused Zac seemed to be thinking. She wondered if he was about to crack another joke.

"What's a prom?" he asked.

The question was unexpected, but the answer came readily. "It's a school dance. Usually happens around this time of year. Bianca is missing it. I think it's been on her mind."

"You're missing it too?"

She was, of course. "Yeah."

"Well, maybe we can have a little fun. It won't be the same, I know, but let's see if we can make this special."

She squeezed his hand. Her life had become defined by these moments. There was no more steady-state. No more routine. One minute she could be fighting for her life, the next enjoying a moment like this. And so she was learning more and more to be *in* the moment. To deal with what was in front of her. Right now they were in Segovia, about to have a day of touring the sights, much later that night it was the club and a few moments of normalcy before the action began.

She tried to relish it.

"Remember we're from America," she said, looking out at the city beyond. "Idaho. It's the easiest cover." Nani had managed to fabricate something that resembled American passports, but Jess hoped they didn't have to show them. If it came to that, if they actually had to produce the fake IDs—whether they passed scrutiny or not … they were already in trouble. Her goal was to remain as inconspicuous as possible.

"You know where we're going?" asked Zac.

She checked the tablet, peered across to the corner they would turn down, matched the street she was seeing live to the images on the screen, committed it to memory and put the tablet in its temp satchel. Where they needed to go was down at the next corner and a few blocks in; the small boutique Nani and Bianca had researched and determined was the best place for them to get the things they'd need for the club, and for the day there in Spain. The store was small and Nani could kill the alarm, which meant they should be able to break in discreetly. Jessica's Anitran clothes looked almost institutional and Zac, with no shirt and the ripped Kazerai pants, looked like he was rolling in from a brawl or an all-night bender. It wasn't as if they wore costumes, but neither did they look exactly like the touring American teens they would claim to be.

"Yeah," she said. "Let's get there as quickly as we can."

They looked at each other. Again she squeezed his hand.

"Let's go." And he led her from the woods.

She felt at once liberated and ... naked, walking into the lights, stepping at last onto the sidewalk then the cobblestone street and heading into the quiet town. Their footsteps echoed on the hard surfaces; too loud, it seemed, and the barred windows up and down the narrow street were so close she wondered how many sleeping people they might wake. She knew Spain was notorious for its late-night revelry. The people in those houses were no doubt used to people coming home in the wee hours, walking right by their windows, but it was still nerve-wracking. Everything seemed louder than it probably was.

As if in response to her own thoughts, up ahead at the corner a trio of drunken boys staggered into view. They'd been talking in low voices but apparently Zac heard them in advance. Their appearance made her jump.

"Pretend we're drunk," she said and altered her gait. He put his arm across her shoulder, leaned on her a little and pulled her to his side. She followed suit, putting an arm around his waist and starting to weave.

The boys came their way, not because they saw them or expected a challenge, but probably because that was the way they were headed. In fact, it was only after they'd drawn a little closer that they even noticed Jess and Zac at all.

"Buenas," one of them mumbled, a polite greeting

that had no need of any response. Jess was relieved this would be no more than a simple passing in the night. She pretended to be even more inebriated, almost to the point she barely saw them, and simply nodded her head against Zac's side.

"Hi," he said as they kept walking. His voice made her jump and she squeezed him to be quiet. She didn't look back to see if the boys turned. From the sounds of their shuffling footsteps they didn't; just kept walking, and if they had any question of Zac's greeting they said nothing.

When they were out of earshot she whispered up to him, "Don't speak unless we have to."

"Got it," he said. "Sorry."

"Don't be sorry," she felt bad for correcting him, even for such a minor thing. "It's no big deal." They reached the corner and she thought to drop the drunken ruse, but it felt nice squeezing up against him, the feel of his warm, bare skin, and so she maintained it. He made no suggestion they do otherwise and they went along quietly, walking with his arm around her shoulder, hers around his waist, holding each other close.

Soon they were in sight of the boutique.

"There it is," she said softly. The town was deathly quiet. No more people out and about. Any bars or clubs still open must be further away. The club they were going to later that night was on the other side of town, far out on the outskirts.

"Bee-a-u mond-eh," Zac tried to read the stylishly scripted sign over the door of the boutique.

"Beau Monde," said Jess. "Beautiful World."

"Spanish?"

"French."

"French?"

"Another country, another language."

"This world is so interesting."

A few more casual steps and they were standing at the front door. Clothes displays were in the window, more inside in the darkness, everything covered with heavy bars.

"We should get in quickly," she said. "I don't want to

get caught standing out here in front of it." Anxiously she looked up and down the street. There were dark corners in all directions. Someone could come around one at any moment.

"Push it in?" asked Zac. He stepped to the door and was looking it over. There were a pair of heavy deadbolts, plus the knob. Jess didn't really want to "break" anything, but they had to get in. Sure Zac could smash down the door, bend the bars, knock in a window—hell, he could walk right through the wall. But she wanted to leave no mark.

Or as little as possible.

She came closer and looked over the locks. "Those," she pointed to the deadbolts. "If we keep the door on the hinges we can at least close it and make it look normal while we're inside."

Zac placed his palms experimentally on a few flat surfaces.

"Be careful—"

He pushed in the door. Ever so gently yet ... *Pow!Pow!* the deadbolts ruptured with a frighteningly loud double crack that echoed down the street. Jess cringed, then noticed the door was, as desired, totally intact. Just little notches broken out where the knob and bolts had been. It creaked inward on its hinges and she could see if they closed it back there would little evidence of forced entry.

Her breathing settled, and as she replayed the sharp sounds in her mind she realized the pops were brief and probably not as attention-grabbing as she thought.

"After you," Zac held out a hand. She entered the darkened store and he followed.

Across the threshold he turned and closed the door behind. It fit nicely back into the frame and looked totally closed and normal, even up close. Jess was impressed. No one outside should notice.

She turned her attention to the interior of the small boutique. Light from the street cast deep shadows across racks of displays, distorting shapes, making the fancy mannequins look ghoulish. For an instant it was creepy, a little scary, and she shook off those initial, childish reactions.

"What do we need?" Zac asked. She looked back at him, standing tall behind her—*so tall!*—street lights shining around him from behind, defining his muscled silhouette.

And suddenly new fears took hold. Practical fears. That they wouldn't find anything to fit him.

"How tall are you?" she asked, as if realizing his size for the first time. *Damn!* She shook her head. Zac didn't know how tall he was. Taller than most Spanish men, she was sure. Taller than most men period. Not only would it be hard to find him something, but he was going to stand out like a sore thumb. Of course she'd realized that but it was hitting home right then. He looked so big standing there in the small, dark foyer of the little boutique.

Hopefully Nani would've thought of that.

Anxiously she stepped over to a rack and began flipping through a bunch of men's jackets, finding none that were even close enough to check.

She needed to talk to Bianca.

Fumbling a little she reached in the satchel and took out the tablet, thumbed it and dialed her up. Her friend's image came on.

"Are you at the store?" Bianca asked at once.

"Yeah."

"Good. Your fashion consultant is standing by." She smiled, both eager and excited.

"I'm worried about Zac," Jess spoke to the screen as she went over to another rack and began looking. "This isn't a big place. The stuff in here is nice, but there isn't a lot." She glanced at Zac, who remained standing near the door. "This isn't Big and Tall. Not a lot of stuff for guys his size." It occurred to her this was the second time she was dressing Zac, with a little help from her friend.

Like we're playing with dolls.

On the tablet screen Nani came into view behind Bianca. "I thought of that," she said, confirming Jessica's hope. "I picked this place because they have some items in inventory that should fit. I tried to pick the best possible place that would cover it."

"What do they have?"

Nani and Bianca proceeded to talk her through finding the items she would need. After a little looking Nani was right; there was stuff hidden in there. They did Zac first, managing to find among the selections two full outfits. Jess talked to the girls on the tablet, alternating between holding it so they could see the clothes and shining the light of its screen so she herself could see. Bianca instructed her on what to try then viewed it on Zac. Jess didn't dare turn on any lights in the shop but their system worked. For the day in the city they found him a cool pair of jeans, a nice V-neck T-shirt that looked great on him (he almost looked as amazing in the shirt as out of it), and an even cooler Italian leather jacket with shiny zippers. When they were talking about the jacket Zac was fascinated that here was yet another nationality with a different style and language. They were in a French-named store, in Spain, picking out an Italian jacket. Jess couldn't tell if he was laughing with them or at them at that point.

To go with it they got him a really nice watch, a fat chrome Breitling that looked great on his wrist—Bianca insisted he needed one, that it was the only real accessory for a guy and super important—then there was a scary moment with shoes, but after a few tense failures they got a pair of nice leather boots that fit, which Bianca agreed would work for both the daytime outfit and the one for the club.

And the club outfit ... When Zac had it on and was modeling Jess felt the urge—actually felt an impulse she had to control—to grab him right there. Say goodbye to the girls, turn off the Kel tablet and take him to the ground. It was a suit and vest combo and it was absolutely gorgeous. Again an Italian job, just the right shine, perfect cut (good, because they had no tailor), and he filled it out like a stud. Even Nani was speechless, and for some reason Jess found it amusing, more than anything, to watch the reaction of the geeky scientist, peering over Bianca's shoulder on the small screen as she held the tablet on Zac so both could see.

Once they'd done Zac he went back to the front and took

up a sort of guard, mostly just sitting and waiting, and Jess got down to business. Or, rather, Bianca got down to business. Jess could see the enthusiasm in her eyes as her friend walked her through item after item, trying this or that combination, giving the advice she so desperately loved, crafting her "Project Jessica" into a club goddess. The key was the dress, of course, and unlike Zac there were many options in the boutique to choose from. Jess was the perfect size for all the awesome, skimpy outfits. They went through so many she began to get short with her friend, hurrying her along as daybreak was coming, and when Bianca finally decided with great zeal on what, to Jess, was the simplest, smallest black dress in there she threw up her hands. "All that for this?" But Bianca loved it. Nani, too, approved, and even Zac came over from the shadows to see what all the commotion was about. "Nice," he said, eyeing Jess as she stood there in the simple, little black dress, feeling silly.

From there Bianca turned to shoes, settling on what, Jess had to agree, were a very sexy pair of heels. She was almost embarrassed to put them on and walk around. Next was polish for her nails, makeup, a very few, very key pieces of jewelry—the selection process of which was also painfully slow—but she had to agree these were important details. They were trying to look as hip as possible, as worthy, and everything they were there on Earth for, their entire objective, depended on this. Everything depended on them getting into the club. After doing so many things up to that point by brute force or direct action it felt strange to be gearing up to be sneaky in plain sight. But it was the only way to keep eyes on their target. Jess could tell Bianca felt a huge sense of importance at her contribution to this part of the mission. It would be thanks to Bianca that they looked the part. Which meant it would be thanks to Bianca that they even got into the club at all, meaning Bianca's decisions here could make or break the whole thing.

For her daytime outfit Jess got jeans, a colorful pair of sneaks and her own leather jacket. Short-waisted, black like Zac's and super-hip girly tough. She put those items on as they picked them and left them on, preparing for the day ahead. Zac also got into his jeans and T-shirt.

Finally Jess got a stylish purse in which to put the tablet, then a large leather backpack for the club clothes they'd have to carry during their jaunt around the city that day. She rolled everything up carefully, neatly, and put it in the bag so as not to wrinkle, Zac's jacket and slacks especially, then stuffed in their Anitran clothes, intending to dispose of those later.

At last she was done. Nani informed her the sun would be up in an hour and that the store opened a few hours after that, but that Jess might want to be gone before then so they could leave the store before others saw. Jess signed off and went up front to find Zac. He'd been walking around and was now standing at one of the counters, in his jeans, boots, V-neck Tee and leather jacket, looking drop-dead amazing, preoccupied with something. As Jess walked up she saw what, waving a hand through a misty cloud of competing scents. He'd gotten into the perfumes. She coughed a little. It was like the smell of an entire department store compressed into one small area.

"Smell this," he beckoned. He seemed to be thoroughly enjoying himself. She set the purse and leather bag on the counter, noticing he had out nearly every bottle of perfume and cologne.

"They all smell so good," he said. It was like he couldn't believe it. She wondered what effect the mixtures of musk-ox sweat, mink glands and everything else that went into a modern designer scent had on his heightened sense of smell. Apparently it was extreme. He was completely infatuated.

"No perfume on Anitra?" she asked, taken by his enthusiasm.

He shook his head slowly, caught up in the next scent he'd just sprayed liberally into the air. "We have stuff," he said. He held up a cute, little pink bottle. "This is my favorite. Should I wear it?"

She laughed. "That's for girls."

"I know," he said, as if to suggest he wasn't so dumb as to think it was a fragrance for a guy. *Of course it's for girls!* "But doesn't that mean guys are supposed to wear it? For girls to smell?" Then, when she couldn't stop grinning he looked a little annoyed: "What then? How does it work?"

Impulsively she reached and put a hand to his cheek. The whole area reeked, many of the scents already on him. He'd been spritzing with abandon. She laughed again.

"Girls wear the girl stuff, guys wear the guy stuff."

"Oh," he said, then extended the pink bottle to her. "Can you wear it?"

She took it with a friendly wink, sprayed a bit on her wrists, rubbed them together then lifted her chin and dabbed her wrists gently on her neck. He looked at her inquiringly and she explained: "You don't need much."

He leaned in close and sniffed. A gentle sniff and she tingled—then shuddered as he sniffed closer. The combination of chemical pheromones thickening the air and his very sensual proximity, sniffing her neck so close, nearly touching her tender skin ... was all at once too much.

He breathed deeply of the aroma.

She put down the pink bottle, diverting the suddenly arousing situation. "We should get one for you," she said. Pretending to evaluate them she slid around a couple of the colognes, lifted and sampled a few.

"This one," she decided. He took the bottle she handed him and sniffed it. Then, quite seriously, sprayed a little on each wrist, rubbed them together, craned his jaw forward—just as she had—and ... dabbed his wrists gently on his neck.

She giggled.

"What?" he was genuinely confused.

She made herself stop giggling but couldn't wipe the amused expression from her face. "Guys don't do it like that," she informed him.

He frowned. "How do they do it? Why do they do it different?"

"It's fine," she touched his cheek, again. "You're fine. You're totally fine."

DAVID G MCDANIEL

"Don't let me make too many mistakes, ok?"

"You won't. You're fine."

And for a moment she was smitten, looking up into his bright blue eyes, brilliant in the shadows as they reflected the light outside the store. So precious her tall, unstoppable boyfriend.

She turned to other topics. "We need money," she said. "Check that," she pointed to the register. "There's got to be some Euros in there." Zac cracked it easily, but inside was empty. This worried her, as there was no way they'd make it through this without real money. She didn't want to have to break in and rob another store. Then she noticed a small safe under the counter, below the register.

Could Zac open a safe? Safes were designed to be impregnable; super-thick iron hinges, thick sides and doors—even a small one like this—but her concerns were quickly put to rest. Under her direction Zac gripped the hinges to try and ... *peeled* them away. She couldn't believe it. It was a strain, and was perhaps the first time she'd ever seen him exert real effort, but the fact that he could even do it at all was unbelievable. She could not *imagine* the force it took to peel away that much iron—and so tight against the other part. He was only able to get his fingertips on it, only able to pinch it at the very tips, but away it came. The dull, floor-shuddering vibration the metal made as it groaned in protest—even as he pulled it apart—was testament to the huge power involved.

Zac was like a force of nature.

Inside was cash. They took what she thought they'd need, leaving the rest, her objective not to gain from this, only to get what they needed to complete the mission.

And that raised another small concern, at least when it came to their equipping for the event. In order to get into the club she and Zac—especially her—had to dress incredibly impractical for such an operation. The little black dress and high heels would be a huge hindrance. The idea, of course, was that Zac would take care of it all when the moment came, and that made perfect sense. In fact, looking the part was *all* she was needed for. Zac would capture Lorenzo. Zac would fight their way out of the club. Zac would contain Lorenzo and protect her and get them to safety, then it was over to Satori and Willet. Of course she'd be a huge part of the direction and tactics of this little op, live on the scene, but when you boiled it down her major role was to act as cover for getting Zac in. Eye candy, in a sense, dolled up like some wanna-be club princess. It was an odd feeling to be preparing for that as never in her life had she been anywhere just for looks, but it made her a little nervous at how impractical it would all be. These clothes would be horrible choices if she actually *did* have to do anything.

She finished stuffing the Euros into her purse.

"You wanna get some rest?" Zac asked. "We've got about an hour."

Part of her wanted to get moving, but there might not be many opportunities during the day. There was a nice couch over by the dressing rooms.

"That's a good idea," she agreed. Zac didn't need sleep. An hour might do her good.

She lay down and he sat beside her a moment. Kissed her on the forehead and pushed back her hair.

She looked up into his face, the stubble of his chin prominent in the shadows, like the beginning of a real beard.

"I'll get you up in an hour." He lingered a moment more, hand in her hair, then got up and went back to the front. She lay there in the darkness and quiet of the Spanish boutique, looking at some of the half-mannequins nearby. Wondering how long it would take her to fall asleep.

Soon she was dreaming.

CHAPTER 25:

A DAY IN THE REAL WORLD

BOOM! ANOTHER EXPLOSION ROCKED the metal floor. Jess kept her balance and continued across the room to the archaic wooden door, the one she remembered—a door which was entirely out of place against the riveted green-iron surfaces of the room. Beside the door was a sleek, high-tech access panel, equally anachronistic.

The same memory, she reeled as the absolute reality of the scene overwhelmed her as before, artificial though she knew it to be. Sensations were too strong, too detailed. It was like *being* there.

Carefully she played it through.

There were no windows. Diffuse light came from the same unknown source. The door before her was covered in the complicated runes that, despite their alien curves, looked strangely familiar. She felt she could very nearly read them. The same battle as before took place outside, rocking the walls, pulsing blasts that throbbed with each hit. Another and she steadied herself.

All was as it had been.

Looking down she saw she was dressed in the same armor, in one hand the long, curved sword of blued steel. She studied her hands more closely. Were they even human? Nearly too perfect, too exquisitely formed; pure, unblemished skin, not a freckle or other mark to be seen. She took a big pull of the acrid air. Tactile feedback, the wall beneath her palm, the armor against her skin ... all of it too real.

The panel.

She turned to it as the battle outside continued to intensify. The vibrant edge to the dream remained.

"This way!" a male voice shouted from across the room. She whirled as he called out: "I'm not leaving you!"

Standing there was a man she recognized. She gasped. *I know you!*

Tall, pale, an almost elven face, complete with pointed ears and sharp, angular features; shock-white hair pulled tight into a ponytail that swung high from the back of his head.

Kel.

Perfection he was, a nearly androgynous handsomeness that caused her breath to catch in her throat.

"Come!" He held out a hand. He wore the same style armor as her; black, slightly ribbed, alien. "I'm not leaving you!" His eyes were bright yellow, intense in their demand. She knew this man, wanted to trust him. Wanted to go with him. Only ...

There was something else. Something else needed to be done.

As before the panic came, surging, and she struggled to manage it. For a terrifying instant she remained locked in that other reality, the Kel warrior calling to her, voice distant. Then ...

Another.

"We've got to leave," the new voice said, far more calm than the last. Beckoning her awake.

She sat with a gasp.

It was Zac.

"Easy," he said. "You were having a dream."

He helped ease her to the edge of the couch, gently putting her legs over. He'd been kneeling, hand on her shoulder as he tried to rouse her.

"It's almost morning," he said.

She shook feeling back into her head; rubbed her face. More vigorously. The intensity of the dream kept getting worse.

She looked over her shoulder, out the barred windows to the narrow street. Lamps were still on, though their illumination was fading in the gray-light of the approaching sun.

Time to get back to reality.

* * *

"Looks like they're leaving the store," Bianca studied the street map on the monitor screen. She watched as the blip for the tablet moved away from the boutique, locking their location clearly on the ground. Using the tablet coordinates she could zoom in pretty tight with the Kel optics and, if she scanned the street view closely, could just make out the top of Jess and Zac's head, moving carefully and joining other, slowly gathering pedestrians as the city began to wake. Without the tablet to guide her it was tough to keep them in focus, but with it telling her where to look she could see them in real-time, making their way through the narrow streets. She watched a while, then, as they stopped at some little café, tables just now being set up on the sidewalk—probably to grab some breakfast—she began feeling a little too voyeuristic and decided to turn it off.

"I could go for some waffles," she said absently and put a hand to her belly. The Kel "food" aboard the *Reaver* was enough and she felt fine, no hunger, but her taste buds were in revolt.

"Waffles?" Nani, as always, was busy looking at screens and studying tons of information. It was practically all she did.

Bianca remembered their brief night in the small club back on Anitra; how Nani had actually been fun to hang with. Almost night and day with the present, typical, scientific Nani.

"Yeah, waffles. They're usually for breakfast. Round, though sometimes square. Made of batter, which I'm not sure what *that's* made of. You put stuff on them, usually syrup and butter." She closed her eyes and made a yum sound, licking her lips.

"Sounds tasty," Nani agreed.

"Oh, it is. I want one so bad. I know Jess has the dangerous part of this, but in a way I'm jealous she's down there getting to eat real food."

"You think she's getting waffles?"

Bianca considered it. "Don't know if Spain does waffles.

STAR ANGEL: DAWN OF WAR

But whatever she gets it will be better than what we're eating."

She expected Nani to defend the Kel food, but instead the blonde scientist actually took a moment to look wistful. "I know," she said. "I could go for something with flavor too."

"I'll make you a deal," Bianca came closer and sat by her. "We get through this, we get this all sorted out, and I'll get you some of the best food Earth has to offer."

"Waffles?"

"Yes. Definitely. Waffles."

Nani smiled, and Bianca could see she was excited to see that day.

Bianca was too.

* * *

DAYBREAK BROUGHT WITH IT a beautiful, crisp, spring day. It was absolutely gorgeous. Jess sat across from Zac at a little ironwork table covered with a heavily starched, gleaming white tablecloth, watching as the small wait staff set up for the day. People were beginning to move on the sidewalks, cars in the street. She and Zac each had coffees—café con leches—and were looking over small menus printed in Spanish, waiting on their waitress to return. The dream was still vivid in her mind, the fear of the new day and the challenges they would face later that night, the fear of all she'd done to get herself there, of being back on Earth where she could be found, all the troubles of her life weighing on her but, as the sun found its way onto the white-washed walls of the buildings across the street, illuminating the quaint beauty of the rambling Spanish town—pretty red and white flowers brilliant in a window box, the smells of the café behind her, the sounds and life of a new day ... as the warm, delicious coffee coursed through her and she looked at Zac and he in turn admired this new world ... as these things overtook her the gloom and the fear receded and she began to feel human again. And, in short order, experienced her first joy of the day. She was in Spain, with

Zac, and they were about to have a wonderful time.

The waitress returned. Jess was able to communicate the basics and, with a mix of excitement and enthusiasm from Zac—he was so dying to try the chocolate croissants—they managed to get in their order, the waitress left and when she was gone Zac asked:

"What's that?" he pointed over her shoulder.

She turned and followed his finger, to a poster on the wall a few doors down.

"A poster for bull-fighting." She lingered, trying to read some of the Spanish words.

"How does the guy fight it?" Zac asked. "Aren't bulls way bigger than a man? The picture makes it look like he's waving a cape at it."

"He is. They don't actually fight the bull. It's kind of a dance. As the "fight" goes on they stick pikes in the bull to make it weaker, and to show that they can, I guess. It's all for show.

"At the end the guy, he's called a matador, drives a sword through it and kills it."

She turned back to Zac. "I think it's supposed to prove the manliness of the matador or something. The Spanish like their bulls. They run with them too."

"Run with them?"

"Another tradition."

Zac looked around at the buildings, the people, the cobblestone streets and sidewalk. "There's so much history here," he seemed to marvel. "Our Emperor came from here. He told us this was Heaven, with no other details, but now that I see it … it's just another world like ours. More than ours. Everything is so rich, so alive."

Jess took another sip of the café con leche, savoring the smooth, milky warmth. It felt so good coursing through her, bringing with it a gentle buzz of delight. She sighed.

Zac looked incredibly perfect sitting there in his black leather jacket with his dark hair. An absolute hunk, frankly. She felt pretty cool in her jacket too. Kind of Euro suave. He stared at the poster, lost in deeper thoughts, and she followed his gaze back and looked more closely at the bold colors. The rough lines of the original painting made it look like it was painted using a putty knife.

"It's interesting," Zac drew her attention back to him. "We have a similar animal on Anitra. Different, but not too much. Horns and everything. We also call it a bull, thanks to the Emperor. It seems the Emperor brought most of the language when he came. It's almost like we're from the same place."

"It would be cool to know more about the Emperor's history," Jess agreed. "Who he was here on Earth. It's like he was Japanese or something, but he must've been American. He must've found the Icon in olden-day Boise. Obviously, since it's the one that goes between Boise and Osaka."

"Japanese?"

She shook her head. "Another—"

"Another nationality."

Jess nodded. "It's curious he chose to bring English to Anitra and insist on that as the main language. He brought Japanese names, culture."

The waitress returned with their food. Jess watched as she placed the plates and glasses of juice—too many plates for Zac—thanking her as she did, using her best "Gracias" though the waitress already knew they were tourists. Zac got four plates of croissants and, while he was big and young and could obviously eat, the waitress eyed him with a dubious stare.

"El tiene mucho hambre," Jess practiced, satisfied that she'd communicated the idea Zac was hungry. The waitress smiled, asked them if they wanted more coffee, to which both said "Si", and off she went.

Zac lifted a croissant and smelled it eagerly. "These made me think of the donuts you brought me in the playhouse," he said. "I hope they're as good." And he took a big bite, chewed once and ...

Closed his eyes in absolute rapture.

"Mmm." He chewed more, savoring it.

"Is it good?" she asked needlessly.

"So good," he mumbled around a full mouth. "This is

my new favorite thing."

She watched as he finished and swallowed, two more big bites and the whole rest of the croissant was gone. He placed both hands on the table as the last of it went down, inhaling the ecstasy of its delicious passage.

"Do you even need to eat?" she asked as he reached for another.

"Not really, no." He took a smaller bite, talking as he chewed. "But I like to when there's good food. Or to be polite. They never fully understood us. The Kazerai were an accident, a kind of mad scientist thing where they kept trying to make enhancements to their super soldiers, the Astake. The Astake were the base, and they were already stronger than a normal man, through chemicals and other tricks." He took a drink of juice, another bite, finished the second croissant and picked up a third. Jess took the first bite of her own.

It was, indeed, delicious. Of course, it was a fresh, warm, flaky croissant filled with exquisite chocolate. How could it not be?

"They don't know where we get our strength. We convert energy from somewhere. Dominion—and Venatres— scientists have speculated on the source, like zero-point solutions or some other tap into spatially stored forces. Perhaps locked up in the engines of our cells." Jess found it fascinating to hear him talk technical. "There's energy in everything," he said as he chewed. Talking and chewing on some people was not so attractive. When Zac did it she couldn't stop staring. Especially as animated as he'd become. There was a certain power to his devouring of the food, backed by the very real power of his form. A mouthful of food and grinding jaws on others? Not so attractive. On him it was ... well, it was sexy. "I mean," he held up the last bite of croissant as an example of his point, "if you could convert this to pure energy it would blow up this whole block. Probably the whole town."

She nodded. "E equals M C squared."

He paused. "Is that an energy formula?"

"Yeah." The elements of the formula would be universal,

but Zac would never have heard it expressed that way.

"Anyway, converting a croissant to energy is just atomic forces bound up in matter. How the Kazerai work is different. The Dominion and especially the Venatres scientists have speculated on something else. The idea is that there could be still other energies locked in space itself, vacuum energy—you name it.

"So, no, we don't convert food to energy. We're powered and on all the time. No need for oxygen, food, nothing.

"*But*," he said, "everything still works the same—again, no explanation for how *that* is but I'm not complaining—and my taste buds are going into overdrive on these things."

She watched him eat with gusto, so happy to be there with him. He had a stack of croissants, only croissants. She had a single croissant, but also got eggs and ham; not quite as exciting but, unlike him, she *did* need food, and protein and fat would take her much further than sugar. They had a long day ahead.

The waitress came with their second coffees. When she was gone Jess took a sip of the fresh, hot new one. It tasted so good! Steam came from it in the cool morning air, the day perfectly brisk. Sipping the hot coffee, out on the romantic Spanish street under a deep, clear, morning sky, sitting at the intimate little café, was absolute heaven. Zac continued to plow through the croissants, leaving her time to sit and just *be*. Pedestrian traffic picked up as the morning got into swing, little European cars and delivery trucks passing in increasing volume in the street.

Wonderful.

A group of teens caught her eye. Three girls and two boys, probably her age or not much older. She watched them approach on the sidewalk, coming closer; themselves tourists but not Americans. From their clothes and their style she thought them to be German, or maybe Scandinavian, and as they got close enough to overhear she determined they were in fact German.

Soon their laughing conversation, for Jess, was dominant among the other sounds. They gathered just over Zac's shoulder, behind him on the sidewalk, looking at their phones, pointing and trying to make a decision. Being goofy among themselves. Zac was oblivious to their proximity, blending as they did into the background and conversations all around. The morning street was alive with new activity. But Jess couldn't stop staring.

Couldn't stop thinking how much they weren't like her.

She *should* be like them. Not an interloper. A stranger in her own world. She should be *just* like them. A teenager, carefree, out seeing new places, laughing and having fun, her whole life ahead of her. But she was nothing like them.

She held the fate of everything in her hands. And whether or not her whole life was ahead of her, or even what that life might hold ...

Sadness gripped her. Unwanted, unexpected sadness. The same sadness that was with her these days, ever ready to pounce, and she just wished the German teens would make a decision and go away. Go get on their next train or whatever. Eurail it out of there, hit the next hostel or the next fun stop.

She could never be part of that. Never, ever again. She would never again have a chance to be that carefree teenager with a pure, unspoiled view of the future.

"Wow," Zac brought her snapping back to the present. He'd finished all the croissants. "That was good."

She shook it off and took a bite of egg. The food was already cold in the morning air. Out of her peripheral vision the teens finally made up their minds and crossed the street, slipping through traffic with shouts in German and continued laughter.

Finally they were out of earshot and soon enough out of sight. Jess took a sip of coffee.

It, too, was cold.

"Where should we spend the day?" Zac smiled, oblivious to her heartache. He tilted his glass and finished his juice. Put down the empty. "We've got a whole day to kill."

"I don't know," Jess fought the bitterness. "But whatever we do let's make sure it's fun."

CHAPTER 26:

EVENING'S DAWN

BIANCA DRAGGED THE VIEW at her console and expanded it, pretty much the same way you'd adjust the image on any touchscreen from Earth. The alien Kel controls were easy to use once you knew what you were looking at. Nani had been a great teacher.

Bianca looked to her left.

"They're getting close," she said. She and Nani had been watching a group of hikers pick their way through the woods, getting closer and closer to the landed Kel fighter.

Nani nodded, caught up in the information at her own console. "Seems like they're finally looking for a place to set up camp?"

"Probably," Bianca looked back at her own screen. She and Nani were alone on the bridge—alone on the ship; everyone else down on the ground—and for a moment Bianca found it interesting how used to all this she'd become. Surrounded by alien technology, aboard an alien starship, looking out a crystal-clear video dome with the whole Earth spread out below, her home planet, outer space all around; tapping and directing the advanced monitoring systems to watch the activity on all screens ...

She had to remind herself how completely out-there it all was. Beyond *National Enquirer*. Way beyond. They were in control of some truly amazing stuff. Apparently the human animal could adapt to just about anything. Once you got used to it ... it just became normal. The way things were.

"They're still pretty far away." Nani had been in contact with Willet and Satori aboard the fighter, keeping them informed of the possible intruders as the hikers picked their way closer through the woods. The hikers were far from civilization and heading more or less directly for the landed Kel fighter. No one knew exactly how to handle a discovery, if the small group continued and actually found the Kel craft, but so far everyone was just hoping they would stop moving deeper into the woods and that would be that. The biggest fear until then had been that the fighter would be seen from orbit, maybe a satellite or something, or from a plane or helicopter flying overhead. So far that hadn't happened. Now, ironically, the least of their concerns—that actual people would stumble on them in the remote location—was starting to become a reality.

Bianca zoomed in as far as she could, switching to a thermal to see the hikers as they moved beneath thicker tree cover. There were four, what she was guessing to be two boys and two girls, and if the small group saw the Kel fighter it was over. Satori and Willet would either have to catch them or knock them out or something.

Nani shook her head. Then: "Wait. They're stopping."

Bianca checked. "It looks like they're starting to unpack." She watched as they walked around, what she guessed were the two boys going to find a place to pee. The images were small—even the Kel technology was limited in what it could resolve in real-time—but clear enough to tell what the kids were doing. She watched as the girls started unrolling one of the tent packs and decided they were, in fact, setting up camp.

"Whew," she whistled. Nani called to inform Satori. The hikers were still a good mile or so from the fighter, but it seemed so close on the screens it was still nerve-wracking. Everything at that altitude was crammed into such a small area.

Earth was huge.

Bianca zoomed out and panned around. No other activity to be seen. They'd only spotted the hikers as they got close. Up so high, looking down from orbit, scanning around like a live Google Earth or something, she was startled to realize just how massive the world truly was. She and Nani were scrolling over an area of only a few dozen square miles—small if you pulled back even just a little; so tiny you couldn't see it if you looked at the whole of Spain, just a dot on the map—and yet, zoomed in all the way she had to slide and slide and slide the screen, fingers swiping and pinching to change the focus, looking at hundreds if not thousands of acres.

At times in the past she'd wondered how there was enough room on Earth for all seven billion people. Now she was starting to get a real sense of just what was available. There was *lots* of room on Earth. All seven billion people could probably stand in that one little field down there.

"These guys are like ghosts," Nani commented, and it took Bianca a second to realize she was no longer talking about the hikers. In Nani's mind that threat was handled and she'd moved on to other things. The hikers were camping. No one else in sight. Time to keep digging.

Nani was always digging. The whole time they'd been here at Earth, digging and digging. Even back on Anitra, where Nani had already discovered all there was to know about the Kel starship, she was digging for more. Bianca recalled hanging with her in the lab. Back then that was all she was doing, hanging, but now she was trying to help. To participate in this little mission with epic implications, yet Nani was leaving her in the dust. It was like she couldn't keep up.

"Who are?" she asked.

"The Esehta Bok." Nani looked over screens of info. "There's nothing on them. Literally, nothing on the networks I have access to. And I can access everything by now. I see why the Project are so desperate to get their hands on them. The Bok have managed to do so much yet remain hidden the whole time.

"It's incredible."

Nani would've been awesome to have in school. Bianca studied her as she in turn stared at her screens, completely caught up in what she was reading. Nani wasn't much older than her, probably mid or late twenties or something. That was ten years, sure, but not really that much. She could easily pass for a teen with the right makeup, the right clothes. It was cute how awkward she was. Kind of the same way Jess was awkward, now that she thought of it, only more so. Neither of them realized what assets they were wasting. A girl only had so many years, and neither Nani nor Jess were putting their looks to good use.

Actually Jess wasn't wasting hers so much any more. Now that she was zeroed in on Zac, her true love, it seemed, she was finally shaking off any misguided hesitations and going for it. Bianca was proud.

Of course their current circumstances weren't exactly lending themselves to a proper romance. She'd much rather be advising Jess on the details of how to proceed with Zac, not watching a bunch of monitor screens and formulating a high-stakes kidnapping. Earlier that day had been fun. Helping pick their clothes, accessories, etcetera. Deciding on their look. For that short time she'd escaped into fonder memories; being back on Earth, in school, working hard to craft her dorky friend into something more.

She looked over at Nani. "Zac sure looked hot in his suit, didn't he?"

"Hmm?" Nani didn't track at first with the transition, then she did. "Oh, yeah," she agreed, not taking her eyes from what she was doing. "He's a handsome guy."

Oh, yeah. He's a handsome guy. The way she said it was automatic. Like the way you'd tell someone; *Oh, yeah. Pretty flowers*, when you really didn't know much about flowers or, probably, didn't even really care. Not surprising. Nani probably *didn't* know much about guys. Nor did she really seem to care. Her time, her brain power, was devoted to one thing and one thing only:

Knowledge.

Bianca smiled at her. She still wasn't looking up from her screen. As if brushing Bianca aside with a wave of her hand; *Go away, kid. Ya bother me.*

With a wistful smile she turned and looked out to the Earth.

Zac had been easy to dress. Bianca was worried, though, that they hadn't gotten Jess everything she needed to kill. She was afraid that, once the two of them got to the club, Jess wouldn't be let in. Not because she wasn't gorgeous. Rather, because Jess wouldn't pull it off well enough without instruction. It just didn't come natural for her, and she could easily blow it at the door by being shy or acting dumb or something.

"Jess looked good too," Nani said randomly. Bianca turned back to her. The glow of the soft purple light only enhanced her youthful features. Nani was pretty. "With that dress you picked she's going to fit in just fine."

Bianca looked at her. Maybe she *was* paying attention.

Nani tapped more things on the screen. "I'm sending Satori an update. There's not much new at this point." Then: "They must be bored. Sitting down there, quiet, no instruments. Wonder how they're passing the time?"

Bianca sniggered, then realized—much to her amusement—Nani was serious. The snigger broke the screen trance, though, and Nani's eyes were now on her.

"Um, I'm sure they've thought of a few things." Bianca even went so far as to wink. A knowing little nod for Nani.

But there was no sign of understanding. "Yeah, probably," the scientist girl agreed. Then she leaned back, taking a rare moment to look out into the black depths of space.

Bianca cocked her head. This bore further discussion. "You realize they're in love, right?"

A pause. Then: "Satori and Willet?"

"Yeah."

Nani studied her, and for an instant Bianca wondered if she did. Then Nani said: "Yeah, I mean, I know it. Satori mentioned him a few times when she was at the complex. You could tell. He came there once. Willet was in the field a lot."

Bianca stared at her. Nani added, as if starting to realize she might be missing something: "There's a lot of tension between them. Like they're mad at each other. Don't you think?"

Yeah. "Sometimes that's the best thing for a relationship. Two lovers, angry, tension high, alone in a confined space. Sounds like a recipe for a makeup, if you know what I mean."

Nani clearly didn't. At least not fully. Bianca decided to

let it go.

"Show me more," she changed the subject. "Show me some more of how this stuff works."

"The ship?"

"Yeah. I want to know how to fly it." She smiled. "I might be a starship captain one day."

* * *

"I'M STILL ANGRY," Satori tried to look it and failed.

Willet frowned. "But not at me, right?"

"Yes at you! You're the cause of this!"

"Me?!"

The console beeped. Again. Willet turned and checked it. Nani sending more updates. He acknowledged without reading and turned back to Satori.

"Yes you," she said. "If you didn't constantly agree with her we wouldn't end up in these messes." She pushed him in mock frustration. "*You're* the one that ran off with her to the Crucible. I was against that. It's been downhill from there."

"You know she's considered a hero," Willet protested. On impulse he reached and ran a hand through her bright red hair. It was in disarray, clumped and tangled and sticking this way and that. He smoothed some of it back. Her gorgeous lips were moist and plumped from being kissed. For a moment he lost himself in her. *She's so beautiful.*

She turned up one corner of her mouth and it only made her more desirable. Satori was perfection, at all times. Willet often had to pinch himself that she was even interested in him at all.

"Yeah, yeah," she said. "Hero. Sure. But she's had her run. Even heroes wear out their welcome and this time she's gone too far. You know it. I know it. Yet here we sit. Going along with yet another crazy scheme."

They lounged close, in the most comfortable part of the fighter, which wasn't very comfortable at all but they'd managed to ignore the awkwardness of the accommodations. Both of them were flushed with desire, having been in and out of each other's embrace for the last hour, interrupted by reports from Nani about hikers and other "important" things.

Willet shifted to the side. "Yeah but this time it was actually Nani's idea."

"You believe that? Jess has been leading this from the start."

"Maybe," he had to agree. "But every other thing she's done seemed crazy at first. Then it all worked out. Maybe this time is no different. I'm willing to believe."

"Don't tell me you're falling for that Prophecy crap."

"No. No. Just ... there's something to her. Even you have to admit that. She's like ... nothing. Just a girl. But you know that look in her eyes. You can almost feel it." He made his point: "And there's no denying what she's done."

The console beeped.

"Dammit!" he snapped his hand to it and caught himself before shutting off the connection altogether. Instead he acknowledged the message—checked it briefly to see that it was, in fact, mostly unnecessary or more of the same— then ack'ed it and turned back to Satori. Nani was getting annoying.

"She's turning out to be a real busybody, isn't she?" Satori shook her head at the console screen. Nani had been feeding them regular updates though there was very little change. They, in turn, were maintaining strict instrument silence. A few minutes ago the mild drama of the approaching campers had come to an end, he and Satori interrupting their kisses each time a message beeped in to pay attention to the oh-so-important possibility that four people out for a hike might actually reach them in the next hour if they kept walking the way they were.

"I only wonder how she's going to handle it when the *real* stuff starts happening," he nodded to the console to indicate Nani. "She's never done anything more intense than research. When the real action hits she's gonna saturate us."

Satori smiled. "Like a newbie on her first mission," she leaned toward him. "If your record is any indication, I think you'll handle her just fine."

She kissed him. Satori had been a newbie once, a junior officer fresh out of the academy when Willet himself was a newly minted field operator. He'd led her on her first mission, where they first met; afterward she'd gone on to command tanks and rise to the level of field commander— reversing their roles in short order and coming to be in charge of him as he continued to lead recon units for the Venatres. Each had pursued their own decisions. Willet liked being on the ground, in the field with a small unit sneaking around behind enemy lines. Satori liked directing massive firepower and blowing things up.

Each was happy.

He kissed her.

Even back then, on that first mission, there'd been a connection. It was many missions, many transfers and many postings later that they actually did anything about it, but both knew back then they were destined for each other. Willet wasn't sure if he believed fully in the idea of soul mates, but Satori seemed to make a perfect case for it.

She kissed him.

The console beeped and now he did shut it off.

And with a wry grin took her into his arms.

* * *

JESS SHRIEKED in absolute glee. Like a girl half her age. She hadn't had this much fun in forever, she thought, as her feet touched the floor of the cage on the carnival pirate ship ride—just as it hit bottom and swung out hard on the other side. She grunted as the far end of the ship soared overhead, everyone in *that* cage floating for an instant as it peaked in its arc, bodies flailing inside the cage high above, silhouetted against the dusk sky ... then they were swinging back and, *unnn!*, through the bottom and everyone in her cage was being thrown into the air once more.

"*Woooo!*" she screamed with abandon, holding the bars as her feet came light and she floated free at the top. Vertigo squeezed her. For those few seconds as they reached the peak and began the next descent it was like being in free-fall. No restraints in the cage, dangerous—no ride like this would exist in the States—it was about as thrilling as she could've imagined any carnival ride could be.

"*Yeah!*" Zac enthused as they swung back through their arc, up and out the other side. He stood beside her, laughing and screaming with everyone else. You had to be careful to be in the right position as it came down, legs under you, or risk getting slammed to the floor as the ship crushed through the bottom. Jess wondered if the experience was really as much fun for Zac. She didn't know how he could actually be so thrilled, but if he *wasn't* having a blast he was faking it with abandon.

"This is so much fun!" he yelled as they shot out the other side. Four other people shared the cage with them, Spanish teens, screaming and laughing as the curved pirate ship swung back and forth in long sweeps, like a mighty pendulum. "We don't have anything like this on Anitra!"

For a moment his comment worried Jess, but no one there likely spoke English, at least not well enough to understand, and even if they did there was too much chaos, the statement too innocent for anyone to pay attention. She glanced at Zac as they hit the top of the arc and vertigo seized her again. He was laughing, pretending to fly, totally into it, no idea he'd even let that slip.

Maybe he really *was* having that much fun.

The next plunge and surge through the bottom whisked away her concern and she was right back into it, screaming along with everyone else in the cage—Spanish, English—whatever—their shouts merged in the universal language of "thrilled". Back and forth; back ... and forth. *Whooooosh* through the propelling wheels at the bottom, shooting up and ... floating free, hanging to the bars in dizzying delight then ... plunging through the drop again and ... *unnnn!* up the other side, hanging and ... back through, only to be flung once more high into the air.

Too soon the ride was winding down. Laughter became chuckles, then excited conversations of how awesome this or that thing was or how so-and-so did this when that happened and how ridiculous this one looked when ...

Jess caught some of the words, translating more from their faces and gestures. Soon everyone was filing off, the next throng of riders heading eagerly up the stairs to get on. Zac stayed near, pushing against the backpack she wore, filled with their things. Protective of her in the crowd. She felt him jostling along behind her, allowing himself to go with the flow and be pushed and shoved with everyone else in order to appear natural. He could, of course, sweep them all away with one arm, but did an amazing job of being human. No one would've thought him a Terminator or something, marching brusquely along without regard for those around him. He got bumped back and forth just like everyone else. She smiled over her shoulder.

This whole trip to the fair had turned out to be beyond perfect.

"Let's get something to eat," he suggested as they reached the ground and the crowd thinned.

"Again?"

He shrugged. "I want another one of those Nutty Buddys."

Already he'd had three of the chocolate-covered cones since they'd been there.

"All you've eaten all day is sweets," she said, heading them for the vendor.

"Those are the best things."

"At dinner you are *not* going to just order dessert."

"But we still *get* dessert, right?"

She smacked him and he pulled her close and she laughed. It was fun smacking him. She used to smack Mike, but not much. He would always wince and pretend harm, then she'd have to pretend to be sorry. Not Zac. Zac could never be hurt. He hugged her to him, feigning anger, and she laughed with the thrill of it.

She looked at the bodies all around them on the dusty field; the noise, the peals of laughter coming from all quarters, everyone lost in the pleasure of the fair. It was like a dream, walking with her arm around him, his around her.

They got his ice cream and found a free bench where they sat as he ate. She leaned into him and looked across the fair grounds at the pirate ship, the tallest ride there—no Ferris wheel at this small carnival—whipping back and forth with its next set of riders, ends jutting high into the sky with each swing, silhouetted against the setting sun. The carnival lights were on, strings of white bulbs everywhere, and in the fading sunlight it was magical. If she concentrated she could hear the riders' screams coming from the cages, distinct from the other noises and voices filling the festival.

She closed her eyes and let the sounds blend into one. A cool breeze blew, tingling her cheeks, strands of hair dancing randomly across her face. Music, laughter—sounds played across her mind's eye. Somewhere high overhead the steady rumble of a jet found its way through, echoes of power far away, bouncing across the sky. Barely audible over the insanity of the fair.

And the smells ...

The smells in the air were amazing. All sorts of foods, the occasional perfume or cologne—including their own—Zac, lovable, precious Zac, still smelling like an entire frickin department store, but she loved it—and the smells of ...

Earth.

She could scarcely explain it, but there was a distinct smell permeating everything. Whether it be the trees, the dirt, the grass—the smell of Earth was all around her.

Zac put his free arm across her shoulder and held her to his side as he ate. Lost in his own thoughts, or simply letting her have hers. Letting her be. She pulled her legs up onto the bench and curled tighter against him. The leather of their jackets crinkled and rubbed together as she pushed into him.

This was what life was about. Everything else one did, every other thing was keeping the wolves at bay so moments like this could be enjoyed.

She sank into it, relishing it. All of it.

She'd earned it.

After what seemed an eternity, eyes closed, sitting in

blissful peace, listening to the sounds of the fair, smelling the smells and all else, Zac shifted and she felt a sudden chill on her lips. She opened her eyes to find him kissing her with his ice-cream mouth. She shuddered with the thrill of it and together they smiled, lips pressed together. He withdrew and she reached and wiped a little chocolate from the corner of his mouth. Licked it off her finger.

It was a totally spontaneous kiss, not tentative or stolen or in a moment of stress. A date kiss, (despite the surrounding purpose of their being there this was their first real "date", which was how she chose to view it and nothing could change that), filled with love, and as he kissed her again, gently, lips cold, she realized it was official. If there had been any doubt before (there wasn't, really) it was now one hundred percent confirmed:

Zac was her boyfriend.

She put a hand on his leg and they kissed again, passionate this time, intense and, at some point, quite suddenly ... both of them giggled. From the pleasure, from the happiness of the moment, from the tingling cold sensation, the chocolate ice-cream taste—whatever the cause they giggled at the exact same moment, together. And the fact that they both made the same silly sound simultaneously, mouth to mouth, almost identical, made them laugh louder, and as they did they pulled back to look into each other's eyes, laughing right in each other's face. Pure mirth twinkled in his, taken with the hilarity of the moment. The power and the feel of his sweet breath, so close to her own, was intoxicating. She let the feeling wash over her. Their laughter subsided and she curled back against him, looking out across the joy of the fairgrounds. He hugged his arm tighter around her, content, and they sat that way for a long time.

The sun set, the lights twinkled, people laughed, the energy of the carnival wafted through the air and Zac was the first to break the serenity.

"What kind of uniform is that?" he asked. Jess followed his gaze to a pair of nuns walking through the crowd. Admittedly unusual, though for her she'd failed to take notice. For Zac they must be quite strange.

"Nuns," she said. "There are a lot of Catholics in Spain. Nuns are Catholic."

"What are Catholics?" he asked. "And what's a nun?"

Jess shifted against him; snuggled closer. The air had cooled, the sun gone completely from sight into a clear, deep horizon, beautiful orange right at the edge of the world, darker and darker upward in increasingly deep bands of blue, all the way up to the black of night. The carnival was ablaze in electric light.

"The Catholic Church," she said. "Catholicism. That's the name of a religion. Catholics are members of the Catholic Church. Nuns are sisters in the Church. Men are priests, women are nuns."

Zac watched the nuns with interest. "Catholicism is the Earth religion?"

"One of them."

"What do they believe?"

What do they believe? "Well, I guess if I had to summarize, they believe in one god, who had a son, and his son came to Earth and, by God's will, died for our sins."

"His son died for our sins?"

"The idea is that if you believe God's son died for your sins then you'll be forgiven and live forever."

Zac reflected on this and Jess wondered what his next question would be. So many seemed to be begging to be asked. How do you know God's will? Who was his son? Why only one god? Why did his son have to die? Does that mean you can sin all you want then believe right before you die? If God is God, why not just forgive everyone's sins *without* having your son die? Did that mean God wasn't God and someone else was making the rules? If not, if God was the ultimate rule maker, then why have a son at all? Why not just have everyone believe in you? Why allow people to be flawed at all?

Instead he asked: "Just the people of Earth?"

That was more interesting than any of hers.

"I don't know," she admitted. "I'm pretty sure the Bible says God created everything."

She kept giving him new words. But he rolled with it.

"The Bible? Is that ... the writings of Catholicism?"

She nodded. "It says God created all. Presumably that would include the trillions of other planets out there." She'd never really thought along these lines. "It only talks about his son coming to this one, and only at a specific point in our history.

"Maybe God sent a trillion versions of his son to a trillion different worlds. Over the course of a few billion years—at the right time in each world's history, right when civilizations became aware, so the people of that time and place could hear his message, again and again—so each race had a chance to believe and save their immortal souls." Even as she said it, though, she heard the cynicism in her voice. She didn't want Zac to think she was insensitive to the beliefs of others. Usually she wasn't. Only, the last year had changed her perspective in so many ways. She wasn't sure what she believed anymore.

She softened her tone. Amended: "I guess it would apply to any person or any intelligent being anywhere or at any time.   Anyone who believes in the son of God could have eternal life."

"What do the other religions of Earth believe?"

"Lots of stuff."

"So you're not Catholic?"

She shook her head. Wondering at the evolution of religion on Anitra. She knew the deal with the Emperor and the Dominion, but what about the Venatres? What did they believe?

But the moment was too peaceful to bother. She didn't want to think any more about such things.

Zac continued to reflect, watching the nuns buy cotton candy and meander back into the crowd. In unison they bit carefully into the pink and blue puffs, bright splashes of color against the stark black and white of their habits.

It reminded Jess of a joke.

"I've got a joke." She sat a little straighter.

Zac seemed happy for the distraction. "What is it?"

She cleared her throat. "What's black, white and red

and has trouble going through revolving doors?"

"What's a revolving door?"

What's a ...

Maybe this wasn't going to be funny after all. "It's a door on an axle," she said, "like a post. It turns as you go through it. One person can be walking in one side and another walking out on the other, without having to wait."

Zac nodded. "Ok," he said. "What's black, white and red and has trouble going through revolving doors?"

She prepared her delivery:

"A nun with a spear through her head."

And Zac actually laughed. Right away.

She smiled, surprised he got it so quickly. "Bad, right?"

"Absurd," he said. "But I like absurd."

And she liked him. Zac was so much like her in so many ways, and the fact that he could so readily laugh—genuinely laugh—at a joke with two alien references in it, nuns and revolving doors, was testament to the connection.

He kissed her on the forehead.

Asked:

"It's getting dark. Should we get changed?"

And she realized it was nearly time for the fun to end.

CHAPTER 27:

DINNER PLANS

JESS FINISHED brushing the last bit of nail polish onto her pinky finger. Bianca had picked dark blue, claiming it went best with the outfit and the accessories she would wear that night. She finished the last, careful stroke, held out her hand and turned it back and forth, looking at the results. The color was a little off in the fluorescent lighting of the public restroom but it did, indeed, go with what she was wearing.

Not bad. Her toes, too, sparkled with a fresh coat from the same bottle. She looked down and curled them up, flexing to catch the best light. *Not bad at all.*

All right. She closed the polish and put it back in the bag, waved her hands in the air a few times, blew on her fingers and grabbed a brush. *Brush your hair until it shines!* Bianca's words echoed in her head. Jess had checked with her briefly before starting to get ready and that was the one thing her friend seemed unable to emphasize enough: brush! There was no way to take an official shower and wash her hair, and after days aboard the ship with nothing but ionizers to clean by, Jess had to admit her hair was looking pretty flat. Clean, but flat. Bianca said it was one of the key things and it had to look luxurious. Especially for this club. It had to look like she walked out of a salon with hundred-dollar bottles of conditioner.

She tugged and brushed and tugged and tugged, working out the tangles until the brush began to make a nice clean pass each time. She brushed and brushed and brushed, recalling that old beauty tip of brushing your hair a hundred times before bed. She was probably way over that by now but kept brushing, each side, top to bottom, again and again, and ... her hair actually started to look better. What had been a dull brown when she began started to get some luster. Those auburn highlights Bianca kept saying she had were starting to show.

It felt weird to be standing there in the dingy bathroom, barefoot on the cold, icky floor—she tried not to think about it—in just the little black dress, brushing her hair vigorously in front of a smudged mirror, a huge bag of clothes and other crap on the counter in front of her. It wasn't a heavily used bathroom but the other women and girls that came in and out during her time getting ready mostly ignored her. None gave her more than a cursory glance. Off and on she'd had the tablet out, and at one point was on it talking to Bianca when one came in. For a moment she freaked, then realized it wasn't that unusual to be talking to someone on such a device. Of course in this case that someone happened to be on a spaceship orbiting the Earth, but the other bathroom visitor certainly had no way of knowing that.

So as weird, as absolutely exposed as it felt, to be getting dressed there in a public restroom, preparing for a mission against the world's most secret organization—in direct competition with the world's most powerful government— coordinating it all with humans from another world via an ancient alien starship—getting ready to go have dinner with her accomplice, a human boy who was hardly human at all … as much as all that sent shudders through her every few minutes, there really wasn't anything about it obvious enough to give anyone a clue. Just a teenage girl getting dressed in a bathroom on a Saturday night. An American, on vacation, too far from the hotel or simply sleeping on the train, carrying all her stuff in a bag and heading out to the clubs, making do the best she could.

Perfectly normal.

So weird.

"How's it going?" Zac's voice startled her from just outside the door. He'd been standing out there asking every so often, long since ready himself. When he first announced he was dressed she'd gone to the door to get his street clothes, only in her dress and just getting started on all the other stuff—ten times what Zac had to do, what with nails and hair and makeup—and at the door she took his bundle of clothes so she could stuff them in the bag with the rest and, as she did, got to see him in his full get-up ...

Wow. Just ... Wow.

Again it hit her. Zac was a stud among studs. In his shiny Italian suit, amazing silk shirt and swanky boots. Not only would they wave him into the club with no question, the doormen would probably give him a tab and ask him to be their club spokesman.

Gorgeous. If ever a guy could be called gorgeous, Zac, in that suit, and that shirt, and those shoes, was it.

"A few more minutes," she said, same as last time he asked. They were really in no hurry at that point. It was still way early for the club and they were going to dinner beforehand, but she understood how annoying it could be to wait on someone. Normally she wasn't one of "those" girls, taking forever to get ready, making their boyfriend or husband wait painfully, but thanks to Bianca—who Jess knew was right in insisting on it—her prep routine for this particular outing was extensive. Everything had to be just right. As perfect as possible. And now, having seen Zac, she knew she *really* had to step up her game. If it were going to be even remotely plausible to see her on the arm of such an Adonis of a man, she would have to be more than she ever had.

She brushed her hair a little longer and stopped, satisfied. There was no way to style it so she would just wear it straight, long and shiny, and after the thorough brushing it actually looked good. She admired it, happy with the results, then took out the few little boxes of jewelry they'd chosen for her ensemble. Carefully she clasped on each piece. A thin, sparkly necklace that fit snug, little diamond ear studs, a similarly sparkly anklet, a few tactically matched bracelets for one wrist, a single, thicker bracelet for the other.

It all looked perfect.

Now for makeup. *God!* Still not done. She shoved the brush and empty boxes in the bag and rummaged for the next items on her list, growing impatient. *Next time I'm coming back as a guy.*

She wasn't normally a makeup girl. Usually she wore none. Fortunately she had some experience putting it on, for if anything about this required skill, makeup was it. All the rest she could just do as she was told. Shoes she could put on, she could put on the dress and the jewelry. What Bianca picked out she could simply wear. Hair she could brush. Nails she could paint without much skill. Makeup, however ...

With the makeup she was on her own.

She thought to check in but decided that would just be an unnecessary distraction. Bianca was liable to start giving her all sorts of extra instruction. With a glance at the tablet she decided she'd do it first and get the check-out after. Even Bianca agreed she had a natural beauty that actually did better with *less* makeup, and so she kept it simple and, in short order, was smacking her lips and putting a few final touches on her mascara. She stepped back to study herself in the streaked mirror beneath the bad lighting.

She looked good. With the hair, the little bits of jewelry, a few other accessories, the little black dress, the nails and now the makeup, she actually looked pretty. *Real pretty.* For a moment she blushed in witness of herself.

Time for the expert opinion.

She flipped on the tablet and made contact.

For a long moment Bianca simply stared. Nani crowded to look over her shoulder, then Bianca asked Jess to hold the tablet this way and that so she could see different angles.

She passed with flying colors.

Jess found herself actually feeling proud. Bianca approved of what she'd done, no corrections. She signed off, stuffed and closed the big bag with all their things, put the tablet in her stylish purse, along with the remaining cash, grabbed some paper towels to clean up the area, wiped the bottoms of her feet and slipped carefully into the amazingly expensive heels.

There. She looked at herself in the mirror, a few inches

taller now. Carefully she took a few experimental steps in the sharply angled shoes. To the left, to the right. Forward, back. Like the makeup heels were mostly foreign to her, as she hardly ever wore them, but she'd worn them enough to pull it off. Embarrassingly she'd practiced in heels way more than she'd actually worn them outside the house. In her room, walking and squatting, turning; practicing for a moment just like this. Yet one more part of her confused youth, never knowing why she tried to get good at so many things but glad for those impulses now. Many of the things she'd learned as a kid had already been put to the test on this crazy adventure, ever since first meeting Zac.

After a few bends and turns she stood straight, brushed her hands over her dress, smacked her lips one more time, grabbed the purse and the big bag filled with their clothes and went out to meet the man of her dreams.

His eyes went wide as she stepped into the harsh lights outside the bathroom. She stopped, set down the bags and stood before him, feeling herself blush as she turned one heel in nervously, striking a sexy pose. The dress was short and the top showed cleavage, bare shoulders and all. A lot of bare skin. Suddenly it all felt very revealing.

"You look amazing," he said in hushed tones. Both of them stood where they were, a few feet apart, neither moving.

Then she did, stepping closer in the heels, feeling extremely alluring and not sure whether she was loving or hating it. It felt strange to be on such display.

"You look so grown up," he said. She smacked him.

"I *am* grown up."

"I know, but ... wow."

Zac just kept staring, doing a poor job of concealing how taken he was. She felt her cheeks getting hotter.

It felt amazing to have him look at her that way.

"So those are stylish?" he pointed to the heels.

"Very." She turned first one then the other so he could see, front and back. Of course they were also hugely impractical, as was everything else she was wearing, and part of her still fought with the notion of putting back on the jeans and tennis shoes. But there was no way that would work for what they had to do, and so impractical and stylish would be the uniform of the evening.

"Don't worry," said Zac. "I'll handle the tough stuff." He seemed to understand exactly what she was thinking. In truth there would likely be little for her to do. Zac *would* handle the tough stuff. All of it. Nothing on Earth could challenge him. Her role was to get him to the target and help along the way. When it came time for action, she would become baggage. There were no tickets for this concert; entrance was based solely on the whim of whoever was at the door. The pressure, therefore, was on her. Zac's was the easy part, considering what he was capable of. If they got inside the rest was easy. Cake. All they had to do was get in.

She swallowed down the nerves that kept trying to overtake her. Maybe they could find a way to sneak in after all. Maybe they'd just end up hiding in the bushes and taking their chances.

Zac continued his admiring scrutiny, unabashedly, looking her over as if he couldn't get enough. "This black outline around your eyes ..." He reached a hand, careful not to touch.

She swallowed, holding still. "Eyeliner."

"It brings out those little flecks of gold." His finger hovered. "The color is amazing in this light." Close but not touching. And in that moment, around the nerves, around the fear, she felt so sensual, so desirable, she *wanted* him to touch. Everywhere. To grab her, to touch all of her, to rip away the dress and smear away that which she'd just spent the last hour making ready.

She felt the pulsing of her heart.

"So pretty." Then Zac, too, seemed to feel the intensity of the moment and snapped from whatever gripped him.

He fumbled in his pocket and held up his tie.

"We got this," he showed it to her, "but I don't know how to tie it. I've seen others wearing them."

Jess reached for it, happy for the distraction. She extended her arms to his neck and he leaned forward. Even with the extra inches from the heels he was a head taller. Deftly she turned up his collar and slipped the tie around.

"Ok," she said. "Stand up." He did and she came closer and pulled the ends until they were about right, then began tying.

"Do women wear these?" he asked.

"Not usually." The tie Bianca picked was, of course, perfect. A handsome combination of color and pattern that made the suit and shirt pop. She finished, snugged the knot, turned down his collar, smoothed it, slipped the end of the tie inside his jacket and laid her hands on his chest.

"You look very handsome."

Another couple walked by, arm in arm, out for a nighttime stroll in the park.

Jess took her hands from Zac and picked up the bags.

"Let's go to dinner," she said. "I'm starved."

* * *

"So the hour is ten local?" Zac glanced at the chunky, expensive watch. It looked great on him.

Jess leaned across the table to look at the face.

"Yep. You're reading it right. DJ Fujito goes on at midnight. That's about two hours from now."

Zac nodded and took another swig of his Cruzcampo beer, the one recommended by their waiter—his fourth so far—and another bite of manchego cheese. They were in a cute little tapas bar, an old, open-air structure. Vines and strings of tiny white lights cris-crossed the ceiling, which wasn't really a ceiling at all, just wires running back and forth, something on which the vines could hang. Through the gaps you could see the night sky and there, right in view over Zac's shoulder, rising in the near distance, was the lighted dome of a Catholic cathedral. At each table candles flickered, small torches burning in holders on the stone walls. Completing the serenity a cool, gentle breeze wafted through the restaurant, carrying the wonderful smells of food and wine.

Like everything else that day, it was magical.

Spanish families and a few other couples filled the place, out for their traditional late meal on a Saturday night, laughing and loud, most of the couples engaged in more intimate conversation. The Spanish were night-owls, both young and old and, one and all, had a certain gusto for life. You weren't likely to see American families out in this number having so much fun openly for all to hear. Especially not that late.

The corner table where she and Zac sat was a bit quieter. So far they'd been able to chat easily. In a way it gave them their own little bubble of privacy while still being out among the festivities. Tonight was apparently a minor holiday, the celebration of some local saint—thus the carnival—and everyone was having a good time. From the look of it Jess suspected the Spanish rarely needed a reason to have a good time. It was no wonder they lived longer. They were so full of life.

The waiter came and asked Zac if he wanted another cerveza. Zac tipped his glass with a thirsty smile and said Yes, thank you. The waiter appreciated his enthusiasm and was off to fetch another round. Now that Jess had been spending time with Zac in the regular world, *her* world, she saw that he truly did not know a stranger. Everyone took to him as soon as he spoke or nodded or smiled and he, in turn, was abundantly sociable and interested in them. He'd been walking around all day making friends. The ice cream guy. The ride operator at the carnival. The waitress that morning, the ticket taker, the waiter tonight, that old lady selling flowers in the street, the shopkeeper ...

Who's the visitor here? It was as if Zac was getting along better than she was.

The waiter returned with his fifth beer. Zac handed him the empty and made some joke about Jess not drinking which, remarkably, was understood by the waiter, who laughed along at her expense then left again.

"Thanks a lot," she grumbled.

"You know I'm just teasing." Zac took a big drink. "This stuff is good. Goes with the cheese, just like he said it would."

"Do you think it's a good idea to get drunk?"

"I can't get drunk," he said, and she figured that would be his response. He frowned. "I kind of miss it, actually. At least being able to."

"You used to get drunk? Before you were a Kazerai?"

"Sometimes. Being an Astake was tough. Used to go out and get loaded on the Emperor's sake."

Jess recalled her own brush with sake, during her time with Darvon back in Osaka. Too young for getting that loaded, that was for sure. Not that anyone was probably ever old enough to feel like that. *Ugh.* She was too young for most of the things she'd done in the last six months.

Zac wasn't legal to drink either, technically—near as they'd figured his Earth age—but he had a certain bearing about him, either from the transformation to a Kazerai or something else, that made it easy to think of him as older. The waiter hadn't even asked.

She took another bite of her delicious paella, followed by a sip of her own drink. A coke.

And for an instant, looking across at Zac, she had that weird sensation she sometimes got. That strange, almost out-of-body sort of consideration of just how powerful he was. Mostly she forgot, or kept it in the back of her mind, like a little nugget of logic or a fact, not really anything to dwell on, just something to be aware of, but every now and then, such as now, it occurred to her quite starkly just how far beyond human he was, and when it did it nearly buzzed her right out of her head. There he was, indestructible, sitting in a chair eating cheese, drinking beer and talking like a normal guy.

Using his napkin.

It was like sitting at the table with Superman. Zac truly was that strong. She'd seen it. Knew it. Yet in these normal settings, doing normal things, it was easy to forget. She stared across the table, over the flickering candle at his broad shoulders, made wider in the Italian jacket, sleeves hugging his biceps; sturdy neck atop a tall frame. A normal guy his size could go on a rampage in that little tapas restaurant and hurt a lot of people before the crowd got him under control.

Zac would kill everyone in the place.

Bring the entire restaurant to the ground. Bring down all the buildings around them, collapse that cathedral shining in the night sky through the vine ceiling. All the buildings in town, all the people, smash any army they brought against him, take their bullets, their missiles and all else. Kill thousands before he could be stopped. If he could even be stopped.

He would be a one-man cataclysm.

She watched him chewing another piece of cheese.

He smiled at her. "What?"

"Nothing." She stirred around some of the paella, then looked up: "Wouldn't it be fun to start a life here?" She looked higher, into the night sky, at the tranquility all around. Stars twinkled up there, far above.

"Here?" He followed her gaze around the fire-lit comfort of the restaurant. "Sure. I could totally get used to living here."

Desire nagged, and as she felt the absurdity of the idea gain purchase she dragged herself back to the present. Now that she was back, on Earth, among the people of her world, the very things she'd already ruled out—knew could never, ever be—teased her. Everything was so quiet right then, so peaceful. Everything was going so well. Everything they were about to do was because they'd decided to do it, not because she was reacting to something in order to survive. For once the trouble she was about to get into was her own decision and, right now, she could decide not to do it. It was easy to imagine the current peace and tranquility going on forever.

But it wouldn't.

"Your eyes are sparkling," he said and she pulled her attention back to him. Stared into his; ice-blue, reflecting the tiny flame on the table. She wondered how hers looked. Especially to him.

Sparkling?

He leaned forward. "They keep getting more of those little golden flecks," he peered into them. "Maybe it's the

makeup, or the lighting, but they're definitely changing."
He looked a little embarrassed but continued:

"You're so beautiful, Jessica."

She felt herself blush; couldn't hold his gaze. "I don't
know why you think so." It was a dumb, automatic-type
response, but she couldn't help it. Despite the fact that
she *did* feel gorgeous in the club dress, despite the fact she
knew how he felt about her, it was hard to ignore so many
years of being down on herself.

He leaned back against his chair. "You don't know why
I think so?"

"I just ..." She brushed some of her hair behind one ear
and glanced to the other side, keeping her eyes down. "I
guess I never thought of myself that way." Then, trying to
joke it off: "Girls are naturally insecure."

"I could explain my infatuation if that would help. Maybe
give you a few facts to back it up. About how your smile
sends a tingle through me every time I see it." Reflexively
she smiled and he put a hand to his chest, as if to still
his beating heart. Of course she tried to stop smiling, to
take the attention away but she couldn't and the smile,
frustratingly, persisted. He left his hand over his heart:
"How your eyes are like these otherworldly lights, like tiny
stars I want to dive into. Every time I see them they're deeper
than before. About how you give off this gorgeous aura I
can't explain. It's like you're something else, something
bigger, something amazing and I can see it almost as well
as I see things with my eyes." He leaned forward. "Did you
know you have an aura?"

"Stop." She really did want him to stop.
Kind of.

"I can't believe I'm sitting here with you," he sat back.

She regained some composure. "Me either. After
everything we've been through I can't believe we're here,
together, doing this." She held out her hands, gesturing at
the ongoing celebration all around, managing at last to fix
his gaze. "I'm so happy right now."

He smiled. "Me too."

And he reached across the table. Tenderly he took her

hands in his and held them. Then ... rose from his chair, leaned all the way over the flickering candle and ... gave her a kiss.

She closed her eyes with the rush of it, inhaling the moment as he lingered; tasting the beer on his breath, sensing the power in him, hidden behind the tenderness. Soft lips, like the caress of silk, an ethereal curtain behind which lurked a lion. She felt a shiver building and pushed it down.

He pulled back and sat. "I've got a good feeling about tonight."

She opened her eyes and let the shiver go as he took the last bite of cheese, followed by another swig of beer.

"You know," he chewed, onto new things, "as a Kazerai I had this goal of going down in history. Of being someone who made a difference. I wanted Horus to be a name remembered for all time. I didn't know how, but I wanted to accomplish things. Big things. Change the world." He fell into thought. "Now the name Horus is almost like a distant memory." He sat that way a long time, looking beyond her, thoughts settling in his mind; then came easily back to the present. "Maybe Horus won't be a name spoken of in the history books. Horus will just be remembered as another Kazerai that failed. They all failed, in the end."

"You haven't failed," she told him.

He took another drink. "Maybe. Zac, Horus. Whichever. Maybe *I* can still make history. Maybe *we'll* make history."

She agreed. "I don't doubt it for a second."

Then he grinned, dropping the last of that deeper contemplation as he glanced pointedly at his clean plate. Cheese gone, he seemed to be saying. Tapas and bread and all the earlier "dinner" food gone. He'd been a good boy.

He rolled his eyes up to her. "*Now* is it time for dessert?"

She threw her napkin at him.

CHAPTER 28:

IN THE CROSSHAIRS

DRAKE WAS THE INSIDE MAN. "So far they're keeping the VIP area reserved," he spoke discreetly, trying to appear natural as he looked down to adjust the buttons of his suit jacket. He smoothed out the front lapels and reached for his glass on the bar. Took a drink.

"We've got a better look at expectations," Bobby's voice came to him over his concealed earpiece. "Confidence is high. I think we can be sure that's where Lorenzo will end up. If he has his usual compliment there should be five to six."

Drake looked around the interior of the exclusive Spanish club. He'd had to bribe the doorman to even get in. A lot. A lot lot. "I'm gonna need a special requisition for the budget when we're done. Damn this place is expensive!" He eyed the glass in his hand with the splash of alcohol in it. *Could've bought three six-packs for the price of this.*

"Makes you wonder why we're risking our necks." Bobby's voice was clear, but barely loud enough to compete with the thumping pre-show music already blaring in the club. "We should quit and start our own secret society."

Drake laughed. "We do it for the benefits," he said. "God and Country." It was after eleven local but there was hardly anyone in there. Spanish clubs were notorious for starting late and going later, many running hard well after sunrise. DJ Fujito, the act for which Lorenzo would appear tonight, was "scheduled" for midnight; all in all an early show time. Drake doubted Mister Fujito would even come out before one. Lorenzo could show up any time.

Drake had three agents in street clothes milling about outside, a half-dozen more in commando gear in the surrounding woods. The club was removed from town, out in farm country with only a few roads leading to it.

The highway system connected one of the access roads, foothills just beyond that. Mostly they were remote. Which would work well as, other than the handful of untrained bouncers and club security, once shit got ugly there would be no legitimate response for many key minutes. Once things went down it would just be them and Lorenzo's guys. The Project didn't believe any of the Bok would be armed with anything more than pistols, if that; they were likely to arrive in sports cars, dressed flashy and making a scene—a bad habit for members of a secret society, but one which this younger breed had been getting more and more sloppy at. Allowing, of course, Drake and the Project to tighten the noose. If all went according to plan, tonight they would cinch it all the way. They might get not just their leader, Lorenzo, but several other key players as well. If the opportunity presented itself.

"Echo One moving to the south side," came that agent's voice. One of the three in civilian garb working the outside parking lot. By the end of the night the club would most likely have more people outside than in. Even now, though the interior was near empty, there were dozens of people in the lot, mostly kids and young adults, standing by cars or mopeds or hanging in small groups, smoking and talking and generally trying to be seen. Most of them would never get in. Most wouldn't even try.

In truth Drake and his team couldn't have asked for a better venue. Remote, late, trendy—they would have as good of conditions as they could to corral their targets, tranq them, stuff them into a pair of inconspicuous vans and wheel them off into the night. From there they had a whole system set up ready to move Lorenzo back to American shores.

The hardest part would be the capture.

They obviously didn't want to kill anyone, though that was not out of the question. Their objective was Lorenzo, and if others got in the way they would do what they needed to secure him. They'd debated tailing him, or watching for his arrival and nabbing him then, but ultimately settled on this plan. In a situation where not much made sense, this plan made the most. Drake was in the club to watch and feed info, confirm the target then, when the show was over and Lorenzo went to leave—or if he bolted sooner—the others would be waiting outside to take him down.

Very low impact.

Right.

Nothing ever went according to plan.

* * *

THE TAXI BEEPED ITS HORN as the light turned green and was off, hugging the bumper of the car in front of it, swaying through the roundabout and racing up the next street, similar little beeps echoing all over the city. In the back of the cab Jess leaned into Zac, eyes in her lap.

They were on their way.

"I don't know," she spoke to Bianca's image on the Kel tablet, keeping her voice low though the cab driver was preoccupied with his sprint out of town, listening to music on the cab's radio and otherwise too distracted to care what the girl in the backseat was whispering into her fancy electronic gadget. He probably didn't speak much English anyway.

Nani appeared on the screen.

"I've managed to locate their signals on the ground," she said. "I'm tapping their feed directly. They've got one guy inside the club and more outside. Check the tablet when you're in and we'll give you updates. I'll send new info as I have it."

"Pretend to check your email or something," offered Bianca. Jess realized doing this same thing ten or fifteen years ago would've been way too conspicuous. Now, thankfully, using the alien tablet looked almost normal. At least from a distance. No one would probably give her a second look.

Still, she would try to keep the screen as concealed as possible. The data Nani sent would most definitely not look like email.

"I don't have any more info on Lorenzo and neither does

the Project. They're waiting and watching same as you will be. They think the VIP area has been set aside for him. In fact they're pretty confident that's the case. Lorenzo should be obvious once he and his entourage arrive. The Project expects him to be with others."

Jess glanced up at Zac, sitting tall beside her in the shadows of the cab's backseat. It didn't matter how many agents or how many Bok were in Lorenzo's entourage. The only trick—the *only* trick—would be getting Lorenzo out alive if things turned ugly. Hopefully Zac would be quick enough to avoid deaths.

"I think they're planning to wait till the show is over," Nani went on. "You might want to act then too, or right before. I think it will be the best option. Everything will be happening at once and you'll have the best chance to get out with Lorenzo."

"Ok."

"And Jessica?"

Nani's pause stretched.

Jess asked: "Yes?"

"It occurred to me that the agents in there might recognize you. That may have occurred to you too."

It hadn't.

"It will be dark, and they're obviously there for something else, but we both know from looking over their records they've passed a lot of info on you." Nani looked worried on the small screen. Zac perked up. "Just keep that in mind. It's possible one of them might ID you. If so they may see you as a target of opportunity. Try to blend as best as you can. If I can point any of them out I will. Just ... be careful."

Great. Now she was even more nervous. As if it wasn't going to be challenging enough, getting into the club and pulling this off, now she had to watch that she didn't get spotted. Zac would never allow anything to happen to her, of course, but was her presence going to throw everything into jeopardy?

I can't believe I'm doing this.

Bianca came on the screen. "You'll be fine, Jess," she

said and, to her surprise, Jess found it reassuring. Just words, but her friend's genuine confidence was inspiring.

"Thanks, B."

"Hey, guess what?"

"What?"

Bianca was looking at another screen on the bridge, off to the side. "We're tracking you. I can see the top of the cab. Stick your arm out the window and wave."

"Shush," Jess looked pointedly to the front. The cabbie didn't seem to hear.

"Just do it."

"Bianca." But she realized her friend would probably not relent. Best to just do it.

She stuck her arm out the window and waved. On the small tablet screen Bianca waved back, looking to the side.

"Hi. I see you."

Jess pulled in her arm.

"I'm signing off." And she shut off the tablet.

Beside her Zac looked ahead out the windshield at the traffic they were zipping through. Smiling in the shadows.

"She's funny."

* * *

"I REALLY HOPE she can get them in." Bianca watched the cab from overhead, making its way through the Saturday night traffic on the Spanish streets. It was leaving the outskirts of town and heading to the hills. She watched the car weave this way and that, wishing she was down there with them.

"She's so amazing," she said. "I love her to death, but she can be a real dork sometimes. Those Spanish studs will see right through her. It's all going to be up to her."

Nani kept doing what she was doing, working at her screen. Bianca had just thrown a string of lingo at her but rather than ask questions Nani said: "You know she's actually a bit of a legend. On Anitra."

"Jessica?"

"I don't know how much you've heard, but the last time

she was there she nearly brought our enemies to ruin. The Dominion are still recovering from her last visit."

"She mentioned stuff, yeah. But she acted like it was no big deal. I mean, I could see the way people looked at her—especially those guys where we first ended up. The Conclave?"

"To them she's an angel."

"They were a little creepy. Otherwise I didn't really get the idea she was a legend."

Nani glanced up briefly. "I think they'll be just fine. They shouldn't have any trouble getting Lorenzo. Big question will be, what do we do with him once we have him? That's when the real fun begins. How do we make him talk? I've never interrogated anyone before. Maybe we can hold him as ransom."

Bianca wasn't sure about that either. She had no idea exactly *how* strong Zac was, but from the footage of him in the park fighting the monster Kang, she knew for a fact he would find no challenge on Earth.

Which made the sneaky part all that much more important. If they couldn't get into the club, if they made a scene and got kicked out, they might never get Lorenzo clean. If the Project guys got to him first, or if any sort of fight broke out, they risked killing or losing them and that would leave them nowhere. It was kind of like trying to catch a cat or something. You first had to get close, then you had to move fast. Zac was more than capable of snatching Lorenzo, the trick was going to be getting close and moving fast, before the Bok dude could bolt.

Idly she switched through a few controls at the console.

The Kel inputs were super versatile. From one console, with the right actions, you could move through all options. The same console that acted as a scanner could be a computer, a weapons control center, or it could bring up all the controls you needed to fly the ship. Nani showed her much of that, along with giving her permissions, which felt a lot like being handed the keys to the car. A very, very expensive, very fast, very dangerous car. From where Bianca sat she could do so much more than simply watch

DAVID G MCDANIEL

a tiny cab darting around corners and through traffic.

"They're arriving," she said, noting the taxi's progress. It was finally speeding down the long access road to the club, no doubt eager to drop Jess and Zac and get a new fare.

In no time it was pulling into the crowded lot.

Bianca leaned back.

"Here we go."

CHAPTER 29:

DAWN OF A NEW AGE

COLD FLURRIES flitted through the night, sticking to Kang's unblinking eyes as he stood with Cee-Ranok atop the platform at the edge of the dreadnought berths. Cee was bundled in furs, small, steady shivers detectable to his heightened senses, he with his own fur wrap loose about his shoulders, decorative only, long white hairs of whatever Kel animal it came from blowing in the chill breeze. An affectation for him, nothing more, nothing useful in it, yet he wore it with a certain sense of pride, a mark of belonging.

The mechanical sounds of construction filled the air, buzzing electric arcs and booming blows as workers fitted out the last of the mighty warships that would travel to the stars. Spread out before them was the invasion fleet, making ready to use the information gained from his Icon. Lights shone in the berths, sparks showering here and there behind blast walls, shooting out as brilliant streamers and fading into the dark as they fell.

After days of non-stop activity the fleet would soon be prepped for departure. Cee was wasting no time. The armies that would go were ready. The Kel were always ready, staging war games constantly at the whim of their leaders. This was the way the Kel lived. Kang relished it. These were a people he could rule. And while this would be no war game, preparations for what they set out to do were no different.

Partly their rush came from Cee's desire to follow through before minds were changed. She had the backing of the War Council and didn't want to lose it. As well she had the minds of the populace and, like the military, risked losing that too if delayed. The Kel, as a whole, were in a state of uncertainty following what were already being called— much to Cee's impotent rage—the Prophecy Uprisings.

There was as yet no "uprising" in particular, not one that Kang saw, but there were apparently enough stirrings that had Cee in a state of panic. Any mention of the Prophecy was squashed mercilessly at every turn, a campaign Kang fully appreciated for its ruthless thoroughness, but the fear was that, now that the seed had been watered, a long dormant seed, sewn long ago, it was growing. As far as Cee was concerned the only way to handle the talk of such things was to overwhelm it. Completely blot it out with new expansion beyond the ability for any prophetic notions to overtake. To put the focus of the people back on new conquest, back to new enemies other than themselves.

And so it seemed she could not hurry the completion of the fleet fast enough. To hurry this monumental event. In fact, and incredibly, they would probably on their way by tomorrow.

Kang was familiar with prophecies. With how they could weaken the minds of a populace. He looked at Cee and smiled, even as her attention was thoroughly caught up in the activity spreading across the vastness before them. Only too happy to do his part.

* * *

THEY'D REACHED THE CLUB. After exiting the cab Jess and Zac meandered across the dusty parking lot; a forced, leisurely stroll, feeling like she wanted to sprint everywhere, the lot already filling up with people hoping to get in. Zac slipped into the woods for a moment to ditch the bag with their clothes while she waited. She debated marking the area where he hid it but decided there was no point. After the events of tonight went down they weren't going to need the bag or anything in it.

She took a deep breath. Zac returned and stood beside her, looking across the lot at all the cars, motorcycles, scooters—dozens of mopeds and scooters—people everywhere. Most everyone was young as far as Jess could see, teens and twenties. A few older people were scattered here and there but not many. The club was a free-standing building in the middle of nowhere, single floor, lit with cool neon and harsher lights from the lot. Four bouncers stood in black suits outside, guarding the black velvet ropes that led to the door.

Nervously she eyed them. Their most immediate barrier. A silly barrier, to be sure—Zac could throw all four meat-heads into the woods with a single toss—but the threat of the doormen was very real. If this little operation was going to work she and Zac had to get by them, legitimately, with no fuss, and make it into the club.

And again she found herself wondering at the plan. Should they just sneak into the woods, put back on the more sensible clothes and wait for Lorenzo to arrive? She shifted in the uncomfortable, impractical heels; felt the hug of the tiny dress. That seemed an easier way to go about it. They already knew from Nani that the Project— their de facto opponent that night—had guys stationed in the trees. If Jess and Zac also snuck into the trees and hid they might spring out at the right moment ...

But if they did that they risked missing Lorenzo altogether. Or being seen by the Project. The Project also had a guy in the club, according to Nani, which meant they, too, felt it was key to have eyes on Lorenzo in that setting. If the Project got Lorenzo then somehow slipped away unseen ... Jess and Zac would be faced with way more complications and unknowns. They had to lay eyes on Lorenzo first, and grab him before the Project could. Nothing was guaranteed, but Jess realized that by doing this, dressing up, playing make-believe and being on the inside—where they could watch and move before anyone else—they had the best chance. Even with Nani listening in on the Project's conversations the Project might still pull some unexpected move and slip away, with Lorenzo, before anyone knew it. Leaving Jess and Zac sitting in the woods twiddling their thumbs, wondering just what the hell happened. Jess couldn't shut off the endless reel of figure-figure-figure running through her head, looking for all sorts of ways to change the plan, but the harsh reality was that nothing had changed and it had come to this:

They had to get by the doormen.

Finally forcing her to admit the idea of that, more than anything—being cool enough to be admitted—was making her more nervous than anything else.

Zac took her hand, pretending to be unaware of the doubt knotting her guts. "Shall we?"

She swallowed.

But he knew. He had to know. How she felt. She could sense the reassurance in his grip as he led her on a straight path through the people in the lot, a little too much purpose in his step. No one seemed to notice, and soon they were merging into the end of the line to wait their turn. Others trickled in behind, laughing and cavorting, having a great time—nothing at all to worry about. For them this was going to be a great time. A night to remember.

Boy was it.

Music issued from the club. It was a strong beat, a danceable rhythm similar to the kind played by DJ Fujito. It wasn't him but it was just as hooky, and through the door each time it opened, as new, trendy people went in, Jess could see strobes flashing and others inside.

She took another deep breath and looked up. Into the night, away from that place.

It was an amazing evening. High, thin clouds striped the dark sky in deep shades of gray; stars, lots and lots of stars higher still behind them, making the dome of the atmosphere seem more enormous than usual. As if, that night, the horizon stretched higher and further, casting a vast majesty over everything, driving home the reality of just how small their little corner of the world was. Far above she could make out a tiny, blinking light against the other points of brilliance, an airplane, probably all the way up at cruising altitude, thirty-thousand feet or more—way up there—passing slowly across one of the bands of gray, methodically slipping in and out of view, lending its own touch of perspective to the backdrop of distant, twinkling suns.

A stiff breeze swept across the parking lot and made her shiver, interrupting her reverie.

Zac slid his arms from his suit jacket and handed it to her. "Here," he said. "You've got goose bumps."

She took the jacket and glanced at her bare shoulders. Her skin looked smooth in the dim light, but no doubt he saw all the little bumps she could only feel. She thanked him, put on the large, expensive jacket and held it closed at the front with one hand. The sleeves flopped well past her fingertips, but the lining was luxuriously silky, radiating the residual heat of his body and warming her instantly— making her shiver for altogether new reasons. There were so many things wracking her nerves right then, yanking her emotions in every possible direction. The goose bumps hadn't been entirely from the cold. In addition to everything else she was terrified.

She forced a smile as she smoothed the sleek Italian jacket, all the way down to where it hung at her knees. She wondered if Zac would notice the smile was forced and made herself relax. At that a real, softer smile touched her lips. Tenderly he put a hand to her head—then seemed to realize what he was doing and withdrew.

"Sorry," he apologized, checking where he'd touched her. He knew how anal Bianca had been over everything, including Jessica's hair. "Don't want to mess up your hair."

But there was nothing to mess up, really, though she made no comment. She just continued admiring him. Beneath the suit jacket Zac wore the vest and, of course, now that he was out of the jacket the shiny vest over the dress shirt with matching tie looked as amazing on him as everything else. Zac truly was one of those guys that looked great no matter what he wore. He could rock anything.

She gave him another smile and pretended to study the line in front of them. A group of Spanish girls stood next ahead. Three of them. Slowly bodies shuffled forward as at the door the next hopefuls were released. With barely concealed scrutiny Jess watched the bouncers making their selections. One couple got the boot and she struggled to see over and around the people in the way, trying to discern why. Hoping not to make the same mistake. Was it their clothes? Their attitudes? The couple looked as pulled together as she and Zac. She swallowed. Were they foreign? They looked like they could be. Earlier, watching from the lot, she'd seen a small group of obviously American boys get sent away. At the time she had to admit she wouldn't have let them in either; they were loud, brash, acting cocky ... like they'd just cause trouble and spend no money. Now she began to wonder if it was because they were American. For an instant her mind began to race—debating trying a French accent or some other stupid idea she'd probably never pull off—then she noticed the three girls in front of them eyeing Zac. Blatantly looking him up and down, giggling among themselves. How long had they been doing that? Zac didn't seem to notice. He was in "ready" mode, gaze well above their heads.

Jess looked at the girls and, to her sudden consternation, found herself jealous. It was hard to tell exactly what they were saying to each other, but in that moment every bit of her past study of the Spanish language, every recall, every word, came flooding to hand. She couldn't understand the particulars but the cute little Spanish girls were most definitely commenting on, and staring at, the muy guapo Zac.

Jess looked away, trying to pretend not to notice. Fuming inside.

Then one of them spoke directly to him.

"You a fighter?" the girl asked in broken English. It was a cute voice, and the one asking was the cutest of the bunch, such a cute little accent coming from her cute little face ...

Jess wanted to punch it. Quite surprised by the strength of the urge.

She was *definitely* on edge.

At first Zac didn't realize the girl had spoken to him, but before Jess could act he glanced down.

"Me?"

The girl looked up at him, put her chin down, big brown peepers rolled up to look at him from beneath obviously fake lashes. So precious, so dainty. She made little boxing motions with her tiny fists. "You know," she jabbed the air. "Fighter."

The others giggled.

Jess watched for how Zac would handle this, not wanting to say anything or start anything, especially now. They were so close. A cat fight with a bunch of club-girl wannabes would definitely get them kicked out. Up ahead a group of well-heeled clubbers were permitted past the stuffed suits guarding the velvet ropes.

Zac cocked his head a little at the girl, confused.

She looked to her friends and Jess could see she was looking for a translation. It occurred to Jessica the girls must've overheard she and Zac speaking to each other, thus deducing he spoke English. Clearly their English wasn't that good.

One of the other girls spoke better.

"Because you look like you fight," she said, and puffed up her shoulders and chest like a big muscle-man. Then she pointed to her cheek, then to his in the same place, to the small scar from his fight with Kang. Faint, nearly healed, but visible. Jess had to admit it was not in the place you would likely get a scar unless you'd been punched.

Zac touched the scar, unsure what to say.

"I was in a fight." He looked to Jess for help, and she struggled with the indignant rage she was feeling that these little hussies would flirt so openly with him right there in front of her. They weren't even looking at her. *I'm right here!* she wanted to scream. *He's my boyfriend!* She wanted to throttle them was more like it. *I'm wearing his jacket! What the hell?!*

But the girls were next and, whether from the silly way they were acting, their age or some other factor, they got dismissed. No pause for consideration. The doormen waved them ahead for inspection, the girls suddenly remembered why they were there, shifted their attention from Zac to the doormen, batted their eyelashes and smiled—probably making it worse for themselves by doing so—and were denied. Of course they exploded with anger. Jess found their bitchy fury amusing, deriving some small satisfaction from their misfortune as one of the doormen had to "shoo" them away, clearing the ropes. As that commotion was unfolding she took off and handed Zac his jacket. No need to take any chances. Wouldn't want the doormen thinking she looked dumb wearing it, no matter the reason. Zac put it back on, eyes on the trio of girls who now stood off to the side refusing to leave, making a minor scene, continuing to complain of the horrible injustice as the doormen returned to their task, deciding to just ignore them.

Jess and Zac were next. No one else stood between them and entry to the club. Nervously she stepped up. The doormen were too cool for everyone, or acted like it, hardly deigning to look anyone in the eye, even the ones they admitted. Zac was taller than all of them, making it hard to look over his head and still appear natural, but they tried. Zac was taller than everyone, actually, even the tallest of the young Spaniards Jess had seen that night, and as they stood there waiting to be judged she finally—*finally*— felt the confidence she'd been seeking. It washed over her, in that most crucial instant, surging out of nowhere; almost a certain haughtiness—that their entry was a given—and even as she felt it, satisfied with having achieved that calm at the last possible moment, the guys were holding back the ropes and letting them pass.

And they were inside.

CHAPTER 30:

DJ FUJITO

"THEY MADE IT," Bianca's eyes roved over the incoming data, checking it right along with Nani. "I can't believe it."

"You didn't think they would?"

"I mean, I guess I thought they would. I don't know. Hoping is more like it. I kind of thought it wouldn't be that easy. Like maybe they'd have to figure out a different way. Like have Zac tunnel in or something."

"Tunnel in?" Nani smiled as she tapped and checked inputs. "I guess that *would* be more in line with the way things seem to have been going." Then: "Maybe we were due for a break."

"Maybe."

Nani tapped a few more things and looked up, to the larger screen. "Okay," she scanned the various overlays, "now we watch. Let's see what else we can find out." And she was back to her personal screens. Tapping away.

* * *

"I LOVE THIS!" Zac shouted, loud enough for Jess to hear above the pulsing thunder of the club's sound system. Of course he could probably yell loud enough for everyone in the club to hear, but in the face of the absolute sonic volume hammering the space Jess wasn't so sure. She could barely hear her own shouts—though Zac heard her just fine. As it turned out his super hearing and super voice were coming in handy. Kind of like the way Han Solo and Chewbacca talked to each other though neither spoke the other's language; Zac could easily talk loud enough for her to hear and, in turn, could hear her clearly when she spoke. How that was true, how he could hear her normal human voice and still take the staggering volume with those same, extra sensitive ears was beyond her. His super hearing must've been as impervious as the rest of him. She felt like her own ears would soon bleed.

DJ Fujito was laying down the beats through the million-amp sound system and the crowd was loving it. He'd finally come on and was as good as any of the sample tracks they'd listened to back aboard the *Reaver*. Jess watched Zac's enthusiastic expression, in rapture with the music. She had to admit she loved it too. Sound energy moved the club; you could actually feel it, and she was reminded of the drag races in Las Vegas, an event that seemed so long ago. The volume here was similar, though unlike the Top Fuel dragsters there were high notes, and she was learning it was the high notes that hurt. Bass you could feel; treble stung.

Standing there among the clubbing elite she felt like a minor star. Now that they were in, now that the most difficult challenge was past—the doormen—she felt practically regal. Drink in hand, heels giving her a few extra inches, little black dress hugging her curves, showing plenty of skin. Thin bands of jewelry glinting in the club lights. For once in her life she actually felt beautiful. Really felt it, not just hoping she might be, or that someone else might possibly think so, but had the uplifting sensation that she, Jessica Paquin, was someone truly desirable.

"Earth is so awesome!" Zac was nodding his head, not quite dancing but almost. He'd checked his jacket at the door, looking stunning in the club lights in his stylish vest, shirt and tie. It was hard not to be affected by the deep rhythm. Jess looked around to make sure no one heard his slip. They didn't. No one else was even trying to talk, or if they did were shouting directly into each other's ear or making hand motions. If anything they just danced or stood and watched or typed away on phones. Dozens of tiny little screens glowed everywhere, scattered throughout the club's frenetic illumination.

To Jess everyone looked either drunk or high.

Lasers fanned the air, smoke machines added brilliant definition to the colored beams, black lights made the whites glow and the dark moments between were filled with strobes flashing in rapid staccato, blasting everything to a mind-numbing pulse. Overall wildly painful, seizure-inducing fun. In the midst of that madness she had no idea how she and Zac were supposed to pull of their mission.

"Do you see the VIP area?" she yelled, knowing she'd made sounds but unable to hear.

"Yeah," Zac pointed over everyone's head, to a place across the room. She wished he'd bc a bit more discreet.

"Let's get closer," she suggested. That was where the Project expected Lorenzo to be. Gently she took him by the arm and directed him, picking carefully through the throngs. They both had cold glasses of coke. Jess held the icy glass in one hand, arm crooked, holding Zac by the elbow with her other. She took a sip as she excused herself with nods and smiles, guiding him ahead of her and moving in his wake. As he made his way slowly at her direction, parting bodies politely, she thought of one of the ancient vampires from Anne Rice's novels, pushing carefully through a crowd so as not to break anyone.

Zac would so destroy a vampire.

She guided him over and stepped up to a higher part of the club, near a bar with some space, stopped and turned to lean against it. She put an elbow on the slightly wet surface. From there they had a clear line of sight to the roped-off VIP area.

Suddenly she wondered how Lorenzo rated. Why didn't he have to come through the door like everyone else? Did the Project agents have to get past the doormen? She looked around.

Where are they?

As Fujito mixed one track into the next she put her coke on the bar and took the tablet from her purse. No new updates from Nani. Their blonde overseer had been keeping them regularly informed.

No, wait. Something new was coming in. Nani had identified the agent in the club. Only one, as it turned out. It was Drake. The leader of this operation and, ironically, also the guy in charge of the op that failed to capture Jess in Boise. A wave of nerves passed over her, though in truth it didn't matter who was in the club with them. It could be the President of the United States; that didn't change what they were there for or how it would go down. They were getting Lorenzo and they were getting away and no one was going to stop them.

Zac would see to that.

Nani sent her Drake's picture again and she made a fresh study of it, glancing up from the tablet discreetly as she did, peering around the multitudes. Smoke drifted, lights flashed, bodies pressed or moved erratically. Pumping this way and that.

Unless Drake was right in their vicinity it was hopeless. She'd never find him.

She turned off the tablet and put it back in her purse.

DJ Fujito was a young, androgynous Japanese, long hair bleached in a few places, combed across half his face, spiked in the back. She knew it was a "him", though the more she watched in the hazy conditions she couldn't be sure. Gender bending had never looked so real. He had a lights guy, equally ambiguous, who shared the riser with him and seemed to derive great importance from his role as laser-shooter-strobe-guy. On either side of the small stage was a cage with a barely-dressed Japanese girl, dancing furiously to the music. Jess wondered if they traded with different girls throughout the set. She hadn't noticed. Just watching them pump and grind, as hard and as steady as they were, was exhausting. She couldn't imagine actually doing it.

"There he is," Zac pierced the grip of the music. His voice had such inhuman clarity amid the pandemonium. She looked up at his strong jaw, followed his gaze over the heads of the crowd ...

And saw him.

Lorenzo. Entering the VIP area.

He wasn't looking at her, of course he couldn't be, not in that crowd and across that room, yet ... his gaze seemed to pass right through her. Through both of them; Zac too. It was as if Lorenzo could feel them, though his focus didn't linger, and the smarter part of her told her he hadn't seen them nor did he even know to look.

How could he possibly?

So why did she have the sudden terror of being seen? Of being picked from the crowd. She looked up at Zac and was dismayed by his expression.

He felt it too.

He didn't look down, though, didn't know she was looking at him; kept his eyes on Lorenzo, watching their target arrive with casual importance. The Bok leader made his way coolly to the couches in the VIP area, entering from some hidden door behind it or some other entrance unknown to them. At any rate he did not walk in through the front of the club.

Turned out it was a good thing they were inside after all. They might've missed him otherwise.

Several others trailed him with the same casual confidence, like Russian mobsters or something; people who knew this was their place and that no one, absolutely no one, would mess with them. Quite the contrary. Others would fear them.

And she felt her first tinge of worry.

Lorenzo and three other guys about his age, plus one girl, all of them dressed uber cool, swank—however you described it, these guys were wearing a thousand dollars worth of clothes each. Had to be. Comfortable, easy fitting, minimal yet ... beyond rich. They sat easily in the luxurious VIP seating, reclining, almost as if they saw everything while barely deigning to notice what was going on around them.

It was all very much beneath them.

"Seems pretty cocky," Zac commented, and his voice was easy and confident. Jess steadied a bit as he added: "Suddenly I think I'm going to enjoy this."

Yeah, she thought. *It will be fun stuffing him in a bag or something.*

Then it hit her like a bolt.

This guy, Lorenzo Fertiti, leader of the Esehta Bok, was, through the distant past, through many generations of

humans, directly connected to the Kel. Until then talk of
the Bok had been just that: talk. Pictures, information.
Now here they were, here *he* was, and ...

For a shuddering instant he *looked* Kel. Like the elfin
images from Nani's records.

Lorenzo wasn't Kel. No way. The Bok had been human
from the beginning. Still, the image was impossible to
shake. He and his cronies exuded a sort of other-worldly
presence that made them *feel* alien, though they'd surely
been on Earth through a line of humans a thousand years
old.

Then she spotted Drake. Quite suddenly, no longer even
looking for him—having almost forgotten the Project at the
arrival of the Bok elite—moving toward the VIP area far
too deliberately, and when she recognized him she looked
quickly away.

"There's Drake," she hissed, thought for a minute Zac
hadn't heard the tiny sound—a hiss that was utterly lost in
the thunder—but he did.

"I see him," he said, keen eyes already making contact
and following the Project agent as he, in turn, zeroed in on
Lorenzo. Blatantly moving against the crowd toward the
newly arrived Bok. Drake was closer than expected, having
chosen the same section of bar from which to view the VIP
area, and Jess wondered how she missed him earlier. No
matter. Now that he was right there and focused on the same
target she had to avoid eye contact. Zac might be safe but
she wasn't. This guy once led the operation to capture her.
No doubt he'd reviewed tons of photos of her, building the
Project's dossier, and would be sure to recognize her—even
dressed as she was, appearing in that improbable setting:
in the midst of a Spanish club, in the middle of their secret
operation, when the last time he knew her location for sure
was in a suit of armor in Boise, popping out of existence
with an Icon. She felt so utterly exposed, more than she
thought she would. Fearfully she slipped tighter against
Zac, hiding herself behind him. He stood taller—if that was
possible—shielding her as inconspicuously as possible.

But she couldn't stop peeking. Looking around his

midsection furtively, like looking around a tree.

Drake held one hand to his ear, obviously speaking into an earpiece, alternately listening and moving his lips in what was clearly a shout. He was handsome, probably close enough to the right age to be in there without attracting too much attention under other circumstances, but with his plain suit and standing there yelling into an earpiece he was a complete sore thumb. If he was trying to be undercover he was doing a terrible job. Jess had to admit the conditions were strained, but come on.

Surely they could do better.

Nani was listening to the Project's channel; Jess had the idea to check the tablet to see what Drake was saying. She pulled it from the purse and thumbed it on. There were, in fact, updates, posted by Nani just moments ago. The Project agents had spotted Lorenzo and company arriving in sports cars and entering through the back entrance. Drake then relayed what he was seeing from inside, which Nani in turn relayed to the tablet, and as Jess glanced back and forth between the straining, concentrating Drake, able to know what he was saying as he said it, right there on her Kel tablet, she felt a little smile turn the corners of her mouth. Not only did she and Zac have the upper hand in terms of physical force, they had the upper hand in terms of situational awareness. They knew more of what was going on than the Project did, and when it came time to act the Project would be left empty-handed.

She watched Drake trying to hear. Pushing the earpiece to his ear ever harder. Lorenzo *had* to notice.

Then, suddenly, Drake turned in her direction. Covered his free ear with his other hand, so obvious now it was almost painful to watch and ... was suddenly looking right at her. He hadn't seen her yet, hadn't focused, but his eyes, randomly, were right on her.

And she realized she shouldn't be staring. She shouldn't be looking back. Now was the time to look away. Head peering stupidly around Zac, rest of her hiding behind him, staring right at Drake like playing hide-and-seek—like she'd somehow forgotten what the hell she was doing—

which apparently she had—Drake right there in easy view
...

   She'd blown it.

   He focused all at once and she realized it was too late to
do anything but stand there and hope for the best, hope
she got lucky. Otherwise he would surely see her ducking
to hide ...

   But luck was not on her side.

   He saw her.

CHAPTER 31:

THE SUMMIT

OSAKA SPRAWLED within its walled confines, dark buildings crowding against the tall barriers at every edge, casting long shadows beneath the rising sun. Outside the walls stood a vast emptiness. The expansive plain surrounding the city did not even have trees, for as far as the eye could see.

Lindin watched from the windows of a large command 'thopter, taking it all in as they banked above the land of their—possibly former—enemies. The waterborne carrier on which they'd arrived, part of a military escort that was as much ceremony as it was function, had anchored with the fleet off the coast of Dominion lands, releasing a swarm of the Venatres ornithopters with their dignitaries and leaders, which now flew along the major waterway leading to the city itself.

Osaka.

Lindin looked ahead to their destination. The wings of the giant flying machine beat the air with a titanic whump, the shielded walls of the executive cabin unable to block the tremendous noise utterly. This was a large, heavy beast, and it took a lot of mechanical action to hold it aloft.

Lindin rode with the president and several of the Venatres top brass. Not all Venatres leaders had come, certainly, but enough were among the convoy that a Dominion trap at this point would be quite damaging. But none expected the Dominion were laying a trap. The Dominion had issues of their own, their entire leadership gutted—not once but twice in the past half-year—and Yamoto, whom the Venatres came to see, was all that was left of that original hierarchy. The Dominion were hurting. A summit, with new agreements, concessions and understandings was, in truth, needed by them far more than it was the Venatres.

Soon the 'thopter was curving down, angling toward the aerodrome at the city center. The two tallest spires, Vivitak and the Tower of Light, jutted high into the air, several dozen floors higher than the next nearest skyscraper, the aerodrome waiting to receive them just outside the inner compound. Perched on a massive landing pad near the top of the Tower of Light was one of the Dominion airships, one of the few left at the moment, after Kang flew most of them across the ocean for his ill-fated attack on Venatres lands.

Lindin knew the Dominion were relieved to be rid of their invincible ruler. Even those refusing to obey orders, those generals staging a coup back in Midbay—yet one more element of decay facing Yamoto—were glad Kang was gone. When the beast disappeared with Zac there was a collective sigh of relief across the globe.

For a difficult moment Lindin fought a barely suppressed rage, inflamed at the thought of what happened with the Icon and, most critically, the starship. But he could not afford to continue to be consumed with it. Not now. Not here. Before them lay opportunity. For now he must hold it aside in his thoughts.

Much could be gained from an alliance with the Dominion.

As they curved around the tall buildings he watched the large airship perched atop its pad until it was out of sight, seeing it from many angles as they passed behind, around at a near distance and below. The Dominion airships were yet another advanced technology the Venatres had been unable to replicate. And yet, in many ways the Venatres were more advanced than the Dominion. The Dominion had a mad-scientist streak running through them, with more than a few examples of advances that did not fall in line with the rest of their knowledge. Subsequently many of those things had become mysterious or arcane—though they themselves had invented them. The airships. Plasma cannons of unparalleled power. Raza energy to tame the mighty Kazerai.

The Kazerai themselves.

Now they'd lost all their Kazerai, and nearly wasted all their airships. And their greatest treasure, the Holy Icon itself ...

That Lindin had. And they knew it.

He wondered how important it still was to them. Wondered if it would be part of the discussions later that day. Surely it would become the topic of *some* discussion. He doubted, however, if it would be put on the table right away.

If things went well, however, that conversation might be one to welcome rather than dread. How far might an alliance go? After so many decades of so much conflict, how easily could they wipe the slate clean? Ideologically there were differences. Big differences. But there were also many things over which to come together. Could this truly be the dawn of a unified world?

Perhaps, in that place and at that time, an alliance might actually herald great things. Monumental things.

As they landed and the heavy wings began winding down Lindin imagined how the Dominion technology and their own might be blended.

How, perhaps, Anitra might, eventually, become one world, united in a greater cause.

* * *

HOURS LATER, THE SINKING FEELING of discovery had finally passed. Drake had definitely ID'd her, there was nothing he could do and, thanks to Nani, Jess knew it. She'd been checking the tablet feeds and knew that, in fact, the agents were talking about her and, if anything, her unexpected presence was throwing an extra layer of stress into the mix. A big layer. They'd been poised to kidnap one person on foreign soil and now here was a second, unaccounted for—a target of extreme opportunity—Jessica Paquin, teenager from Boise, whom they wanted just as badly and ...

What to do?

And so they'd begun working feverishly to incorporate her into their plans, having no idea their harried conversations were being tapped; no idea Jess knew what they were up to. In fact, she wasn't even sure they knew she'd seen them. It was quite possible they didn't. When Drake first spotted her she looked away casually—even as her blood chilled—and yet it didn't appear he realized she, in turn, knew who he was. And why would she? The possibility had not, apparently, crossed his mind. It was looking more and more likely that her furtive glances in his direction had gone unnoticed.

Of course, the fact that she was there at all, an uncanny "coincidence" that flew in the face of chance, must've tipped him somehow, even if he wasn't saying so to his partners. He had to be suspicious. After being at the top of their Most Wanted list Drake must realize there was no way Jess could just happen to be at the same club—all the way over in Europe, no less—that the Project was staking out. Therefore, she concluded, whether it looked like it or not they *must* suspect her. More than that, they had to be a little afraid. Right? She would be. If Jess *did* know what they were up to, which was the only logical explanation— unless they thought her somehow connected to the Bok, which would bring its own sets of confusions—if she *did* know then why did she willingly put herself directly in the middle of their operation? They'd come after her once, back in Boise, and she, one girl, faced with an onslaught of well-armed, well-funded agents had, essentially, handed them their asses. Weren't they just a little afraid to find her there now, smack in the middle of their operation? Right as they were about to make their move? Was she about to snatch their prize again? This time with no suit of powered armor, just a little black dress and a fancy purse. How could she possibly?

If they only knew.

She stared up at Zac. He stood tall beside her, sipping a coke. She held her own ice-filled glass, moist with condensation. Like the glass she was sweating, flush with the exertion of dancing.

She leaned back and put her elbows on the bar.

Since Drake's discovery she'd been trying desperately to push herself into the role of club rat, to blend thoroughly, hang with Zac and pretend to be there for the music, the DJ, the drinks, the experience—anything but what really brought them. Anything to make them appear completely natural. In order to do that the only thing she could think of was to dance. The exact thing she did *not* want to do, had not wanted to do from the moment she knew they were coming to a club and, though she was nervous and embarrassed—so embarrassed—she made herself get out there. Filled with dread she dragged Zac to a spot on the floor and ...

Danced.

On top of everything else; the fear of being discovered, the sheer magnitude of what they were there to pull off, the desperate need to blend in, the self-conscious uncertainty of actually dancing ... she couldn't have imagined a more agonizing mix of emotions. Shy terror? Embarrassed fear? It was nearly too much. Once she began letting go, however, once the initial awkwardness eased ... much to her surprise it got easier, came more naturally until ... it started to be fun. Now, after hours on and off the floor she'd been dancing with abandon, working up a healthy sweat and feeling, in a word, awesome. In fact the dancing actually helped ease the other, darker emotions and she was, incredibly, having a great time. There was nothing else to be done until the critical moment came and so, as always, if it was time to have fun, then, why not have fun? By then she was fully in character; a girl and her boyfriend out at the club and nothing more. So what if Drake knew she was there? It didn't matter. Not even a little.

And so she danced.

Before tonight she never really had. Definitely not like this; not at a club, not with a boy. Gymnastics, tricking, ballet when she was little, even martial arts ... she knew how to move, especially in structured movements, it just felt embarrassing to let go. Once she did, however, it turned out she was good. Zac too. He was a great mimic and super coordinated. Of course he would be. He did what the others did and more. Even some cool original moves. Watching those around them, following Jessica's lead, and together they'd been dancing the whole night, making stuff up, even jumping around, which was hilarious and fun, getting more and more creative, totally getting into it and having a blast. At first small, simple movements, awkward expressions and knotted nerves, those turning eventually to goofy smiles and the occasional laugh, then gut-busting laughter at each ridiculous, increasingly exaggerated, sometimes silly move, all of it gradually becoming more ...

Intense.

At some point Zac took off and pocketed his tie, rolled up his sleeves and took it to the next level. Jess followed his lead. Dancing up against him, grinding and turning in the little black dress as the furious beat drove their motion, flipping her long hair side to side, across him, feeling incredibly sexy as the night wore on, making deep, prolonged eye contact over her shoulder, back up against him, more and more bold in her actions—he gripping her hips and grinding right along with her. They alternated, face to face, her palms on his chest, looking up into his pale-blue eyes, glinting exotically in the colored lights; short, dark hair and the stubble of his beard; rugged, handsome, young—impossible to look all those things at once yet he did, and more than once she had to catch her breath.

And he was as into her; an intensity in his regard that made her rush with a transcendent sort of fulfillment. Time and again he ran his hands down her arms and over her hips, brushing her skin, roughly then lightly, around her butt and up her back to her bare shoulders, over again and down and it was the most exciting thing ever.

By the time they finally broke from the last round of dancing and returned to the bar she was flushed from more than just the exertion. Shivering with a cold sweat. Several times, in fact, during the heat of it, she forgot why they were even there. Totally. It was just she and Zac, blood coursing through every inch of her, desire, pumping so hard, music crushing all other realities, frenetic lights obliterating the world ...

In those moments their real situation was far, far gone from her mind.

She pulled her eyes from him and took a drink. Glanced in Lorenzo's direction—only a glance—then flicked her eyes back to the crowd. She wiped the cold, wet glass across her hot brow.

Zac wasn't sweating. Physical exertion, dancing—these things were nothing for him. He wasn't even breathing differently. She steadied her own breathing; watched as he also took a drink. He'd had six cokes already. *Where does it go?* Probably just evaporated inside him somehow, with his crazy metabolism. His gusto for food and drink was insane.

Casually she let her gaze wander more slowly across the chaos of the club, back to Lorenzo and his entourage in the VIP area. None of them danced. They hardly moved, in fact. Even in the body rocking, absolute-edge-of-overwhelming environment, constant strobes and laser lights, they remained stoic. Unaffected. She suspected Lorenzo knew Drake was there. Somehow she was convinced he'd also seen she and Zac. Watching him gave her the creeps. Almost like he *was* some kind of super-chic movie vampire, or one of those self-aware guys from the *Matrix* or something. Not like a real-life, ordinary person.

And as she watched him without watching she realized how absurd it all was. It was like everyone was just playing along. Everyone knew. Drake knew she was there; Lorenzo probably knew they were there; she and Zac knew Drake and Lorenzo were there. Everyone knew what everyone else was up to. And if they didn't, they should. She almost wanted to wave. "Hey! Catch you after the show! No, literally. Catch you after the show. Get it?"

Life is never dull.

She took a deep breath and leaned harder against the bar. It was super late. Probably not long till sunrise. Local time as reported on the Kel tablet was just before 5 am, and after dancing hard for the last several hours and being up the day before—on high alert much of that time—she was exhausted.

It was not an unfamiliar feeling.

The last six months of her life had been filled with such

extremes, and she was quite ready for the action to begin and this mission to be a wrap. Standing there sweating, cooling off, sipping her cold coke, she was most definitely "on". She pushed a few damp strands of hair from her forehead. Adjusted the delicate purse with the tablet in it. When they started dancing she threw the thin strap across the other shoulder so it wouldn't slip off. Her last check-in with Nani brought no new news. It was pretty much down to waiting now for the right moment.

"He's onto us," Zac commented, sipping his own coke casually. The music was as loud as ever, the lightshow intense, no sign of DJ Fujito winding down. Would they go past sunrise? Spanish discos were legendary, but this was nearly too much. "He keeps looking at us," Zac said, indicating Lorenzo, "then he looks at Drake. He knows."

She and Zac had been talking off and on about the possibility, trying to figure out if it was just their own worry of exposure, that sort of imminent vulnerability when you were spying on someone and couldn't tell if they knew, or if Lorenzo truly did know they were there. The Bok leader's focus remained mostly on the DJ, and when he did look away it seemed he always looked at them and at Drake. More than that, though, the thing that bothered Jess was the way he did it. Not an ounce of concern in his eyes, no worry whatsoever in his expression or in his mannerisms. Just a casual look, confirming their current location in the club, then eyes back to the show. Almost like making sure they weren't going anywhere or hadn't left. It was creepy. No sign he was about to bolt, or that they made him nervous, or even that he wondered what they might be up to. And so it was hard to tell if he actually saw them or not. How could he and not react? With the confirmation of Zac's instinct, however, and the fact that, even then, in that same moment, Lorenzo looked at them and she could *swear* he saw her—and this time the corner of his mouth turned up ever so slightly—the reality of it locked into place.

He knows we're here for him.

And so it was official. Everyone knew. The icy chill she got watching Lorenzo, however ... it was a feeling she wished she could make go away. He was cocky, you could almost feel it he was so cocky, but it wasn't just that. Lorenzo wasn't just full of himself. He exuded some sort of tangible awareness that was difficult to dismiss. As if he had good reason to be cocky. And that bothered her.

She looked up at Zac, who in turn watched their prey. Zac wasn't worried. At least, if he sensed Lorenzo's overconfidence he didn't show it. Just sipped his coke, standing there so tall, so strong—a god among men— waiting to make the grab and get out of there.

Jess pulled the tablet and checked for updates. Satori and Nani were coordinating, Satori ready to fly in and meet them once they had Lorenzo. When the set was over and as the club was emptying out they would move to the VIP area and grab him. Zac would dismiss any interference as needed, stun Lorenzo and get he and Jess out, with the prize, before the agents had a chance to react. So far their communications indicated the Project was sticking to their plan to nab Lorenzo outside, which meant when Jess and Zac moved—inside the club—the only one to offer any resistance would be Drake.

"How much longer is he going to play?" Jess was starting to grow exasperated. Fujito just kept going and going and going.

Even as she said this he wrapped it up. As if her mere question triggered the finale. With no fade or even a change in tempo to indicate the set was winding down, he finished. Just like that. The strobes and lasers stopped, left the club for a moment in the half-dark, the bass drubbing crescendoed and ...

The music ended.

The resulting silence was almost as numbing as the sonic assault. Jessica's ears rang and it took a few seconds to realize the new sound filling the darkened space was the crowd cheering. Maybe they'd been cheering all along. She couldn't tell. All she knew was in the wake of the rhythmic pulse there were now cheers. Quieter by far yet loud in their own way; hundreds of voices raised in an exultant roar. Like they'd all just gone through an exhilarating journey.

Which, in a way, they had. For a few moments Jess forgot herself in the energy of the moment and cheered along with them. A rush, a sense of belonging with those who'd been through it with her, those who experienced the amazing.

But she and Zac were there for far more important things. Their night was just beginning.

She stuck close to him as the crowd continued to roar, until the steady cheering degenerated to shouts and hollers for encores. DJ Fujito and his dancers simply took their praise with curt little nods and beaming white smiles, not moving to play any more music. There would be no encore. Many in attendance had already taken the cue or were simply too tired to care and had begun heading for the exit. Nervously Jess watched Lorenzo in the VIP area, wondering how quickly he would leave. He knew people were there for him. How soon would he run? She glanced at Zac, who watched Lorenzo and his small group with calm regard, shoulders squared, looking over the heads of the crowd, then she glanced across at Drake, who was on the other side of the dance floor, back to speaking quite obviously into his "concealed" earpiece.

"Stick close," Zac advised and put an arm around her. They put their drinks on the bar and took a few steps forward. Brighter lights came up, exposing the ugly of the club interior and the zombified stares of the clubbers. Milling about, bumping into each other as they slowly began to leave.

"I don't trust the Project guys," Zac explained. "They might make a grab for you while I'm preoccupied." He looked down at her. "I don't want to add a rescue to our kidnapping tonight."

Jess took a deep breath. Trying to put herself entirely in his hands. It was hard, however, not to be tense. Hard not to want to do something, hard not to *expect* to do something. But at this point all she could do was stay out of the way and watch as Zac took care of business.

More and more people disappeared as she and Zac wandered in a seemingly aimless pattern among them, moving closer to the VIP area. So far all was going perfectly.

Drake remained alone, the only agent in there, watching, not yet realizing what they might be doing. Sizing up this new, additional opportunity. She and Zac were getting closer to Lorenzo and the club was emptying, leaving fewer and fewer people to get in the way. Lorenzo remained, reclined in his seat just as he had been for the entire show, comfortably aloof, sipping a clear drink, working the VIP area to its fullest. Now that the music was off he and his cronies were talking among themselves. Chuckling little ha-ha chuckles as they spoke in short, inaudible sentences, the others chit-chatting among themselves; rich young assholes, acting as if the rest of the club was beneath them or, more to the point, as if it didn't even exist.

Not running at all.

That should've made Jess more confident, not less. Lorenzo was now not looking at them at all. This made it easier, right? As if Lorenzo had put them entirely from his mind—though she was certain he knew full well they were there and drawing nearer. Now that the club was empty, she, Zac and Drake among the few left—moving oddly closer with their focus on the VIP area, shooting nervous glances at each other and at Lorenzo—it should've been so obvious to Lorenzo that he needed do *something*, or at least pay attention. Get up and get out of there. Shout at them; demand to know what they hell they were doing. Ask if he could help them. Anything but sit there plainly ignoring them, not even looking in their direction.

His arrogance was palpable. Such that the confidence his failure to run should've inspired in Jess instead raised other concerns. Other ... fears.

Yes.

She was starting to feel a little afraid.

Then Lorenzo stood and ...

Looked right at her.

Not at Zac.

Not at Drake.

Straight at her.

And as his eyes fixed hers she tingled all over; goose bumps that went right through her, rippling across every inch of her skin.

That same corner of his mouth turned up in a smug sneer.

Oh yes. He knew all about them.

She gulped involuntarily. Fought not to shake.

Then felt Zac's arm around her.

"Stay here," he said, took a step toward them and waited.

At that Lorenzo's entourage rose behind him, similar sneers of overconfidence on their young, perfect faces. Lorenzo stepped from the VIP area to the dance floor, so pretentious it was sickening. Moving like a cat, not ten paces away, followed by the others, arms out at their sides and grinning. Like the bad guys in an old Kung Fu movie and this was the showdown. Only these guys were for real. And, to Jessica's creeping horror, looked far more dangerous.

Nervously she looked at Zac, standing tall before them. Casually he stared the Bok down, no fear of his own. She swallowed.

And saw the Kazerai as if all at once. Saw *Zac.* As if she'd somehow forgotten. Not one man, as he appeared. Not one against five. Those were not the odds. Not simply one strong guy against five badasses. Not even close. This was five against a thousand. Five against a guy who could peel the hinges off a safe. Five against a guy who could leap a hundred feet straight in the air. Who could pummel suits of powered armor to scrap like they were nothing. Bullet-proof, fireproof. This was Kratos, the God of War, versus babies.

She had a reality check.

Looked back at the assholes.

Now it was her turn to grin.

She felt so sorry for them.

CHAPTER 32:

HIGH IMPACT

WITH BARELY a glance in Zac's direction—though Zac was clearly the one about to jump them—Lorenzo stopped, still several paces away, looking deep into Jessica's eyes. A stare that felt like something tangible, like he might actually, somehow, pierce her mind. His sneer expanded.

"See, Merci?" he said to the Bok girl on his right. As if confirming a suspicion. "It's not her." He shook his head almost imperceptibly. "Nothing special about this one."

Merci agreed, flashing her own, knowing sneer: "Nothing at all."

Lorenzo chuckled. Jess swallowed.

Time seemed to stand still.

Then his expression straightened.

"Well don't just stand there," he spoke directly to Jess. "You came to bang," and he held his arms out invitingly, twisting his head just a little to the side; an audible *crick!* of his neck as he flexed.

Gaze on no one else.

"Let's bang."

Before she could move, before anyone could move, he threw out an arm, a harsh snap in the direction of Drake— who stood off to the side watching. And as Lorenzo's elbow locked it was as if he hurled something, though nothing left his hand; nothing physical, at least, only a shimmering wave—it had to be an optical illusion—warbling the air like an invisible bolt of lightning.

Straight at Drake.

Bam! The Project man went flying. Backward across the dance floor, struck hard by a wall of force.

That was no illusion.

What the ... ?!

As if punched, doubled over; lifted from his feet, an

unseen pendulum hammering through his gut in a mighty arc—extending directly from Lorenzo's outstretched palm. The blow sent Drake tumbling, landing on his back and sliding, unconscious or dead.

That fast.

Lorenzo had never really taken his eyes from her. Now his sneer screwed into an expression of sadistic purpose as ... he cast both arms in front of him, the same way he just did to Drake.

Too late to react.

WHOOOM! Jess cringed but it wasn't for her, and she felt an overwhelming ripple in the air as the wave front hit, striking ...

Zac.

He went flying.

No!

Then a shout. Inside her head:

<Fear me!>

Lorenzo.

And she froze. Utterly. Stunned, swallowing a spike of terror even as ...

His hands were snapping directly toward her and an electric tingle pulsed her spine ... *WHOOOM!* it slammed her like a shot and she, too, was flying. The world spun and she felt a sharp triple-crack as she smacked the floor, elbows and tailbone—managing to catch her head before it hit—sliding in a disorienting whirl of lights and sound. She came to a squeaking stop, bare skin gripping painfully against the dance floor.

Somehow she hadn't been knocked out.

And suddenly she was enraged.

Shock, awe, fear, pain—those things snapped away in an instant as the rage consumed her; the coppery smell of blood filling her nostrils, like a blow to the head. Demand for retaliation surging. She would crush Lorenzo. To oblivion and beyond, and continue crushing him until he was completely destroyed.

Bastard!

She rolled in a rush to stand, fell, struggled to her feet,

slipped in the ridiculous heels, spun in place, tried not to fall again; the room whirled and she made herself stand steady, so full of anger she wanted to kill. She held her arms out at her sides and got her bearings.

It was like she'd been punched in the face.

"*Zac!*" How the hell did Lorenzo knock him down?! She checked her nose for bleeding. There was none.

"You okay?" There he was. *Zac!* Behind her. She turned and he was there, the room still spinning, his own eyes wide with disbelief; checking her with urgent concern.

"I'm fine," she lied, aching all over. Her ears rang.

She stabilized. Zac locked gazes with her.

Neither could believe what just happened was real.

"What was that?" he asked. "I was *not* ready for that."

Jess shook her head at the memory of it. At the echo of Lorenzo's voice in her head—*how did he do that?!*—wondering if she'd just imagined it. *Fear me!* It was Lorenzo and, some impossible way, he'd spoken inside her skull.

He spoke in my head!

She oriented herself and found the VIP area.

The Bok were gone.

The last stragglers in the club choked the exit, screaming to get out. Obviously freaked by this supernatural display of power. It must've looked harsh from their perspective. To judge by their extreme reaction it did. Drake lay unmoving on the floor, right where he'd been thrown.

The clock was ticking. Jess took off for the VIP exit.

"Come on!"

* * *

"Where is she?" Nani tapped across several screens, enlarging this, scanning that, even as Bianca squinted at the tiny, chaotic images of bodies and vehicles filling the parking lot around the club. "Do you see her?" The whole place had erupted in chaos.

"She's still inside," Bianca kept coming back to the indicator for Jessica, frighteningly still in the midst of what had, almost instantly, become a full-on panic down below.

"What just went on in there?"

Bodies were rushing everywhere. There was no sense to be made of the confusion. Bianca shook her head as she reviewed the scans and screens for which she was responsible. "I don't know." She'd expected some kind of reaction from the people in the club when Zac moved, if for no other reason than it was a blatant kidnapping, and if he had to use any of his super strength then that would only add to the chaos, but this ...

It was like the whole place had lost it.

"Where's Zac?" Nani wanted to know. She was scanning her own information. Tons of it. "Why aren't they moving?"

Bianca was at a loss. "Not sure."

"They're not answering."

"Shit," Nani was growing frustrated. "I knew I should've laid in more contingencies. Shit!"

They'd hung it all on Zac. They couldn't get a decent scan into the club and so had been monitoring the signal from the Kel tablet, the marker for Jessica's location. It wasn't moving. Outside the club all hell had broken loose and hordes of people were in a state of chaos, the ones closest to the building rushing from it, bodies fleeing in all directions. Once started the rush only seemed to multiply. There were smaller groups congregated further away, watching things unfold with a rising sense of curiosity, but the panic was spreading. Even at the best resolution Bianca couldn't make out expressions from overhead, only the larger details. Already she'd spotted a dozen dark-haired girls in little black dresses running this way and that, cursing her own lack of foresight for not giving Jess something more unique to identify herself by. *Wouldn't have mattered*, she realized. The madness on the ground was proving impossible to follow.

It was obvious the planned action had gone down; they could hear the Project agents on their channel franticly trying to get a response from their inside man, Drake, to no avail. Jess appeared immobilized too. Where was Zac? How was *he* immobilized?

What's going on in there?!

Then the Bok sports cars began taking off—along with several others. Many cars were suddenly fleeing the scene, including the half-dozen exotics parked directly outside the VIP entrance. Those had gone hot and began streaking away through the crowds—actually running people over in their haste, or knocking them out of the way, no regard for human life—ripping into the night and heading off in seemingly random directions.

"It's too much!" Bianca was suddenly frustrated, almost to the point of tears, as she failed to zero in on what mattered—watch the Bok? Keep looking for Jess?—the whole thing unfolding faster than she could track. Should she follow one of the Bok cars? All of them? Which one was Lorenzo?

It wasn't supposed to go this way.

Why aren't they answering?!

The impacts of the cars with a dozen or so fleeing people in the parking lot sent the panic to whole new levels. Bianca found herself frozen for an instant in morbid fascination, zeroed in on the fallen bodies, wondering if they were dead. Like some kind of sick, voyeuristic internet video, with drama you just couldn't look away from. She snapped herself back to the task at hand. No time for that.

Nani kept cursing. If the nab had gone down, as it must have, where was Zac? They should be emerging, Lorenzo in hand. Did they come up with a different tactic? If so why didn't they tell them?

"Should we send Satori?"

Nani shook her head. "Not yet. Let's make contact."

Things were clearly moving too fast for Nani as well. Between the both of them they were unable to pin any exact thing on which to focus, anywhere to put their attention. Nani's hands flew over the controls.

"I'm trying to tag what I can," she tapped away, cursing each time she made a mistake or thought of something else. Her sudden and obvious frustration when she'd been so competent till then, was disturbing Bianca as much as anything else.

Answer! she willed the motionless blip on the screen.

Where her focus kept coming to settle.

Jessica.

Get up!

Down below Bianca caught a few figures moving with purpose against the grain, heading into the club, not away.

The external Project agents.

But her eyes kept coming back to the dot. The little, blinking signal that was her friend. Laying in the middle of the club.

Not moving.

If the Project guys got to her ...

Jessica! Answer me!

* * *

"THERE!" Jess ran as fast as she could in the heels, around the rear of the club, out the VIP entrance and through the scattering crowd, pointing after one of the Italian sports cars fleeing the scene. "Is that him?"

Zac flew up behind; stared into the night, taillights of the car dwindling into the distance. The echoing whine of an upshifting V-12 drifted back across the shouts and screams, smell of scorched rubber hanging in the air. Other expensive cars were racing off in all directions.

Zac seemed to determine that wasn't the one, then turned his attention to another, then another, about as far away, heading up a different route.

"That one," he pointed. "That's him."

For a strained moment he and Jess looked at each other, shouts, screams, movement all around. The panic was spreading fast.

"Can you catch it?" she asked.

Zac started, stopped.

"I can't leave you," he said, looking back and forth between her and the rapidly dwindling car with a sense of urgency. "The agents are still here. Other Bok could be—"

"Never mind," Jess was frantic. The car now seemed impossibly gone.

Her fury spiked. *He* can't *get away!*

He couldn't. She wanted Zac to try, to just go, but she knew he was right. He wouldn't. It was too dangerous to leave her. She was the Project's next target of opportunity.

People were screaming, running; it looked like the Bok hit some pedestrians as they fled. Jess saw bodies laying in the near distance. The club parking lot had become a madhouse.

"Can we take another car?" Zac was casting about, looking for a way to keep up the chase. Jess could almost hear a massive clock ticking louder in her head, Lorenzo disappearing for good with every thundering tock.

They'd never get another chance.

Move.

"There," she pointed across the lot to a group of Spanish boys gathered around a few fast-looking motorcycles. Jess started for them. In the distance the sing-song of Euro sirens had already begun. She scanned the group of bikes as she ran toward them, cutting through the disorganized crowd, settling on the one that looked the fastest. There were no cars in the lot that would catch Lorenzo but ...

Yes! She rushed up on one bike in particular, a street-legal Moto GP. A big one. One of the boys was on it leaning back, hands on the tank, looking cool in a white T-shirt and leather jacket—holding court with his entourage in an animated discussion of the events unfolding all around. He recoiled as Jess and Zac rushed up on him out of nowhere.

"Give me the keys," she stuck out a hand, Zac right behind. Before the boy could move Zac had him by the collar, lifting him free with one hand, steadying the bike with the other.

So much for pleasantries.

Jess checked the ignition. "Wait," she told Zac. "They're here." She grabbed the handlebars.

At that Zac tossed the boy aside, kicking and screaming. A hundred and fifty pounds, ten feet, one hand, not so much as a grunt of effort. The rest of the crowd stumbled away in the face of this display of superhuman strength. Jess was already throwing a leg over the custom machine. As she did the short black skirt tugged up and she nearly fell, caught herself, reached awkwardly with one hand and ripped the skirt in frustrated impatience. Legs free she straddled the bike, scooched forward on the seat and noticed the badge on the all-black speed demon: *NCR M16*. A Ducati, a tricked-out version of an already fast road bike and, if memory served, it would smack the shit out of any Italian sports car.

But they were already precious minutes behind.

She turned the key and thumbed the starter. The engine caught with a throaty surge, still hot. She bripped the throttle, feeling the mass of the powerful engine between her legs; turned to Zac ...

He was gone. *Where the ...*

She found him on a nearby Vespa. Straddling the baby-blue scooter, one hand on the handlebars, the other holding keys. A boy—the owner, presumably—was in a full sprint away from him, looking back fearfully at the big, dark-haired guy that was stealing his scooter. Zac sat on it, keys in hand, knees nearly to his chest and squashing the tiny scooter with a very serious, very determined look on his face, searching for the ignition.

Ready for action.

"How does it work?" he called urgently.

Though the circumstances were far from funny Jess nearly laughed. It would've been a bitter laugh. She nodded to the seat behind her on the Ducati:

"Get on."

Zac stood from the scooter. "Should I just run?"

She shook her head and nodded again to the small area behind her.

"Get on."

Zac came to her.

"Yours does look faster," he said and threw a leg over. As he mounted the bike his full weight pushed it down, hard, and for an instant Jess worried it might be too much. She scooted all the way up against the tank.

It'll be fine.

The carbon-fiber dream bike weighed barely more than Zac himself, but with upwards of 200 horsepower on tap there was no doubt that, even with both of them, the Ducati would tear up the road like a cheetah with a tazer up its ass.

She bripped the throttle, clutched and stabbed it into first. As she did the heel of her fancy shoe caught the engine case. She wriggled it away and it caught something else. *Damn!* Angrily she kicked that one off, then the other, angry at the shoes, angry at the dress, angry at the delay—angry at everything right then. Why she'd come so unprepared for action, knowing everything *always* led to action ...

Lorenzo was now long gone.

Should they just ...

Zac reached an arm around her, holding himself close—it felt more like he was holding *her* close—grabbed the bike's frame with his other to steady them and was ready. His feet were flat, firmly on the ground. She took a deep breath. Between her legs was an idling demon with unprecedented power, at her back sat Superman.

How could she fail?

I'm getting that bastard.

She twisted the throttle, fanned the clutch and ...

They were away.

Whoa!

Even with that little bit of gas the bike pulled hard, sucking up a hundred feet of parking lot in a second and sending the crowd before them scurrying and leaping to the sides. She stayed on it, aimed toward the exit, let the clutch out all the way and they were off, surging ahead in an alarming rush. Zac dragged his feet the whole way, touching left and right as they launched, the bike leaning back and forth with the uncoordinated take-off—like a set of human training wheels as they shot out onto the road. It must've looked frighteningly ridiculous; an angry clown missile, big Zac on the back, holding a girl at the controls, demon bike searing the air with its killer whine and insane acceleration.

But they were off. Jess swerved around a departing car as Zac finally lifted his skidding feet and she held the bike straight, charging ahead in first gear, not daring to shift. As they cleared the car and she saw the open road she grabbed a bigger handful of throttle and was rewarded with an even greater surge. The Ducati was wound *tight*. As she twisted the throttle the bike's nose pulled up, effortlessly, front wheel clearing the asphalt as it worked against Zac's counterweight, pushing ahead with its own unrelenting force as it came over backwards ...

She reacted. The unexpectedly high wheelie freaked her out and she rolled the throttle shut, too fast, nosing down hard.

Poompf! the forks stabbed to their bottom stops.

"You got it?" Zac asked from behind. They were still moving fast in first gear.

This is no dirt bike, Jessica's mind flashed to all those races, all those 85 cc bikes she rode as a kid. The Ducati worked the same, but was so many orders of magnitude beyond its smaller cousins it was nearly unreal. Plus with the heavy Zac on the back ...

She had to get control.

"I've got it!" she yelled and leaned further forward. Zac got the idea; shifted his weight with her, leaning down as she hit the throttle again. She realized there would be little moderation on this high-strung beast. It chirped and shimmied as the rear tire spun—there was no winning—but the front wheel stayed mostly down this time as she ran it all the way up to redline and, working to keep it at the edge of traction, front wheel hovering, clutched up to second. *Unn*, it dug in and pulled hard in the fresh gear, tacking on more insane speed. Now they were really moving. Second got them to a hundred and fifty klicks and as she curled her toes under the shifter and snapped it to third—speedshifting this time without the clutch—they lunged again. *Unnnh* closing on two hundred and she popped it short to fourth, then hard through the next two gears—*bang! bang!*—sucking up the night road faster than she could process. There was nothing out there this time of morning, no real curves, just one long straightaway, and as she peered ahead over the small fairing, eyes squinting, tearing—the suddenly frigid night air blasting her senses—she began to shake. At that speed her hair whipped about her head, a thrashing halo of insanity, lashing her bare shoulders, painfully stinging her face.

"You got it?" Zac asked again, voice right behind her, strong and at ease but with an edge of real concern.

Of course he was at ease. He was, after all, invincible. Where this was freaking her out—and they hadn't even spotted Lorenzo's car yet—he had the luxury of being fearless.

But she knew what he *did* fear for.

Her.

"I've got it!" she yelled and bent to the task, tucking tighter, as tight as she could; gripped the handlebars, forced her muscles to be still, all five senses overloaded.

In turn she felt Zac squeezing her. "If you don't then I've got *you*," he said. "I won't let you get hurt."

It was a nice sentiment, and she believed him, but there in the open, flying into the pitch, screaming into the night—the feeling of imminent impact was beyond reason. Could he actually save her if she lost control? Maybe. What if something popped out right in front of them? Too fast to react?

"There he is," Zac pointed. She could barely see anything through her assaulted senses and watering eyes. "I think he slowed a little." Zac noticed all the things she wasn't. Couldn't.

Then: "Can you go faster?"

She could.

"Hold on!" her voice was barely audible, even to herself. She couldn't see any lights ahead but if Zac saw them ...

Time to find out what you can do. She felt the bike; twisted the throttle and, amazingly, it surged in top gear like it was nothing. Massive acceleration even without a downshift. A 300 pound bike with 400 more pounds on it. Gone. Hurtling ahead with a lunge that didn't stop. Stretching its legs to 270, 280, 290 ... 300 ...

And she chickened out.

That number was big and the world around her had

become nothing more than howling blackness and vertigo—backed by the sphincter-spasming fear of a sudden, violent collision. This was a long, dark stretch of asphalt that could disappear in a flash. Impact would come in an instant. Death ... immediate. The lighted gauge before her was a mere measure of the velocity of her doom.

"He may have seen our lights," Zac noted. He didn't judge as she rolled it back below 250—still insane. "I think he did. He's speeding up."

And she saw it. At last. Red taillights in the distance. Just a glimpse, but it was enough to give her hope.

"He knows we're back here," Zac confirmed. "He's running." Then: "Curves."

The taillights, which Jess had only just brought into focus, whipped away suddenly to the right, out of sight.

Shit!

CHAPTER 33:

A SINKING FEELING

"SHE MUST BE HURT!" Bianca could no longer imagine any reason why Jess wasn't moving or answering. The dot that was her friend was still stuck. Just laying there. Bianca's mind raced, unable to draw any conclusions. Nani was also frantic, trying to piece together what went wrong.

Clearly Lorenzo had *not* been captured.

"I don't understand," Nani was checking in vain. "Where's Zac? Why is he letting her just lie there? Did he leave her? Did he chase one of those cars? Did we miss it?" Again she was cursing herself. "Why! Why did I send them off like that?"

The police had arrived, Guardia Civil, just two cars but more were on the way. People had definitely been killed in the chaotic departure of the sports cars through the densely packed crowd. As yet Bianca and Nani still didn't know what went down in the club. The Project agents were inside. According to the Project's own radio traffic they'd just got Drake on his feet and were as confused by the events as Nani and Bianca. However, it was becoming clear the Bok had done something to Drake. Knocked him out somehow. As Bianca listened to their radio chatter she began to worry they'd done the same thing to Jess, and even to Zac, and that both were lying in the club hurt and unconscious.

How did they knock out Zac?

But if Drake was okay maybe Jess was too?

Then Jessica's signal moved.

* * *

THE CURVE FED down to the highway, one of the Spanish Autopistas, and with a gut-wrenching heave to the right—

Jess shouting at the heavy Zac to "Lean with me!"—they were flying down the ramp at a radical angle, nearly on their side—Jess holding her feet tight against the hot engine case in fear of dragging bare toes on the obscenely fast-moving asphalt—knee out and praying to live through this night. But the fat racing tires gripped like a tarantula and they were over the crest, rising with a little vertigo-inducing lift, down into the merge, straightening at the last possible second and crunching through the bottom at speeds the onramp was never designed for. Onto the highway, leveled out and blowing past a handful of early-morning commuters—cars that were probably going 70 miles an hour or faster yet looked like they were standing still—on the throttle hitting supersonic speeds and rising.

The sheer velocity thrummed through her with a shuddering rush.

Out in the clear on the flat, wide multi-lane she rolled them up, hammering the shifter—*bam!*—*bam!*—blitzing beneath the highway lights so fast their alternating pools of illumination became a psychotic strobe. Flashing a hundred beats per minute, the effect surreal. Like having an out-of-body experience, floating free as the bike absolutely sucked the highway into its maw, snapping left-right through traffic. She blinked furiously in the bitter, howling wind, tucked behind the small fairing, fighting to keep her eyes open, hands stinging in pain as the cold, high-speed air cut across her knuckles like a knife. Beneath her the engine roared. Hot, primal, hungry for more.

She gave it to it.

Able now to at least see, if only a disorienting, flashing, hair-stinging blur, her confidence rose. The highway was wide. There was room to move. She uncorked the Ducati all the way. Twisted the throttle to its stop, top gear, Lorenzo's low-profile sports car in her sights dead ahead. The Italian race bike was a high-power rifle and she was aiming it straight on target: *Bang!* Riding the bullet, clearing 300 klicks and on. Faster. 310. 320. 330 ...

She pulled to the right around a car in the middle lane, Lorenzo weaving sharply up ahead. Left around a truck;

what would've been an easy drift at sane speeds, now a power-lifting yank, hanging off each side of the bike, back and forth, Zac pulling with her. Left. Over and ... right. Then right to the far lane. Left around another semi-truck and another, straight on between two more rolling side by side, up the centerline between them at plus-one-hundred miles an hour and out the front like a missile being fired between their hoods.

Shooom!

They were gaining.

Lorenzo must've sensed it and veered hard toward another exit—smacking up the ramp in a shower of sparks, flying off the highway into the night. At the speed he was going if that ramp dumped to any sort of an intersection or curve it was all over.

Jess prayed that it did.

But his red lights whipped out of sight and were gone high above, even as she pulled them over in pursuit, heaving Zac's weight behind her, centering up the exit ramp and slamming them straight into it ...

Whuunn! she grunted as the suspension caught their huge inertial mass, the bike hitting the grade at speed, carbon hardpoints sparking as they banked and dragged, way out on the edge of the envelope.

Now she was into it.

She had the soul of the machine, as she always did in her races as a kid—eventually, in every race, she got it, and when it came it was hers. Indeed. When it came and she knew the machine she could extend it to its limits. Beyond. And she had this one.

Even Zac was a little freaked.

"You got it?" he yelled as they charged up the ramp and off the highway, a tinge of extra volume in his voice.

Boy did she.

"I've got it!" her voice was completely inaudible. Hair a wild medusa's mane, a thousand tiny snakes stinging her eyes, stinging her shoulders, her frozen cheeks. She wasn't even sure she could truly see any more. Not with her eyes. Some other sense directed her.

WHOOOA! she shot them up the top of the ramp and over, catching air ...

BOOOMP! the bike hit on the other side and bottomed out under their weight, and with a slight hook to the right the road was clear and straight—as Lorenzo would've known.

Of course he knows. This is his turf.

The car was dead ahead and again they were gaining. And as Jess realized they were close she began thinking ahead to the next phase. The whole reason they were chasing him: to catch him. Under other circumstances she would have no idea how to stop a car with a bike, but she had Zac. Get him close enough and it was all over for Lorenzo.

Out of her peripheral vision, such as it was, she saw the dark mass of the mountain range to their left, looming against the gray-light of a gathering dawn. Could almost sense Lorenzo in the car ahead, almost feel him, desperate to lose them.

You're mine.

* * *

DRAKE CONTINUED shaking feeling back into his head. The room was still spinning but he was aware enough to grasp the facts: Lorenzo got away and so did the girl. On top of that, the Spanish police were arriving and the whole club was about to get locked down. If they were going to have any chance of getting out of there without incident they needed to do it soon.

Bobby walked up to him. A few of his other agents were there, the rest out in the lot or in the woods, relaying information which was basically useless.

This Op was screwed.

How the hell did he do that?! He rubbed the back of his head.

Whatever Lorenzo did, whatever he used, some electromagnetic device concealed in his sleeve or some other advanced weapon or—a frightening possibility, actual psionic powers—they had to take a serious look at reports they'd previously dismissed.

The Bok were hiding more than a few secrets.

"Take a look at this," Bobby got his attention, holding out what looked to be a tablet or a large phone. Drake squinted and rubbed the bridge of his nose. He took the device.

"Recognize it?" Bobby asked.

Drake turned it over in his hand. It had an unusual feel. Like some kind of sturdy composite, like aircraft-grade materials or something. It had a screen, a flat back. No branding on it. None. That alone piqued his curiosity. *No brand.* Could it be some kind of custom job?

He looked to Bobby, hoping he had an answer.

But Bobby didn't.

"I just found it," he said. "I can't seem to turn it on. There isn't a button."

Drake turned it over. Didn't see any either. No ports, no camera eye, no audio holes or any other way to interact with it. At least nothing obvious.

What the hell is this?

He was beginning to get a creepy feeling holding it.

"I tried dragging the screen," said Bobby. "Nothing."

Drake looked at the purse in Bobby's other hand. A clubber's stylish purse, thin strap broken. Probably in the melee.

"Was it in that?"

Bobby nodded.

"Wait a minute." Drake looked to his other agents, moving about the club, looking for other clues. One of the bouncers had come over and was so far assuming the Project agents were official, but that wouldn't last. The cops were interviewing people. They needed to get gone.

Drake took out his phone, keyed it up and began scrolling through the discreet photos he'd snapped of Jessica and her tall friend. He stopped on one.

"There." He held the phone and looked closely. "There," he touched it lightly on the screen. "The purse. It's hers. And look at this one," he moved to the next photo and there Jessica was using the tablet. The very one they now held in their hands.

"This is hers." He held up the tablet. "This is Jessica's."

* * *

JESS STABBED THE BRAKES, locking up the rear tire in a fishtail skid. The ass-end of the Ducati slid out before she could balance it with a nose-dive at the front and whip it back online. Ice shot through her veins in that instant, colder than the air on her skin as she veered them around the tractor that had just come into sight dead ahead. Hulking and deadly, ambling down the side of the road—directly in their path as they crested a sweeping country curve.

She felt Zac's arm tensed around her as she straightened on the other side. He'd been prepared to lunge with her to safety but held, giving her that split second to react—trusting her as she downshifted in a blitz—*click—click—click*—tire smoke from the skid drifting past.

She was in the zone. The terrifying instant passed and she cracked the throttle and lurched back to speed, lofting a mid-height wheelie through two gears, the front settling gently to ground as the acceleration crested and they hit the next corner.

It was an insane speed on the winding, dark road. Ahead through breaks in the mountains and the forested side steppes the sky was getting lighter, but only slightly. Useful sunlight was still far away.

Lorenzo's Lamborghini—she could see it clearly now as they closed the gap—drifted hard in front of them, around tight corners, his own tires giving off smoke as he alternately locked the brakes and stabbed the gas. Zac had gotten good at working with her on the bike, pulling it over left and right as she did, dropping his knee out with her side to side, leaning radically back and forth; left curve, right curve, left, left—harder; straight, hard; brakes and down right again, Jess curling them through long, upwardly winding roads, curve after curve. Never letting them drift so close that Lorenzo could jam the brakes and ram them up the Lamborghini's tailpipe.

There was no doubt now. They were going to catch him and Zac would beat the snot out of him. Not kill him, which Zac could no doubt do with a pinch of his fingers; just a little extra pain for all the asshole Bok leader had put them through.

She was furious at what he'd done back in the club. *How the hell did he do that?!*

It was like some kind of a Jedi Force punch or something. She wondered if the Project knew anything about it. Could all the Bok do that? Or just Lorenzo? One thing was certain, these vampire wannabes were definitely hiding something.

And she was going to find out what.

Their pace was way too fast for the road but Lorenzo recklessly kept it up, nearly going off the shoulder on several turns. Jess hung tight, wondering what he feared. They were alone. With that little trick of his why didn't he just stop and take care of them? He must not've thought he could because he kept going, determined to elude them. An effort that wasn't going well as she continued to close the gap. Maybe he was just having fun? Anger burned hotter. As his brakes flashed on and off ahead of them, brilliant red in her vision, she was nearly close enough at some points to make out the Lamborghini bull logo on the back; could nearly see the back of his head through the slit that was the rear window.

The sensory assault was now just part of the background and she was in the flow. Nothing to do but push; far, far past the edge. Not even inside her own body anymore, it seemed. She knew she was frozen, hands completely numb, knew she could barely see, barely feel, but none of that mattered. Like she'd become detached from the whole thing. "On" in a way that would've been beyond an easy description. But she was coming to expect this when pressed. Rather than shrink, rather than retreat when challenged she pushed out, rejecting fear and marshalling whatever force kept her going. And for a strange, disconnected moment, amid the absolute intensity of the chase, she thought how strange she must seem. So vulnerable whipping through the chill

night on a racing machine in nothing but the skimpy
black dress, by all rights a flower that should've long since
wilted. But she hadn't. The flower had become an oak,
and the greater part of her, however impossible, however
improbable, maintained that terrible focus; reaction beyond
anything human.

She was getting to know this other Jessica.

"I can't jump off without wrecking us," Zac said loudly as
he leaned with her into a long left-hand curve. "No matter
how I do it," he paused as they hit the end of the curve
and swept harder into another, Jess downshifting to keep
the bike in its powerband. As they straightened at the end
and she banged up through the gears he continued, voice
amazingly clear through the roar of wind and machine: "If
I get off we crash."

And it struck her: Was this even necessary? Everything
had fallen apart and she let it. After Lorenzo did ... whatever
he did, knocking she and Zac down, the absolute rage of her
reaction was probably not the best solution. Why hadn't
she collected herself and called in the cavalry? Surely there
would've been a better solution than this impulsive, deadly
chase. Couldn't Nani and Bianca just follow Lorenzo from
orbit? At the time it seemed so urgent, especially there on
the ground; as if they were about to lose him for good. Now
that her blinding rage had cooled she was starting to think
more clearly, and what she realized was it was time to turn
things around. Call in the troops and end this. They were
certainly far enough from civilization. With a quick call ...

Her heart sank. All the way out the bottom. All the way
to her gut like an iron anchor into a pit, down to the road
and dragging her with it. Concentration left her entirely for
an instant and she nearly crashed.

"Got it?" Zac steadied the bike as she wavered, holding
them on course, off the shoulder and out of the trees.

Ahead the gap with Lorenzo stretched.

"The tablet," Jess said in disbelief, voice lost utterly in
the wind.

But Zac heard.

"Damn," he hadn't noticed either. "We left it, didn't we?"

It was over.

* * *

"Is she alive?" Bianca wanted to know. She glanced desperately between Nani and the moving blip on the screen that was the Kel tablet. At least Jess was up and moving around. What else could Nani tell from the readings? What went wrong down there? Bianca made herself breathe. Would they now have to rescue Jess and Zac from the Project guys? Her heart beat fast in anticipation.

Nani fumbled through screens, tapping up information.

"I'm not getting the right bio signatures on the device," she said, growing alarmed. Bianca went to stand by her at her console. Did that mean Jess was sick?

"Are you ready for us?" Satori's voice came suddenly over the channel. For a moment Nani froze, then found the right action and put Satori's face up on a section of the domed viewscreen across the bridge.

"What's going on?" Satori asked, red hair and beautiful face perched atop her black uniform collar. Behind her Willet could be seen in the shot, both of them sitting aboard the Kel fighter. Ready. "We're listening to the feeds."

"We don't know yet," Nani kept working.

"They're still in the club? Lorenzo got away?"

Bianca shook her head. "We're trying to figure it out."

"I don't think they're in the club," Nani sounded bad. Bianca turned to her. Nerves rising higher.

Something had happened.

Nani shook her head slowly. Repeated: "I don't think they're in the club." Then: "Someone else has the tablet."

"What?" Bianca was suddenly terrified. She rushed back to her console.

"Jessica isn't holding the tablet. Someone else is. Not her, not Zac."

"Did she drop it?"

"I'm sending a signal to clear it. We can't take any chances."

"But," Bianca's heart was absolutely pounding in her

chest, "where is she?"

Satori's image watched them both from the screen, eyes looking back and forth. "Are they okay?"

Bianca couldn't believe it. It was her job to protect her friend. Her one and only job. To scan the club, keep them in sight and not lose track of what they were doing.

And she'd failed.

She stared with wide eyes at the screen before her, at the milling crowds of people, at the arriving police and the police already there and the cars and more and even more people from the club and the Project agents probably among them and people going in and out, into view, out of view, standing in groups, running, walking, leaving, coming ...

Nowhere.

Tears stung her eyes and she wiped them impatiently, tapping her screen in a rush and straining to see everything all at once. Scanning and scanning, scrolling and zooming.

Jess was nowhere to be seen.

She'd lost her.

Satori was rising to action. "Should I just fly there? I'm going to fly there."

"No." Nani leaned back, trying to take stock of the situation.

Jess and Zac could be anywhere.

Satori's voice was impatient: "I'm flying there—"

"No!" Nani got her composure. "Don't. This is bad but ... we've got to think this through. If someone got them you might scare them underground then we'd never find them."

"How could anyone 'get' Zac?"

"I don't know!" Nani had become far more emotional than Bianca would've expected. Bianca looked up from her screen. In a way Nani's over-emotion helped calm her own frustrated terror.

"I don't know," Nani said more quietly. "Maybe they managed to give chase. The Bok scattered after whatever happened in the club. Maybe Jess and Zac went after them in those initial moments. Zac could've chased them."

"What about Jessica?"

"I don't know. Give us time to scan through the videos. I've got a lot of tags out there. Maybe we can pick them out by looking back. I can code something to scan the images. That should give us a clue. If they left the club and we can find out how ... maybe we can find a way to track them"

"We should've had more fail-safes." Satori's tone was not accusatory. But what she said was true.

Nani shook her head in disbelief. "I know. I didn't give this enough thought."

Satori agreed. "None of us did. This is my fault."

Nani still couldn't believe it though. "Zac should've been able to pull that off with no issues," she said. "Something isn't right."

"What the hell happened?"

"We've got to figure it out. We can figure it out."

Tentatively Willet tried to add humor to the moment. "Sounds to me like everything's going as planned," he gave a lopsided smile. "As in, this is yet another big mess we'll have to figure or fight our way out of. Business as usual."

The joke bombed. Totally.

Bianca put her face in her hands so no one would see her cry.

* * *

THEY'D BROKEN OUT onto the upper edges of the mountain pass, a steep grade to their left, a plummeting drop to their right. The drop got more alarming as they went higher, racing up the snaking, increasingly narrow road, a wide, misty valley opening up below in shades of gray and black. Sunrise had probably hit elsewhere but it was still very much night there within the shadows of the towering peaks. Jess hugged around a sweeping lefthander and broke past the last rocky outcroppings, a tall forest climbing the side of the mountain to their left, the valley far below to the right. It was a spectacular view and a million bad things made it impossible to appreciate.

She was hard on it, more determined now than ever to make this connection. The Project or the Spanish Police or someone would have the Kel tablet by now and any hope of secrecy, if any remained, was gone.

They had to catch Lorenzo. This may be their only chance. He would go far, far underground after this if he got away.

Up ahead the Lamborghini set a nearly untouchable pace but Jess was hanging with it on the dangerous road, into the groove and gaining.

"That's it," Zac said from behind as she heaved them up and over from a sweeping left to a sweeping right, pegs down and tires shimmying; nerve-wracking little slip-grip moments as they hit loose pieces of gravel on the mountain road.

There were no more straightaways.

"I'm going to end this," Zac gripped her a little tighter and she began to tense for whatever he had in mind. "Get ready."

They snapped out onto a section of tight curves, in clear sight of Lorenzo, who surely had to be checking his mirrors at every turn, watching their headlight sweep back and forth behind him. She felt Zac ready himself for whatever he planned ...

"Let go," he said and she did so without question, knowing they would crash even as ...

He leapt.

Not from the bike without her but, from the bike *with* her. In an instant his arms were securely around her and the two of them were flying up and away, high into the air, still moving forward at an insane speed, arcing over the road even as the bike scrunched under the force of Zac's launch, pitched left and right, back and forth, unable to fall due to the extreme gyroscopic effects of the wheels and it's momentum but trying to very badly, lost its direction and shot off the road like an arrow, clear out over the gorge below. For a surreal moment Jess watched it from high in the air, arcing to a freefall of her own in Zac's arms, the headlight and little red taillight angling out over the valley forest; a dark missile, flying until it began to cartwheel right before ...

Booom! it hit the cliff across the way, just beneath the Lamborghini as it hooked hard around the next curve. No explosion to speak of, just a little fireball from what gas remained, but at that speed the impact sent pieces of motorcycle, rock and dust ejecting in every direction.

Lorenzo had to have seen it.

Then they were into the treetops and Zac was cradling her tight through the blackout of collision, branches cracking around them. She felt the rapid deceleration, then tumbling as Zac did what he did; shielding her from harm. They rolled through a flurry of dirt and leaves, darkness and a few slivers of moonlight until ...

They were sitting.

In the forest.

Without delay Zac uncurled her in his lap. She sat straighter. He checked her over.

"You okay?"

She was.

He leaned back and gave a lopsided grin. "That was fun," he took a precious moment to reassure her.

Then he was shifting her gently from his lap to the ground and standing. "Stay here," he said, looking off in the direction of the fleeing car.

And he stepped back and ...

Leapt. Straight up, bursting through the canopy overhead, arcing off into the distance like a rocket, leaves and dirt poofing away from the thrust of his feet, the actual ground giving a little pulse as he launched his weight upward with such force. Gone from sight in that first superhuman bound.

Gone.

The forest was deathly quiet in the wake of his departure. Gloomy. She looked around. Nothing moved. Nothing made a sound. Her entire body buzzed from the fury of the chase, frozen through and through. She felt like she was still in motion; had to steady herself. She shivered and looked down at her hands. They tingled madly from the incessant vibration of the handlebars. Absently she touched her fingertips together, feeling the strange, soft sensation, studying her perfectly painted blue nails as she did. Sign of another life, it seemed, a ruse meant to make her look normal. After a time, she knew not how long, she looked up through the breaks in the branches, up to the early morning sky high above. It was crystal clear.

And she was all alone.

CHAPTER 34:

THE SITUATION GETS WORSE

THE MORE DRAKE LOOKED at the tablet device the more alien it appeared. In his position he was well aware of the various bizarre and unexplained things his government hid from public awareness, things people could only guess at, and this thing here was definitely an oddity.

He was pretty sure it did not come from Earth.

Bobby concurred. "That's an advanced composite," he reached and tapped the back of it as Drake continued turning the tablet slowly in his hands. "We'll have to analyze it. Definitely custom, if not full-on alien." Bobby knew most everything Drake knew, about the girl, about everything. He knew what happened back in Boise, knew the girl's connection to the shiny chrome transit devices, which were *definitely* alien, had been scrambling along with the rest of them to come up with a good explanation for how she suddenly appeared in the midst of their Op tonight and everything else so wrong about her involvement. Bobby, therefore, knew when something wasn't quite right. And this tablet definitely was not, in any way, right.

Drake handed it back to him.

Maybe that guy Jessica was with was alien. All they knew for sure was that, in the confusion, the two of them— Jessica and the tall stranger—took off with the Bok into the night and were gone. Spotting her there tonight Drake's first thought was that she was connected to or working with the Bok after all. However there were too many signs that she wasn't. Already the Project was convinced the Bok were after *her* following the Boise incident. Drake and his team had been watching to see if the Bok would make a move on any of the girl's family, or try in any other way to make a grab for anything she'd left behind.

The next thought, then, was that Jessica, too, had come

for the Bok. Which was equally absurd. Yet, one of those scenarios had to be true. Coincidence was right out. Whichever the case, Jessica was the one the tablet belonged to and, if it did prove to be alien, she was therefore in this far beyond anything Drake would've guessed possible. Just a few short weeks ago they figured her to be little more than an accidental participant in what was turning into a web of impossibilities, one that was shaping up to be so broad in scope Drake had begun to wonder what they would find next. Ready to believe anything. Now they'd found Bok throwing, apparently, telekinetic energy from their hands. Could it be? Mere weeks before that, alien powered armor leaping off into the void using alien quantum devices. He was no longer ruling anything out.

Now Jessica shows up, here, of all places, after disappearing in Boise, and goes running off with or after the Bok, the Project's arch nemesis. Following them or chasing them.

Probably chasing.

His gut told him, as it had been all along, that his original assessment of Jessica was correct. That she was just an unwilling player in something far beyond anything for which she had a real understanding. A completely normal girl.

Somehow, some way, though, her reactions were all wrong.

Rather than cringing from the strange things happening all around her, rather than running from danger, she was attacking. Once Drake could talk to her he would find out. If he could get her out safe he would. Right then, though, she was part of the game and her fate would fall as it might.

Across the club more of the Spanish Guardia Civil were entering, moving about, checking this or that but mostly just standing around hitching their belts and looking equal parts silly and deadly serious in their funny black hats.

They had no ideas.

Drake could tell that look when he saw it. All they knew were the facts, sketchy as they were. Likely their report at the moment was something along the lines of, a fight broke out in the club, people panicked, the panic spread, a small group involved in the fight ran out, got into exotic sports cars and raced off in all directions, killing or injuring innocent bystanders as they did, adding to the panic and turning the whole early-morning club event into a chaotic crime scene with no clear motive. Just a random sequence of events that led to a few deaths and took a simple fight to a new level.

Drake studied the Spanish police discretely.

So much more than that.

"We should get going," he said to his small group. "Send the signal to extract. Let's get that analyzed." He pointed to the tablet in Bobby's hands.

Bobby nodded, mind on entirely different things. More impossible things.

"Looks like it's true," he mused.

Drake knew exactly what he was talking about. The telekinesis, of course. How had Lorenzo knocked him flying, the girl and her helper as well, with nothing but a dramatic gesture? The Project had previously suspected the Bok of such knowledge, but until then had no real proof of any actual ability. Now, Drake had to admit, they quite likely did.

He shook his head. "Sure looks like it."

* * *

It wasn't supposed to happen like this.

Jess shifted to the side against the tree where she sat cross-legged at its base, leaning into the trunk. A bird chirped loudly, up above in the branches, then stopped just as abruptly.

The forest was awake. The sun had begun moving ever so slowly into the sky, still below the lowest ridge but casting its light beautifully into the clear blue morning, details of the forest visible in steadily brightening hues. Birds were singing, animals scurried here and there, though not too many, most staying well clear of the alien intruder. She barely moved but her presence was noted by all. There was a chill in the air, the morning seeming to get colder not warmer in those first few hours as the day began. A wide gap in the canopy overhead showed a clear patch of sky; deep, serene, cloudless. A pale, white, three-quarter moon stood in sharp relief against it, reflecting the rising sun. Bianca and Nani were up there. Somewhere. Jess wondered if they could see her. Wondered if they'd managed to follow her stupid, impulsive little sprint clear out into the remote countryside. Wondered what they were thinking.

As she sat there waiting all the physical aches from the race to that spot, all the little things lost utterly in the adrenaline of earlier, began to throb. Those pains were minor, however, compared to the fear of the moment; the sheer helplessness of having no way to know. Over the last however how long she'd been sitting there that loneliness had only grown, developing a sharp pain of its own. She was used to taking action but right then could take none, nor did she have any information whatsoever on which to act. There was nothing at all to do but wait. Zac was gone. She had no tablet with which to communicate—no anything with which to communicate. She was completely, completely alone. In the middle of nowhere. Everything depended on Zac's return, and she was about to go crazy waiting for that moment.

In that vacuum of inaction, especially so hot on the heels of the furious pursuit of Lorenzo, her mind had begun flitting anxiously from subject to subject. No matter how she tried she couldn't steer her thoughts toward any calm center. Could find no point of Zen from which to gather herself and wait patiently. Foremost among the thoughts assaulting her, frustratingly, were thoughts of Christmas. Christmas Eve. Recollections of this exact same feeling of impatience, just like the one she had now; when she was much younger, the same feeling, such vastly different circumstances; nervous anticipation, staring out the window down the street on that magical night, waiting for Nana's car to turn the corner at the end, signaling the imminent arrival of the opening of presents. Until that moment every minute was agonizing, every car that turned the corner a terrible tease that left her aching. Now and again she'd hear a noise off in the forest and think it was Zac, only to realize it wasn't, further inflaming that same sensation; the agonizing wait on Christmas orbiting tightly about her psyche.

Reminding her of a life that was forever lost.

There were other things. Awful doubts. All the way back. A mental exercise that was dangerous, she knew, and yet in that terrible, beautiful place, high up on the side of a mountain in the middle of nowhere in Spain, nothing at all to do and her entire life hanging at the edge of a cliff—both literally and figuratively—she could not arrest her rambling mind. All those little branching decision points where she could've chosen differently, perhaps should've chosen differently, all the way back to before Zac's arrival and especially after, so many mistakes, so many places she could've done better, had better, been better, happier; all the times she failed to act, even as a child, the ways she forfeited happiness as a result of timidity or fear; how now, in the midst of the truly fantastic, she'd *over*-compensated, pushed through and so far past fear and timidity she now wondered if her actions had circled back around to some form of foolishness. As if listening to the fear would've actually, at some point, made sense.

Regret is a dull and rusted blade. The lyrics of the song echoed in her head. Another: *I say goodbye to my weakness, so long to the regret, and now I see the world through diamond eyes ...*

One thing was certain: She needed to focus on something else.

It was cold. Maybe she could throw her attention into that. She hugged her arms tighter around herself; stretched and pulled at the tatters of the stupid little black dress, trying to cover as much skin as possible. Looked herself over. Somewhere in the chase, or the insane leap from the motorcycle, she'd lost one of the bracelets she'd been wearing. The thicker one. The thinner bracelets on the other wrist, and the necklace, had managed to hang on. The anklet was still there. She fingered it idly, then returned her arms to their tight grip across her chest.

Vigorously she scissored her legs back and forth against the ground, spontaneously, determined all at once not to be the effect of her situation, to keep taking action, digging through the layers of fallen leaves and underbrush, down into the dirt then, once she'd sunk her legs in an inch or so, piled the leaves back over until no skin was exposed. Maybe that would act as some sort of blanket. She sat that way for a long time, feeling at last a small bit of heat being captured beneath the leafy mound, warming her legs and feet ever so slightly. She shivered.

It was still cold.

* * *

BIANCA STARED AT THE SCREEN like a zombie. They hadn't yet spotted Jess or Zac in any recorded images from the club exterior, which at once made her feel better—knowing she hadn't been a total loser and just missed them watching it live earlier—and totally crushed that they were nowhere to be found.

They were officially lost.

She sniffed and rubbed raw eyes with the heels of her palms, stretching the skin around them and trying to focus.

She and Nani were pouring over images and video captured during those frantic moments after whatever happened in the club. From police band traffic and that of the Project they'd begun to learn more of what went down. There was a scuffle inside that started everything rolling. Project radio traffic was not too specific, but from what they could tell the Project now knew the Bok used a weird power of some kind to knock Drake out. "The girl", Jessica, was definitely gone. Bianca wondered if the Bok had done something similar to her and Zac.

She'd argued with Nani, loudly—wishing she hadn't been so angry—to just fly down and find them, but Nani, ever the voice of reason, made her understand they could see no better down there than they could from orbit, and the panic it would cause would only make things worse, not better. Satori, too, called, wanting the same thing; to fly there, scour the area, use the Kel technology in full view and to full effect, find Jess and worry about the rest later. After all her resistance leading up to this Bianca was amazed by the passion Satori obviously felt for the welfare of her friends. Though the red-headed commander never really wanted to do any of this in the first place, now that the chips were down she seemed all about doing whatever was needed to save them.

But Nani talked everyone out of it. Kept making them understand that would create more problems than it solved, that if Zac was still on the mission the fighter was exactly where he would go and so Satori leaving that spot was not a good idea and other sound reasoning and, ultimately, though part of Bianca resented it, she knew Nani was right. They all did.

And so the last however long had been a lot of Nani arguing with everyone, while at the same time pouring over this or that bit of information, trying new scans or trying to capture this or that feed or signal, giving Bianca things to review, like cyber detectives using all the Kel technology at their command.

So far nothing.

Bianca had been applying Nani's enhancements to run through video after video, image after image, adding her own scrutiny to what the computers could find. Amazed, with all this, how difficult the exercise was. Shouldn't they just be able to find them? Every Earth movie always had the CIA or the FBI or whoever using satellites and gadgets to zero in on people in impossible ways, finding them no matter how well they hid. The Kel technology was way beyond any of that. But movies were proving, apparently, to be movies, and the magic button was so far nowhere to be found. Human error was to blame for this fiasco, and Bianca blamed herself—blamed all of them, really—for not insisting they prepare in advance for more things that could've gone wrong.

And again she asked herself, as they all had: *What*

happened to Zac?

On the images, cycling through, cars and scooters and motorcycles and people leaving, police cars arriving and other cars and vehicles that weren't police cars, at least one of them was a news van that was recent. Bianca was convinced if Jess and Zac left it was shortly after the incident inside the club.

Actually, for all they knew Jess could be lying somewhere out of view, out cold in the woods or …

Bianca swallowed.

But Zac couldn't die, she didn't care *what* power the Bok had, not after what she knew he'd been through, and he wouldn't leave Jess. The Project *and* the police were in and around the club, the Project discreetly, and neither were talking as if anything like that happened. Drake was still alive. In fact the Project had quite clearly reported across their channels that Jessica left the club and was gone.

Which meant she and Zac could be long gone, depending on how they went, covering so much ground by then with so many possibilities of direction that it became an even bigger, nearly impossible challenge. Maybe they would find their way back to Satori and the Kel fighter hidden in the woods. Maybe they were on their way there now. If they chased Lorenzo and lost him that would be the next logical thing to do.

But what if they'd captured him?

Then they'd also need to get back to the fighter.

Either way that would—should—be their destination. In the meantime Jess and Zac were lost and anything could've happened.

"The Project agents are leaving," Nani said, still doing ten things at once. Bianca overheard their comments on that broadcast. Nani tapped in a live feed of the parking lot, yet another screen on the massive wraparound dome of the bridge that was starting to look like a missile command center, information and videos of all sort becoming difficult to sort through for two people. Bianca's eyes were starting to hurt. Nani, however, was in the zone.

"There," she found the car that belonged to the Project,

moving toward the exit to the lot even as the communication came that they were leaving. "Wait," she checked something else and frowned. "Great." It wasn't great. She overlaid the tracking blip that was the Kel tablet. Right atop the car the Project was driving. "As we feared. They're the ones that got the tablet." She looked to Bianca, then turned back to the image of the car leaving, winding slowly out of the parking lot, finding its way clear and out to the road.

Nani sighed. "Maybe it's better that way. At least now we have a good way to track them. If a random person or even the police got hold of it … At least the Project will keep it quiet." And with that she was back to her console.

From the corner of one eye Bianca watched the car leaving; pulled back that scan to see it heading out toward the highway. After a few minutes she shook it off.

And saw something on one of the static images before her. One she'd looked at twice already but this time, right as she looked at it, her eyes went straight to a cluster of bodies at the upper left. Something odd about it. Two people, standing close to a group surrounding a few motorcycles, others in the crowd doing other things. What was it about them? From above it was hard to gauge height or other features and, frustratingly, she'd already discovered how many dark-haired men there were at that resolution and from that perspective that looked like Zac. There were just as many girls who looked like Jess.

But these two caught her eye where before they obviously hadn't. She ran the corresponding video, moments before the image, through it and beyond and …

One of the guys, image tiny but there it was, grabbed a guy on a motorcycle, lifted him with one hand and tossed him away. A girl standing beside him then got on the motorcycle. The action was nearly lost among the rest of the activity but …

There it was.

"That's them!"

* * *

"SHE KNEW we were going to be there," Bobby said from the back seat of the car. He rode with Drake and two other agents in a non-descript sedan, heading down the Autopista into the rising sun. Drake sat in the front passenger seat.

"She had to," Drake agreed. They'd been puzzling over the entire situation, more so now that they were clear of the scene and driving along in relative peace. There was rarely any real "peace", but this was one of those moments to sit and think.

Slowly Drake looked over the tablet in his lap. It had to be Bok. Which meant it could, in fact, be alien. Not of Earth. Something from the Bok's fantastic history.

Drake was dying to get hold of them. To crack their organization and its secrets.

What the hell did they do back there?! He couldn't get over it. Would never get over it. That invisible wall of force ... More technology? Was it truly generated by Lorenzo? Some sort of psychic manifestation? Or did he possess some other form of alien device, something that could project energy; a concealed gravity gun, perhaps, that could knock things down. It certainly wasn't beyond the realm of possibility. Nothing much was at that point.

Drake held the tablet up in the early morning sun and studied its edges. No sign of entry points, no battery case, no buttons, no nothing. Just one smoothly formed surface with a screen on one side.

Did the Bok build it? How? Or was it something from their past? A thousand-year-old device brought to Earth when the first of them came?

Maybe it wasn't Bok at all.

"Sir," the other agent in the back with Bobby got his attention. He was the head of their delta unit. "My guys are telling me they got one."

Drake turned in his seat.

"Lorenzo?" That would be an epic coup.

But they weren't that lucky.

"No, sir. One of the others. Went to ground in the city after fleeing the scene. They picked up some local police traffic and zeroed in on the chase. Managed to get to him before the locals did."

It wasn't Lorenzo but Drake was satisfied. This was perfect. Anyone from within the Bok organization—not just a wannabe mercenary they employed but a real member of the Bok—was a huge score. This could be big.

"Where are they taking him?"

"On their way to the safehouse."

Drake looked down at the tablet.

Wondering just how much the girl knew.

There was now far too much at risk. "Institute Alpha Protocol," he said. "We'll meet them there and see what we've got."

"Yes, sir."

Alpha Protocol would severely cut their ability to communicate. It was, in essence, a total blackout. The only way to be absolutely sure. The Project's methods of encryption were tighter than any in the world, but in the face of these events Drake wondered if they'd somehow been hacked. Too many things didn't add up. They were, after all, dealing with something that was quite possibly *out* of this world. He looked down at the tablet in his lap. If the girl had access to technology that allowed her to tap their comm channels and know what they were doing ...

So much may already have been compromised. For all he knew the tablet was a listening device. Or a tracker. Likely as not it was both.

Time to run silent.

CHAPTER 35:

DOWN ON THE FARM

CRACK! a big branch broke somewhere far off in the woods. Jess jerked alert; snapped her head around the trunk she'd been leaning against, toward the noise. A few more cracks, then a voice:

"Jessica!"

It was Zac.

"Here!" she yelled, jumping up. At last. She shook off the leaves, brushing frantically at her filthy legs.

"Hey!" He ran up, shirt untucked but mostly still on, shoes and vest gone. He came to her in a rush and grabbed her up in a hug. She squeezed him back, absolutely relishing his sudden presence. It felt like she'd been sitting there forever.

He pulled back to look down at her, still holding her off the ground in his embrace. She craned her neck around his broad chest, peering into the forest the way he came.

"Did you catch him?" she asked, impatient. "Where is he?"

He set her to her feet. "I didn't catch him," he said and her heart sank. But Zac continued. "He kept going the way he was, didn't try to turn around. I got the idea to follow him, to see where he would go, thinking he might lead us somewhere. I mean, that's what we're trying to find, right? Bok bases or anything like that? Once he knew we were off his tail he slowed but kept going." Zac shrugged a little, hoping the decision he'd made was okay. "I was curious to see where he ended up."

Jess had been expecting Zac to return with their prize, bound and gagged and ready to take back to the others.

But maybe this was better. "So where did he go?"

"A farmhouse." Zac nodded his head in the direction from which he'd come. "Not far, actually, in a straight line. I think that was where he was headed when we were chasing him. Maybe he was hoping to face us with backup. Some of the others were there."

"From the club?"

Zac nodded. "Two were there when Lorenzo got there, three more arrived right after him. I watched them a while then decided to come see how you wanted to handle it. It looked like they were waiting for more, but I can't be sure. I can be back there in no time, but they might not stay long."

Jess sighed.

Now what?

She probably would've done the same thing. If Lorenzo was gathering with the rest of the Bok then this might, indeed, be an opportunity to go all the way. Find out what the Bok were all about and stop them cold. After all, as Zac mentioned, wasn't that the point of capturing Lorenzo in the first place? To find out more? Well, here they were. Rather than snatch Lorenzo from the club they'd chased him all the way to his hideout. Or a hideout. And so did they take the time to muster the rest of the troops and hope he and the Bok stayed where they were? Should she and Zac go get Satori?

She looked off through the woods, imagining the distance they'd covered, hoping Zac knew the way back to the Kel fighter.

It had been a long chase.

She took a deep breath and turned her eyes to his, understanding why he came to check with her. Why he didn't act on his own. Things had changed. Dramatically. But the reality was clear. They would have to continue this leg of the mission themselves. There was no time for anything else.

I'm so tired, she thought, suppressing a groan.

She pulled herself straight.

"How far?"

"Close," he said. "Like I said, I can get there in no time if that's how you want to do it."

She had no idea how she wanted to do it.

"It's a farm?"

"Up on the mountain. Looks abandoned. To be honest I think it's just a rally point."

Her mind drifted. She'd been sitting in the cold forest long enough that most of the adrenaline had drained and she was exhausted. She wanted Lorenzo more than ever, but the thought of another chase, any kind of engagement, made her ache.

Then there was the persistent, low-level fear instilled in her during the encounter at the club. A strange, oscillating set of emotions; hatred, the desire to destroy, matched by an uncertain apprehension that Lorenzo could harm, which drove a strong counter-impulse to run. To flee him and his kind. And though she'd already chased him so aggressively, though in moments of terrible clarity she imagined his neck in her hands, an unreasonable urge to kill ... that counter-impulse to flee flared within her.

She recalled Lorenzo's voice in her head.

Fear me!

She looked up. Zac saw the turmoil in her expression and wanted to ask more, wanted to know what troubled her—she could see that he did—but instead he tried to boost her in typical Zac fashion.

"I know it may have screwed things up," he said and grinned, a mischievous little grin, "but taking that motorcycle and chasing Lorenzo was a pretty baller move."

She was too exhausted for funny, or thought she was, but the prodding look in his eyes, the little turn at the corner of his mouth ... a smile washed over her and she felt a teeny bit better.

"Yeah," she agreed. "It was pretty baller." What she'd done, the way she'd ridden a race-ready machine to its limits and beyond, under those circumstances ...

Yeah. Pretty baller.

Zac stood back and put his hands on her shoulders.

"When the rest of the Bok show up, if they show up, the whole group may take off again." He glanced back the way he'd come. "This may be our only chance. I wanted to come check with you, but we need to figure out what's next. Do I go?"

Jess rolled her neck. Tried to stretch out the kinks.
How did she forget the tablet? Such a stupid mistake, even
in the midst of the chaos. That should've been foremost in
her mind, like not forgetting your keys. She and Zac had
so much technology, so much at their disposal, the Kel
fighter, the *Reaver* itself yet, somehow, they were on their
own. Bianca and Nani must surely be watching, but how
to get them a signal? As a child of the 21st century she
was so used to being in constant contact, always able to
communicate with anyone when needed, always able to be
reached. This sense of isolation felt very, very empty.

And then there was that other, nagging fear. She looked
into Zac's face, needing to know yet … not knowing how to
phrase the one thing at the front of her mind.

She swallowed.

"Do you think you can stop them?" She didn't want it to
sound like she doubted him. She didn't. God knew he was
strong enough. Only, it was just …

Before she could explain, before she had to, he laughed.

"Of course," he said, voice unconcerned. Free of
reservation. He knew exactly what she was worried about
and yet he himself had no worry at all. "I was off balance
when he hit me with … whatever that was he hit us with.
Neither of us saw it coming. I sure as hell didn't. We know
how it played out from there. First thing I had to do was
make sure you were safe. While I was doing that they got
away. Fast. Real fast."

"You weren't … knocked out?"

Zac shook his head. "Just knocked me back because
I wasn't expecting it. It was nothing. I'll have to adjust
for it if they do it again, which I'm guessing they will, but
it won't be a problem. I think Lorenzo sensed what I was
capable of. It looked like he was afraid, actually, when he
saw I wasn't affected. I wouldn't be surprised if it was why
he ran as fast as he did.

"Anyway, that card has been played. There are no more
surprises. This time I'll be ready. Now I know what they
can do."

Jess inhaled, letting her breath out slowly.

This day might never end.

"I wonder if they can all do that? Or ... other things." She didn't tell him of the speaking in her mind. *What if they can freeze us with a thought?*

Zac shrugged. "We should assume so. It was something different, that's for sure. I've never run across anything like it." Then: "Of course, I doubt they've ever run across anything like me." And he hazarded another grin.

She looked into his eyes. Impulsively she hugged him. Pulled herself all the way in, squeezed tight and held on, head against his chest. He hugged her back.

His confidence was contagious.

After a long moment she spoke, though she maintained her embrace.

"Let's go get them."

It only took him a second to process the "let's" part of that; not the plan he was expecting. She felt the hesitation in his silence.

"I don't want to wait here in the woods again," she explained, worrying he would make her. "I can't. I can't wait here wondering how you're doing. What's going on."

To her relief she felt him nod. "I'll bring you," he said. "But I'll leave you nearby while I take care of them. No getting involved." He released her and looked into her eyes. "Okay?"

She nodded.

Tenderly he stroked her cheek. She saw the expensive Breitling watch was still intact, even after all the jumping around. He smiled at her and no more words were exchanged. There was no need. They knew exactly what came next, knew exactly what needed to be done. He gathered her up in what was becoming a familiar position, one she'd come to love, held her firmly yet gently in his arms, all limbs accounted for, protected, head against his shoulder, the beat of his heart steady in her ear. The pace of that mighty heartbeat barely changed as he ran, through the trees, up steep ridges and down, leaping across the occasional gorge or creek, into the forest, weaving, smooth—

so smooth, considering what they were doing—keeping her safe, getting her at last to the clearing near the farm.

They loped the last hundred yards or so and he set her down at the edge of the woods where they faced out on a big farmhouse, the nearest edge just a few dozen paces away. There they crouched. A pond was to one side, naturally formed or decorative, it was hard to tell. Trees dotted the yard, a large barn in the near distance. Spreading out on the far side and plunging off into the valley below was a vineyard, dead vines and wild growth snaking over rows upon rows of latticework. What was once no doubt a thriving little winery. The sun was up, several spans above the horizon, the last mist of the morning burned away.

The real point of interest, however, were the cars. Seven of them Jess could see, maybe more out of sight; shiny new sports cars; Lamborghinis, Ferraris, a few convertibles, one McLaren, all belonging to the crowd of elite-looking young Bok who stood near them. Such a contrast in the rustic setting. A few million dollars worth of colorful, exotic machines dotting the yard, slung low and managing to look both menacing and extremely impractical all at the same time in the tall grass. The Bok just looked bored. Some of them she recognized from the club, though they were a little far off to see faces distinctly as they milled about, talking among themselves. Lorenzo was on a phone, having an animated conversation. It looked like he was mad.

Zac shifted beside her in his crouch, ready to get started.

"There's a few more now," he noted. "Sounds to me like they're talking about leaving." Of course he could hear their conversations. "Lorenzo is arguing with someone about what happened. The rest seem more interested in what they're going to do tonight. Sounds like they want to go back into town for the carnival or a parade or something."

Jess looked at the Bok, in their super swank clothes, trim, fit, handsome and, in the case of the girls among them, exquisitely beautiful. Like some kind of ultra-cool twenty-something clan with a dash of trust-fund-baby entitlement, standing around idly, more worried about what popular thing they were going to do next than any real possibility of danger. Their overconfidence, their obvious attitudes—such affected posing made her sick.

She couldn't wait to see them smacked around.

Zac added: "Lorenzo is not happy with what he's being told."

Jess watched Lorenzo the most. He was, indeed, having an unpleasant conversation on his cell.

She scanned the wider area, the whole of the farm property and surrounding woods. They could risk waiting and follow him to wherever he went next, but maybe they should take down everyone right now. Brutally if needed. Nab Lorenzo, see what else they could find there at this little farm hideaway then get him out of there—there was no way anyone would be able to follow as Zac carried them back over the mountains. Take Lorenzo, get back to the fighter and get this whole mission back on track.

"I think we have to nab him," she said. "Before something else changes. They're going to bolt again and we might lose him this time."

"Agreed."

Jess looked up at Zac as he in turn studied their targets. She looked back at Lorenzo. "Go in fast," she said. "No slow approach. I'd say take them all down so no one can follow. I don't care if you kill them if you have to." She didn't, really. She hoped Zac didn't. "Get Lorenzo, come back and get me. We'll see what else we can find here then get the hell out of here."

"Got it." And he rose to go. On impulse she stopped him with a hand on his arm. Looked at him, a little sheepishly, but he got her intent. He leaned in and gave her a kiss, held close and said: "This won't take long."

She nodded. He stepped back and stood.

And this time, giving the Bok no time to even become aware of his presence, he was among them. Crashing from the forest in one move, leaving her safely far behind, leaping across the distance as only he could, upon the first Bok before anyone saw him, leaned in and braced for the same sort of telekinetic punch they'd used before.

None came.

Crack! the sound of his fist hitting the first guy's head echoed sharply across the field. That guy went flying. After seeing Zac punch multi-ton armored units around like they were toys Jess wondered what sort of restraint it took to punch a man and not vaporize his skull, but somehow Zac did it. With a small spray of blood the Bok went flying backwards.

Despite the "gentleness" of the punch, however, she was quite certain he was dead.

They certainly didn't reckon on Zac.

Lorenzo yelled. Fear in it. Others yelled, suddenly in action, not knowing in those first few instants what they were dealing with. Zac hit and probably killed the next guy. Out of nowhere here was the man from the club, moving like a jacked-up superhero, two of their number already on the ground.

Crack! another went tumbling, out cold or dead. *Crack!* another, Zac a blur as he skidded and lunged, cutting back and forth across the randomly placed group that was now dispersing as they dove for cover or took up useless fighting stances. Jess could see Zac was reining himself in with the strikes, probably not thinking it smart to kill all of them.

Crack!

But Lorenzo saw what was happening.

Whooom! He threw out his hands, just as he had before, knocking Zac flying. As Zac was leaping for another Bok, eyes not even on Lorenzo, the force came at his back and hurled him tumbling away on the same trajectory, completely missing his target. Jess felt a ripple in the air from the blast—even from that far away.

Whatever Lorenzo did at the club was no fluke. His power was real.

But Zac gained his footing as the others shouted, two of them leaping at him as he oriented himself, then another, throwing out their hands in similar fashion to Lorenzo and knocking Zac back before he could get set.

And there was the answer.

The other Bok *could* do what Lorenzo did.

Of a sudden she heard a throaty *Vrrrmmm!* as an engine

caught. She jerked and saw Lorenzo was in his car.

No!

Things were moving too fast. She heard the car grind as he slammed it into gear and was off, gravel spitting, the Lamborghini fishtailing for traction in the soft yard, whipping away in an expanding tail of dirt and grass that shot out over the melee behind him, onto the long driveway, accelerating impossibly fast on the bad surface, flying down the sloping path to the mountain road below ...

Crack! the sound of another skull cracking. The rest of the Bok, still four standing she could see, maybe more out of sight—she hadn't done a proper headcount before all this started—surrounded Zac, the fifth going down hard as Zac hammered him to the ground. She cringed as the body hit in a solid thump of dirt and gore.

That one was dead for sure. Zac was frustrated, she could tell, and in the face of their unusual resistance his restraint was questionable. No Bok would live through this morning. She could see that now.

Zac was anchoring himself as best he could, but they were jumping around in exaggerated karate-like motions; creating a scene that had become brutal and ultra-violent fast. Zac was trying, but he could no longer control this the way he wanted. Even now, distracted by the loud, hurried departure of Lorenzo—she could see the indecision in his face, even at that range, not knowing whether to give chase or stay and make sure she was safe—the small group took advantage and shoved him with invisible walls of force. All four of them at once. His feet dug in, raking gouges as he was pushed backward, and before they could deliver another he was at one of them with a leap and that man went down in a bloody spray.

Definitely dead.

"Your friend is really something."

Jess screamed. Fell to her left; scrambled to get away from the girl standing suddenly right beside her. *Where did she come from?!*

"The Old Guard is saying you're the one," the girl went on, a sneer of confidence on her face. Having a conversation as if she hadn't just stopped Jessica's heart cold. It was Merci, the girl from the club. Matrix-style braids, snaked and tied in loops that stood out from her head. She didn't immediately close the distance between them as Jess stumbled backward and fell. "Lorenzo doesn't believe it," she said. "Neither do I."

Now she stepped closer and Jess scurried, on her palms and heels, slipping, trying to get away but hampered by the underbrush.

The girl shook her head, pretending disappointment. "You're weak."

Jess found her footing and ran. Out of the woods, around the back of the farmhouse. As she hit the grass at a sprint she caught a glimpse of Zac swatting the Bok like flies— there were more, it turned out. More than they thought. Zac was slowed by their ability to push back but Jess had no time to consider it, fleeing at full speed and desperate to find her way clear. At once terrified beyond reason and humiliated to be running like a child. But the terror was winning this battle and she was on it full bore, heels kicking out behind her as she flew. Out of the edge of her tunnel vision she saw Zac grab a yellow Ferrari and flip it over on top of his assailants; thought she heard gunshots; then she was around the back of the farmhouse and heading for the other end, past the pond, looking frantically for a place to hide ...

Whoooom! a tingle ripped up her spine and the blast sent her tumbling to the side, the world a sudden blur as she left her feet and went hurtling through the air ...

Splash! she hit the surface of the pond and went under.

It wasn't deep but she struggled to get her bearings, the force of the blast completely disorienting. Cold water was up her nose, everything a dark haze as she flailed about, trying to feel the bottom. She found it with one hand, twisted hard to the side, got a foot down, then the other, pushed off and stood. Her head surged above the surface and she took a gasping breath of air.

Then a splash beside her as the girl leapt in, Jess still trying to blink away the water enough to see, and the girl had a handful of her long hair right at the scalp and was jerking back. Jess cried out sharply in pain.

"*Who is he!*" the girl was demanding, yelling right in her ear. And as Jess winced, squinting hard against the sting, she vowed not to scream again. She would not give this bitch the satisfaction.

"Who's your friend!" the girl thrashed her head. Jess tried to resist but couldn't. The girl was not much bigger but seemed stronger somehow. Vaguely she heard yells on the other side of the farmhouse, the sounds of the fight.

Zac! She wanted to call to him, but he was completely occupied with his own struggle.

It was just her and the girl.

"You may not be special," the girl said with false calm, "but he is. How does he move like that?"

Jess grunted behind clinched teeth, refusing to speak. Then, unexpectedly, the girl shoved her head forward, plunging it beneath the water. Jess thrashed, panicking, trying in vain to break the surface so she could breathe. She knew the thrashing would only shorten whatever air she had in her lungs—she hadn't even had a chance to take a gulp before the girl pushed her under—but reason played no part in this. She wanted oxygen. Now.

The girl yanked her clear. Jess swayed in her tightly clinched grip, gasping hard, scalp aching where the girl squeezed the handful of her hair like a vice.

She grated: "Tell me who he is! Where is he from?"

Jess didn't know why she said it: "Go to hell."

And she was back under. Freaking. Knowing what it meant to die. The girl held her; Jess tried to kick, tried to sweep her legs, to use anything she knew to bring her down, to loosen her grip, but the girl was impossibly strong and Jess could do nothing.

She was about to drown.

Then her head was back above the water, the girl was saying something Jess couldn't hear behind the pounding in her ears, red rage rushing to cloud her watery vision as fresh oxygen rushed to fill her depleted cells and ...

Something snapped.

With a roar that boomed in the air—from deep within her lungs though she scarcely knew she made it—she surged from imminent death to that other place. That other Jessica. In the same instant she squatted and spun, hair twisting painfully in the girl's grip, jabbed an arm upward in a single lightning move *whap!* and had her assailant firmly by the throat. A sudden, furious action, palm open and grabbing the girl's neck in a thundering, wet smack. It happened so fast she had it before the girl could throw up anything in defense. It happened so fast Jess herself didn't even know what she was doing until it was done. In reaction the girl released her hair, both hands coming for hers.

Too late.

Jess no longer cared about hair. This wasn't about getting free. This attack was no threat, no ploy to get the girl to stop what she was doing. This was no slow choke. This was the killing blow. One contiguous, determined move, full malice behind it, full intent, hand jamming into the girl's neck as hard as she possibly could and continuing, thrusting all the way to the spine as her fist clinched, gripping in a bloodlust of sudden power, one goal in mind and the absolute decision to do it:

Kill.

Even as the girl's hands reached Jessica's wrist her grip was closing as hard as it could, as hard as it possibly ever could—a squeeze so filled with rage the girl's throat collapsed instantly in her grasp, fingers closing and digging in, yanking free like grabbing a handful of dough, pulling away with a ferocious jerk beyond any physical power she should possess, skin ripping, tendons and ligaments fighting to hold things in place—to no avail. Whether a normal human could've achieved something so extreme mattered little. Jess was not normal in that moment and this girl was about to die.

It was over in an instant. The girl's eyes so wide by now that Jess thought they would pop from her head, hands grasping at the torn, bloody gash where her throat used to be, staring at her killer in mute horror. Staring at her own throat, which was now right there in front of her, where it most definitely should *not* be, held firmly in Jessica's grip. The gasping became feeble, a bloody, gurgling sound that escaped the bloody hole that was once a neck, and with a stagger and a few more impotent flails of her arms Merci, poor Merci, fell to the side. *Sploosh.* Her body slipped beneath the water and sank, floating just below the surface, clouds of blood billowing from the ragged gash, thickly, like deep red food coloring, staining the water in a swirling cloud of death. Lapping gently into Jessica.

In no time she was standing in a pool of it.

She blinked. Looked at her still outstretched hand, gripping the bloody pound of flesh, purple-grey, tubes and veins, little chunks of arteries and pale white skin ...

She tossed the lumpy mess into the pond.

Staring at her blood-soaked hand.

At the blood in the water all around.

Soon she noticed the sounds of fighting had stopped. Everything on the farm was quiet. Just an abandoned old farmhouse, high on the mountain, a breeze blowing gently, morning sun shining warmly on a pleasant day, not a soul making a noise.

Slowly she turned. Little ripples of sound broke the silence as the water splashed red against her skin. And there, standing on the shore, was Zac. Watching her, clothes torn, flecks of blood on his own skin, a look of disbelief on his face. Had he seen what she just did?

He must've.

Her dress was shredded; wet, black tatters clinging to her. Whatever possessed her, whatever power, whatever impulse drove her to do what she'd just done was fading. She could feel a retch building.

She shuddered. All at once. Shook violently for a second, so hard she splashed the water; got it under control and stood staring at him, little shivers continuing to wrack her. Wondering how long she could maintain.

Wondering how long until she fell completely apart.

Zac, too, looked as if he was trying to come to grips with what had happened.

"I killed them," he said. "All of them."

But that wasn't what shocked him. Zac had killed before. Many times. His shock came not from the murder of the Bok. His shock came from this. He *did* see what she'd done, and ...

It shook him.

She looked at her bloody hand, then back at him.

"I had to," he said, almost as an afterthought.

She stared at him.

Fading fast.

CHAPTER 36:

HEALING

"THERE MUST BE SOMETHING," Bianca paced at the front of the bridge, near the edge of the domed view screen, alternately glancing at the screen-in-screen displays showing different overhead views of the Earth's surface and directly at the Earth below, peering hard at the Spanish peninsula, bright in the fresh morning sun. The shadow-line of sunrise curved far out in the Atlantic, inching slowly across the ocean toward America.

She and Nani had grown more and more frustrated as they failed to turn the image of Jess and Zac into any real leads. The Project had decided to go silent, no more info available through those channels. The last word was that they'd captured one of the Bok, not Lorenzo, and were laying low, no doubt trying to make a plan of their own. Hours after the incident the police had no more reports on any deaths or arrests, which at least meant Jess was probably still alive.

Bianca stared vacantly at the panoramic domed screen, a spectacular view that was no longer stunning in the least. No more magic in it. Especially not now. Just the Earth, stretching all the way side to side. Huge. Impossible to see every detail.

So huge.

Never had that fact hit home more than now.

Jess could be anywhere.

Among the other police reports was the report of a theft, a motorcycle, and she was convinced it was the one taken by Zac and Jess. Frustratingly no details were yet available; the police on the scene had so many more important bits of information to file there was nothing yet in the records on that one. If Nani could just get the owner's name or the info on the bike registry or anything, maybe she could use that to do something.

Maybe.

"There must be something," Bianca repeated in the tense silence.

"I'm looking!" Nani snapped. She looked immediately apologetic. "I'm looking, ok?"

"I know," Bianca tried to suffuse a bit of calm into the bridge. "I'm just thinking out loud. We're doing everything we can. I know."

"They're both smart," said Nani. "Zac has incredible strength. Between them ..." she shook her head. "They'll either go back to the fighter, or they'll turn up or get our attention somehow. Personally I think they're chasing Lorenzo. It hasn't been that long. I expect them to show up any time, ready for Satori to pick them up and get back here to us. We may be worrying for nothing."

Bianca hoped she was right.

* * *

JESS COULDN'T get the last stains of blood from her palm. She scrubbed and scrubbed in the running water, checking her killing hand again and again. No matter how she scrubbed ... she couldn't get it clean. Either hand.

Couldn't make them stop shaking.

Somewhere upstairs Zac ran a hot bath, looking for clothes, looking for towels, claiming she needed to clean off, needed to dry off. Needed to rest.

She just wanted to wash away these damn stains.

The water ran steady from the old iron faucet, over her hands and into the deep, chipped, porcelain sink; a lulling sound, filling the quiet emptiness of the abandoned farmhouse, failing utterly to block the images of the bloody massacre laying outside.

She looked up, into the dusty mirror on the wall over the faucet. Into her own face.

The face of a killer.

Her hair was a wet mess, tangled about her head. Strands nearly covered one eye. She didn't push them away. Didn't care. Water dripped slowly down her chin; her skin itched but she didn't scratch. Just stood there, absorbing her own image, seeing someone familiar yet ... not. A girl who felt no regret. A girl who felt only an aching numbness, so deep, so thorough ... she wondered if she might care about anything ever again. How could she?

Most of her makeup was gone, from the pond, from the race through the night ... from everything. Her mouth hung partly open, still damp, bottom lip trembling. She thought to wash away the rest, or wipe her lips with the back of her hand. Instead she just let them hang, mouth open, lips heavy, staring back at herself, hair in her eye, across her cheek, water running ...

She was a killer before today. Had killed in the name of the Cause before. Never like this. Never so brutal, with her bare hands. Now she'd ripped a girl's throat from her neck. And whether justified or not, now she'd done it all. Killed in all ways. To be standing there at the age of sixteen—at any age—wearing that crown, was all at once more than she could bear.

"Come." Zac was beside her. Visible from the corner of her eye, appearing from the nothingness of the hall. He held out a hand. When she failed to move or change in any way he reached gently and turned off the water. The resulting quiet was palpable and she continued to stand there, unmoving as the last drips faded into the silence.

She wasn't catatonic; she knew that. A zombie, yes, but not entirely. It was just ...

She wanted to curl up in a corner and be left alone.

Zac led her, checking her with worried glances as they walked. They passed through the modest foyer, complete with a small chandelier that hung from the second floor, everything kind of dusty, kind of unused but not utterly so; old furniture visible out in the living room as they went to the stairs, wooden steps creaking but sturdy, up to the top, turned down a long, quiet hallway with a carpeted runway and a few doors, ending at what had to be the master bathroom.

Inside was an old claw-foot tub. A big one, right at the

center of the room. A spacious room, as bathrooms went, black-and-white tiles on floor and walls, white porcelain sink and more iron fixtures. Morning sunlight streamed through a dirty, paned window looking out over the forest side of the house, little dust motes twirling in the orange beams. Dust that had probably lain undisturbed for a great, long time, stirred to action as Zac brought the old room somewhat to life, drawing a bath that steamed visibly. There was hot water. Apparently the old farmhouse wasn't entirely dead.

"I'll make a fire," he said.

And he left. It was quiet in the bathroom. She heard him moving about a few rooms away. For a long time she simply stayed in that spot, just inside the door, mesmerized by the little waves of steam on the surface of the tub.

She went over to it. Stripped off what few bits of the dress remained, the nice underwear she'd picked at the boutique—all she had left at that point, soaked and ruined—dropped it all on the floor and stood there, naked. The necklace was still on, the thin bracelets, the anklet. She slipped off the bracelets, but found no energy to do more. She left the others on and stepped in.

The room was cool, she noticed, the contrastingly sharp sting of the tub's heat bringing her into focus. It burned hot on her feet and legs, halfway up her shins; a deep bath and it felt good. And for the first time in what seemed like forever she felt a sense of soothing. For a long moment she just stayed like that, staring out the window, back to the door, in a daze but becoming aware enough to realize she was standing there on full display, and wondered for a moment if Zac might walk in.

He didn't. She could hear him still moving about a few rooms over, clanking this or thunking that, but whatever he was doing occupied his attention and he didn't return. Slowly she squatted, down into the water, feeling its hot, defining edge trace a line across her skin as she settled deeper. Soothing, intense heat below the line of the water; cool, crisp air above.

She sat all the way. Pushed back into the sloping curve

at the rear of the large tub and extended her legs all the way out. Her feet didn't go to the other end. It was the kind of tub you could stretch all the way out in, at least someone her size, and she put her arms in and sank lower, all the way until the warm water rose to her chin, lapping gently as she lay still and everything settled. The little waves of steam began to tickle her nose.

After a bit she held up her hand. Turned it front to back, scrutinizing palm and wrist. Water glistened, dripping from her skin; no sign of blood. Any stains she saw earlier must just have been an illusion. The product of an overtaxed mind.

She lowered her arm back into the tub and looked over her body, distorted and undulating beneath the slowly moving water. Dirt from the ordeal had begun to float free, clouding it. She rubbed at the most persistent spots and they came clean. Looked around. There were no washcloths, no soap. No towel in the room. She assumed Zac would bring her something, if there was anything to bring. Hard to believe the abandoned house would be stocked. She rubbed more, found scrapes, one bruise. The polish on her nails was still fresh, not even a day old yet, some chips but otherwise shining bright blue as she wiped away the grime. A stark flash of color, fun; an attempt to look pretty that stood in direct opposition to the way she felt.

She slid further down, head in the water, face just breaking the surface, hair floating about her shoulders and her scalp. She wiped her palms across her face a few times, getting rid of the last of the makeup, and for a long while just floated there, the water oh-so soothing, body rocking ever so gently, hovering against the bottom of the tub, swaying back and forth in the waves each time she moved. She closed her eyes and listened to the muffled silence of the house, gradually losing the tiny connections to the aches, the pain. The world.

And finally felt herself breathing.

"Here's a towel." Zac's voice was dull beneath the water. She opened her eyes. Raised her head slowly, seeing him standing in the doorway across the room. He held a plain white towel and seemed hesitant; unsure what to do next.

Apparently the house was stocked after all.

"Come in," she said, wondering whether she really wanted him to. Did she want to be alone? Did she want him to see her naked? Even beneath the somewhat cloudy, distorted surface of the bath? No matter; now that she'd asked she couldn't take it back.

Still he seemed hesitant.

"You sure?"

She was.

Slowly he entered, found a hook for the towel inside the door and came to stand beside the tub. Awkwardly. He tried not to look down, tried to look out the window, at the forest, at anything but her. Then, realizing how stupid that must seem, fixed his gaze on her eyes. She looked up at him, chin in the water, eyes turned up, ends of her hair drifting softly about her shoulders; stretched out in the tub, floating, completely naked. Raw before him, feeling suddenly liberated that he could see all of her, every inch, and yet he'd already seen so much, seen her in so many ways, so many more significant, more important ways— after all they'd been through the nakedness of her skin hardly mattered.

In a way it only made that deeper bond official.

"Sit," she told him. The large bathroom was nearly empty, just an old toilet and a bidet, the sink and the tub. He settled himself to the floor and leaned against it, one arm on the side, head next to hers, and as he looked into her eyes, too close now to be distracted by anything else, he seemed finally to relax.

They sat like that for many minutes, so comfortable, so natural, the hot water soothing. Jess soon found herself in a sort of rapture. Terrible events had transpired, terrible events were likely on the horizon, but in that moment, as she'd learned to accept—moments were to be lived, the good with the bad—in that moment she and Zac were one.

It felt right.

"I'm not sure what to do next," he said quietly. "I should probably get us to Satori before—"

"Shhh," Jess shook her head slowly. "Let's not talk about any of that for a bit. Okay?"

"Okay."

For a second it looked as if Zac had another idea, was going to make another suggestion related to their plight, but routed his thoughts elsewhere and said instead:

"You did what had to be done."

"I know."

"We both did."

"I know."

"Whatever powers they have ..."

"Shhh," Jess held a wet finger to her lips. "Let's not talk about it."

Zac was at a loss. There was so much *to* talk about, so much to discuss, so much to figure out ... she could see it was difficult for him to turn his mind from it. Knew it was. Because she was having the same trouble. But she wanted to. Needed to. Needed to put it all far away, if only for a little while.

He sat there staring at her as she, in turn, stared at him. Studying his face in the soft glow of the morning sun; strong, perfect—as handsome in that proximity as at any range. Zac was so perfect. So sweet. He cared for her so very much.

She felt undeserving of it.

"I want to help you," he fairly whispered. She focused, realizing she'd been looking into his face, thoughts somewhere else. Beneath the admiration of his stare she looked down, dipped her chin in the water and let a little flow into her mouth, tasting the heat.

"From the moment we met." He searched for words. "I don't know." He almost gave up. "I can't describe it. It's like you're a girl out of time. A girl ... but not. Something greater. I know you hate it, I know it bothers you when people talk this way, but I can see why they think you're an angel."

She lowered her chin more, keeping her eyes on his.

"I mean, you're here, you're very much here, and yet it's almost as if you're beyond us. You're walking around, feeling undeserving," he echoed her thoughts, "incapable, wanting out of what you've fallen into, all the while not realizing you've got wings."

He looked away, trying to make sense of the things he, himself, barely understood. Trying to make her understand. "It's like you're reaching back, trying to pull the rest of us forward." He thought a moment. "You deserve everything anyone can do. People have tried. Darvon. Me. Satori, Willet. Now Nani and even your friend, Bianca. You have support because you *deserve* support, Jessica. Don't ever doubt that you deserve it. Don't doubt that."

The sudden intensity of his admiration was more than she could bear.

But the absolute tenderness of the glimmer in his eye, on the face of such a powerful man—a super man—one who would fight the world for her, and had and was openly making his declaration to continue to do so, made her heart break. Here he was, trying to make her understand what she meant to him—when he likely only partly knew what *he* meant to *her* —*so much!*—and, frustratingly, she could think of nothing to say. Nothing that would touch him the way he touched her.

Nothing that would tell him how deeply she loved him.

And suddenly she was lying naked in the tub. The nervousness she'd expected to feel came crashing in on her now. It was sudden, it was strong, and there was nothing she could do. Right there, right there in front of him, no way to rise up and hide, no way to turn or cover up, no way tactfully to ask him to leave—especially now that he was sitting there so comfortably at her invitation. She was dirty, she was ugly, and he was right there, an arm's reach away, leaning over the tub, talking calmly. For him nothing had changed. No realization had come over him. She'd invited him in and he came and there he sat.

She swallowed. Worked to corral these suddenly embarrassing thoughts, heartache turning to a flutter of nerves, hoping he wouldn't notice the change.

"I sometimes wonder myself," she said, hoping to talk her way through it. "I know my life, how I grew up. It's kind of hard to fit that image with what I've become. I mean, *am* I destined for this? Am I meant to be a savior? And a savior of what? So far all I've done is run around and mess things up. I mean, if I'm supposed to be here, if I'm supposed to be doing something ... what is it?

"*Is* this part of some plan laid down by a priestess a thousand years ago? Am I the agent—the angel—of her prophecy? There's no doubt I've managed to get myself into the middle of *something*."

The tub was cooling off. Still warm, but no longer the soothing heat of moments ago. Dirt and pond remains had spread out, remnants of makeup, until the water was now a light, sooty gray. And right there beneath it, clearly visible, was all of her.

Now the moment was thoroughly awkward. She wanted to get out.

Rather than blurt a sudden request, however, she stared at him a little longer, tried to be calm, tried to recreate the earlier tenderness. Then, after what seemed the right amount of time, asked: "Can you bring me the towel? I think I'll get out. The water is getting cold."

He rose and went across the room to get it, eyes shifting from her face to his objective without so much as a glance to anything else. He was definitely being a gentleman.

She watched intently as he padded away, across the tile floor in his bare, muddy feet, Italian slacks torn and dirty, the shreds of the shirt he'd worn at the club in equally bad shape.

Hugging the curves of his muscular back.

And as he reached the towel hanging on the hook, in full view across the room, head to toe, another feeling surged. A brand new feeling, entirely displacing the nervous desire to run and hide, or even the previous desire to be pure and open before him. Something else altogether.

It was the desire to grab him and drag him into the tub. Right then, right now, and she had to catch her breath as the powerful urge swept through her with a sudden, fierce shudder she could barely conceal.

Then he was on his way back, eyes politely raised, towel

in hand. He extended it for her to take, turned as she did and headed for the door without so much as a glance back.

"The master bedroom is across the hall," he spoke as he left. "I've got a fire going. I found some clothes."

And he was gone.

After a long hesitation, during which she worked to get her mind on track, she rose, shakily; unsteady shakes that accelerated with the shivers that gripped her in the cold air. Outside the sun was rising toward late morning but nothing had warmed. At least not that she could tell.

It wouldn't have mattered. The cold air on her soaked skin was only exacerbating the thrill racing through her.

She patted herself dry and wrapped the towel around her, all the way up, over her shoulders, under her chin. It was a big one, like a beach towel, thick and soft. It smelled a little musty but she held it clenched about her and pushed it up to her face until the shivers steadied and she was still. She stepped from the tub, cold air on her shins and ankles, cold tiles beneath her feet. Steadily she splat-splatted across the slippery floor, out to the hall and onto the worn carpet, feet drying as she walked.

Firelight shone from the master bedroom and she walked to it. It was the next door up, and as she turned into the room she found Zac kneeling, tending a fireplace. A big fireplace, even for a big room, rising nearly halfway up one wall. The fire in it crackled with soothing heat that could be felt from the doorway.

He looked up, using one of the iron rods to push a few blazing logs around. And for some reason, as he did, she had another of those "Zac" moments, wondering if he even needed to use the rod. He could no doubt just adjust the logs by hand. She already knew he was fireproof. Maybe it was just easier to use the rod. Certainly it made him seem more human.

"Hi," she said.

"Hi," he returned.

The exchange felt shy. She was already back to feeling nervous, the harsh blast of irresistible lust fizzled.

She entered. Stepping from the carpeted hall the wooden

floor of the room was warm from the fire, the whole space giving off an immensely soothing vibe. Zac had obviously worked hard to make it comfortable. She could see some of the clanking and banging, in addition to starting the fire, must've come from the fixing of the bed, the placing of new sheets, the drawing of curtains and his other efforts to create a relaxing space for her to rest.

She was deeply touched. And smitten all over again. Kneeling by the fire, all he'd done, all his concern ...

"Obviously we shouldn't stay long," he said, poking the logs, "but you need to take a few minutes and recharge. Sleep if you can. I know you're not ready talk about what we need to do, and maybe now's not the time, but you need at least a few minutes. Rest, then we'll figure it out."

But she just stood there, halfway in the room, huge towel hugged around her, covering her from chin to knees, naked beneath, watching him.

Not moving.

Not daring.

Much of her exhaustion seemed to have left her.

He rose, satisfied with the fire, went to the bed and turned it down. He'd even covered the pillows with lacy cases.

When she continued to just stand there he sat on the edge and looked across the room at her.

"I know sleep is probably the last thing on your mind," he said, and she wondered if he had any idea what was actually on her mind. She looked for signs as he continued: "You're driven," he added. "I know. But please, for me." He patted the bed beside him. "Please just let yourself rest. Just a little. I won't let anything happen while you do."

She wavered; nervous—so nervous—head buzzing with a million thoughts. Outwardly calm, inwardly in turmoil ...

And all at once was above it.

The buzz continued, there was no doubt of that. She could hear it. Conversations flying around inside her skull. Doubts. Fears. Nothing was silenced. Yet ...

She was above it. Drifting, in a sense, out of that inner conflict, all the way to ... inner calm. A center. A place from which everything finally made sense. A place where there were no more doubts. A place where the contemplation of that which did, in fact, make absolute sense and which she would, in fact, do, gave her a deep, shuddering thrill.

Unsticking herself she made her way to the bed, slower than she might've walked otherwise, deliberate in her steps though not exactly a sultry, sexy walk. Enough, however, so it should've been clear by then what she had in mind.

Somehow she thought it probably was.

Zac sat at the edge of the bed. Watching her. Waiting. She reached him and stepped close, then closer. Right into the V between his knees, brushing his legs apart with hers and stepping all the way up against him; looking down over the top of her towel, directly into his upturned face. He in turn looked up into her sensual gaze and ... swallowed.

Superman was starting to look a little nervous.

So was she, she knew, but the last shreds of timidity were falling away. There would be no rejection, of that she was certain, and the realization of that gave her the confidence she needed to push beyond her final fears.

She shrugged the towel from her shoulders and dropped it to the floor.

Zac didn't look down. He kept his eyes on hers, though his face was right at her chest. She reached and held his jaw on either side, locking his gaze.

After a long moment, standing there, just being there, doing nothing more than looking into his eyes, she bent slowly and ... kissed him. A tender touch of her lips on his. Once. Holding his cheeks lightly. Then again, slowly, another brush of the lips that rushed instantly to a deep, open kiss, pulling him into her with every bit of desire she restrained.

The world around her moved.

She released him and he strained toward her but she held him, at a tantalizing distance; leaned in slowly and kissed him again. Softer this time; then again, so softly, breathing into him as she did: "Zac." Deeper, more passionate.

She pulled back, face inches from his.

Looking deep into his eyes.

"Now is our moment," she told him.
And he took her to him.

CHAPTER 37:

THE TICKING CLOCK

"SO WHAT'S HE SAYING?" Drake entered the safehouse in the lead, Bobby and the others in tow. The rest of the agents were in the main room, a few noticeably absent. Those few were likely in the rear room with their "guest".

"So far not much."

"How were they planning to get out of the country?"

"Nothing to go on yet."

Drake motioned Bobby for the tablet. Bobby handed it to him and Drake in turn handed it to one of his specialists.

"Take a look at this," he said and the man took it.

The other agent continued: "All we know so far is what we saw: the Bok all scattered in different directions, no known destination. We've been monitoring traffic on all channels, specifically the local airports and even a few ports that are close enough." The agent looked to the army of screens in the converted living room, each displaying information, manned by members of the team, watching and listening for any sign of unexpected departures. They of course had no info on any of the Bok and so could not flag them closely, but at least they could watch for unusual, last-second passenger requests, or flight plans or other signs, especially if several were made at once, cross-reference those for clues and see what materialized. So far nothing. Drake was sure they'd already chased more than a few dead-ends.

"Maybe they're not leaving the country," Bobby suggested.

One of the techs nodded. "We've been checking information through the Pyrenees passes. It's possible they went west, toward Portugal, or east or even south, though with the time elapsed any of those crossings would still be unlikely as of yet. We're watching police channels."

"What about the girl?" Drake was nearly as keen to get Jessica as he was Lorenzo.

"We think she and her male friend fled the scene."

Drake rubbed his scalp. This wasn't going at all as planned. "Have you brought headquarters into the loop?"

"They were informed of Alpha Protocol. So far no break of silence on their end, so we have to assume no additional information there."

Drake sighed. In the rear of the house he heard a thump and a muffled scream.

"Has our captive tried," he fished for a description, looking back down the hall toward the interrogation room, "anything? Has he been able to use any ... power, like Lorenzo used in the club?" The man he spoke to was one of the agents that had been with him at the club, though he hadn't witnessed the Bok directly. Only Drake experienced the full, direct power of what Lorenzo did.

"Not so far. At least, not that we can tell. We have him quite immobilized, so it's possible it requires some form of gesture, or use of the body."

"No devices?"

"None yet."

Drake felt his skin crawl. If the Bok used no devices to generate the weird field then that meant the power came from them directly. A frightening thought.

But maybe it was something embedded. Some ancient technology the Bok had embedded beneath the skin, within their bodies, that hurled the wall of force. Or maybe this guy they'd captured couldn't do it. After all, only Lorenzo had done it for sure. At least as far as Drake knew.

Another shout from the back and he cleared his head.

"Let's start piecing together our next steps."

* * *

NOTHING ELSE MATTERED. Not right then. Jess saw every opportunity missed, every chance that had passed, everything that might still be, the whole world open before her. It was a fresh look, filled with all manner of possible

futures. Nothing she'd done, nothing that had gone before
...

Nothing else mattered.

Zac lay with his head on her shoulder, looking down
across her breasts, hand on her tummy, brushing her skin
idly, finger going now and again in and out of her belly
button. Both of them had been quiet for what seemed like
a long time. She hugged his heavy head with one arm,
stroking his short, black hair, breathing in the musk of his
powerful presence. On her back, staring up at the ceiling,
he stretched out beside her.

She was clean. Spiritually and physically, clean. The
bath earlier cleansed her body, the last hours had cleansed
her soul. Zac's own body had at first been dirty, from the
ordeals of the day, but slowly they'd cleaned him too, here
and there along the way. His feet were the dirtiest, and at
some point she'd used a towel to wipe them thoroughly,
that simple action alone hugely sensual, leading to yet more
passion. Everything was sensual right then. She was like
a raw nerve. But she was finally satisfied, at last able to lay
naked with him without any impulse driving her other than
to simply be. For his part it seemed Zac could go forever,
a product of the Kazerai infusion, no doubt—as even the
most horny teenage boy would've given up long before
then—but he was more than content to lay with her, quiet,
being together in the purest, most magical way possible.
Beyond his obvious stamina, and much to her complete
and utter joy, Zac had proven to be completely normal.
At least in every way that counted. Though she had no
real-life example with which to compare, and perhaps he
was much better than most—she had no way to know—she
deemed him fully human, fully normal. Absolutely perfect.

She could not have been happier.

"You're normal," she said it as if a revelation. After
everything to that point she was finally getting herself
together enough to think. To step back and appreciate the
events of the last however-many hours. The thrill running
through her would not abate. Not that she wanted it to, she
didn't want it ever to, but the alternating giddy sensations

and shuddering thrills coursing deep within her were starting to make her feel like she'd transcended; not just a temporary rush, but an actual rise to another plane. One filled with pure bliss. She couldn't come down. It was like the world held still that afternoon. The day was theirs and nothing could impinge upon it.

A smile stretched her face until it ached. She let it run its course. Little butterflies danced in her belly, harder like dragonflies each time Zac's fingers passed across her bare skin, back and forth, ever-so-gently, stirring them to a tingle she never wanted to forget. She wanted to burn that feeling into her mind; to have it, to relive it whenever she chose.

"Normal?" His hand came to rest on the patch of skin just bellow her naval.

She was recalling the ridiculous conversation with Bianca back on Anitra, imagining Zac as some sort of freak. Which he most definitely was *not*. A freak of perfection, maybe. Every inch of him. *Wonderful*. Every inch drove her desire, every piece, every part. At times that day she could hardly believe he was real.

When she didn't respond he sounded a little sad: "I guess I was hoping for something a little more."

What?

"No," she said hurriedly. "No, not that." She reached and hugged his head with both arms, holding his cheek to her breasts. "Not that. You're not normal."

Face smooshed against her in her grip, his eyes turned up to look into hers. Shimmering, ice blue in the afternoon sunlight that streamed through cracks in the curtains, brilliant beneath his perfect, dark brows; brows that curved up just a little at the edges, the exact right amount and all sexy-like. *So handsome*. She kissed his forehead.

Now he looked confused. "So I'm *not* normal?" he said through his smooshed lips.

"Stop. It's just ..." she began. How best to put it? "You're so super. You crack tanks in half, Zac. Come on. Put yourself in my place. Imagine you're me." She knew he wouldn't make a joke of it. "I was a little afraid, that's all."

"Afraid of what?"

Suddenly she was shy. *How can I be shy now? After all this?* She released him a little. "I mean, what if you didn't work like normal guys? Or something else was weird? I had no idea what to expect." He waited for more and she admitted: "I don't know! You're normal. Ok? And that's exciting."

"So I'm normal." he confirmed, acting resigned.

She smacked him. "You're amazing, alright?" She leaned her head forward so he could see all of her face. "Amaaazing," she rolled her eyes, all the way up in her head, making a totally amazed face. And Zac laughed and all was good. She flopped her head back to the pillow and looked up at the cracked, peeling ceiling, smiling to herself and so happy right then. Somewhere off in the house a clock ticked. Like an old grandfather clock.

Zac *was* amazing. Once her mind was made up and she jumped over that cliff she threw herself into the moment with every bit of pent-up desire, every ounce of her own passion, holding nothing back. Why go all the way and not go *all* the way? She, of course, had no idea what she was doing, other than a million internet views, magazine articles, overheard conversations with other girls, unwanted advice from Bianca, Amy, different advice from Mom, sterile text books and any and all the usual sources available to and bombarding any teenager. With only that to go on she feared, at first—and thankfully only a little—she'd get it wrong. But there was apparently more to it than all those things, and while experience probably went a long way toward sex, there was no denying the sheer power of instinct. Especially here where that instinct was backed by such passionate desire, fighting desperately to be unleashed. And so once loosed, once the bottle was uncorked, the day cascaded forward in a giant, cresting wave, crashing between intensity, tenderness, laughter, and even the occasional tears of disbelief that any of it could actually be happening. She had no idea Zac's own experience nor did she ask, but through it all he *was* amazing, unbelievably so, and the way he fulfilled—exceeded—every dream, every hidden impulse, like he somehow knew without having to ask, or her having to say, though he also asked and she also did say, and she asked him and he told her, his every desire, no being embarrassed, all inhibitions gone, throwing themselves into each new thing ... the way he fulfilled was so surreal, held her in such ecstasy, so high and for so long ... in her greatest moments of lucidity that afternoon she wondered if something broke. Wondered if the utter, absolute joy of it—over-joy—had actually kinked something out of whack. Was this normal? Would she be stuck that way forever?

Ahhh, she sighed, hugely content.

If only that were possible.

"*You* were amazing," Zac said quietly.

She stroked his hair; buried her nose in it and kissed his head. The fireplace crackled, flames low but still guttering, no longer giving off much heat. Off in the quiet of the house the clock ticked, methodically slow, echoing from the wooden walls. *Tick. Tock. Tick. Tock.* If it was truly a grandfather clock someone must've wound it. Maybe the Bok, when they were there earlier that day? Or maybe it was electric. There was electricity in the house. The farm was definitely used.

"It's getting late." Zac seemed to sense the moment had turned. Jess shifted uncomfortably.

The feeling of ecstasy started to fade.

But she was determined not to lose it. Not now. Not ever. To hell with the Bok and to hell with everything else.

"I'm hungry," she said, changing the subject before anything bad could happen.

Zac inhaled. "Lorenzo will be back with more firepower—"

"I'll cook us something," she ignored him and rose, laying his head to the side and sliding to the edge of the bed.

He sat up to his elbows.

"We should go get Satori," he persisted. "This was probably not the best use of our time."

No. She was *not* going to have that conversation. Not

going to let the magic of this slip into a discussion of practicalities and things they should've done or should not have done or things they now ought to be doing.

"I need to eat," she said. "I'm hungry and we're going to eat." And that was final. She rose from the bed, turned and stood beside it. Looked him over as he sat there leaning back on his elbows, stretched out naked in all his length, all his glory, feet hanging over the end. He looked at her with those ice-blue eyes; always glowing with a light of their own, it seemed. Studying her. Wanting to do one thing, conceding for now to follow her wishes. She could see he would not argue. Not yet, anyway.

But the moment of their disagreement was coming.

"There must be something in the kitchen," she announced. More practicalities crowded in. She stood there, completely naked, wondering what to wear. There was nothing left of her clothes. Nothing she would put back on. Somewhere during their lovemaking she'd taken off the rest of the jewelry and now had on absolutely nothing. Zac's shirt was torn and filthy and ruined. She would've loved nothing more than to throw it on and walk around with it hanging to her knees. Cooking them a nice meal, wearing his oversized shirt, lounging about, just the two of them after a day of passion.

That wasn't an option.

Frustrated she went to the room's large closet.

"There's some old shirts and a few overalls," Zac said from the bed. She reached and opened the door. "They looked clean," he added. She kept her back to him as she looked in the closet and shuffled through the few options. All the same size: men's medium. Probably belonged to the once farmer. No female clothes to be seen, just three tan shirts and two pair of denim overalls. Nothing that would fit Zac, not even close. She took a shirt off the hanger and put it on. On her it was big, kind of like she wanted, but it wasn't Zac's. It only hung halfway down her thighs, and it stunk like mothballs.

She would have to pretend.

Shouldn't be hard, she thought as she angrily rolled up

the sleeves. *This is all one big game of make-believe.*

She turned to Zac, hating the sudden dissatisfaction crawling all over her.

"I'll see what I can find and make us something," she worked to keep things positive.

"Okay."

He remained reclined on the bed, watching as she left the room and went padding down the long, carpeted hall—heels stomping harder than she wanted against the wooden floor beneath.

But she couldn't take the emotion out of her step.

CHAPTER 38:

DESPERATION

"THEY FINALLY filed their report," Nani said as she flagged a new bit of information. "Let's see what we've got."

Bianca walked over to stand behind her. Put a hand on the back of her chair. Bianca had been pacing, exhausted but unable to make herself rest. Jess was lost and until she was found—and safe—there was no way she could sleep. It was late in the day down on Earth. Everyone had now been up a full day or longer. The dark edge of sunset could be seen moving in from the east, heading toward Madrid. They'd been monitoring feeds, piecing together any picture of the incident below they could sift from the noise. The whole exercise was turning out to be far more complicated than Bianca ever would've imagined. Now it looked like Nani had the police report they'd been after.

"The motorcycle belonged to a Ramero Campione," Nani read from a screen. "Apparently a rare model. It had a tracking device, embedded in the frame." She looked over her shoulder at Bianca. "Which means we can probably find it."

Bianca felt a surge of energy.

"Where is it?" she stood straighter.

Nani's nose was in the screen, looking through everything she could find, tapping and cross-checking, dragging and reading.

Nothing.

"The tracking info isn't part of the report," she sagged a little.

Bianca refused to let her hopes be dashed. "Can we find it through the manufacturer or something? I mean, everything's on the web these days. Can you find it?"

Nani straightened, rubbed her eyes and threw out her arms in an involuntary stretch. Bianca stepped away from the chair to give her room; stepped around in front of the console. Nani leaned back for a moment and let her lids close, then began rubbing her temples as Bianca watched. After she kept doing that for what felt like a long time Bianca almost snapped, almost asked her what the hell she was doing, but even in her depleted state realized that would be uncalled for. Nani was as tired as any of them and, honestly, she'd been doing all the work. In truth, as frustrated as she was, as angry, Bianca realized she could not ask for a better companion in this. Nani's compassion, her intelligence, her dedication, were amazing. Though they'd only just met she felt like Nani was already a lifelong friend.

With one more glance at the beautiful scientist she turned and went all the way over to the edge of the domed screen, stood and looked down on the Earth below.

She's alive, she told herself.

She had to be alive.

* * *

Zac could smell whatever Jess was cooking, wafting down the long slope of the yard, coming directly from the kitchen ahead; a savory aroma that permeated the air, hints of things he couldn't identify but definitely could not wait to taste. He walked slowly up the hill toward the house. The delicious flavors first caught him as he was finishing the unpleasant task of dumping the bodies of the Bok, mixing delicately with their exotic perfumes and colognes. There was as yet no stench of death among the Bok, just the smells they'd been wearing when alive. The smells of leisure; the very scents Zac found so intoxicating when discovering them in the boutique with Jessica. Those smells did little, however, to mask the carnage. So many bodies. He recalled how they seemed to keep coming, attacking from every angle. Maybe they'd been in the house, or the barn. Maybe in the trees. Once the fight began it was way more than he'd first thought.

He tried to clear those images from his mind. Disposing

of the dead after battle had never been part of a Kazerai's duties, and while he'd seen plenty of fresh death in his short life he'd never dealt so closely with the results of his power. It wasn't often he fought unarmed or, especially, unarmored men. Blood, lots of blood, shattered limbs, skulls and faces disfigured beyond recognition, glassy, staring eyes—where eyeballs remained. All of it the result of his gruesome assault. Despite their unusual "powers" the Bok were definitely human and died just as easily. The additional forces they'd been able to manifest in their defense had completely frustrated his efforts—and quickly his desire—to manage his attack. He'd wanted to knock them out, or otherwise incapacitate, mainly since any one of them could've been a source for finding out more. None of that worked. When the fight began things degenerated fast, options flew away and he was left with ...

That. He glanced over his shoulder at the giant mound of dirt at the forest edge. The burial pit.

Out in a little ramshackle shed he'd found a few shovels and hoes, broke them all as he used them well beyond their capacity, switched to his hands and quickly plowed out a massive hole, rounded up all the bodies and parts—including the girl Jess killed in the pond—threw them in and covered the whole thing up. He'd been sure to grab whatever they had on them, wallets, phones, keys, in the event any of it might prove useful. The rest went into the hole.

He turned and looked at the large barn building, where he'd put the Bok's personal items, then paused for a moment as he neared the house. He stood in place and turned to face out across the rolling hills, across the vineyard, out to the mountains beyond.

An inspiring view.

So tranquil.

Hard to believe the massacre that occurred there. He inhaled deeply of the fresh mountain air, the tang of old wood and fresh dirt—overlaying it all the amazing smells drifting down from the kitchen. A breeze blew from that direction, lightly, tingling the skin of his back. And he found himself amazed—amazed that he could still be amazed, after all these years—how perceptive were his senses. Able to feel pleasant things like wind, while simultaneously being able to withstand so much. He could feel a tiny bug on his back; tell you when it lifted a leg. No human could do that. He could also take a cannon to his back. No human could do that either. The absolute range of strength, of perceptions, available to him was staggering. The Kazerai truly bordered on the magical. Even the Dominion scientists had never fully understood them, or even tried, letting the mystique of the great warriors slip instead into the realm of Holy Decree. The great Kazerai, Hands of God.

Zac closed his eyes.

Before setting about his grisly but, he felt, necessary task he'd pulled on the torn slacks, the one piece of clothing still reasonably intact. For a moment he felt them on his legs, feeling with them all the things that were wrong with the current situation.

Being there, still being there, doing what they were doing … it made no sense, but he wasn't sure how to steer Jess back toward action. Spending the day together as they had, as wonderful—as absolutely wonderful—as that was, so completely fulfilling, had cost them valuable time and left them dangerously exposed. At least that time could've been used for her to rest. Of course he was entirely complicit, as eager as he also was, as full of the same desires. He loved her. More than any girl he'd ever loved. In truth there had really only been Kitana before her, Zac never had many girlfriends, and though Kitana had been forced on him, an arranged marriage—so young, both of them, to be husband and wife—he had, in fact, loved his bride.

But not like Jess.

No one like Jess. There was something about her that was a complete and total lock. A feeling he could never explain. Jess was the one, and Zac truly could not think of a life without her. Which only made it worse. He loved her so much, so incredibly much, wanted her so much … it made it harder. That whole afternoon, such a mashup of unbound hedonistic satisfaction, fulfillment beyond his most fervent hopes, squashed together with a gnawing impatience to keep moving ... it had his head spinning.

She had his head spinning.

And so he was guilty. A fact which did not make what they were doing any less stupid. It was never too late to change your mind. To get your head on straight. Yet, after giving in to their passion and jeopardizing an entire day, they were now getting ready to have a leisurely dinner. All at her insistence. He knew she needed to eat. Whether a fast bite, something simple or an elegant spread, she was human and hadn't eaten in a day. He tried to rationalize it that way, all the while realizing those were empty excuses. He could rationalize it all he wanted, the simple truth was they did what they did because she'd decided that was what they were going to do and he, unable to resist her even a little, went along. It had been that way from the beginning. What she wanted to do she did, and so did he. Therefore if he didn't find a way to get her mind back where it belonged ...

He opened his eyes. Looked out across the spectacular vista, seeing far, into the distant hills, all the way to the mountains which were slowly becoming shrouded in an evening mist. There were no people in that slice of view, no human constructs of any kind. This old abandoned vineyard and winery occupied a remote section of mountain. The narrow road leading to it far down over the next hill had barely any traffic on it. No sounds of humanity, no machines anywhere other than the occasional car or truck passing on the main road much farther below. Peaceful.

The night would likely bring a sky full of stars.

She's probably wondering where I am. The sun was heading for the mountains. He turned from the beautiful view and walked the rest of the way to the house, following the aromas as if they were an invisible finger, beckoning him onward to the tasty finale. He climbed the last of the hill and approached the house.

At the back door he announced himself:

"It's me."

Jess called from the kitchen. "In here."

He went inside and found her at the stove, stirring three pots, all kinds of other things spread out on the counters around her. It was a major production. She turned and smiled as he entered, continuing to stir.

"Almost done." She tasted a spoonful of one pot, decided it needed a little more of something and reached for a shaker. "Wanna set the table?"

He did. He wanted to do anything she asked. Everything.

And that was part of the problem.

May have been *the* problem.

Why am I so infatuated?

He was utterly hers.

He paused a moment, taken with her, lost in her image, then went over and stepped up behind her, pushed her fragrant hair from the back of her neck and kissed the soft skin at the nape. She shivered. He let her hair fall back, closed his eyes and breathed in her heavenly scent. The old farm shirt had a definite odor of its own but hers—her distinct, incredible aroma—thoroughly displaced it. So strong was it, to him, that he barely smelled the shirt at all. For him it was only her and the amazing food.

He cleared his head and opened his eyes. Asked:

"Plates? Forks and knives and things?"

She nodded. "Rinse them first. Everything is dusty." She reached for a glass on the counter and took a drink. He noticed she'd opened a bottle of wine. He looked more closely around the kitchen. It was like she was trying to put everything out of her mind. Refusing to let anything ruin this special moment she was determined to create. "The food is actually fresh," she said as she stirred, "Not much here, but there was bread and stuff, and meat and cheese and even fresh vegetables. Someone keeps the place stocked, though it doesn't look like anyone has eaten here in a while. All the pots and things are dusty. They must throw food away if they don't use it. Weird."

Zac rummaged around in the cabinets. He found plates, selected two of the prettiest, largest ones, rinsed them in the sink and placed them on the table, then went looking for glasses.

Jess pointed, glancing between him and what she was doing. "Wine glasses are up there. You want wine? There's plenty."

Zac got down two, then remembered she had one, put the other back and set his on the table. He checked drawers for silverware, found what he needed, rinsed and put them by the plates.

"It smells amazing."

"I hope you like it."

She put down the stirring spoon, reached for the open bottle of wine, gathered up her own glass and turned to him with a gleam in her eye. With deliberate steps she moved from the counter, bottle and glass in hand, walking with a sort of swagger on the balls of her feet, over to the table to stand beside him. There she put down her glass, reached and picked up his and held it as she poured from the bottle—a deep, clear, red wine—rolling the tip expertly as she finished. She handed it to him, set down the bottle, got her own glass and held it up.

"To us," she said. They clinked a toast and took a drink. She smiled up at him over the rim and he could see she wanted a kiss. He bent to her, savoring the soft tenderness of her lips, the taste of wine on her breath.

"To us," he held close, words quiet, sincere, and she blushed. He kissed her again, lingered, then she kissed him once more and went back to the stove. As she did he stood straight and turned his gaze to the kitchen's large flowerbox window. Outside was the rolling green yard, shadows in the orange sunset. The beauty, the vast distances. Everything so wonderful, so refreshing. Jess working so hard to craft that special moment ...

All of it a mirage.

"It'll be ready soon," she informed him. He turned his attention to her. To her back, where she stood cooking. Beautiful hair, soft waves, tangled and falling to a point just below her shoulder blades. Posture perfect, hair hanging a little bit away from her back as she stood working at the stove. Without meaning to his eyes locked to the curve of her figure, tracing her perfect waist beneath the farmer's shirt, her hips, all the way to the backs of her bare legs where they appeared beneath the edge, along her calves and down as they curved just as perfectly to her ankles, her heels, one slightly off the floor as she bent that leg forward, putting her weight on the other. All of it tantalizing shades of brown in the fading sunlight. Hair, shirt, skin. Much to his consternation he found himself fighting the urge to take her, right there, right then, knowing she would welcome it. Knowing he had to be strong for them both. He wanted to enjoy this little fantasy too, this little slice of heaven, yet was unsure how to do it while the idea of even standing there in the kitchen—contemplating any of it—flew so hard in the face of reason.

"Good," he found his voice. "I can't wait to eat."

"You can never wait to eat." She looked over her shoulder and smiled. Then she turned off the stove and began putting the meal together.

Of course he could handle anything that came up. Maybe he'd killed most of the Bok. Could that have been all of them? And maybe, now that Lorenzo got away and he and Jess had no more clues, maybe it was best to just sit there and wait till the Bok came back anyway. Nab them and see what they could find from there. But he didn't really think so. And in fact Jess hadn't suggested that. She hadn't suggested *anything*. So far she was simply refusing to face the reality of their situation. Or seemed to be. Almost like she was trying to enforce her own reality. Her own little world. And that was what gave him pause.

He wanted to support her. But soon the real world would come crashing in. He was surprised it hadn't already.

"Let's light candles," she decided as she made preparations, positioning food items on trays, getting out various utensils with which to serve, moving back and forth across the kitchen in a deliberation of activity. She dug through a drawer, producing what had to be a lighter of some sort. She held it like a gun, clicked the trigger and a small flame burst from the tip. She let the trigger go and the flame went away. Handed it to him.

"I think I saw some over there," she showed him a section

of cabinets and went back to plating food. Zac went to them. The old kitchen was large, lots of cabinet space, both high and low; stained wood, sturdy and well-made.

"This isn't my best work," she said as he found the candles. "I don't have everything I need. If we were back at my place I could make you an *amazing* meal."

"If it tastes anything like it smells it will be amazing, trust me." He placed silver holders around the center of the table and stuck the tall, red, stick candles in them.

Jess began bringing over serving trays of steaming food, arranging them on the table. "I know you'll like it," she said. "It's just, this is the first time I've cooked for you and I want it to be special."

She went back to get the rest as he used the lighter to light the candles, each tiny flame bringing new life to the gloom of the gathering night. Soon he was holding her chair as she sat with her glass of wine, then he walked around and sat at the corner directly across from her.

She raised her glass. "To a new beginning," she said. "To the start of a better life."

He clinked with her and took a drink. She took a longer pull, closed her eyes to savor it, then set down the glass and began serving. He watched as she put noodles and bread and vegetables and a meat of some kind on his plate, piling it high. There was a sauce to cover things, butter and garlic to spread, spices to shake and plenty to eat. He found himself licking his lips, waiting as she finished and served herself, then she was saying "Bon appetite" and it was time to dig in.

The flavors were, indeed, every bit as good as they smelled.

Better.

"Wow," he paused long enough to compliment her, to make a face as he savored the first bites of each item. She ate her own eagerly—she had to be starving—apparently satisfied with the way things turned out. He chewed and shoveled, watching as she in turn watched him with what could only be admiration—and an unconcealed happiness with his quite obvious enjoyment of what she'd prepared.

She was so beautiful, even more so in the light of the flickering candles. He didn't think she could be more perfect.

"Try some of this," she handed him another dish. "It's called caprese. Tomatoes and cheese. Normally you'd eat it first as a kind of appetizer, or even a meal, but I figured we're too hungry for courses."

He took the plate and tried it. Red vegetables covered with thick white cheese and a dark sauce, a leaf on top of each. He ate half of one, leaf and all. It was delicious.

"Mmm. So good."

"Balsamic vinegar. It's the best." She went back to her own plate and continued eating. Of them both she was the one who needed the food. For him it was simply a pleasure.

So good.

For a while they fell into a sort of earnest quiet, no sounds but the gentle clink of silverware and hungry mouths chewing. For Zac it was a little slice of heaven. He tried not to think of anything else.

After a long stretch of that wonderful silence Jess broke the spell.

"Does fire burn?"

Zac looked up as she finished what she had in her mouth and took another drink of wine. Her glass was nearly empty.

He chewed and swallowed. "What do you mean?"

"When you touch fire. Does it burn?"

"You mean does it hurt?"

"Yeah." She took another drink. "I saw you reach across one of the candles when you were lighting them. I don't think you noticed, but the flame touched your arm. A normal person would've jerked away. I mean, I *know* you can take it. I've seen you get shot by a plasma cannon that can vaporize a car, for crying out loud. So I know fire, especially a candle, doesn't do you any harm. I'm just wondering if it burns. Do you feel it?"

He shrugged a little. "Pain isn't the same as it used to be." It was a good question, and one for which he didn't have a great answer. More of the Kazerai magic. "Fire doesn't hurt, but I can tell it's hot. It's hard to explain. It takes a lot to feel pain like I remember it. Kang hurt me. That was painful." He lapsed into the recollection of that.

She nodded. No further questions. Took a long drink, put the glass down but didn't resume eating. He could see her drifting. Fading in and out as she struggled to keep up the façade. Conversation, dinner, being together, pretending not to have a care in the world. This was all fantasy. One he could see she was, perhaps finally, having a hard time keeping up.

Then her gaze drifted back to the present and she smiled and said: "Your beard is growing." Small talk. Then, curious: "How do Kazerai shave?"

"Shave?"

"Yeah. What do you use to cut your beard? I'm assuming a razor wouldn't do it."

He wasn't sure. Again, a good question.

She persisted. "Fancy laser? Do they have a special Kazerai shaver?" Gentle laughter, then, as she held up a gun finger and made little *pew!pew!* sounds, pretending to wield some tiny device that shot off beard hair. Zac laughed with her, polite, but also a little sad.

"Fact is," he shook his head, "after the conversion our hair doesn't grow. The process in the Crucible kind of freezes us. Everything just sticks the way it is. Most Kazerai are retired before anything has a chance to change. Guess I've been going on long enough for things to evolve. Now my hair is growing."

She zeroed in on one word: "Retired?"

"Kazerai aren't kept around long." And all at once he realized he was talking as if this were an ongoing process. Which it wasn't. He was the last Kazerai. There would be no more after him. "New ones were made," he said, switching tense—feeling a twinge of loss as he did, though he wasn't sure why he cared. "Old ones were retired, never more than a few at a time. All part of Dominion lore. They alone possessed the method to kill us, so when it was time to be "retired" that's what they did."

"And you guys let them?"

"They made us believe we would ascend to Heaven as part of the process. Most went willingly."

She drank more; took a few bites.

Then spoke quietly: "I'm glad that's all part of the past."

Her role in the demise of that system could hardly be understated. Before her arrival the Dominion was on its way to domination of the entire world. By the time she left their entire mythology had been undone. Dramatically, with authority, burned away in nuclear fire.

But her observation about his beard was not lost on him. The subtle changes to his own physiology were beginning to trouble him. Beard. Hair. Other things. There was no doubt he was outside the known parameters of Kazerai existence. In addition there was the fight with Kang, the multiple transfers with the Icons, the coma, the exposure to the cold vacuum of space, direct stellar radiation—all things a Kazerai had never had to endure. In short he was far down the road of his existence, farther than he was probably ever intended to go, at a place that had never been mapped. Never experienced. And so he had his own questions. About beards and hair and other things.

Could he be near the end? The hypothetical but never-before-realized burning out of the Kazerai flame?

He looked into the flickering candles, watching the little fingers of fire shrink and expand in the gentle movements of air.

All things were temporal.

But he was here, now, with the girl he loved, the girl he would cross time for—and in some ways had—and he would not give these things thought. Death waited everyone. Neither of them were immune. And though there were many things they should be doing right then, many wiser things, if he made himself relax he could, indeed, enjoy a meal and her company. He could enjoy this moment. Just as she wanted. And so he resolved to do so. To relax, to immerse himself in her creation, to be there for her, enjoy it with her. Confident she would find her way back to reason soon enough and they would be on their way.

Even as he decided this, however, she announced

suddenly:

"Let's just stay."

He blinked. Realized that, while he'd been lost in his own thoughts she had as well. Sitting there pondering.

Coming to an impossible conclusion.

Her words reverberated in his head.

"We're just two people," she tried to explain. "What do we matter? They don't need us. We tell Satori to take the ship back. They can take Bianca home. It's what they all want anyway. Let Anitra have their starship back. Kang is gone. We don't have to worry about that anymore." She looked at him, eyes suddenly glistening in the glow of the tiny flames.

Desperate.

"The Bok won't get past the Project," she said. "There's nothing more we can do to stop that war. When I don't return they'll forget about me."

Zac didn't know where to begin. "Jess, they saw you in the club. The Project and the Bok. Lorenzo knows you're here. Drake knows you're back."

She shook her head. "Let's stop all this running."

"Jessica ..."

"We were meant to be together!" All at once she was angry. Sad. "Somehow, some incredible way, we've found each other. You know it. I know it. Why keep running? Why ruin it? Why keep after this? Why? Let's find our peace and live together. Zac! Let's do it. No more risking our lives. We've done enough. Now is our time.

"Let's find our Happily Ever After."

She looked at him pleadingly. He felt his head shaking back and forth, just a little, and made himself stop. He needed to tread lightly. She took a long drink and finished the glass of wine, shaking, on the verge of tears, looking to him with those big, beautiful, gold-flecked eyes, needing him more than she ever had, more than she'd probably ever needed anyone, and he had no idea what to do.

She reached for the bottle. On top of everything else the wine was no doubt adding its own impairment, skewing her already exhausted, clouded, emotional judgment.

She poured a fresh glass, hands continuing to shake, then put down the bottle. She held up the glass but didn't drink.

"It's okay," she told him.

"Jess, I—"

"It's fine. I know I'm talking a little crazy right now." But even as she said this she had to look away. So badly did she want it to be untrue.

She composed herself. Sat straighter and put her glass on the table. "If we *do* stay ... I'll do the dishes." She tried to chuckle but it just ended up making her voice hitch. He remembered their earlier conversation, aboard the ship, laughing at who would do the dishes if they settled down and made a life. A little home somewhere, Jessica and Zac, she in the kitchen doing the dishes, he out mowing the yard. He almost quipped, I'll mow the yard, but couldn't. Not in that moment.

The sadness in her expression was too thick.

"We can't stay here," he said, as gently as he could. "This house belongs to people who want us dead."

"Not here," she waved a hand, dismissing the idea with red-rimmed eyes as if it were clearly a silly one. "Obviously not here. We'll find somewhere. Somewhere else. Make a life. We'll be like Bonnie and Clyde." She lifted her glass, tears welling as she laughed into it and took another drink. A pained laugh. He could see she was starting to lose it. Not that she particularly had things together up to that point, but right then she was headed for a breakdown.

"Look," he leaned closer. "I'm sure Bonnie and Clyde were a great couple." The anguished look on her face made him think maybe they weren't. He went on: "But we can't stay. A lot is depending on us."

But even as those words left his mouth a certain bitterness took hold of her expression, killing the impending tears.

Maybe that hadn't been the right thing to say.

"I'm tired of being depended on," she said brusquely. The transformation was instantaneous. "I want my life back." Of a sudden she had that hard look in her eyes. The gold flecks flickered, more brilliant than ever, and Zac felt himself pull back. He knew how strong she could be; knew how strong she *was*. He wasn't fooled by the image before him, that of a seemingly fragile girl, holding a glass of wine with trembling hands. If he made a mis-step he might lose her. And if he did ...

Consciously he regrouped. Told himself they'd come too far, done too much already for her to quit now. This was temporary. He had to believe that.

She took another drink. "I'm tired of living my life dictated by the emergency of the moment. One thing after the next after the next. Don't you see?"

Then she softened her position. Temporary anger replaced by an earnest desire.

"You know me," she said. "Just like you I've dreamed of stars and planets, other worlds and, honestly, what does it matter? Compared to all that, we're nothing. Even on this one world we're nothing. A comfortable home, a good meal, being surrounded by the people you love—*those* are the important things. I gave all that up, yes, but I can have it again. We can have it right here. On Earth. Right now. You're the one I love, Zac. As long as we have each other that's all we need. Don't you see?" She swallowed. Spoke more gently: "I want to know you. *You*, Zac. I want to know all about you. I have so many questions! After all this, after everything we've been through, we know so little about each other. We've been through so much more than anyone. Even people who are together their whole lives never go through as much as we have. But as deep, as well as I know you I still don't *know* you. I know so little about who you are. What you were like when you were younger, your favorite things. I want to know all that. I want to know everything, Zac.

"I want to know *you*."

"I want to know you too," he leaned toward her again and took her hand. "So much. Everything, all things."

"Then let's stay," her voice fell to a choked whisper.

He wasn't sure whether to keep talking or just be quiet. Not take this up right now; not in her current state. But he found himself trying to reason. "Everything has to be

DAVID G MCDANIEL

defended," he said. "That's why we're doing what we're doing. If we stop, now, none of this will last. Too much is in motion. If we do what you're saying, if we drop out of the equation ... Things will not remain the same. Any peace we have won't last. We'll just get drawn back in. We can't simply run away."

Rather than rail against him, however, she was silent.

He forged on. "The decision was yours," he said. "Every step of the way. We're here, now, in the middle of this because of decisions *you* made. I, for one, think you've made the *right* decisions.

"We've come too far not to continue. Whether we like it or not we hold far too much responsibility. Just like you said on the ship. We're responsible now. We can't hide."

"It's not hiding," she insisted. It was almost a pout.

He searched her face, wondering if she was shutting him out. "We're far more important than either of us dreamed we would be," he went on. "Too much is in play. If we don't finish what we've started ..." He could only shake his head, uncertain of everything. And as he felt himself pushing for a continuance of their surge into danger, trying to make her see that they must, like it or not, go forward, fear swept unexpectedly over him.

What if she was right?

What if she was right, just as she'd been right at every other turn? Was it really running away? Or was she onto something?

So far he'd been supremely confident in his ability to protect her. But on this little adventure there'd been too many close calls. Like the Superman and Lois Lane story she told him once before, he feared the ease with which she could be lost. Strong as she was, as indomitable as was her will, she *was* fragile. At least in form, and she could die so easily if he failed to protect her. By urging they go forward, by insisting they forge further into what would no doubt be ever more deadly situations, he was, by his own hand, putting her at risk.

Should he just go on without her?

"Anitra can take care of its own problems," she continued

to rationalize away their involvement. "My world is a mess. There's nothing more we can do." She looked deep into his eyes. "You're safe." And again it struck him, as if he'd somehow forgotten; though he'd done his part for her, for others, *she* had also saved *him*. "That's all I ever wanted," she implored. "To save you, after you saved us. I mean, what are we even trying to solve? Why keep doing this?"

Her gaze fell. Weary, exhausted. She was so tired. And not just physically.

"I mean," she sighed, "it's just too much. Any silly ideas I had about changing the world ... too much."

Should he just drop it? Was he pushing for something in which he didn't really believe? Was he just being automatic, encouraging conflict when maybe, truly, things at that point were best left alone? Multiple worlds, huge, complicated systems, governments, millions, billions of people, secret societies holding God knew what enigmas, a race of ancient aliens that could be a future threat ...

What could they possibly hope to do against all that?

Were they right to keep after it?

Should they just run away? Hide for the rest of their lives?

But there was more at work here. More to Jessica, more to him.

More to *them*, though he could hardly fathom the depth of his convictions when it came to that.

He knew only that there was.

He relaxed his posture. "From the time I first saw you, I knew you had a destiny. Don't ask me how. I know this isn't the end. This is not all you have left to do." He squeezed her hand. "Sometimes," he said, "the next step is hard. Sometimes it seems impossible. So many people give up when faced with great challenge. They know what they have to do but they stop. They don't take the step. Sometimes doing the right thing isn't easy. Things get uncomfortable, things get hard, people decide to quit and then they're done. Their journey ends. They live the rest of their lives wondering what might've happened.

"No one truly fails, Jessica. They just quit. You know

that's true. Here, now, the decision is yours. I want you
to know I'll do whatever you say. I love you. I'm here for
you." He put his other hand on hers and held it with both.
"If you want to go somewhere and do dishes and have me
mow the yard, I'll do it." That got the smile he was after; a
fleeting turn at the corners of her mouth. It gave him hope.

"I just don't think you should quit."

She looked down, no longer able to hold his gaze.

At length she said: "I don't know what I think anymore."
The room flickered in deeper shadows. Outside night had
fallen. The shifting light of the candles only seemed to
enhance the confusion on her face.

She pushed back her chair.

"I'm tired," she announced. "I'm going to get some sleep.
I can't think about this right now."

At that she stood, a little of the old Jess in her expression,
an endearing gaze, resolute; the strong poise he knew and
loved, and it renewed his faith.

She came around and stood beside him. Ran a hand
through his hair. He turned in his chair to look up at her
and she kissed him. For a moment she lingered, fingers
twirling against his scalp, thoughts far away. He sighed to
himself. She was all that truly mattered. And she was right.
With her he could do anything, live any life, be anywhere.
As long as they were together. Standing there beside him
in the candlelight she *was* an angel, and he never wanted
to leave her. Never.

She kissed him again and went upstairs.

After she was gone he listened as the floors creaked
overhead and she got into bed.

Then, when he could hear she was settled and breathing
gently, fast asleep, he let himself relax. Enjoying the
peaceful quiet of the house.

He finished the wonderful, delicious meal.

It was the best he'd ever had.

CHAPTER 39:

THE BOK

HANSEL WAS NOT HAPPY. As the major domo for the Bok castle/ HQ there in Spain his regular duties were rather light, and he'd grown used to fat compensation checks from his mysterious employers, the Esehta Bok, in conjunction with a mostly ceremonial militia presence. He headed their local commandoes, maintaining and training that force, ensuring it was well-equipped and ready for use, but rarely was he called upon in that area of the world. The Bok employed many for such purpose, some on retainer, some outright mercenaries hired as needed, but at the various Bok strongholds there was always a force. It was a conceit of theirs, Hansel believed, to be ready at all times for small wars or minor conflicts. He knew little of the Bok's real purpose, but what he did know was that they really only used their small armies to conduct raids now and again, globally, on the quest for yet more arcane knowledge or artifacts to add to their treasures. Rarely did they fight in defense of their own holdings. Not surprising, really, as no one knew where they were. The Americans knew of their existence, or so he'd heard, but had no knowledge of their whereabouts. Perhaps a few others knew of them. Mostly, as far as Hansel knew, the Bok were the greatest secret society of all time. No one had any idea where to find them.

That had apparently changed.

Lorenzo was still storming about the castle, had been since his return, scorching up through the castle courtyard in his fairly dinged and dirty Lambo, flustered and yelling as soon as he leapt out. Hansel had so far not been consulted, but he could see that moment was upon him and was not looking forward to it after everything he'd overheard. From the sound of it Lorenzo and several of his young cronies, many of whom Hansel knew, had confronted some kind of powerhouse of an individual at the farmhouse, one of the Bok safehouses not far from the castle. Prior to that they'd scattered from a nightclub near Madrid and, damningly, one of them had been captured. By the Americans, it was believed. The rest got away, but when they converged on the farmhouse they were attacked and, presumably, killed by what they were now calling the super warrior. None save Lorenzo had returned or been heard of since. As if proof of their demise all their phones were still pinging at that location. Unmoving. Just a great big pile of them, all in one spot.

Dead or captured, thought Hansel.

And so Lorenzo was furious. And a little scared, Hansel could see, which gave him a small measure of grim satisfaction. He never liked Lorenzo, not from the beginning, when the young Bok took charge; a self-important asshole who brought more of the young Bok upstarts under his wing, instilling in them the same arrogance. Lorenzo rapidly became an anomaly, less like the rest, more like a new breed, uncovering hidden secrets the previous Bok had no knowledge of or had simply decided to leave buried. Hansel knew not where Lorenzo found what he did, but the new Bok leader shared only with his younger cronies, raising them up, teaching them things Hansel had never seen nor would even have thought possible. Moving things with their minds, battling with projected force and other parlor tricks that were not really tricks at all. Hansel watched them, out on the grounds, in the training rooms of the castle, practicing with these new abilities, walking around pompous and full of themselves. He'd come to fear them, in fact, after what he'd seen, and that fear eventually turned to resentment and finally hate. He'd never been particular fond of the older generation either, the ones who originally hired him, but these new elite were insufferable.

Of course he had no real options. This was the sort of "job" you didn't just leave. Not with his position. He would be rich for life, wealthy enough for any man's desires, but true freedom would never be his.

"Hansel!" Lorenzo's voice called from the other room,

echoing from the rough stone walls of the castle. It was the summons he'd been expecting. With a shiver of dread he went.

"I'm here," he said, rounding the corner and entering one of the larger rooms, where Lorenzo stood with Franco, a member of the Old Guard. Franco was an athletic sixty-something with a thick mane of gray hair, and would probably have been the next leader of the Bok if it hadn't been for Lorenzo's bloodless coup. The two men were alone. Fire raged in a giant pit at one side of the archaic room, casting hard orange light over everything, giving a subtle shimmer to it all. Shadows danced on every surface.

Hansel took a deep breath. He liked the castle. The Bok built this one long ago, as they had built others, maintaining it in their possession through the ages, across changing governments and legal institutions, kept, on the interior at least, in fantastic shape. Tapestries draped the walls, ancient wooden furniture here and there. This particular room had a vast, Moorish rug covering the center. Hansel continued over and stood on it, near Lorenzo.

"You've heard everything, I'm sure," Lorenzo held a glass with a red liquid in it. It wasn't wine. In addition to whatever bizarre, psychic manifestations he and his so-called New Bok (or as Hansel liked to call them, "Rude Bok") cultivated, they also took enhancement drugs and drank and consumed rare foods and plants, all in the name of ultimately honed physical perfection. Despite how much he despised them, Hansel had to admit they were all in great shape. And their powers ... those were quite real.

He nodded. "There've been a lot of raised voices."

"I didn't get to see much of this super warrior," said Lorenzo, "but he went down easily enough in the club. He and that girl chased me all the way to the farmhouse. I have no idea how they followed me. Their bike went off the road. I *saw* them crash." Even after all the intervening hours Hansel could see Lorenzo was shaken. "Whoever that guy is he came to the farm and ... I can't speak for the girl, but when I left he was shredding us like some kind of super freak." Suddenly he snapped. "Dammit!" he threw his glass across the room into the fire, where it popped with a muffled crash.

Franco spoke: "You can't ignore this," he said, earnest. He and Lorenzo had been arguing. "She *is* the One. Our priestess said one would come. You cannot deny this is her."

"I can and I will!" Lorenzo shouted at him. "False hope! Our priestess could *not* see the future! That witch *caused* our troubles! Why would I pay attention to anything she said now? There is no 'One', and this girl certainly is not it!"

"Then why do you seek her?!" Franco had fire of his own.

"Because she knows something! She had that damn suit of armor! She took both devices back in the States and popped out of existence! She crashed our raid on the Americans with something we've never seen, took *our* property—that technology is ours!—and—poof. Gone. So where are they? I want to know what she knows!

"Now she shows up here—of all places!—chases me with that freak of a bodyguard, raids our land and, as far as we know, kills everyone. I want answers!" He turned to Hansel and Hansel suppressed an involuntary swallow. "And you're going to get them. Go to the farm, kill that freak and bring me the girl. Don't let her get away. Kill her if you have to but don't let her get away."

Franco looked alarmed. "You can't kill her!"

Lorenzo ignored him. "If they're not there find them. If they're gone track them down. I don't care how."

Franco had other fears. "If they've found the vault—"

"No one's found the vault!" Lorenzo was clearly fed up with the elder Bok and his resistance. "Even if they *do* find the vault there's no way for them to get in. And even if they did get in," he seemed to consider the possibility, a slight worry passing across his expression, and as it did Hansel began to wonder just how strong this super warrior could possibly be, if Lorenzo thought there was a chance, however slight, he could break into a vault with a multi-ton door and three-inch-thick bars, but Lorenzo was finishing his thought: "it doesn't matter. The real prize is not there. They're looking for ancient Kel technology. Looking for us. They have no idea the treasures we hold, and they're not even close." His demeanor morphed in the firelight, closer to his usual, haughty self. If Hansel didn't know how real, how fantastic the Bok truly were, it would be easy to dismiss Lorenzo's cryptic statement as delusional hubris.

But the Bok were for real.

Hansel, however, was more interested in the immediate. "I have only two choppers on site and about a dozen commandoes. Are you saying you want a raid on the farm? Tonight?"

"I'm saying I want him dead!" Lorenzo directed his impatience at Hansel. Hansel bristled. "Go there! Find him! Kill him! Now! It couldn't be more simple!"

"If this freak killed the others," Hansel refused to be cowed, "then how strong is he? Can he be killed?" Much as he hated them, the young Bok that had been killed on the farm—if they'd been killed—were no minor threat. If one man killed them all …

"Everyone can be killed!" Lorenzo was beside himself. "I have no idea how strong he is, but when you find him you shred him with everything you've got. Understood?"

Hansel glared at him. He would do it, of course. It was his job. But he did not have to respect the man giving the command.

"Save the girl," Franco added his own order to the mix and Lorenzo whirled on him. Now it was Franco's turn to wither before the young Bok's murderous stare, Lorenzo glowering, contemplating something terrible. He turned back to Hansel.

"Kill the freak. Bring me the girl. Kill her if you can't." He looked back and forth between Franco and Hansel. The blazing fire crackled and popped. "I'm going to Cairo," he announced, and started across the room.

Franco watched him go, boring holes into his back. "Cairo!" Hansel wondered if the elder Bok would give chase. His fury was peaking. "Cairo! You've issues to deal with here!" Lorenzo kept walking, not looking back. Franco accused: "You've done this! Your greed has exposed us!" Lorenzo didn't turn. He was almost gone. "Now the Prophet is here!" Franco shouted. "She walks among us, yet you intend to kill her! You encourage it! We are a thousand years old! Forty generations of Esehta Bok!" Lorenzo reached the corner, not slowing. Not caring. "This is the sign! You will single-handedly bring about our ruin!"

The impetuous young Bok rounded the corner, still not looking back, and as he passed from sight into the dark hallway beyond said simply, voice coming to them as an echo:

"Shut up, old man."

* * *

It was the dream again. Jess stepped across the room, explosions rocking the floor; went to the archaic wooden door set against the riveted green-iron walls. Beside it was the sleek, high-tech access panel.

As before she played things through, working in some subtle way to take control. The door was covered in complicated runes that, she was now convinced, were written in the same language as those from the *Reaver*. It was the language of the Kel.

The battle outside rocked the walls. Gunfire, lots of it. More than before. Another big blast and she steadied herself. She was dressed in the same armor, in one hand the long, curved sword of blued steel. It was she that held the sword. She that wore the armor. But *she* was not Jessica. Not a girl from Boise.

Someone else.

But who?

Mind racing, she studied the shiny access panel and had the idea to look. Slowly she bent to the panel until she could see ...

Her reflection.

At the sight of it she gasped and pulled back.

Not me at all.

Only ...

It is *me.*

Carefully she leaned in for a closer look. *So vivid!* The image before her was shocking but she held steady and looked herself over. Face strikingly beautiful, barely human ...

Kel.

She was Kel. It was her own eyes she peered into. Brilliant yellow, almond-shaped eyes, wide in shock at her own apparition. Staring back in disbelief. Jaw and cheeks a collection of angular perfection, slightly pointed ears peeking from a wild tangle of shock-white hair.

It was like wearing a mask. Like looking at herself in a mirror while she wore a perfect, face-hugging mask.

But this was no mask.

Who am I? Her image was youthful, though as she stared into the reflection of her eyes she felt far older than her current sixteen years. In fact, looking into the depths of those golden orbs she could've been a thousand.

Like a mage.

A few thin, dark symbols, traced precise lines around her left eye, a few more along her right cheek. Inhumanly gorgeous. A pure, flawless being, beyond any human standard.

Like an angel.

All this she saw in an instant, heart racing as an explosion spiked the air and hammered her ...

Awake.

She sat bolt upright. Struggling for breath.

She was in bed.

BOOM! another explosion. *That* one was real. Orange light flared in the room, a fireball outside the window that sent her diving off the far side. She hit the floor and rolled, fighting all at once to get her bearings.

What's going on?!

A cool breeze blew through the open window, an acrid tang drifting in with it. There was a haze in the air. After the flash of the fireball the room was dark again, it was still night, though as her eyes adjusted she could see the sharp, flickering light of flames raging outside, casting harsh shadows across the walls. Sound now, a forest fire of some sort, cracking and popping loudly outside in the yard.

She rose and ran. Staying low, out of the room, feet thumping the carpeted wood floor as she sprinted for the stairs at the far end of the hall, hoping there was some natural explanation for this but not believing there could be. She almost screamed for Zac but wasn't sure that was a good idea yet. She made the stairs and flew to the bottom, tagging only three before she hit the floor in the foyer and took cover, eyes darting in every direction.

The light of the huge fire outside dominated through the front windows and the milky panes of the front door. The size of it definitely matched the volume.

She was panting. *Where's Zac?!* With a second's more hesitation she hurried to the front door, skidded up against it, stood to the side behind the frame and ... opened it. Slowly. Sounds flooded through the crack. Cautiously she leaned her head around, opened the door wider and stuck it all the way out, peering into the chaos outside in the yard ...

She felt her mouth go slack.

Across the way, on the hill, sat two military helicopters, burning. One on its side, nearly upside down, blades snapped. The other burning more furiously but upright, four-bladed rotors drooping, flames consuming everything. Both were mere shells of what they must've been. Gutted. She didn't recognize the model but could tell they were medium-sized troop transports, configured for military use. Her mind tried to place them and she marveled at the fact she was even doing so. Smoke blanketed everything, shifting, capturing the orange lick of the flames, enhancing it, transforming the dark field into a localized version of Hell. She saw bodies now. Sprawled in unnatural poses, visible in the fire, silhouetted in the shells of the choppers; other lumps in the shadows or off in the darkness, littering the field.

Suddenly she noticed two on the ground not far from where she stood. Uncomfortably close.

"Jessica."

She screamed.

"It's me," Zac walked out of the smoky shadows.

She looked at him in shock, in horror. He walked up and just stood there, wearing nothing but the torn suit pants, looking no different than when she last saw him at dinner.

She struggled to speak.

"We were attacked," he said.

"... Who?" It was a stupid question.

"I'm pretty sure they were sent by the Bok." He looked over the field of destruction. Stated the obvious: "It got messy."

Jessica's head was on a swivel, looking; spotting more dead people. She saw them now more clearly. Commandos in Kevlar armor, assault rifles, helmets—the works. These guys would've done a SEAL team proud.

Suddenly she wondered if they were. "You're sure they were bad guys?" What if Zac had just killed a bunch of Spanish or American special forces?

But Zac had no doubts. "When they landed I walked up with my hands over my head and they started shooting. Jumped out as fast as they could and lit me up. Opened fire and kept coming. I made no sudden moves, did nothing to provoke them. Even gave them a second to reconsider.

"Their intent was clearly to kill me."

She could see the hard set to his jaw. If Lorenzo sent them ... surely they must've had some idea what they were in for. But they wouldn't have known the extent of Zac's strength. Could not have. Even after that day, after Zac killed them en masse, how could they know? She looked over the field of dead. More Bok mercenaries, just like back in Boise.

Zac was unscathed. Still she scanned him, finding no marks. She'd seen him shot before and knew there would be none. It was obviously a quick battle. She looked over the remains. He'd made short work of this little assault force. Fires still burned mightily in the choppers and she wondered if anything had yet to explode, adding to the inferno.

As if in response to her thoughts ...

BOOOM! a small fireball erupted within one. She cringed and ducked but this time didn't scream. Smaller bursts followed, going off in a *rat-tat-tat* staccato as a box of bullets caught fire. She felt a hand on her shoulder and Zac was guiding her inside. Next thing she knew they were standing within the relative quiet of the dark foyer, door closed, Zac before her.

"Are you okay?" he asked. First things first.

She nodded. She wasn't, really, but she nodded anyway.

He was willing to take that and move on. Clearly their hand had been forced.

He looked into her eyes. "You need to see something."

CHAPTER 40:

THE VAULT

"So we think it's actual psionics?" It was exactly as they feared.

"If our captive can be believed." The agent in charge of the interrogation briefed Drake in the front room, sharing what they'd found so far with everyone present. "And I think he can. He's become very candid in the last half-hour. He's verified other points we can confirm independently."

Drake nodded. This was the first time they had an actual Bok in custody, not simply one of the Bok hires or mercenaries. Which meant it was the first time they had one to question. One of the elite, if Lorenzo's own propaganda meant anything, and so far this "elite" captive seemed to be buckling under the Project's interrogation techniques, no different than any other mere human.

"And he doesn't exhibit the same abilities? Why isn't he using them? Why not knock you down and break free?"

The agent shrugged. "A few times it looked like he was concentrating, trying something, but he's so constrained, so jacked up on the drug cocktail we've given him—if he *does* possess any psychic power he hasn't been able to use it. Maybe they have to move their arms." The agent shrugged again. "At any rate, he's too far gone now to try."

Drake sighed. "So we don't know how Lorenzo did it, only that he can. At least from what we saw. And that this guy back there," he nodded toward the rear of the house, "claims he can too."

The agent nodded.

Drake turned to Bobby. "Get me everything we know on psionic experiments. Anything we've proven. Psychic manifestations, whatever."

Bobby turned to go. Just then another agent came forward from the back room, the chief interrogator's assistant, sleeves rolled up, signs of having been at his unpleasant task.

"We just got something else," he reported as he entered. All eyes went to him and he announced: "One of the Bok hideouts. Up in the hills, not far from here.

"It's a castle."

* * *

A CHILL WAS IN the early morning air. Jess had pulled on a pair of overalls from the closet, over the farmer's shirt, cinched them at the waist with a fat leather belt, rolled the legs up to mid-calf and now walked across the yard following Zac. The rising sun lit the sky from below. She followed in silence.

Echoes of the dream flickered hauntingly across her mind's eye. Would not be still. So vivid, now more than ever, the vision of herself in the reflective panel, looking for all the world ... no, not just looking, *being* ...

Kel.

Who am I?!

The dream made no sense; was pure fantasy, yet ...

Zac led her toward the large, barn-like outbuilding, and though she tried to dismiss the dreamscape imagery she could not stop the flashbacks. As before it felt too real. Too unlike a dream. Too tied up in the events of the world all around her, a memory that had no clear connection but that was, nevertheless, authentic.

She trudged along. Working on forgetting.

A cool mist hugged the ground, grass damp with dew, smoke drifting across the field from the fires of earlier. Little flames still flickered in the blackened hulks of the helicopters, their giant, ugly forms blighting the lush green yard, but otherwise the rage of the inferno was gone.

She and Zac walked on in silence, grass scrunching beneath their feet, dew so heavy it soaked her skin all the way to her ankles. It was a beautiful, tranquil morning, marred only by the carnage of the earlier events; dead bodies lying in sight, men in helmets and soft armor twisted at unnatural angles. As Zac neared the barn most of that passed from her peripheral view and all she could see were the old vineyards far ahead, overgrown and untended, sloping away to a deep, miles-wide valley, bordered on all sides by majestic, soaring peaks. Thick morning mist laying like a low cloud over it all. If she tried, from that vantage she could almost imagine a morning on the farm, in its heyday, people awake and going about the business of the day. She was certainly dressed the part, a barefoot farm girl in overalls, out to milk the cows or otherwise start the morning with chores. An old tractor sat rusting to one side as they rounded the corner and Zac led her to the barn's large entry doors. At that point a few of the Bok sports cars came into view. Various colors of high-end machines, standing out like sore thumbs against the rustic backdrop. Zac pushed aside one of the barn's tall, sliding doors and entered.

Inside was more of a cask cellar, really, above ground, at least the parts that could be seen in the gloom. Some of the developing sunlight had started to find its way through cracks. The whole space had a strong, musty smell, dirt floor strewn with a thin covering of old straw. Aged equipment hung here and there, other pieces sitting unused among a bunch of large, wooden barrels.

"I was looking around," Zac said as he led her into the dark. "Right before I heard the helicopters fly in I found something. Back here."

His voice was amplified in the large, cluttered confines, no other sounds to compete with; no birds, no animals, no breeze, their feet nearly silent on the hard dirt floor.

He led her through a door toward the rear, into a ramshackle wooden corridor. "This was more than just a safehouse," he said.

They reached the end of the hall and a wall. A little light came through a few broken planks along the sides. To Jess it looked like a dead end. Zac did something with a concealed knob and the wall swung back to reveal a set of stairs. Inside the small landing he reached and pulled a chain and a dim, bare bulb came on overhead, swinging from its cord. It cast feeble illumination down a long flight of stairs that led into the ground. Shadows slid back and forth with each swing as they descended, ominous, the incandescent bulb lighting the way harshly from above.

At the bottom was a massive bank-vault door.

Like the entrance to a steel bunker or something—a high-tech, fortified contrast to the old-wood, aged architecture of everything leading to that point—it was pulled from its hinges. Hanging away, leaning to the side at an odd angle and falling into its recess. Shiny steel casings gleamed where they'd been sheared like sheet metal and peeled away, along with other signs of trauma; solid steel pins the size of pipes forced back, bent, sheared or popped through their retaining notches. The door was feet thick, most likely weighed many tons yet there it sat, broken open like she might've forced her way into a locked Scooby Doo lunch box or something. She stared wide-eyed at Zac. She knew what he was capable of. Had seen it. But this, somehow, took the cake. This ...

This was beyond anything so far.

Just what were his limits?

"I seem to be getting stronger," he said by way of explanation. He felt it too. And he, like her, was at a loss.

Carefully he reached a hand for her. She took it and stepped with him over the threshold, following nervously as he found a switch and flipped it on. The interior of the chamber came alive in the white/green of industrial-grade fluorescent bulbs.

"I didn't have a chance to look at much before they came," he said.

Nervously Jess scanned the room, tensing, feeling as if an army of telekinetic madmen might descend on them at any moment. Inside was clearly some sort of operations center, maps on the wall, desks with files and all sorts of neatly organized, high-tech items. All of it shiny, hard and sterile.

Her eyes were drawn to one of the maps.

And as she recognized what it depicted, as she saw the info written neatly upon it, her blood ran cold.

CHAPTER 41:

MOMENT OF CRISIS

"THAT'S A MAP of your country, right?" Zac pointed. Jess couldn't believe what she was seeing.

It was indeed. And, right there with it ...

A street map of Boise.

Right there on the wall. In a high-tech underground bunker, in the mountains outside Madrid, in the lair of the enemy; right at its heart. A map of her home town. And there, inked with red circles, arrows and written notes, was her house.

My house.

She began shivering.

"It looked like what you told me about," said Zac. "What you showed me on the ship," he pointed to the area, referencing, of course, the maps of the U.S. she'd shown him aboard the *Reaver*. He had, indeed, identified it correctly, though he was having a hard time understanding why she was so shocked.

Then he seemed to get what she was looking at. "Wait." And he, too, realized what she already had.

"Is that your house?" He was incredulous. Then: "What are they doing with maps of your house?" He looked closer, reading the writing, the notes, the scribbles—everything.

Stiffening with a certain, dawning rage.

Jess scanned and scanned again.

Fear compounding.

It wasn't even a small map, a subset of some larger thing or an afterthought or something else—which would've been bad enough. It was a big, color map, dominant on the wall, with details, covering a major section. There were other maps as she turned to look around the room, clearly other points of interest to the Bok, but the map of her home appeared to be as major as any of the rest.

If not more so.

The empty feeling in the pit of her stomach grew. A great, yawning emptiness, that horrible feeling of being violated. How long had this been here? She turned her attention to the table beneath the map, then to the desk; stepped to it, opened and started rifling through drawers, faster, even as Zac's own anger built. He began looking with her.

"What the hell were they doing?"

As he spoke she found a folder. With plans. Printed plans, detailing an operation to take out the Americans—the Project—and raid the house belonging to the girl.

Me.

Inside the same folder were pictures. Snapshots of Mom. Dad. Amy. She had to struggle not to drop them.

"Is that your family?" Zac asked from over her shoulder. Slowly she handed him the pics, feeling sick. He took them, looking at the faces of the people that were most important in her life.

With a surge of will she pulled herself together. Turned back to the contents of the folder and devoured the pages, the schematics, pouring over everything in a rush, unable to read quickly enough. The Americans they spoke of were definitely the Project. The Project likely didn't know the Bok's plans, however the Project were smart enough to assume the Bok would try *something* and so, according to what was written here, had been keeping surveillance on Jessica's home in Boise. It was proof of exactly what Nani said; the Project suspected the Bok were watching for her.

She looked up. Digesting that bit of information.

The Project were trying to protect me. Or at least they were trying to make sure the Bok didn't get to her first.

She resumed her aggressive read. Flipping pages, flipping back. Zac straightened, clearly lost, deciding to wait for her to comment. The Bok wanted her. They believed she might be hiding something at her house, or might've left something, and they only became aware of her, apparently, around the same time as the Project. This whole set of information here was hasty, recent, put together following those events. Obviously, though, the Bok were doing a better job of spying on the Project than the Project was doing spying on them. Following events in Boise the Bok quickly made her a prime target.

She looked up at the map.

Important enough to plan an operation to watch for her return.

"Check this out," said Zac. She turned to him, the stack of shuffled papers gripped tightly in her hands.

"This is Spain, right?" He was standing at another map across the room, that one framed.

She went closer. Stood beside him. The map was, indeed, a map of the country they were in. The Iberian peninsula. A satellite photo. Shades of green and brown, lines for elevation, faint demarcations for borders but otherwise a true image.

"Look at these," he pointed. The map had red dots on it. Not many, each with small, typeset print beside it. He touched one in particular. "This is about where we're at, right?"

It was. A red dot, right there near where they should be, practically on top of Madrid at that scale. She peered closer. Read the name beside it: *Jeklakt*. For a flash it sounded Kel, and she dismissed the thought as soon as she had it, then ...

Would that be so strange?

The Bok *were* Kel. Or, more precisely, humans that had been part of a Kel rebellion in the distant past. Now here was a location with, she was suddenly convinced, a Kel name. That wasn't an Earth language, she was pretty sure. *Jeklakt*.

"Is it a base?" Zac touched the map. "You think that's a marker for this place we're in now?"

For some reason she didn't.

"This is just some kind of way station," she said, meaning the farm and the vault. She pointed to the dot. "That's bigger. Close to where we're at, but bigger."

Beneath the map was a small safe, bolted to the wall. A safe within a safe, if you counted the room they were in as a giant safe.

"Open that," she said. Zac did so without question. Didn't look at her. Didn't pause. No careful peeling of hinges, no subtlety. Simply *BANG!* his fist was through the metal door and yanking it away. It was so loud, it was dramatic, and she squinted from the force of the impact, turning away as he tossed aside the compromised door. Metal pieces hit the floor with an echoing clang.

She shook it off.

Inside were binders. She fairly snatched them out, setting aside the other papers in her hands as she tore into this new trove of information and, in no time, had found a reference to the map on the wall. Impatient to make a connection she rifled through the laminated sheets, glancing up at the map, down at the binders, piecing it together, wondering why the Bok would arrange it this way—with a safe inside to keep the details so obviously in sight yet ultra secure. It had a feel of arrogance to it, like a constant visual reminder of territory.

The whole place reeked of arrogance.

She found the location they were currently, the farm, then its relationship to the bigger, main base not far away. The red dot on the map. A castle, right there in Spain.

Jeklakt. It had a name.

A *Kel* name.

Where Lorenzo fled.

It must be.

"Look," she showed Zac. "Here it is." As she suspected, not far. "Right up the road. It's a frickin castle. One of their bases." She touched it. "That has to be where Lorenzo went."

Zac turned at once, very nearly about to go—that instant—but hesitated and looked into her eyes.

Remembering all that was at stake.

"I can't leave you," he said. Then, rethinking everything: "We need to make contact. This has gone on long enough. We need to find a way to reach Nani."

"It *has* gone on long enough." Jess hated the Bok so much right then. "I'm tired of their shit. I'm tired of all this. We—you—can end this right now." And she decided.

"We're going." She touched the map again. "This is not far away. Not at all. They have to be there. We're going and we're going to stop them."

Too much time had been wasted.

"They're no match for you," she marveled at the intensity of the fury building within her. So mad, almost seeing red, ready to rush off to grab the Bok herself.

Kill them, insisted her passionate bloodlust in that moment.

But she had to bring some reason to bear. Zac was shaking his head. Subtly, but his resistance was clear.

"We've seen that," she said. "I don't care what crazy powers they're using. We keep the heat on and get them now. Before they scatter." She thought of the dead commandoes up above. "If they haven't already." Worried the Bok may already have fled far and wide.

Zac, however, as determined to settle the Bok score as was she, had deep reservations. "Jessica," he put a hand on her shoulder; implored: "It doesn't make sense to keep this up."

But she pointed to the dot on the map. "They're right here." They were close. "We can end this."

"I can't keep letting you put yourself in danger," he tried to argue. "Not anymore. Last night, when I was walking around, before I found this, before they came, I had time to think. And I realized you're right. About everything you said over dinner. It's time to end this. Time for you to stop risking your life." He swallowed. "I won't let you. I'm indestructible, you're not." He was trying to be firm. Not confident whether he could, in fact, tell her what to do.

She appreciated that he feared her. It meant he would do what she said. It also meant she must be absolutely sure of her own decision.

"*You* were right," she told him. "I wasn't making any sense. I was being emotional. I'm past that. We have to follow through. End this. The time we've lost is my fault." She kicked herself for the wasted day, feeling her own change of heart acutely, the swing to a sudden impulse to finish what they started—so different than her desire of last night to run away, to just put the whole mess behind. An irrational fancy, that idea, and she saw that now; silly, driven by no sleep, compounded by the day with Zac—a day that absolutely blew her mind, to such an incredible degree, loosening and shifting her entire universe ... But none of that mattered. She could never go back. She'd already realized that long ago and it was time to stop getting distracted.

It was, as she pointed out, time to end this.

"Jessica ..."

She held him with a steady gaze. Anger drove her current frame of mind, she had no illusions of that, but her enraged determination was not unreasonable. She knew that as well. She couldn't name it, but she could feel it, and this impulse for closure rocked her. The absolute affront of the attempted commando assault, bent on killing them, the discovery, right there in that room, that the Bok, in fact, had their eyes on her and her family, with malign intent; confirmation that the Bok were out to get her; Lorenzo's attempt on them in the club; the girl's attempt to drown her right there on the farm ... Her mind was made. The Bok were here. She was here. Zac was here.

The time was now.

The Bok's day of reckoning was at hand.

"We have this." She gestured around the interior of the vault. Filled with information. Who knew what else waited at the castle. Maybe the Bok *did* have other Icons. Other artifacts. Knowledge of the Kel. Surely they had other secrets.

"We have you." She gave that a moment. Then: "We're just down the road," she pointed to the map. "Minutes away. We're going to put an end to this." She stood straight, chest inflated with fresh determination. "We know where Lorenzo is and we're getting him. No more waiting."

Zac's distress was clear. His untouchable power, however, was just as obvious. There was no way he could fail. Not against the Bok. And, like an Alpha Male Great Dane or something, fully with a mind of his own but, in the final bargain, a follower of his master's wishes, Zac would do as she said. He would follow. Her decision had been made; the command was given.

She only hoped she was right.

* * *

CEE-RANOK STRODE aboard her shuttle, followed by two personal guards; elite warriors in ceremonial armor, long rifles held across their chests as they marched in step. Her bishop trailed to the side, the shuttle door closing behind as they entered.   The shuttle was well-appointed, the Tremarch's private coach, and she absorbed the change as they transitioned from the stark metal corridor of the dreadnought to the softer interior of her private craft.

She continued on across the entry room, to the forward seating area where her captain waited.

"Make ready to depart," she said and went to her in-flight throne, a large, ornate chair that dominated the small space. It faced a screen that covered the entirety of one wall, making the wall look transparent—as if looking through a floor-to-ceiling window directly out the front of the craft. At present it looked out on the interior of the hold in which they were docked.

"At once, my queen." The captain left for the front, for the cockpit, to get them underway.

Cee keyed the screen and an image from the dreadnought's bridge appeared. Voltan was there, along with Kang. Kel crew manned stations in the background, preparing for departure.

"We're aboard," she announced.

Voltan turned to face her.

"Very good," he said. "All craft have checked in. Once you're clear we will move to our departure point."

Cee inhaled. More excited than she had been in a long, long time. They'd done it. Taken this potentially dangerous situation, the arrival of Kang, and turned it into what promised to be the birth of a grand empire. They'd cracked the device brought by him and made its information part of their systems, enabling their craft to travel to the stars with a specific destination in mind:

Kang's world.

Anitra, he called it; where waited a real enemy, one the Kel could conquer. One that was being handed them on a platter, ripe for the taking. New territory. A new empire to be forged. Her people would have direction again, purpose.

It was the dawn of a new age.

* * *

LINDIN LOOKED out the panoramic window, over the city of Osaka. Capital of the enemy and there he was, high in a room in their own Tower of Light, being shown every courtesy.

He took a sip of the hot sake that had been provided, enjoying the serenity of the lavish setting. It was so unreal to be standing at that spectacular vantage, looking out over the surrounding fields from inside the city walls, fields where not so long ago he and the Venatres army were engaged in a fiery campaign to invade. Strange as all this was it had, surprisingly, not been that hard to move on. After arriving for the summit he and each of the delegates from Venatre were given a similar room, there on that floor, and, following the discussions of the day, he'd chosen to retire and recharge. Absorb a little quiet and collect his thoughts. Some of the others chose a tour of the city.

All day the focus had been on this historic meeting and the promise it held. Their entire world had been shaken in so many ways over the last half-year, from the complete ruin and upheaval of the Dominion's core leadership to the wars and counter-invasion that followed, the arrival of Kang and all the damage that caused, now a coup among the ranks of the Dominion generals overseas—still fighting, still waging war in Venatres lands—followed by the discovery that the Venatres had been hiding something so advanced as to be world-changing:

The starship.

As a result Anitra, the entire world, was in a massive state of flux. Anything, truly, at that point, was possible.

And now the near impossible was happening. Venatres senior leaders were in Dominion lands, talking peace. That very day. The first round of discussions had gone amazingly well, almost as if events leading to that moment were enough to entirely shock both sides out of previously held beliefs, enough to knock loose fixed positions such that each of them, Dominion and Venatres alike, were ready to figure out how to coexist.

To take their world to the next level.

Lindin inhaled the pleasant scents of the room. Despite the monumental progress he wasn't foolish enough to believe he would not be held accountable for his role in the loss of that same starship. It would return eventually, of that he was certain. Jessica and company would bring it back; they would not stay away forever. There would be an accounting for all involved when it did. In the meantime the burden was on him. Would Jessica and her band of thieves show up suddenly? More than that, once they did, how *would* the Venatres get the starship back?

That was perhaps the bigger question.

Deliberately he calmed himself, letting the harsh sake do its work.

All that would come later. For now, talk was of the future.

For now talk was of a united Anitra.

CHAPTER 42:

ALL SYSTEMS GO

JESS BRUSHED fluttering strands of hair from her eyes, hooked them behind an ear and squinted into the sun as she and Zac made their way up the winding mountain road. They'd taken one of the Bok Ferraris, a brilliant, lime-green 458 Spider convertible—the first set of keys for which they found a match—and she drove. She glanced at Zac in the passenger seat as she hugged them gently around a tight curve. He filled the small cockpit, looking awkward in the bucket seat with his knees against the dash. Like a basketball player trying to enjoy an exotic toy, one that just wasn't designed for anyone that big.

She brushed more strands of hair from her eyes and looked ahead.

After a few mis-steps she got the car started, got used to the controls—buttons, paddle shifters and all else that made the Ferrari a Ferrari—then got them moving down the long dirt road and wheeling out onto the steep mountain pass. They wore their seatbelts and she drove normally, not racing, taking it easy, trying not to attract attention.

An impossibility to say the least.

No matter how low-key they tried to act they were absolutely screaming for attention. The Ferrari was a bright green splash of *Hey look at me!* their clothes not much better. She wore the old, mothball-smelling farmer's shirt and oversized overalls; Zac the dress pants from the club and nothing else. There was no time to hunt other options. Zac had buried all the Bok—not that she would've put on any of their clothes even if he hadn't. So there they were, dressed like hobos, Zac shirtless in the cool morning air, Jess sixteen and looking like she just stepped off a 1970s farm, driving a lime-green Ferrari through the Spanish hills. An odd combination by any standard. Frumpy and disheveled, dirty, incomplete, cheap wardrobes in such a high-end machine. But there was no one around to look closely. Hardly anyone was out at that time of day, especially that far in the middle of nowhere. They'd passed only one other car.

Around the next curve they headed up a steeper grade and she tapped the paddle shifter down a gear.

She'd never had a car of her own. Never even had a driver's license. Now here she was, touring the Spanish countryside in a quarter-million-dollar exotic, her handsome, perfect boyfriend at her side. The man of her dreams. A gorgeous, sunny day, the morning filled with promise, fresh, fragrant air blowing across the open top, long strands of hair whipping about in a delicate dance. Living the dream.

She couldn't have felt worse.

She hated everything right then. Her life. Her situation. It was difficult to see any future where she might once again find joy. One free of the endless battles that must be fought. From here on out she would have to win her way to everything. It made her bitter. Crushed at all she'd lost, all she'd given up, each decision leading her there, to that moment, a moment of sheer desolation, any shot at normalcy gone in a most permanent way. These feelings struck her now and again, sure, ever since she began the mad journey that was her current existence, but never had they impinged like they were right then. It was crushing. Absolutely crushing. Waves of sadness, crashed upon by anger, drenched in outright terror, smack in the middle of that glaring, horrible contrast in which she found herself:

Wind blowing. Wonderful feel in her hair. Sunshine and the engine burbling happily up the slopes. Spring smells, the beauty of the setting all around, fighting to be noticed. Demanding to be appreciated.

Driving the bitterness so deep.

She might never know happiness again.

For an instant she nearly laughed but choked it back. Knowing it would turn to tears.

Desperately she struggled to offset these feelings with

reason. Everyone had to fight for what they had. Of course that was true. You didn't eat, didn't have a roof over your head if you didn't work, if you didn't somehow contribute and exchange with the society that in turn gave you the means. By and large, though, the culture from which she came, her life until now, was one of freedoms. Luxuries. The "battles" they fought were mild. Not even battles at all, really. To survive you went to work. You cooked dinner. Figured out how to spend your free time.

All that, for her, was gone.

Now she had to find her place in the world. Her *new* place. And she had no idea what that would be, where the search would lead, where it would end. For now all she could do—*all* she could do—what she *had* to do—was keep going. Relentless. Going, and going.

And going.

What would they find at the castle? More guys with freaky powers? Another Icon? Other Kel devices? And what was the Bok's interest in her? Beyond the obvious. Whatever it was they wanted to get their hands on her.

Yes, she thought with grim determination, *but I'm going to win that game.* And that was really all she had left. Anger. A contest of wills. And so she'd embraced it, was letting it run the day, and so what if better ideas were to be had, more careful strategies. At that point she didn't care. She had Zac. Zac was a god, he was hers, and she was mad and she was going to unleash his wrath.

Oh, yes. She was about to go kick some ass.

She debated turning on the car's stereo, seeing if this particular Bok, the owner of the lime-green Ferrari, had anything worth listening to. Maybe something fast, something metal. Something to amp her up, take her mind from things, if only for a short while. The beautiful drive was not near distracting enough.

She didn't bother.

She just wasn't in the mood.

* * *

KANG GAZED INTO the depths of space, seeing far and wide, counting and recounting the Kel ships within view. There were many. Any one of them, even the smallest cruiser, could devastate Anitra from on high. There would be nothing either the Dominion or the Venatres could do. Even combined, their forces united, those two "global" powers could be so easily picked apart from above.

But it was not his intention nor his goal to ravage the Anitran infrastructure, leaving little behind, nothing to rule. Armies waited out there in those Kel ships, some of the vessels purposed with that specific task, acting as transport for the troops that would finish the job, that would conquer rather than destroy, and so when the time came the Kel were prepared for that as well. As they were prepared for all things. They were a race, a culture, built for war. What they set out to do was what they were made to do.

The Kel were solidly in their element.

He let his eyes rove the bristling, lethal curves of one of the other dreadnoughts. There were three in this armada, two in addition to the one on which he now stood. The forward viewscreen out which he gazed was giant, the activity of the bridge noisy behind him; conversations, footsteps, preparations.

The dreadnoughts were behemoths. Titans of firepower and armor, each carrying their own small fleet of fighters, squads of ground units and Kel special forces. One of *those* could utterly crush Anitra. The armada that had been tasked for this historic campaign was well beyond anything needed, yet it was merely a subset of their overall might. It struck Kang again just how warlike were the Kel, how much of an army they maintained when they, in fact, had no foe. He could see why Cee had been so eager to take advantage of this opportunity. During his time on Kel, waiting, Kang read their history, noted the unprecedented expansion of their might since restoring themselves and their capabilities following their crushing civil war of a thousand years ago. It was clear they needed something, and soon, on which to act. A place to direct that impulse for the fight. He'd come to believe the nature of the Kel was not entirely driven by culture but was quite possibly genetic. The urge toward combat, to dominate, to rule. All urges Kang could fully admire.

Earlier the fleet had begun moving slowly away from the homeworld, a grand imperial march into position, a place from which they could safely use the engines that would propel them across the incredible distance to their target. Kel was out of sight behind, no other celestial bodies close enough to be seen, and so it was into a vast field of stars he gazed, a vast field of potential, the vessels slipping further from the world's gravity well to the spot from which they would launch their assault.

The invasion would be made easier, of course—if it wasn't already easy enough—by the fact that he ruled one half of Anitra already. The Dominion was his to command; his first objective would be to announce his return and bring them quickly under his yoke. The fall of the Venatres would come easily after that. Days. Maybe even hours. He chuckled, getting a few nervous glances from nearby Kel on the bridge.

He would become both Emperor *and* God.

How they will lament me.

"This is a momentous day," Voltan said in English from behind. The Kel Praetor had walked up a few moments before, standing to look out as was Kang, waiting for the moment. Voltan had taken time to learn a bit of his language, among other things. Voltan's words were in accented English but clear. Kang wasn't sure whether to appreciate his efforts or despise them. Voltan switched to one of the translation wands.

"When we reach position I will give the order," he said, reiterating what Kang already knew. Voltan was to lead the invasion. In Kang's mind, however, the chain of command had not been entirely clarified, and he intended to use the most glaring oversights to his advantage. *He* would lead the invasion, *he* would call the shots and Voltan would go along. "Once all craft are assembled on the other end we will begin our assessment of your world," the computer voice said as Voltan's voice spoke behind it.

A recap, nothing more. "The Fetok of my world will present no challenge," said Kang, using the Kel's own word for humans. *The Tolerated.* Kang himself might've been considered one of them at one time. Human.

No more.

Now he was neither human nor Kel. He was a new breed, and with him at their head this army of Kel would bring Anitra to heel. Then move on to the next. He looked at the thousands upon millions of multi-colored points of light salting the black universe before him. Bands of them everywhere, as far as you could imagine, worlds upon worlds, so many that must be just as ripe.

Anitra would be but the beginning.

Voltan nodded. "If all is as you say."

Kang tried to read any subtext to that statement in Voltan's expression, in his one eye, that infuriating eye patch making him somehow more warrior, not less. The Kel were incredibly human-like in many ways, but there were subtleties to them Kang knew he'd not yet mastered. Emotions were the same, but did Voltan harbor doubts? Carefully hidden ... hopes? Some twisted desire that Kang was wrong and this failed? During briefings leading to this moment Kang, now and again, thought Voltan suspected him of lying. Of not being entirely honest in his descriptions of what waited at the other end. As if, somehow, Kang might have something there, ready to massacre the Kel and take what they could, then find their way back to the Kel homeworld and do the same. It was an absurd idea, for so many reasons, but it seemed as if Voltan suspected *something*. Like he didn't trust Kang fully, if at all.

Not that it mattered. Kang *did* intend to use the Kel and all their resources, and was sure that intention had so far been quite clear. They knew what was on his mind. And he knew what was on theirs. This marriage would not end with a happy union. But there *would* be a union. Once all was said and done and the smoke cleared it would either be with him on top, in charge, or him destroyed, removed from the equation and the Kel holding all the power.

He did not intend to be destroyed, or to be removed.

He grinned at Voltan. Wide, showing lots of teeth. He could feel their pointed tips against his bared lips.

"All is as I say."

CHAPTER 43:

THE CASTLE

THEY ROUNDED THE LAST BEND, following the scribbled map Jess drew back at the farm showing the way. And there it was. The castle. A classic stone structure, not uncommon for the region, old and weatherworn, partially in ruins at the top of a small rise, built up against the rocks, looking out over a wide, panoramic vista in three directions. Jess slowed as it came into view, feeling suddenly vulnerable. Far too visible in the lime-green sport scar on the narrow road, and all at once she was thinking about everything they could've done different. They could've gone for Satori, as Zac wanted. Could've just left, gone back. Could've stopped further up the road and walked in.

She worked to convince herself—swallowing hard several times, nerves shooting to the fore all over again as she stared at the ominous castle, waiting up on the rise ...

This was the only way.

There was another hill between them and the grounds, and as they passed behind it the castle slipped from sight, then popped back into view and they were on their way up, last chance to turn around, all alone on the desolate entry road.

"See anything?" she asked, on high alert, scanning the scrub trees, the wide, grassy grounds, the castle ramparts— everything in her field of vision, all of it clear and sharp in the bright morning sun. Glimmering, fresh and pristine beneath a cloudless blue sky.

"Not yet." Zac looked just as intent, eyes darting across the landscape, sweeping the castle.

"Do we just drive up?" she wondered, realizing they hadn't really decided how they would make their final approach. Now they were here and they needed to decide how to take the next steps. Probably they should sneak the rest of the way on foot. "Maybe we should—"

A sharp flash of pain and the world spun, inverted and upside down; a deep grunt as Zac had her in his arms—she had the presence of mind to realize that much—yanking her free, through the air, blue sky and green grass whirling in her field of vision before she could even process the fact that they were soaring and the roar of an explosion was sweeping up from below; heat, a spike of light and the sudden sound of gunfire.

Heavy gunfire.

Chun! Chun! Chun! Chun! a large cannon ripped the air where they'd just been, world tumbling as Zac held her to him, rolling and leaping, hitting and flipping again, diving, landing, coming at last to a stop with a solid impact, feet out at a crouch, Jess squeezed tightly in his arms. He set her down and she flopped to the side, retched and tried to get her bearings. Her world spun. Everything was spinning. She rolled to her back and put her hands to the sides, fists grabbing at the grass and holding on. They were in a ditch behind a row of small trees.

Chun! Chun! Chun! the stunningly loud gunfire found its way closer, echoing powerful across the land—coupled with the *Whump!* of impacts she could *feel* through the ground. Those were *big* rounds. She grabbed harder, pinching her eyes closed and holding herself still. After a few moments of steady fire she peeked and looked sharply to the right, back pressed against the ravine; saw the burning remains of the exploded Ferrari in the distance. Plumes of terrain shot into the air as the gun continued to track their location, towering geysers of grass and dirt marking each hit.

The tranquil hillside was suddenly a war zone.

Chun! Chun! Chun! the chain gun couldn't zero in. Zac had them safe for the moment. Rounds ripped overhead, orange dash-dots strafing furiously, *Chun! Chun! Chun!* hitting the berm of the ravine above, passing over and hitting the ground beyond. None able to connect. The intensity was overwhelming. The Bok were filling the hillside with heavy rounds. Lots of them.

Chun! Chun! Chun! Chun! Chun! Whump! Whump!

Whump! The big bullets ripped the air, making her cringe tighter into herself. Unnecessary, it was clear they couldn't hit her, but she was so scared. That was no rifle, no handheld machine gun. That wasn't even an ordinary chain gun. That was a military grade emplacement, giant orange tracers and everything. It churned the ground to a maelstrom of choking debris. Like anti-aircraft or something. Anti-armor. Twenty-mil, maybe thirty. Bigger.

Chun! Chun! Chun! that thing could take out a tank with one shot. She was sure of it.

"You okay?" Zac. She jerked her head; stared wide-eyed at him. He crouched beside her, as alarmed as she was.

"Yeah." Her legs hurt, one badly. Probably hit it on the steering wheel as he yanked her free. She looked down and rubbed her thigh. Otherwise she was whole.

"Sorry," he said. "I didn't see it in time." He seemed genuinely angry with himself.

"Zac, you saved me."

The gun stopped suddenly. Zac craned his head, looking all around, scrutinizing the entire countryside.

Looked back at her.

"Stay here," he said. "I'm going to take it out." And he was gone. That fast. No more discussion, no waiting for an answer. She tried to stop him, wanted to make a plan, wasn't done sorting out this new twist but he was over the berm and leaping into the air before she could move, covering half the distance to the castle in one bound. Without thinking she jumped to her feet, to the edge of the ravine, looking past the trees as the gun spotted him and opened up, a whirling stream of fire spitting from the barrel that peeked over the rampart—she could see it now, nestled in an armored mount atop one of the walls; a modern fixture in an ancient setting, seeking out the flying Zac. She ducked but held position as she realized he was its full focus. She saw no other guns and so watched in morbid fascination as the orange tracer rounds ripped the sky, nearly a solid line, bearing down on the small, difficult target that was Zac, dark hair and bare skin until ...

They found their mark.

"No!" she screamed in horror as he was knocked aside, tumbling. That was a *big* gun, and if it could explode a tank what could it do to Zac? Could it really ...

No. He hit a hundred yards off course in a cloud of dirt and was on his feet in the same instant, turning the tumble into a roll into a run, making his next leap as the gun opened up again—she could only imagine the surprise of the gun operators—flying once more toward the castle wall, so high that time, she could feel his fury, a hundred feet in the air, arms and legs out for a landing as ... the gun hit him again, smacking him off his new trajectory.

But that was all. A smack. This time he arced to the side, flipping out of control in the air but still flying forward with massive momentum and ... *crunch!* hit the castle wall further down in a shock of stone and dust—an impact she heard all the way across the field. Instead of bouncing, however, he stuck like a dart, arms punching in and finding purchase.

Incredible. What he could do, what he could endure was just absolutely, unbelievably, incredible. He was getting knocked around not because the gun could hurt him, he was getting knocked around due to simple physics. Fifty supersonic one-pound rounds coming at him each second ... of course that was going to do that. But there was no damage. She felt her eyes stretched wide and stinging in the cool air.

The lives of the gun operators were numbered.

Probably in seconds.

Using his grip he flipped himself to the top and sprinted along the upper rampart, a flesh-toned blur, too fast, too far inside the intended arc of the gun and was upon it. What transpired within the emplacement she could not see nor really even hear, all she knew was that it went silent. Quickly thereafter she heard a giant *clang!* followed by a few smaller bangs that echoed heavy across the field, the unmistakable sound of distressed metal, and she was sure the gun was no more.

In the wake of that the field was quiet. Eerily so. The gentle breeze blew. The leaves of the nearby trees rustled.

Even the small fire from the charred mess that was the Ferrari had burned out and was silent.

She began to worry.

She listened a little longer. Nothing. No Zac. Had he gone on into the castle without her? She knew he was growing more and more fearful for her, worried about her safety. He kept saying so. Was he using this opportunity to go on without her? Hoping she'd just stay where she was? Out of the way? It seemed that was exactly what he was doing: run off fast before she could argue. Intending to just take care of things himself. For him the combined fear of leaving her alone versus taking her with him had mostly driven his relenting to her demands thus far. That and his unnatural desire to do what she said. But now, with her safely in a ravine—with all the enemies clearly in sight, in one place, right there in front of them—he'd seized upon the chance to do what he'd been wanting to all along: handle the dangerous stuff without her.

She listened to the soft rustling of the leaves in the short trees.

Was he hurt in there?

With no way to be absolutely sure worry began to take hold. Impossible. There was no way. Yet ...

Stop! She tried to make herself stop before that line of thinking took hold. But the notion had already begun working its way into her mind. An insidious little idea, eating away at reason as the minutes ticked by, all quiet up on the vast hill, no more activity, no more sign. Could something weird have happened? *Did* the Bok have some advanced technology? Some ancient Kel device that would allow them to injure Zac?

Or even kill him?

Zac! Why wouldn't he come back? At least give her a sign! He could've come up to the rampart and waved or something. Or shouted for her to stay. Or given a signal.

Anything.

The silence of the whispering trees began to kill her.

He was so confident in his own abilities. And why shouldn't he be?

Now the worry was full-blown. She had to save him. She had to know. It was just her, high up on a remote Spanish mountain, nothing anywhere nearby but a castle full of the enemy. She began to wish she'd brought one of the rifles scattered about the farm from the commando team. Anything with which to fight, never expecting she would have to. She stared at the barren castle.

Why did you run off without making a better plan?!

Carefully she scaled the ravine, slowly, little hesitations holding her. She'd been so angry. So filled with misplaced confidence. Now she was scared and felt stupid. At the top of the ravine she reached all the way over, pulled herself into the clear, was out in the open before she could allow herself to stop and ...

Running into the sparse cover of the small trees. There she crouched behind a trunk, hoping there wasn't another gun. All her senses were tingling, set to 11 on a scale of 10. She saw everything, heard everything, smelled everything. Several of the trees had been cut down before the ballistic rage of the emplacement.

Trees would not protect her.

She snapped her eyes across the field between her and the castle. Once she left the trees there would be no more hiding. There was no cover, and it was a good hundred yards or more to the nearest wall. Lots of time in the open, even at a full sprint.

There was a window there, directly ahead, no bars covering it, no glass. An open entry. Near enough to ground level to go through. It was the only way in she could see.

She went for it.

No second thought, up and running just like Zac did, going on impulse, ignoring the throb of her sore leg and hitting a full sprint with everything she had, an action she'd become well used to: running for her life. Dodging left then right around the last trees and out onto the wide open field and only *then* doubting her decision, regretting it even as she forced herself on as absolutely fast as she could, heels thumping the ground, wind roaring in her ears; drawing the castle to her—catching her fall more than once as she hit a dip or stepped in a hole, trying on top of every other thing demanding her panting attention not to injure herself before she even reached her objective. A twisted ankle or a jammed knee at this point would be it. She would be through; laying in the field like a fly in a web, adventure over.

A harsh scoff escaped her as she pounded furiously ahead.

Adventure.

Yeah, that's what this was.

Between checking the ground ahead she kept her eyes on the wall, on the window, on every edge, on every distant opening no matter how high, looking for the glint of a barrel, ready to tuck and roll if needed, to start weaving or anything else she could to avoid a hit out there where there was nowhere to hide.

Closer. The wall was close, what was probably only seconds seeming like minutes, hours, and she turned her full attention to the window through which she would dive. Wind whistled past her ears, legs and arms pumping, the overly baggy overalls flapping awkwardly but hardly slowing what was surely record speed—probably for any human ever—breathing like a locomotive, feet whipping through the tall grass, over the alternating hard and soft ground, determined not to fall.

Determined to make it alive.

And she was there. The last few yards. No shots. Maybe they were preoccupied with Zac. Maybe the only shooters had been up with the gun emplacement. Whatever the reason she'd made it and was unscathed. A little too late she started braking, as hard as she could, jamming her feet ahead of her in rapid succession, digging into the dirt but not soon enough.

"*Uhhnn!*" she shouldered into the wall, precious wind punched from her lungs in the impact. But she was okay. All was good. She took a step back and caught her breath, hands on her knees—then remembered there was no time to spare. Panting, she quick-peeked through the window then dropped back down and pushed up flush against the rough stone wall. Reviewing the snapshot of what she saw. Dark inside. No people. She thought there was the light of another room beyond.

She rose and checked again. Lingered this time when no danger was forthcoming. There was indeed another room, a hall it looked like, through an open doorway. With one more check and a brief listen she hoisted herself over the sill and through, diving to her hands on the other side and tumbling to her feet. A perfect gymnastic tumble and she felt a pang of sadness that all that prior practice in her youth was being put to use for this. But there was no time for sadness. If ever she had to stay "on" now was it.

The room had a stone floor, smoother than the walls. It was dark but her eyes adjusted quickly. The light from the bright sun streamed through the window behind her ...

A man came through the doorway, gun in hand. He reacted as soon as he saw her, jerking the gun up in total surprise but she was quicker. Lunging the long stride between them she had the gun in both hands, twisting the barrel around on him violently before he could apply enough force to resist and ... jerked it with every ounce of strength she had; a spastic motion that snatched his arms before he could respond and, exactly as she hoped, snatched his finger against the trigger.

Bap!Bap!Bap! the muzzle flashed, firing right into his chest at point-blank range. Messy, shocking, loud ... he went down like a rock. She held the gun and it wrenched from his grip as he fell, leaving him dead at her feet and the machine pistol in her hands. She checked it over. Short barrel, something like an Uzi, extended magazine sticking from the bottom of the grip, probably mostly full. It was unsilenced and the echo of its burst reverberated down the stone halls. More Bok would be coming.

She stepped into the hall. Another was there, running around a corner to her right, not far away, gun up and ready to shoot.

She shot first.

Bap!Bap!Bap! he ran into the burst and flipped back as if running into a fist; *Bap!Bap!Bap!* the second group only added to the bloody spray. He flopped to the stones, his own gun clanking at his side. She ran to him, no hesitation, grabbed the gun and slung it across her shoulder. For a moment she looked back and forth between the two dead men, curious she felt absolutely nothing at having just killed them. But she didn't. Even though she was there for that express purpose it seemed she should feel something. But she didn't. It was kill or be killed and the Bok were the ones that made that decision. They'd already tried to kill her three times in the last day.

This was beyond personal.

She had no idea where to go next. Her only thought was to make her way back in the direction of the giant gun in the hopes of finding Zac. Maybe she would intercept him.

With that in mind she ran to the end of the hall—right into another guy coming for her. They surprised each other, as had the last two, and like the last two she was quicker. This Bok took an instant high kick to the chest, an unexpected stab with her heel that knocked him sideways into the wall, dazed for an instant and she triggered his chest right where she'd just planted her foot ...

Bap!Bap!Bap! one burst this time, controlled, zero hesitation. The machine pistol was loud, hammering the air in the close confines of the stone hall as her target spasmed against the wall and slid down it in a swipe of blood.

Three down.

How many more to go?

She hoped her fears for Zac were unfounded. Surely he was still alive, making his own way through the castle. She was reminded that, despite the adrenaline of the moment, despite the overwhelming sense of destiny she felt right then, she was vulnerable. Highly vulnerable. She could die easily.

Crouching a bit she continued, turned the corner and headed deeper into the castle. Jogging carefully—acutely aware, suddenly, of looking like a farm girl from *Hee Haw*, overalls and barefoot, wielding two machineguns and feeling more like *La Femme Nikita*. By all counts not belonging in that place in either capacity. But here she was. Moving as quickly as she dared, on high alert, eyes darting, ears pricked beyond all sensitivity. If a gnat farted she would've heard and shot it right between the eyes. She passed a computer station of some sort, then another, then a larger room, stones rough and imperfect as they no doubt had been at the time of the castle's construction. The bigger room was filled with what looked to be networking equipment, orderly cabling, some of it large, high gauge, probably fiber, all of it lit by red lighting; little lights blinking here and there on various pieces of high-tech equipment. The contrast of ancient and modern reminded her of some kind of super-villain complex, like something out of a James Bond movie, or like Cobra Base from GI Joe, or Doctor Doom and the Fantastic Four.

So far these Bok weren't far from any of that.

Suddenly a sound and she whirled as two more Bok ran from a corner behind, a guy and a girl, guns up and looking for targets. Jess saw them first; held both machine-pistols out, spraying a sustained volley down the hall, arms extended as she kept moving, twin muzzle flashes blasting the walls with light and sound. The girl dropped in a flail of limbs as the guy leapt back the way he'd come. Jess couldn't tell if she hit him or not but used the chance to duck into another room to the side. She ran in looking for others, searching for cover. It was a larger, empty room, more computer workstations on one wall. She checked her magazines and readied the guns, even as she heard a distant, "No!" echo down the hall from the way the last two came. The sound of the voice gave her pause.

No?

The voice continued shouting: "Fools! Stop shooting! Do *not* kill her!

"She *is* the One!"

The One?

And the sound of those words gave her her first chill since entering the Bok's domain.

* * *

ZAC HEARD MORE gunfire off in the bowels of the old castle. After taking out the gun and turning his rage on another group of Bok who came to attack he'd wondered whether he was doing the right thing. He knew Jess too well. Which meant he knew he could likely not count on her to stay put, no matter how quickly he dispatched the Bok. He'd forged on a bit further, determined to lay as much waste as he could before she was put in harm's way, killing several more Bok before deciding, with certainty, that he must in fact let her know what he was doing. She was just too likely to take matters into her own hands. Back at the top rampart his fears had been confirmed.

She was nowhere to be seen.

Meaning she'd come for him.

Seconds after realizing that frightening reality the gunfire began. At which point he'd launched himself toward the source, full effort, an uncharacteristic panic consuming him. Breaking through feet-thick stone walls when he could find no direct path, slaying Bok who got in his way, all but ignoring those that didn't, leaving them behind in his mad rush. Each time a new burst of gunfire went off his hope spiked, that Jess was still alive, fighting for her life—crushed immediately by the idea that *that* series of shots might be the last, the one that killed her.

Then more shots would come. And on he raced. He ran down a long corridor now, tracing the echoes, running so fast he literally ran along the wall, such was his speed that he actually stuck to the extended curve.

He'd never felt the impassioned rage he did right then.

"You will not have this world!" a voice came from up ahead. He was almost there.

"This world is ours!"

"It's not!" an older voice insisted, overruling them all.

Zac leapt from the last corner into a large inner room, a dozen or so of the Bok clustered within—all with guns in hand. Everyone present jerked their heads in his direction, in reaction to his shocking entrance, guns up and aimed right at him. Only a few in the front could've feasibly shot him, but in that initial instant it looked as if they would all open fire, the ones in the rear shooting through the backs of the others just to get him. Such was their aggression, their desire to kill. He could smell it.

But the old man standing before them held them with a shout.

"No!" he threw up his arms.

And there she was.

Jessica!

Directly across the room, on the other side of the cluster of bodies, her own guns up in what had no doubt been a standoff, all of it held in check by the old man. The urge to lay into them, all of them, fought with Zac's reason. He very nearly screamed with the impotence of it. There were too many. Unless he killed them all in one sweep, before any could shoot, before a single trigger could be pulled, Jess could be hit. By a direct shot. By a ricochet in the stone-walled space. She felt it too; she couldn't risk moving any more than him. She glanced furtively at him from across the room.

At the moment, however, all listened to the old man. No one moved. He had a thick head of gray hair and, at least for now, held their attention.

"He is with her," he told them, indicating the freshly arrived Zac. "We don't yet know his role in this."

"His role is to kill us!" one of them shouted, clearly looking to incite the others.

"No!" the old man cut her short. "No. This hate has been caused by Lorenzo. We must think clearly. We *know* what this girl has done." He looked to Jessica. "How else do you think she came to be here?"

No one answered. All were seething. Barely holding themselves still. Zac scanned the scene with his eyes, all of them, everything, darting back and forth, careful not to move. There were a lot of guns in that room. He had to figure out what to do, and fast. The old man was closest to Jess and, while he had no gun Zac could see—and Jess was holding two—Zac was starting to get a very uneasy feeling.

The man took a few more steps. "You all recognize this," he said and Zac tensed as he reached for something inside his jacket, withdrawing and holding up ...

An Icon.

CHAPTER 44:

DAWN OF WAR

DRAKE STARED at the charred remains of what appeared to have once been a lime-green sports car, the bulk of it a dozen or so yards off the road, fragments and chunks scattered at a distance. His eye caught a shiny emblem glimmering in the bright sun among the ruins; a prancing horse. A Ferrari. If he had to guess he'd say what turned it into a shredded mess of expensive composites and exotic metals was some sort of anti-aircraft gun. Not just a fifty-cal. Something big. There were signs all over the ground; hundreds, maybe thousands of large bullet craters. Like a jacked-up Phalanx system or something, spewing many, many heavy rounds per minute. The car was complete toast.

What was most curious, however, was that there were no signs of occupants. Whatever poor rich person or couple had been on their way to see the ancient castle ruins on this gorgeous day, maybe out for a picnic, were nowhere to be found. Maybe they got out and ran before the gun hit the car. He didn't see how, but that was the only explanation. However they did it, Drake hoped they made it far, far away from that place.

Bad things were about to happen.

He signaled two of his team members to close on the hill behind which he hid. The castle sat on a wide expanse of field with no easy way to get close. Certainly they wouldn't chance the gun system that obliterated the car. They were going to have to call in help, which would mean breaking silence. As yet they did not know the extent of what they were dealing with. This castle was clearly not abandoned as it appeared. Their Bok captive was telling the truth: there were people in there, and they were probably more of his comrades.

Up ahead was a ravine. Drake and his team left their vehicles back down the road and came this far on foot, donning camo gear before setting out. Still, even with that—and armament—they were unprepared to do much more. Theirs was a top secret, specialized task force, inserted in-country for one purpose: bring back Lorenzo. The idea being that Lorenzo would lead them to the Bok as a whole. Now, it appeared, Drake and his team had achieved their objective without him. They now had a huge lead on the Bok and their whereabouts.

The Bok castle was right in front of them.

Following up on that was not part of the original mission. They would need to re-assess how to proceed. Reinforcements would likely be needed.

But Drake would first see what he could. Learn what he could before breaking silence and going in for the kill.

* * *

"I've got it." Nani jumped on a new bit of info and Bianca jumped right with her. It had been a full day since Jess and Zac fled the club and she was about to burst. Neither she nor Nani had slept and the stress was starting to wear on both. The usually calm Nani had been short with everyone, including Satori—who continued to push for an all-out sweep of the whole area in full view—but Nani held everything in place while she drilled through what she could, running code-cracking and password-cracking routines on her console, trying to get the GPS info on the stolen bike.

"The tracker. Here it is."

Bianca watched as she brought up the now oh-so-familiar overhead view of Spain, drilled into the parts they'd been over and over and over again, swept along away from the club, far out over the highway, into the mountains, into an area miles and miles from anywhere they'd looked. She tapped and zoomed, tapped again, centered on an area and stopped. Bianca stared at what was a narrow road winding along the side of a mountain ridge, forest and trees on one side, a deep ravine on the other.

There was nothing there.

"There's nothing there," she said it.

"Wait," Nani checked a few more things and overlaid the signal directly. The blip was down in the ravine.

"Oh my god," Bianca's heart rose in her throat. "Did they crash?"

"There are no bodies," Nani was already several steps ahead, checking other info. "That's the motorcycle," she confirmed. "Looks like it went off the road here," she highlighted and marked an area, tracing a line on the screen, "at a high rate of speed, arced over the ravine and impacted the side of the cliff here." And she dotted that area. Bianca saw signs of an impact, exposed gashes in the rock and a few scorched and broken bushes. As Nani panned around larger pieces of the bike came vaguely into view, down in the trees below.

Bianca swallowed. "No bodies?"

Nani shook her head. "No bodies. Zac must've pulled them clear. In fact, I think the fact that there *are* no bodies is proof that this was Jessica and Zac. Zac, at least. No one else could've survived that crash."

"Where did they go?"

"No telling. The crash site is hours old, maybe older. With Zac they could've covered a lot of ground." Nani leaned back; exhaled heavily and ran her hands through her hair. "They could be anywhere."

Bianca slumped into a nearby seat. Exhausted. Crushed.

They were no closer now than they had been.

* * *

ZAC INCHED CLOSER. The tension in the room was a hair-trigger from deadly action. One wrong move and everyone would open fire and Jess would be dead. There were simply too many guns in too small a space. Frantic to get her out of there he imagined move after move that might save her, none workable, none that would guarantee her survival, and so all he could do was inch ever so slightly toward her, hoping an opening presented itself. Ready to at least dive and cover her should the Bok snap. A last-ditch effort that might not work, but it was all he had. For now she was across the room, on the other side of all the bodies, all the guns, and they'd turned their attention back to the gray-haired man near her.

Not liking what he was saying.

"She is the one the priestess predicted!" the man shouted, gripping the newly-produced Icon in his fist. "She *is* the One! You know it! She must be taken!"

Taken? Zac began to grow ever more uneasy.

The man continued, as if lecturing children. "This is her destiny! Foretold by the priestess!" He scoffed at them. "You and your New Age. This is not the Golden Age of the Bok! Lorenzo is the beginning of our fall. He's misled you with his greed. *Your* greed has blinded you to the truth." He bore into them, holding their reluctant attention. "You use these gifts for your own gain, denying them to your fellow man—the very reason we exist! The priestess brought us here for sanctuary!"

"Our 'fellow' man has done nothing but persecute us!" one of them shouted. "Hunted us and killed us!"

"That was a thousand years ago!"

Zac studied Jessica's reaction to all this. He noted she'd lowered her guns; only slightly but definitely lax, caught up in the man's impassioned words. The barrels pointed down as she listened. Zac knew how the beliefs of the Conclave affected her, how she felt about being referred to as a prophet, the harbinger of some past prophecy. Now here was yet another group—a group she hated—calling her their messiah. Or at least the old man was. The others were very much in disagreement. What the man reminded them of was the fact that Jess represented a key part of their legend. Legends that said she was expected; meant to be there. An arrival foreseen by their past priestess, and that they were in danger of ruining that vital prediction.

And as Zac watched these things unfold he experienced a sudden shift of view. All at once and completely out of place with the danger all around. As if his eyes were opened and a veil lifted, unexpected in that setting yet, in that brief breath of silence as the old man and his furious insistence were on pause, the staredown and the anger of the Bok hanging in the air ...

He saw her.

Jessica!

There she was.

Visible in a way he could not at first seem to grasp. He'd always believed her to be transcendent, of course, at least in a sense; had always *known* she was something special. But seeing her standing there now, in those old farm clothes, barefoot, scratched and dirty, guns in hand, listening to the old man rant ... all those imperfections seemed to fade and, as if the arrival of a fiery sunrise, beaming through a morning haze, she shone. With radiance, with a beauty, an absolute clarity he could not describe.

It wasn't that she changed. She didn't. A camera would not have shown some ridiculous, heavenly aura. He knew that. No one else saw it. She gave off no light, no magical glow, yet ...

He saw her. As he'd only ever imagined. Her true form, perhaps, her true self, and as he saw *her* a sensation of supreme wonder came over him.

Followed immediately by the violent, mind-wracking realization that he must protect her. Above all else. She was bigger than all of this, and he must protect her and right now he was failing. No matter the absolute love, the absolute devotion he himself felt for her—no matter what she meant to *him*, no matter how badly he himself would do anything to save her, to be with her—no matter his own, personal motivation, he must protect *her*.

For them all.

For everyone everywhere, for now and for the future and for all time. On whatever her journey held, from whatever might stand in her way, that she might fulfill the destiny she so ardently resisted and which he suddenly perceived in its full magnitude and yet could not fathom. How he derived such a lucid, unwavering conclusion—now, under such duress—he did not know. He knew only that she was meant for something, and he knew it all at once and with unexpected conviction. *You're meant for something!* More than him. More than any of them.

She must be allowed to continue.

She must be saved.

In that, at least, the old man was right, and in one crystallizing instant, an epiphany of the highest order, Zac knew it. What he'd known all along but which now shone for him brighter than the brightest sun. His own role in that destiny, more clear than it had ever been.

He was her guardian.

"She must go," the old man was saying, "that she might free us." And suddenly the man was close—too close—collapsing Zac's vision all at once. Jessica, angel, vision of purity, image of power, stood raw again, dirty and helpless as the man put an arm around her, twisting the Icon in the same motion ...

And was gone.

Bok flew bodily aside as Zac covered the gap in a blur, so fast he hit the spot where Jess was even as the last trace of she and the old man rippled the air; waves of cool wind swirling in the vacuum of their passage.

Too late.

He wavered in their absence and ...

Fell to his knees.

She was gone.

* * *

"Whoa!" Nani exclaimed. "Hold on," she leaned forward, responding to an alert that had just flashed at her console. Bianca felt her heart jump, again, wondering how much more she could take. This waiting had her at wits end.

"That was a QED flash," Nani was suddenly in action. Bianca came closer.

"QED?"

"Quantum device, like the Icon." Nani was already lost in the evaluation of whatever had just pegged her readings.

"The Icon?" Bianca leaned over, looking. Who used an

Icon?

"I'm zeroing in on the source." Then: "It's not far from the location of the motorcycle crash."

Then more alarms went off; like the last only more urgent. More of them. Many more. Bianca sought the cause. This was not good. What was going on down there?!

"What the ..." Nani checked the new signals. "Those are coming from behind us." She glanced over her shoulder, looking out the rear dome of the screen in disbelief. Bianca followed. "Inside the lunar orbit." Nani's eyes were right back at her console but Bianca kept staring into the depths of space, away from the Earth, a creeping fear crawling over her as she sought the source of the alarms. Everything was a field of black. Suddenly she saw a flash, like a shooting star, then it was gone. Nothing she could make out. Then another.

No. Wait.

Something out there glinted, following the flash.

"What is it?" she asked, sensing Nani's growing alarm. The chill, creeping panic continued to inch over her. Tingling all over her body. All through it.

This was not right.

"Oh no," Nani's voice sounded terrified and Bianca felt her whole insides go to ice. She turned to Nani. On the screen were several schematics.

Starships.

"They're like the one back in the Kel system," Nani was utterly dumbstruck. "Dozens of them."

She turned slowly to look at Bianca.

Helpless.

Face like ash.

She swallowed, voice hoarse. Managing only to say:

"They found us."

* * *

KANG STOOD aboard the lead dreadnought looking out. At once surging with impatience, lusting to begin the conquest of his world, excited to finally be here, even as he began to feel ...

Confused.

Floating before them in the near distance was a blue world, for certain, covered in clouds like Anitra, only ...

"Target system locked," the reports began coming in. The bridge of the dreadnought had come to life following the abrupt transition to this new location. "All ships on station." More conversations. "We've reached the target coordinates."

Kang looked around the bridge at the Kel warriors. Their systems, their screens. Green lights, the energy of combat systems prepared for war. He looked back to what lay without. To the side of this blue world in the near distance was a gray/white moon. No other celestial bodies in sight.

That was not his moon.

"We're picking up a diverse language base," the Kel evaluation charged on, reams of data streaming in, activity on the bridge rising rapidly to a fast pitch. The trip, the switch of location, all happened in a flash, and now they were preparing for the fight. "Predominant language is the one we have on file," came the confirmation. "Capturing key transmissions now."

Kang listened to all this through his translation wand. That world out there, whatever it was—it was *not* Anitra— was using English to communicate. Sending electronic transmissions that could be intercepted by the Kel. Which meant whatever English-speaking beings were on that world were advanced. But how advanced? And what creatures? Could that Icon have connected ...

Suddenly it hit him.

This was the Emperor's world.

How had he not known!

Voltan queried his crew: "Are they aware of us?"

As of yet the Kel would have no idea this was not Anitra. Soon, though. Very soon they would. And when they did ...

But did it matter?

Not really, Kang surmised, unless of course the Emperor's world turned out to be far more advanced than his own.

"Yes," came the answer to Voltan's question. "Detection on multiple levels. A detection network is starting to fire across the globe."

Not good so far. Should Kang tell them to back out? Nerves came over him, uncertain fear he'd not felt in a long, long time. If this was not Anitra—and it most certainly was not—then how did he get back? Should he demand a withdrawal and a regroup back at Kel, to re-examine the Icon and discover just what went wrong? Should he tell them what he already knew, before they learned it for themselves?

"Lord," one of the voices rose above the din. Voltan turned to him. Kang did too. This voice was more urgent than the others.

"We have another contact," the Kel operator reported. "Sharing our space."

It took Voltan an instant to process that. "Another contact? A war craft?" Kang could see the commander's concerns on the rise, no doubt jumping to the conclusion that he'd been right, that Kang's world had the firepower to defeat them and would be waiting. In Kang's testimony his world had no starships.

But he wasn't lying.

This was not his world.

The Kel operator looked up. "It's the intruder. The ship from the encounter in Raag orbit."

Now Kang shook off the last of his worry. He stepped toward the man making the report, halfway across the bridge, holding the wand loosely at his side, forgetting all else for the moment. Voltan too was shocked, though at the confirmation that this was the ship they'd already encountered his expression seemed to steady. Kang stopped after only a few steps and looked back out the wide forward screen.

"The ancient ... Kel vessel?" asked Voltan.

Reports were flying, schematics of the craft appearing on screens all over the bridge—just as they had, thought Kang, when the ship first appeared what seemed so long ago, snatching Horus from his grasp and fleeing.

He recognized it. It was the same craft.

"Confirmed."

He looked to Voltan. Realized he was a little more concerned than was the Kel commander. They of course would've expected the ship to run back to Kang's world. After all, that's where it was from, right? Only, this was not Kang's world, a fact which they did not yet know—though they would soon enough—and so for him there was the mystery of why the ship that stole Horus came *here* and did *not* go back to Anitra.

It should, however, be carrying Horus.

And at the thought of that ...

"Destroy it," he said. He remembered the wand and brought it up so he could be heard more clearly: "Destroy the ship."

The crew looked back and forth between Kang and Voltan.

Kang turned directly to Voltan. Impatient for action. "I want it destroyed."

Voltan nodded that he heard, but was not ready to jump so hastily to this spontaneous command. His next question was to his crew: "What is our assessment of the world so far?"

"So far technologies are substantially inferior to ours. By an order of magnitude. No serious threat in terms of projectable offense. Thorough communications infrastructure, on a level with ours, but not hardened. It would be easy to bring their communications down as a first step. It appears that action alone would deal a significant blow to their ability to respond."

"Any other vessels like the one in orbit?"

"None detected, lord. That ship is beyond our own, and far beyond anything we're detecting on the world ahead. It would appear it is, in fact, an isolated example."

Voltan looked at Kang, his one good eye studying the demon, a dozen questions on his mind but none, clearly, worth discussing at present. He turned to his second in charge.

Choosing to continue ignoring Kang's demand.

"Monitor the ship," he instructed. "We'll sort this out as we go.

"Move all craft into position around the target world."

EPILOGUE

JESS FELL TO HER BACK and hit the ground with a crack, vision spotted, familiar copper tang raging in her skull as if she'd been punched in the face. The older Bok stood over her, staggering after he released her but keeping his feet. In his hand he held the Icon. Above him the castle was gone and now, spanning the night sky ...

Stars.

Stars upon stars. Patterns she didn't recognize. A brilliant, multi-colored nebula dominating a giant swath overhead.

It was night. It was afternoon where they'd just been.

They were outside. On a completely different ...

No! This couldn't be happening.

She struggled to rise, horribly disoriented; convulsed and rolled to her right, doubling over even as she saw ...

Saturn.

She collapsed again, this time in shock.

Not Saturn.

A planet just like Saturn but ...

Not.

Rising above distant mountains in the starry sky, gigantic in proximity; brilliant blue, icy rings flying around it at a steep angle, their static, sparkling lines tilted sharply against the horizon.

Not Saturn.

Spastically she coughed; struggled to get control of herself.

Got to get back.

Her limbs weren't listening. She pulled her legs under her to get up. The man was standing nearby. Only, unlike her he seemed invigorated; in rapture, looking to the star-filled heavens, turning slowly in place beneath their majesty and drinking it all in.

"Yes!" he exclaimed. "Here you will find your destiny! Here you will save us!"

And suddenly he had a gun. A machine pistol like the ones she carried, pulled from somewhere inside his jacket. She checked frantically for hers; one had fallen in the transfer and lay several feet away. She became more aware of her surroundings. The other was jammed beneath her, strap twisted across her shoulder. She felt it in her back; jerked around hard to reach it, desperate. Was he about to shoot?!

The man looked down on her.

"Lorenzo was wrong to come here," he said. "This was meant for you." He held up the Icon.

Then dropped it to the ground, even as he pointed the gun at it and fired.

"*NO!*" she screamed as the muzzle flashed in the night. Bullets zinged off the shiny surface and she covered her face; ricocheting sparks, bullets kicking the Icon, making it dance, relentless, splanging the stony ground ...

Her only way back.

She shook it off and rolled over with purpose. The old man continued the barrage as her feet and hands shoved hard against the stones, fighting for purchase, fighting to grab hold of her own gun and bring it around; in a panic to end the madness happening right before her ...

POW!

The Icon popped out of existence.

And the man stopped firing. She froze. For an instant, the briefest of instants as time seemed to stand still, as the man stopped firing and the last shots echoed through the empty air. Simply ... frozen, half risen. For that instant she could not move.

She fell to her knees.

Defeated.

Her way back was gone.

The old man stood in the soft blue glow of the giant planet, beneath the spectacular hues of the star-jammed sky, looking at the spot where the Icon had just been.

Then turned his eyes to her. Anger in them and she

braced herself.

"That whelp perverted our legends!" he said, rapture turned abruptly to fury. "And I let him! But you ... you will fix things. You will set us right. You shall fulfill your purpose!" He grinned like a maniac. "The great priestess has foreseen it!" He was convinced of that. "This is your destiny!"

And before she saw it coming he pointed the barrel of the gun—not at her, but at his own head, before she could act, pushed it hard against his temple, squinting in anticipation.

"I have delivered you!" he yelled. "Our future is in your hands!" Maybe the bullets were out ...

Brap!Brap! he fell in a spray of blood and fire. Like a sack of meat in a crumpled heap, right there on the ground before her.

She stared at his motionless form.

The Icon was gone.

She was stranded.

And the man to blame had just committed suicide right in front of her eyes.

Her world began to collapse. She was alone. The air was cold. She felt it now. Harsh on her skin. Blue Saturn rose majestic behind it all, mocking, the dark silhouettes of mountains stitching a line across its face, impossibly huge, filling the night sky. Over it spanned a stellar nebula that could've been anywhere.

She flopped to her back and stared up at the impossible heavens. A galaxy of stars, filled beyond counting.

She could be anywhere.

Anywhere at all.

* * *

ZAC WAS ON HIS KNEES. Jess was gone. Moments ago the crowd of Bok in the room had opened fire, following his mad lunge to grab his true love, a withering spray of bullets that lasted until the Bok were out of ammo. Vaguely he was aware of them ranged out behind him, standing around

the large stone chamber, empty guns trained on him—
surely wondering what to do next. They'd just unloaded
everything they had, echoes of the discharge of massive
amounts of gunfire still ringing down the halls, yet there he
kneeled, completely ignoring them.

The Bok meant nothing to him right then.

He'd failed.

His nightmare had come true.

Then ...

POW!

Across the room, near the alcove where the old man first
stood. Zac whirled and came to life as the Icon popped into
existence and fell clanging to the stones. In an instant he
had it in his grip. No Jessica, no old man with it, but with
the Icon he could follow. With it he could save her.

Without hesitation he gripped and twisted, preparing for
the transition to wherever she'd gone ...

Nothing.

He twisted again. Looked it over frantically. Was he
doing it wrong? The other Icons worked so easily.

He noticed it was dinged and scratched, badly, almost
like it had been shot. Did they have a gunfight on the other
side?!

Now he had to get there. He twisted again. Studied it
more closely, looking for its mechanism, wondering if the
bullets had damaged it somehow.

They must've.

He stared wide-eyed at the roomful of Bok, barely seeing
them in his desperation, stunned and staring back at
him, guns up, out of bullets and fearing for their lives, not
moving as he in turn fought angrily with the Icon.

This couldn't be happening. He made himself look
carefully over its parts, recalling exactly how the others
functioned. Twisted, exactly as he knew he should, parts
moving exactly as he knew they were supposed to.

Nothing.

He twisted again.

And again.

Nothing.

* * *

JESS LAY FOR SOME TIME. A long time, a short time ... she couldn't be sure. Only that time passed.

At length she heard the light clink of metal. Coming from somewhere beyond that small zone of death and impossible loss. With difficulty she lifted her head. Looked down the length of her body in the direction of the sounds, listening.

Armor. It sounded like old armor. The chink and clank of metal armor, like plate or chain mail, or something equally archaic.

Then a glint beyond the edge of the wide plateau on which she lay and a man came into view, jogging up what could only have been steps. He was followed by another and together they ran shoulder to shoulder, coming directly toward her. At least, they looked like men. Two armored forms, man-sized and shaped, two arms, two legs, wearing shiny black metal armor, carrying what looked to be long pikes across their chests. She gripped the gun; decided to remain as she was, lying on her back, even as she pointed it slowly across her middle, between her feet, lining the men up as she nervously watched their approach.

They saw her and slowed. As yet showing no signs of attack. More like they'd come to investigate the commotion. She lay still, watching.

Soon they reached the dead Bok and stopped. In the reflected light of the blue gas giant she was able to make them out in more detail. The shape and style of their armor was not exactly medieval, though the technology seemed no more advanced. Simple plate and mail, slapping as they moved. Over the armor they wore a sort of tunic, white, with symbols that looked vaguely like ... hieroglyphics. What made this seem more likely were their helmets. Now that they were close she could see the reality of what she'd only thought she saw in the dim celestial light as they jogged closer:

Their helmets were shaped like the heads of dogs.

Long snouts and ears. Like the head of Anubis, old

Egyptian god of the afterlife.

They looked like one of those ancient statues come to life.

And the oddity of that, as she made the connection with something so definitely Earth—in the midst of what was so definitely alien—shook her more than anything so far.

All at once they seemed to notice she was alive and raised their metal pikes. She held the gun tighter.

Hoping Zac would get the Icon on the other end. Hoping it wasn't destroyed. Hoping it went right back to where they'd been in the castle—hoping so many things right then that might save her and yet seemed like utter impossibilities.

Willing Zac to come charging through.

Fearing he never would.

www.ingramcontent.com/pod-product-compliance
Lightning Source LLC
Chambersburg PA
CBHW051429260626
47162CB00001B/19